THE SOLACE OF SIN

Other Books by Catherine Cookson

NOVELS

Kate Hannigan
The Fifteen Streets
Colour Blind
Maggie Rowan
Rooney
The Menagerie
Slinky Jane
Fanny McBride
Fenwick Houses
Heritage of Folly
The Garment
The Fen Tiger
The Blind Miller
House of Men
Hannah Massey
The Long Corridor
The Unbaited Trap
Katie Mulholland
The Round Tower
The Nice Bloke
The Glass Virgin
The Invitation
The Dwelling Place
Feathers in the Fire
Pure as the Lily
The Mallen Streak
The Mallen Girl
The Mallen Litter
The Invisible Cord
The Gambling Man
The Tide of Life
The Slow Awakening
The Iron Façade
The Girl
The Cinder Path
Miss Martha Mary Crawford

The Man Who Cried
Tilly Trotter
Tilly Trotter Wed
Tilly Trotter Widowed
The Whip
Hamilton
The Black Velvet Gown
Goodbye Hamilton
A Dinner of Herbs
Harold
The Moth
Bill Bailey
The Parson's Daughter
Bill Bailey's Lot
The Cultured Handmaiden
Bill Bailey's Daughter
The Harrogate Secret
The Black Candle
The Wingless Bird
The Gillyvors
My Beloved Son
The Rag Nymph
The House of Women
The Maltese Angel
The Year of the Virgins
The Golden Straw
Justice is a Woman
The Tinker's Girl
A Ruthless Need
The Obsession
The Upstart
The Branded Man
The Bonny Dawn
The Bondage of Love
The Desert Crop
The Lady on my Left

THE MARY ANN STORIES

A Grand Man
The Lord and Mary Ann
The Devil and Mary Ann
Love and Mary Ann

Life and Mary Ann
Marriage and Mary Ann
Mary Ann's Angels
Mary Ann and Bill

FOR CHILDREN

Matty Doolin
Joe and the Gladiator
The Nipper
Rory's Fortune
Our John Willie

Mrs Flannagan's Trumpet
Go Tell It To Mrs Golightly
Lanky Jones
Nancy Nutall and the Mongrel
Bill and The Mary Ann Shaughnessy

AUTOBIOGRAPHY

Our Kate
Catherine Cookson Country

Let Me Make Myself Plain
Plainer Still

CATHERINE COOKSON

THE
Solace of Sin

BCA

LONDON   NEW YORK   SYDNEY   TORONTO

This edition published 1998
by BCA
by arrangement with Bantam Press
a division of Transworld Publishers Ltd

Second Reprint 1998

CN 1297

Typeset in 12/14pt Sabon by
Phoenix Typesetting, Ilkley, West Yorkshire

Printed and bound in Great Britain by
Mackays of Chatham PLC, Chatham, Kent

PART ONE

1

Constance Stapleton glanced from the red face of her son to the bed behind him where, spread on the coverlet, lay a number of pictures of nude women in contorted poses. Her eyes remained fixed on them until the boy spluttered, 'You shouldn't have burst in like that.'

She now looked into his eyes, so like her own, the deep brown slashed with the after-glow of his blushing. She had never before knocked on his door, but today he was eighteen: he was no longer a boy, he was a man; young in manly years yet, but already clawing at the baser urges of the man. But then she was glad he was taking an interest in such things. However, if she were to tell him so he wouldn't believe her. They understood each other very well; they were closer than most mothers and sons: close in the places of the heart that needed no voice; close in tastes; and definitely close in resemblance, both nut brown, tall and thin with similar tentative expressions always hovering on their faces, as if something inside of them was striving to escape but found it impossible to push through the surface, though he would not have believed her if she had told him she was glad he was looking at such pictures. Her eyes still on him, she said softly, 'It's all right.'

When he swung round from her and leant over the bed, his fists digging into the glossy photographs, sending bare legs and thrusting breasts into further contortions, she looked at his narrow shoulders and wanted to pull him to her, to grip him fiercely to her and lay her head against his neck and cry. She imagined, for a moment, how upset he would be if he saw her cry. He had never seen a tear in her eyes in his life, and she had never known him cry since he was four and a half years old, on the night she found out about Yvonne and Jim.

Yvonne should have been in the nursery seeing to her charge, but her master had sought her services.

She herself had returned home unexpectedly early from a day in town, and the sight of her husband in their room with a slip of a girl, almost unrecognisable without her clothes, had stripped her bare of the benefit of her convent education and brought her voice tearing and rasping from her throat. It had filled the house and startled the maids. It had scared the pert French nursemaid. It had angered James Stapleton and it had brought Peter running across the landing into the bedroom, there to see his mother, his warm brown beautiful mother pouring out strange words as she stood over Nanny, who was pulling frilly knickers on to her legs and had her chest all bare.

It wasn't until her son had begun to cry that she had come to herself. Grabbing him up into her arms, she had taken him back to the nursery, and there, still in her outdoor clothes, she had sat rocking him until he fell into an exhausted sleep. But she herself had not cried.

The very last time she had cried was on her nineteenth birthday, when Peter was only two months old. She had cried all that day and all the following night, and she felt she would be crying now if the doctor hadn't given her a sedative. Three days later, when she became fully conscious, she realised that in those twenty-four hours she had cried all the tears she should have shed in her lifetime.

'Put them away into a drawer,' she said, again looking down on to the bed.

'I'll . . . burn them.' His head was still bent.

'No, don't burn them,' she said, her large mouth falling into a smile, 'you'll only go and buy some more.'

'Oh, Mother!' He turned his head for his chin to rest on his shoulder, his eyes tightly closed now.

'There's nothing to be ashamed of; it's merely a matter of curiosity.' Constance walked to his dressing-table and picked up the silver-backed hairbrush, one of a set she had bought him for his seventeenth birthday, and she ran her fingers lightly over the bristles as she said, 'Don't let this worry you, Peter, please. Think nothing more of it; it's just a form of growing up . . . When you find the right girl this phase will pass.'

When he made no answer she knew a sense of relief, for what he could have said was, The right girl? Don't make me laugh. After living with you and Father all these years in this set-up you would advocate me getting married? That's what he could have said, but he didn't. And she was grateful, thankful to God that his knowledge of the inner working of their lives had not coloured too darkly the picture of his future, at least where girls were concerned.

When she turned back, the pictures had gone from the bed, and he was standing now looking out of the window, his head and shoulders bent slightly forward. She did not go to him and touch him as she wanted to but left the room, saying, 'I'd get ready; it won't be long before they're here.'

As she crossed the hall and passed the four shallow steps which led up to her husband's study and the roof garden, she paused a moment, her head to one side, listening, and when no sound of typewriter keys being hammered came to her she raised her eyebrows slightly, before making her way to the kitchen.

The kitchen was as modern as one could expect in a seven thousand-pound flat. From its position on the sixth floor, the window faced in the direction of Newcastle Town Moor. You could see part of the moor over the roofs of the houses and the dark blur of the city beyond. Constance liked Newcastle; she liked this controversial north-east and its people. Although her accent, and even her manner, stamped her as a southerner, a foreigner almost, she felt they accepted her. At least, her tentative nature cautioned, she thought they did. But who, after all, did she know here except Jim's relations and the Thompsons on the next floor, with whom they occasionally played bridge? She based her judgement mainly on the attitude of the shopkeepers, the men on the buses, the porters on the stations. She always remembered her first visit to Shields. It was stamped on her mind by a small incident, but to this day the memory brought her warmth. She had peered out of the station on to a bare dull street, and remarked to the porter in some bewilderment, 'Aren't there any taxis?' And he had answered, 'Aw, lass, you want ower the bridge. Here, come on,' and he had grabbed her elbow and led her over the bridge to the other platform as if she were a child travelling under the care of the guard. And she must have appeared in need of guidance because, as he took her up to the solitary taxi standing in the front yard of the station, he said, 'There now, lass, you're not lost after all.' Just a little warm incident. Yet it was strange that her husband, who had been born and bred in Newcastle and who had insisted last year on coming back here to live, had scarcely a good word for any northerner.

In the first months of crazy love, even in the first year of their marriage, she had taken his aggressive attitude towards his own people as a trait of strong character. She had been led, self-blindly, to think that his arrogance was but the outcome of constant struggle and striving to establish himself as a writer. When she found out that this trait stemmed from nothing more than a giant inferiority complex she had felt pity for him; and the pity, she knew, would have made her love grow but for this other thing, the other thing that had become like a disease with him, this thing that besmirched her and made her feel fouled from his touch.

As she turned from the window to make for the refrigerator she realised she'd be sorry to leave this flat, and as she took out a tray of eight glasses containing a mixed fruit salad and considered the seven other homes she'd had during her nineteen years of married life she realised she'd had little feeling about leaving any one of them. But this flat was different. Perhaps it was the place itself. Perhaps it was because she had been more resigned during the last year. Perhaps it was because she knew she could now walk out tomorrow and it would have no adverse effect on Peter.

There now surged up the thought that if she had walked out at any period in Peter's life it would have made little difference to him, as long as she had taken him with her. It implied, as it always did, that she had stayed because she had wanted to stay, that she had stayed because she had hoped against hope that Jim would behave . . . and had he? At least he was more civil to her now. She would not listen to the voice that told her one had to be civil if one thought that by being otherwise one would lose one's only means of support; instead, she told herself he was more settled: he no longer had the urge to get into the car and drive off without a word and not return for two or three days, sometimes even a week. His life was now set to a pattern: he worked in his study until lunchtime; then he took a long walk in the afternoon. He was very proud of his figure. At forty-four he had no surplus fat on him; his neck was thick, but it was muscular thickness, and his sandy hair showed no trace of thinning or greyness. He was careful of what he ate and even more careful of what he drank; except for the times when he would drink himself into a state of ugly viciousness. These bouts would usually precede a long absence from home, but the bouts too had now ceased. Twice a week he went to a club; sometimes he went to a theatre, although never with her. The evenings he was at home he shut himself in his study and worked. That was the pattern of this present life. She had fitted into it without demur, for the moment thankful for the respite. But this period of peace, if not already ended, would be shattered tonight when she told him that they could no longer continue living their present way of life and must give up this flat, and . . . that she was closing their joint account.

She was tossing the salads when the bell rang, and as she

11

went out of the kitchen the study door opened and her husband appeared on the small landing at the top of the steps, and from there he said, 'That'll be Harry. I'll let them in.'

It was as if he had been waiting for the bell to ring, she thought. And very likely he had; he always became tensed up before a meeting with Harry. It was different with Ben. He could patronise his older brother, but he couldn't take such an attitude with his younger one. She hoped Harry wouldn't be in an argumentative mood tonight, because she had been looking forward to Peter's birthday tea – it couldn't really be called a party.

Jim Stapleton tugged at each cuff of his smart woollen jacket before he opened the door, and when he saw his brother Harry and his small dumpy wife standing there, he smiled widely at them. It was an attractive smile. Lighting up his heavy face, it stripped the years from him and placed him firmly in his early thirties.

'Hello! Harry,' he said quickly. 'You got here then. Is the lift working? It was out of order all morning. That's what you get in these places.' He stood aside as he talked and allowed his brother and sister-in-law to enter the hall. 'How are you, Millie? Here! give me your coat.'

'Oh, fine, Jim.'

'Oh, fine, Jim?' Harry Stapleton cast an amused glance at his wife. 'You had symptoms of rickets before we came out.'

'Oh, give over, you!' Millie pushed at her husband; then turning to Jim, who was hanging up her coat in the hall wardrobe, she said, 'And he would have rickets if he had the work I have before me every day. He and Ada make the place look as if we've got a family of ten.'

As yet the brothers hadn't exchanged a greeting, and Harry Stapleton was walking towards Constance, where she stood in the lounge doorway. She was, as usual, leaving the ushering to her husband. He always liked playing the amiable host. That the mood rarely carried him through an evening was beside the point.

'Hello, Connie.'

'Hello, Harry.'

Harry looked closely at his sister-in-law. His eyes level with hers, he asked bluntly, 'You all right?'

'Yes, I'm quite all right, Harry.'

'The head?' He tapped his brow.

'Not a sign of a migraine for the past month.'

'Oh, that's fine. I'm glad to hear that.' He nodded at her. Then looking round the room, he cried in a loud jocular tone, 'Well, where's tall, wide and handsome?'

'Oh.' Constance laughed at the description, which secretly pleased her. 'He'll be out in a minute, Harry; he's just getting dressed. Sit down . . . where's Ada? I thought she was coming with you.'

It was Millie who answered. 'She'll be along shortly, Connie; after five, likely. She's got a new job.'

'Another?' Jim had uttered the word unintentionally and he hastened to explain it immediately by adding, 'What I mean is—' But he got no further before his brother came back with, 'I know what you mean. Well, she can change her job seven days a week if she wants to, and here's one who'll help her. If you have your fling early enough you'll settle down; it's those who are restricted who come a cropper later on. It's been proved again and again.'

Harry did not look at his brother as he spoke, and when he finished speaking he nodded towards his wife, and the nod said, That goes for you, too.

Millie stared back at her husband for a moment. Then she looked up at Constance, and Constance looked back at her, and in the awkward silence, which tonight had presented itself particularly early on in the family meeting, Peter entered the room, and the atmosphere changed.

Harry and Millie shook his hand warmly as they offered him birthday greetings, and Millie, who had been holding a small parcel, handed it to him, saying, 'There you are, lad. It's not much and likely you've got a better one, but anyway, that's what we've got for you.'

Peter fingered the parcel, then impulsively he kissed his aunt on the cheek. He liked his Aunt Millie. He liked her thick northern accent; it was warm and enfolding. His mother's voice too was warm, but in a different way. There was an earthiness about his Aunt Millie that had a soothing effect on him. She was good, honest. That being so, why was their Ada such a bitch?

'Go on; aren't you going to open it?'

He undid the brown paper to reveal a leather wallet and a matching key case; and sticking out of the wallet pocket was a pound note.

'Oh, Aunt Millie.' He bent forward and kissed her again, and she pushed him, saying, 'Go on. Give over, an' don't pretend you're floored by a pound note. We generally put a penny in for good luck, but we couldn't give you a penny, could we?'

He turned now to Harry and said quietly, 'Thanks, Uncle Harry. I need them both, the wallet especially first' – he smiled broadly – 'but it'll be some time before I'll have a use for the keys, I suppose.'

'Oh, you never know. You never know, lad.' Harry nodded at him.

'Come and sit down beside me' – Millie patted the maroon plush couch – 'an' tell me what else you got.'

'Oh.' Peter lowered his eyes for a moment. Then lifting them to Constance, he said, 'Mother—' His words were checked by her expression and he glanced towards his father, who was standing with his back to the wide window, and added, 'and Father . . . they bought me a car.'

'A car? But—'

'It is only a second-hand one.' Constance was nodding her head in small jerks at Harry.

'But where are you going to keep another car with two already in the garage? Good God, another car!' Harry finished on a high note.

'Oh, I'll keep it round the side of the block, Uncle. It won't

14

matter about it getting wet. It's not a very grand one, but . . . but it'll be mine. I wanted one of my own, you know.'

'Three cars.' Harry Stapleton looked at his brother, then at his nephew, and lastly at his sister-in-law, and he said flatly, 'You're daft, Connie. That's what you are, clean plumb daft.'

The remark could have been taken as either censorious or funny. Millie and Peter took the latter view and laughed; Jim, apparently, the former, for his face became tight as he stared at his brother. But Harry seemed not to notice. Drawing up a chair opposite Peter, he said, 'Well now, I want to hear all about it. University: did you get fixed? What's going to happen?'

'Oh.' Peter rubbed his chin with his hand before beginning, 'Well, eventually I want to study microbiology. For now I have been advised to take a general degree in science, to include chemistry and biology.'

'That's good.' Harry was nodding at him.

'If I get it, I could go into industry, or the agricultural side of things, even medicine' – he smiled at Harry – 'for microbiologists are in demand in the National Health Service.'

'You've made a good choice; you're not going to be pinned down to one job for life.' There was a note of bitterness in Harry's voice.

Harry had started in the pit at the age of fourteen and from the first day his one desire had been to get out of it. This he finally managed to do when he enlisted in the Army in 1943. At the end of the war he took a course while still in the Army, which brought him an educational certificate and enabled him to attend a teachers' training college. Now he was a teacher. In those first days it didn't matter that his pupils were the roughs and toughs of the slums of Newcastle. He was out of the mines, he was out of the Army, and he was teaching. He had a status. Moreover, he was the only one of his family that had achieved anything. At that time his elder brother Ben spent his days hacking up carcasses of meat; as for their Jim, he would neither work nor want; a writer, that's what their

15

Jim wanted to be, and in the meantime he managed to get by on an incompatibility with most jobs and the compensating factor of the dole. And then one day, it seemed overnight, their Jim had become a writer. He wrote a book about the very things that he, Harry, was thinking all the time, except the sex bits, and these weren't bits, but great dollops. Jim had set his story on the Tyne, where he had grown up. He had made a backcloth of the river, with its gantry-lined banks, its ships, its factories and yards, its bridges; the fine huddle of bridges streaming upwards one above the other. He had made those bridges live, and he had used one of them as a climax to his story: the beaten man straddling its girders before taking his last leap into the river.

Overnight his brother Jim had become a name. Within a month of the book being published Stanhope Street knew him no more. He moved to London, from where he sent his mother fifty pounds, and she had acted as if it were five thousand. Fifty pounds for keeping him for twenty-four years. The day they made a film of his book she threw a big party. They came from Barrack Road and Gallowgate in their dozens. They couldn't get into the house, so she put a table in the street, and she put herself into debt she never got out of for years.

Then his brother Jim had another stroke of luck. He married his publisher's only daughter, although not, it was understood, to everybody's satisfaction, particularly of the publisher himself. But Jim's luck was in, for the publisher died within six months of his daughter being married, and now their Jim had a wealthy wife.

Harry remembered the first time he had seen Connie. It was when Jim came down to their mother's funeral. He could recall to this day the first glimpse he had of her as she stood by the side of his brother in the dingy front room. He had thought then that she resembled a racehorse harnessed to a dray cart, and subsequent years hadn't altered his opinion.

His train of thought was broken by Millie saying to Constance, 'Are Ben and Susan coming?' and Constance

16

answering, 'Yes, but not before six. He can't get away from the shop before then.'

'And I'll lay ten pounds to a penny that they'll be gone at seven. What do you bet?' Harry was leaning towards Connie, a grin on his face now.

'I wouldn't take you on,' said Constance, smiling back at him.

'No, nor would anybody else,' said Harry, dropping back against the couch. 'That woman and her bingo; honest to God, it's a disease. Our Ben says, she's like a cat on hot bricks all day on a Sunday. Can you believe it?' He looked round from one to the other. 'The mentality of wanting to play bingo six nights a week!'

'There are men who go to the races every day in the season, travelling hundreds of miles between the courses. There are women who play bridge every night . . . including Sundays.' Jim sounded like a lecturer in philosophy explaining a social pattern to a group of young students, and the impression was carried further when he walked to a table and took a cigarette from a box and tapped it on the back of his hand before turning to them again and adding, 'No one should judge another man's actions . . . or a woman's, for that matter, until he has been in a similar situation and noted his own reactions to it. Susan goes to bingo because she finds an outlet in it; also, from what we gather, she has won a considerable sum over the past few years, so therefore —'

'Oh my God! Leave over,' said Harry, still not looking at his brother. 'I take your meaning. All right, all right; look at it from a philosophical standpoint or from any point you like, but to me Susan is a lazy trollop. Well, perhaps not a trollop in that sense or Ben would kick her backside out of the house, but she's a lazy cat and all she thinks about is bingo and clothes, and if she could only see herself in them as other people see her she would have a fit . . . Clothes, and getting out of the house, that's Susan.'

A long-drawn-out breath from Millie brought Harry's eyes

17

to her. Millie had a quirk to her lips, and she said to no one in particular, 'And good luck to her.'

When Harry gave her a push that nearly knocked her off the end of the couch they all laughed, again all except Jim. He turned away and looked out of the window and down into the courtyard for a moment to give himself a chance to get a grip on his temper. His brother Harry had the power to get under his skin like nobody else. He always had the desire to slap him in his mouth, but Harry always managed to do the slapping first.

Jim considered himself a good talker, an interesting talker. When he got going he could hold people's attention, all except their Harry's . . . and, of course, his own family's. Oh yes, his own family's. They didn't want to listen to him, either of them. He turned to see Harry standing by Constance's side. His brother was laughing as he explained something to her, and the sight of her looking happy, even carefree, gave him a feeling that held the bitterness of gall. She liked their Harry, she always had. She even admired him, this schoolteacher at Westgate Road School, he with the stamp of Stanhope Street still on him; a lovely combination. His accent had never changed and he was teaching children, and he dared, he dared to talk down to him, to shut him up. He asked himself now why he had ever come back to this quarter. Why? It hadn't made the slightest difference to his writing.

In those first few months when he had dashed that book off, he had thought perhaps it had. But where had that got him? Nowhere. He was more dry now than when he had been in London, and if it wasn't for one thing he'd go back tomorrow.

As his eyes roamed slowly around the room, he had to add another reason to that which at present kept him in the north: every article in the room spelt money . . . and taste. A man got used to certain comforts; they crept insidiously into his life, until they seemed not to have any value until he was faced with doing without them. He had lived graciously, one could say, for twenty years and he was less inclined to give it up as

18

the years went on. As one grew older the needs of the body didn't change except to become more demanding, and the price he had to pay for satisfying these needs became greater. In his case it meant cultivating a civil tongue – a difficult accomplishment when you wanted to spit venom – and he knew that before tonight was over he'd be called upon to use all his control, because this morning she had received her bank statement, and it was only because she wanted her young lordship's party to go off smoothly that there hadn't already been a showdown.

He moved to where she was standing and put his hand on her shoulder, something he hadn't done for a long time, so long that he couldn't really remember the occasion, and when he felt no stiffening or shrinking from his touch he bent his head forward and said, 'What about a drink? And you, Harry, what'll you have?'

'Oh no, not for me,' said Harry. 'It's too early in the day for that. What I'm dying for this minute is a cup of tea.'

'I'll make one.' Constance moved smoothly away from Jim's grasp. 'It won't take me a minute.'

'I'll give you a hand, Connie.' Millie rose from the couch and followed Constance across the hall and into the kitchen, but once there she did not set the tray or help in any way; instead, she walked to the window and stood looking out, and after a moment she said, 'I've always thought this is a fine view, Connie.'

'Yes, Millie; it's a lovely view.'

How often had Millie remarked on this particular view during the last year, Constance wondered, as she placed five cups on a tray. After taking a silver teapot from another tray already set on a side table, she scooped five teaspoons full of tea into the pot before pouring in the boiling water. Then she looked at Millie's back and asked quietly, 'What is it, Millie?'

Millie turned from the window and, putting her hands behind her, supported herself against the sill, and she gulped audibly before she said, 'I think she's done it again, Connie.'

19

'No!' Constance walked slowly towards her and again she said, 'No!'

'She's brazen and he can't see it; he thinks she's clever. He would soon see it in anyone else, but not her. I've been through her things. I've seen nothing over the past three months. So . . . so yesterday I tackled her with it. An' you know what she did? She just laughed at me. It's a disease with her, Connie. It's a disease. She thinks nothing of it. I'm scared, I'm really scared of him finding out this time, because she's getting more and more brazen. She knows he's daft about her, yet I could see her taking a knife and cutting him to pieces and laughing while she did it. There's something radically wrong with her, but there's only me and you, Connie, who seem to recognise it; everybody else says, isn't she a good sport? isn't she fun? It'll surely finish him when he finds out, as he's bound to do sooner or later. I wish to God she'd go away, run away. You know, when I hear of girls running away from home, I think to meself, Why, in the name of God! doesn't she do it.' Millie now closed her eyes and bowed her head on to her chest and said, 'Fancy saying things like that about your own daughter.'

'Oh, Millie.' Constance put her hands out and gently held the plump arms. She'd always been very fond of Millie; there were even times when she wanted to lay her head on her chest and draw comfort from her. Millie was only a year older than herself but she gave one the impression of motherliness, of warmth and security. And yet her own daughter needed none of these things from her. Her daughter was without heart. She hadn't any heart even for the boys or men she took up with. She wanted one thing from them, and when she'd got it she quickly grew tired of them. It was strange, Constance thought, but Ada could have been Jim's daughter, for their characters were similar. And stranger still, her own son was more like Harry. At some point the wires of heredity had crossed.

'The hardest part,' said Millie now, 'is to put on a good face to him. If I look serious or a bit off-colour he keeps on at me to know what's the matter.'

'Millie! Millie! Here a minute . . . Tell Connie.'

The sound of Harry's voice coming from the lounge brought them both to the table, and as Constance lifted the tray Millie took it from her, saying, 'It's a dead weight. Let me carry it.'

The small gesture, made often before, brought a sense of comfort to Constance. Millie always wanted to take the load; there were so few people, at least in her life, like that.

As they entered the lounge Harry called across the room, 'I'd forgotten about the house. I was just telling Peter how we came across it.'

'Oh, the house.' Millie smiled and nodded to him. Then turning to Constance, she said, 'Oh, aye, I meant to tell you, Connie, for the minute we saw it we thought of you. Didn't we, Harry?'

'Yes, we did. It was funny. We stood looking up at it and we both nearly tripped over ourselves saying the same thing together.' They nodded to each other as they recalled the incident.

'Oh, it was funny.' Millie put her head on one side. 'There we stood saying, "Connie would like this. This is just her type of house." And you know—' Still with her head on one side, Millie looked up at Constance and added, 'It was the kind of house that would suit you. I don't know how I knew it, but I did. And so did Harry. Didn't you, Harry?'

'Well, all right, Aunt Millie' – Peter was standing by her side now, laughing down at her – 'we'll take your word for it: Mother would like the house. But tell us what it's like, and where it is.'

'Well, it was like this,' said Millie. 'We were out for a run last Sunday and we got as far as . . . Oh, what's that place, Harry? You know what I am for remembering place names.'

'Chollerford,' said Harry patiently. 'You've been there dozens of times, woman; Chollerford.'

'Oh well, you go on with the story,' said Millie.

'I know Chollerford,' said Peter. 'It's where the bridge with the fine arches is; up the North Tyne.'

'That's it. We all went for a picnic there, remember? It was years ago, when you came down for a holiday.'

'Oh, I remember it well,' said Peter. 'But go on about this house.'

'Well, we went along to Humshaugh, and right on to Barrasford, had a look at the trout hatcheries and I stopped Millie from going on the ferry.' He nodded at his wife. 'Once she was aboard, I would never have got her off; her and ferries. We skipped Wark-on-Tyne. That was as full as a fairground; you couldn't put a pin on the river bank. We really meant to stop there and have some tea, but we went on and stopped just below Woodpark, near Lea Hall, you know, but this side of the river, and then we thought we'd stretch our legs . . . Well, we found a path and it went in and out, in and out, until it came right out on top of a hill—'

'More like a small mountain!'

'All right, have it your own way. A small mountain.' Harry nodded at Millie. 'One thing, you could see for miles.'

'He said he could see the sea from there, but I couldn't; it's miles and miles from the sea; he was just looking into the sky. It seemed nothing but sky from up there. Grand, it was.' She stopped and made a motion with her hand, then said, 'Oh well, go on.'

'Well, I thought I knew most of Northumberland and had seen it from every angle,' went on Harry, 'but I've never seen such a view in me life as from that rise. I knew Shepherdshiel Moor was away to the south – I've been over that way – but from this point it looked different. You know the moors are wild up there, but I've never seen anything so wild or so beautiful as the stretch of country that lay below us . . . All right, all right, I'm coming to it.' He thrust out his hand towards Peter. 'Anyway, we started to walk again, and there was nothing, nothing, only sky and scree and fell, not a thing. We didn't even see a sheep, did we?'

22

'No,' said Millie. 'And at one point I got a bit frightened; I thought we were lost.'

'You weren't the only one,' said Harry; 'I mean, thinking we were lost. And then—'

'And then you saw the house.' Peter flung his head up and laughed.

'Yes, lad, we saw the house. We came on it suddenly. We came on a path. We could see it had been used before and we walked up it and over the breast of a hill, and there it lay. The sun was shining and the stones looked pink in the light. The same stones as the Roman wall is made of; perhaps taken from it, 'cos it isn't far away. Anyway, between it and us lay a hollow, and there on the far side, on a piece of flat ground beyond a terrace of stones, stood the house. We nearly didn't go near it because we thought someone might be living there. And then a jackdaw flew out of the chimney pot, and that was a good indication that no fire had been lit there for some time.'

'But he knocked on the door.' Millie pulled a face at her husband.

'Well, I just wanted to make sure,' Harry said, 'I could have been wrong. When there was no answer we walked back a few steps and looked up at it, and quite out of the blue, I'm telling you, Connie –' Harry was nodding at her – 'we both said, "Connie would like this." I couldn't get over it, because the fact is you hadn't been in me thoughts at that time. And Millie said the same; she hadn't been thinking about you. Anyway, we looked through one of the windows. Whoever built it was ahead of his time, because those windows were made to frame a view. The floors had old boards about a foot wide, you know the type, and as far as we could make out the walls weren't even plastered; the same inside as out. And at the back, the kitchen – I suppose it was used as a kitchen and eating place – was nearly the length of this room. Honest.' He nodded now at Jim, who was staring at him. 'There was an old black grate in it, with a hook hanging down the chimney.'

23

'And all this reminded you of me?' Constance was laughing as she handed Harry a cup of tea.

'Yes, it's funny, Connie, but I could see you there. I tell you, Millie said the same. We knew what you would do with the place. You know, you have a flair for titivating, haven't you?'

'An old range with a hook hanging down the chimney. Oh! Harry.' Constance jerked her head at him derisively.

'If you could see it you would know what I mean.'

'Well, tell her what happened next,' put in Millie quickly.

'Oh aye. Well, as I said we got round the back and her nibs here wanted to spend a penny.' He laughed as he jerked his head in Millie's direction. 'And across a yard of large paving stones and at the end of a rough garden there were some outhouses, and she makes for one of them. Well, it turned out to be a coal and wood shed. Then she opens another door, like Goldilocks, you know.' His head was now bouncing with amusement. 'But no luck there either. Two more doors to go –' he held up his fingers now, speaking directly to Peter – 'and she opens the third door, and bang! She lets out a squeal that nearly takes me over the roof. And mind, I'm telling you, I got a bit of a gliff on the side an' all, when out stalks this fellow, six-foot-four of him if an inch, with shoulders on him like a bullock and a face that could have been chiselled out of the same stone that the house was built of. I'm telling you, I wouldn't like to meet him on a dark night, but the surprising thing about him was, he took the wind out of our sails by saying quite calmly, as if he was expecting us, "Hello; can I help you?"'

All their attention was drawn now to Millie, sitting with her arms round her waist and rocking herself slightly as she said, '"Eeh!" he stammered. I mean, Harry did. He said, "N . . . no. W . . . we're just lookin' round."'

'I didn't stammer; I was just taken off me guard.' But now Harry laughed. 'He was twice the size of me and it was a lonely spot. Anyway, it turned out that he was there because he was expecting a buyer for the house, but he was all right and he showed us around. And oh, Connie' – he nodded at her and more slowly now, emphasising each word, said – 'it was really lovely. A sort of family house, you know. There were five rooms upstairs, three of them running into each other. And there was this big kitchen, the length of the back of the house, and a big room running the length of the front. It was simply constructed but it had an atmosphere about it. I said to Millie, "This has been a happy house," and she felt it an' all. Didn't you?'

'Aye, I did.' Millie looked across the room into the distance, her face wearing a sadness now. 'I said I'd like to live there, away from everything.'

'About the fellow,' put in Peter. 'Was he the owner?'

'He didn't say and we never asked him,' said Harry.

'He was so big,' put in Millie, smiling now.

'Did he live there?' asked Constance.

'No. There was no furniture in the place.'

'And he had a knife in one hand and this piece of wood in the other,' said Millie. 'And he kept whittling at it.'

'But he hardly opened his mouth,' said Harry.

'He asked you if you were interested in houses.'

'Oh yes, he did. And I said I was, very much.' Harry pulled his nose downwards. 'He was a big fellow; I felt I had to agree with him, you know.' And this caused all but Jim to laugh; he could see nothing funny in his brother's recounting of being shown over an empty house on a fell by a big man.

Turning now to Constance, Harry said, 'Why don't you take a run out there and have a look at it, just for fun? I'll draw you a map. From where it lies I should think it's somewhere between Shepherdshiel Moor, Green Moor and Allerybank Moor, circled by them so to speak. Anyway, I'll do you a drawing before I go.'

'You'll do nothing of the sort.' Jim's voice filled the room. 'Don't be so daft, sending people on wild-goose chases. Who do you think's going to live out there? Not me, for one, and not her, either. What are you trying to start now?'

25

'What am I trying to start now!' Harry screwed up his face at his brother, and looked at him squarely for the first time since coming into the house. 'Man, I'm only wanting Connie to see the place.'

'What for?'

Harry's face wrinkled itself further and his mouth fell open into a slight gape before he said, 'I don't know.' Then on a high note, 'I don't know; just for her to see it. We thought it would make a marvellous week-end place, and being out there it would likely go for a song.'

'Oh, so you don't know why you wanted her to see it. Well, let me tell you we don't require any week-end place. This flat serves us weekdays, and it'll do for weekends an' all.'

Harry bowed his head. His teeth were clamped tightly together. He had come to his nephew's tea party, and if he answered his brother the way he wanted to he would have to walk out of the house before it started. As he raised his head he saw Connie's face. Her large brown eyes were pleading with him, for a moment revealing the pain she usually managed to barricade behind the façade of her upbringing, and because of it he forced himself to say with some calm, 'All right, all right; we'll let it drop. Forget I ever mentioned it.'

It was at this point that the doorbell rang and Constance went to answer it. As she did so she thought it was strange that Millie and Harry should think of her when they saw that house. Tomorrow, if it was fine, she would go and have a look at it. Not that she would ever dream of taking it. If she was afraid to be alone in the town, she'd be more afraid out in the wilds, but it would give her a run out, and would please Harry and Millie.

2

'This is all because that bloody fool mentioned that house to you.'

'It's nothing of the sort.' Constance's voice was quiet. 'Why won't you face up to the fact that we can't go on living as we have done for the last ten years? I've tried to tell you again and again, but you wouldn't listen. Well, now you've got to, because I'm selling the flat.'

'Oh!' Slowly he inclined his head towards her. The pupils of his blue eyes looked black behind his narrowed lids. 'So you're going to sell the flat. No consultation. Oh no! No discussion. Your money bought the flat and all that's in it, and I'm just a kept man . . . Go on, tell me.'

Her straight back pressed tightly against the high-backed chair, she stared towards the mantelpiece as she asked, in controlled tones, 'Do you want me to remind you of how little money you have earned in the last ten years?'

He had been standing to the side of her, and now he came and confronted her, his thick body seeming to swell as he bent towards her, grinding out between his teeth, 'There are times when I'd like to ram your bloody money down your throat.'

She stared into his red fury-filled face. How could two people who had ever . . . ever expressed love for each other sink to this?

'There's always a solution,' she said.

'Oh yes, there's a solution now that your darling boy is out of rompers. There's no more talk about him being the victim of a broken home. Oh, not any more. Because your own dear mama skipped it, everything had to be sacrificed to your son's psychological background.'

'Stop it!' She pushed the chair back and strained her body away from him as she got to her feet. She was an inch taller than him, and so stiffly was she standing now that he appeared short beside her, and there was a dangerous quiver in her voice as she said, 'I didn't ask you to stay, ever, not even for Peter. You stayed because you wanted it easy, because you knew that the royalties your books were bringing in, even up to ten years ago, wouldn't even keep you in clothes, not the kind you have a liking for, let alone running your own car, and . . .' Her chin jerked upwards and she seemed to have difficulty with her words as she ended, 'paying for your particular kind of amusement.'

She watched the flush fade from his face, particularly from around his mouth, leaving a distinct grey line. In the silence between them the gentle chimes of the clock in the hall seemed to groan throughout the room. As she watched the beads of sweat appear on his upper lip she began to feel afraid: he had never, as yet, struck her, but in scenes like this she always expected him to. She made herself turn slowly from him and walk to the empty fireplace, and there, resting her hand on the high mantelshelf for support, she said, 'From now on you can please yourself what you do, but as I've told you, we've been living on the capital for the last three years. The way things are going there'll soon be no capital left.'

There was another silence before he said grimly, 'If you're so hard up why the hell did you buy him a car?'

Her voice came back flatly to him: 'It was only second-hand, and two hundred and fifty pounds, and I intend one of the other two to go anyway.'

His voice was rasping: 'And I suppose it's mine that'll be for the axe?'

28

She turned from the mantelpiece and walked towards the door as she said, 'If you can pay for the garage, petrol bills and maintenance, you're welcome to keep it. Also –' she turned and confronted him from the doorway – 'there'll be no more separate withdrawals. I'm closing the joint account as from tomorrow.'

'Ah! . . . So that's it.' He took three steps towards her; then stood leaning forward, his fists clenched. 'So that's it! We're coming to the crux of the matter now, aren't we? Your suspicious mind's at work again. Well, I can tell you what I did with every penny I took out, if you'll listen. I bought my suit and . . . and then that new overcoat; I also got him that wrist watch.' He thumbed towards the wall.

She looked steadily back at him. 'In the last three months,' she said slowly, 'there have been seven twenty-pound withdrawals and five of ten pounds.' As she turned around, then crossed the hall, she felt that something would come flying at her head, and when she reached her room she leant against the door and cupped her face in her hands, pressing it so tightly that her mouth was distorted. Then she dropped on to the bed and, with her face still gripped between her palms, she buried her head in the pillow, asking herself for the thousandth time why she really put up with it. Why? Why?

Some minutes later, after the outer door had banged and she heard the whirl of the lift going down, she raised her dry, burning face and, sitting upright, drew a long breath.

When the tap came on her door she blinked her eyes rapidly and rose to her feet before calling, 'Come in.'

Peter entered the room and, as she had done, he stood with his back to the door. His face was white, his eyes large. In this moment they resembled each other even more closely. He said to her, 'Why don't you end it?'

'What?'

With an impatient movement he thrust his body from the door, crying, 'Look. Don't stall any more. Remember this is my eighteenth birthday. He's always accused you of coddling

29

me. Well, don't coddle me any more. Let's talk this thing out.
I say why don't you end it, why don't you leave him? I . . . I
heard what he said about your mother leaving your father. I
never knew that; you never told me. Do you mean that you've
stayed with him all these years because of me? Look.' He pulled
her round to him. 'It drives me bats just to think about it. Look,
Mother, for Christ's sake—'

She bowed her head and shivered saying, 'Don't use that
expression, Peter.'

'Well, it needs something strong to make you understand.
Tell me . . . tell me, have you really stayed with him because of
me?'

She looked at him squarely now and answered, 'No, no; not
really.'

'You're sure?' His voice was soft.

'Yes. You see, he wasn't always like this. He's . . . he's unsure
of himself, always has been. He needed someone—'

'Stop it! Stop it!' He turned from her now, tossing his head
as if to throw off the image she would present to him of his
father. 'I know all about what he needs; I haven't lived all these
years not to know what he needs, or what he thinks he needs.'
He turned to her swiftly again and said slowly and emphati-
cally, 'I know all about it.'

It was on the tip of her tongue to say, You can't. Oh no,
Peter, you can't know all about it. Her boy was just eighteen.
Surely he couldn't know about the thing that plagued his
father, surely not. Oh God, surely not. But she daren't go into
it, in case . . . in case.

She had thought that the plaguing was over three years ago.
She had been simple enough to imagine that, because he had
actually gone on his knees to her and begged her to forgive him,
promising that it would never, never happen again, that it was
over. It took a lot for a man like Jim to go on his knees to a
woman, but he had done so. Yet he had not asked her for
comfort. He had not come to her room, or taken her to his.

Peter was saying, 'One thing he was right about, you should

30

never have bought me that car if you were hard up.'

'You shouldn't have listened, Peter.' She glanced at him over her shoulder. 'Anyway, I'm not hard up.'

'If we're living on your capital it won't be long before you are, will it? Now look.' He came and stood in front of her again. 'Think of yourself, just for once. In two months' time I'll be going to university. Make a clean break, divorce him. That's what to do, divorce him. You know –' he shook his head slowly at her and his eyes travelled over her face – 'you could have anybody. That's what I've always thought. Why, when surely you could have picked anybody, did you pick him? You're beautiful now, but when you were very young, eighteen, nineteen, when you married him you must have been . . . well' – he shook his head, searching for a word – 'startling.'

Her lips moved into a trembling smile and she put out her hand and touched his face, saying, 'It's nice to hear someone say that, although it isn't true, it's just how you see me. I'm thirty-seven, Peter, and I feel sixty-seven, and I can't imagine ever again feeling any younger.'

'Don't be a fool.' He pushed her almost roughly. 'Look. Do what I say, make a break. I've been thinking a lot about it lately and my mind won't be at peace, especially when I'm away; in fact, I won't be able to settle to work knowing you're here and miserable.'

'Durham isn't far; you'll be popping in.'

'But . . . but I thought you were going to give up the flat. You said—'

'Yes, I'll have to sell this place and look for something much cheaper, but it'll still be here in town.'

'Why don't you go and look at Uncle Harry's house?'

'Oh.' Her smile widened a little. 'He was entertaining, wasn't he?'

'Shall we go tomorrow and have a look at it?'

She turned and stared at him for some seconds, then nodded, saying, 'Yes, but it'll be no use to us, to me. It sounds right away in the wilds, and there'll be no electricity, water, or sanitation, and I couldn't possibly live there on my own. You know I couldn't.'

'No, of course not.' He nodded in agreement. 'But anyway, it'll be an outing. Let's take some food with us and make a day of it, eh?'

She did not tell him she had already thought of going to look at the house, but answered, 'Yes, I would like to get away for a day.'

'That's settled then.' He leant towards her and kissed her on the cheek, resting his lips against her flesh for a moment, and at the door he pointed down to the lock and said, 'I'd see to that if I were you; he might come in rolling.'

She made no answer, but slowly undressed herself. In whatever condition her husband returned she would have no need to lock her door against him. He might rail against her but he wouldn't come into her room. As she had pointed out to Peter, she was thirty-seven, and the age limit necessary to satisfy his plaguing was eighteen, or as far below as he dared to go.

3

'Are you sure we're going the right way, Peter?'

'Yes; he said it was a good twenty minutes' walk before you came to the track.'

'It seems more like two hours to me.' She laughed. 'Let me help you with the hamper.'

'No, I can manage. Watch where you're putting your feet; this grass is slippery. It's a good job you put on flatties.'

'Yes, it is.' Constance stood for a moment on the grassy slope to get her breath, and again looked at the miles of raw beauty stretching away to the left of her as far as the eye could see. To the right the land was hilly, cutting off the view, except that of the valley just below her, which led to another rise. She was moving on again when Peter's voice called to her, 'Here it is, the path,' and she sighed as she said to herself, 'Thank goodness.' She had never walked so far in years; at least, not this kind of walking, slithering and slipping crabwise across hills, then climbing again, only to slither and slip once more.

'It must be over the rise.' He pointed excitedly ahead. Then, his step quickening, he hurried along the rough path. She followed more leisurely, and when she saw him stop she knew he had seen the house. He did not turn towards her, nor did he speak when she came to his side; then she, too, gazed at the house.

She was tired, hot, and thirsty, and her mind was in deep

trouble. But if only to bear out Harry's and Millie's impression of the place she felt she should feel a stir of excitement in her, but there was none. Peter was looking at her and she returned his look and smiled, but did not speak. Neither did he. But he was showing enough excitement for the both of them, and she let it go at that.

Down yet another slope, over the flat grassy level, on to the slab terrace, and there they were standing by the front door. It was an oak door, browny black, the weatherboard at the bottom worn away. It had a black iron handle in its middle as you would see on a church door. Peter had laid the picnic basket on the uneven stones of the terrace and now, taking her hand, he pulled her towards the right-hand window, and they both put their faces near the panes and peered in. Then they went to the left side of the door and examined the room through this window.

'It's as Uncle Harry said, it goes the width of the house. The front door must open into the middle of it. Look, the stairs are over there.'

She shaded her eyes and saw the stairs, immediately opposite the front door, it would seem. Then her eyes travelled to the fireplace. It was merely a projection into the room of the wall itself, built of the same stone. Even the mantelpiece was an uneven ledge of stones. When she again looked at Peter her eyes were smiling, and she said, 'They were right, it has something.'

'Let's go round the back and see if we can get in.'

'No, no; we wouldn't want to run into the big fellow.' Her smile broadened. 'If he scared Millie he might do as much for me. Let's have something to drink. I'll lay it out on the doorstep; it's big enough to act as a table.'

She stood waiting by the large square step until he brought the basket and then, spreading a plastic cloth on the stone, she laid out their meal, and after removing her dustcoat she folded it lengthways, and they sat on it and ate.

From the age of thirteen, Constance had travelled; she had become well acquainted with the scenery of Switzerland,

Austria, Spain and France. As the guest of particular families she had spent all her holidays in one country or another, but never, never had she seen a view to match the one she was looking upon now. The land, sloping to a river, or running stream, looked wild and frightening, even on this warm summer day.

Yet even as she thought how terrible it would be living here in winter she knew that, terrible or not, she would have to see the house and maybe even experience such a winter. Yet in further contradiction she heard herself say in an unusually brisk tone, 'I just couldn't live here, Peter, not on my own. However would I get to a road? And the loneliness—'

'Of course not. Of course not. Who's talking about you living here? But . . . but it's grand, isn't it? Wonderful; and not a soul to be seen. Not a house to be seen.'

'There must be a house nearby belonging to that man, the owner.'

'Yes, it'll likely be down that side.' He pointed along the length of the terrace to where the land looked wooded. Still keeping his hand outstretched, he now said slowly and quietly, 'Look there. Do you see what I see?'

Constance leant forward in front of him and looked along the terrace, and at first she saw nothing but the dark line of trees. And then she noticed the girl emerging from the shadows. When she stepped on to the terrace she saw that she wasn't more than eleven or twelve.

Both she and Peter, rising to their feet, waited until the visitor approached them.

'Hello.' The greeting had a personal touch as if they had met only a short time before. 'You havin' your dinner?'

'Yes.' Constance inclined her head. 'It's such a lovely spot. Are . . . are we trespassing?'

'Trespassin'!' The round blue eyes twinkled. 'No, you only trespass further down in the valley' – she pointed in the direction of the river's downward course – 'you don't trespass up here. That's what Vin says.'

35

Constance glanced at Peter and they exchanged a smile. Then they both turned to the girl again. She was very thin, not like a robust country child at all. Her hair was a light brown and her skin had a porcelain tint to it. Constance said to her, 'Would you like a sandwich?'

The girl examined the picnic lunch, then raising her eyes again to Constance, a twinkle deep in them, she said, 'No. Ta . . . thanks; but I wouldn't mind a piece of that cake. We only have cakes for Saturday tea, maybe sometimes on a Sunday, if there's any left over. Mother just bakes them once a week.'

'Of course! Help yourself.' With a motion of her hand, Constance indicated the table.

The girl's fingers hesitated over the four pieces of cake on the paper plate and her glance darted sideways up at them as she selected the smallest piece. And then, after she had bitten into it, she pressed her lips tightly together as she munched. Almost straightaway and nodding her head, she said, 'Aye, it's nice.' Her voice was a mixture of Northumbrian and . . . Constance wavered in her mind before deciding that the other part of the child's accent was Scottish, although it wasn't quite that.

'What's your name?' she asked.

'Moira.'

That was it; Irish.

'Do you know who owns this house?'

The mouth spread wide from the small teeth. 'We do, it's ours. We're sellin' it. There were some bodies after it yesterda', but the woman wasn't for it because she was born lazy, Hannah said. It was the water; and no lavatory. Look!' She pointed towards the end of the terrace from where she had come. 'Not twenty yards around the corner there's a stream, and it comes out of the rock hand high.' She placed her hand on a level with her small chest. 'And a big flat slab to stand on. You don't get your feet wet, not like ours down beyond. Come and see for yourselves.'

Constance and Peter again exchanged amused glances; then

36

they followed the girl as she rounded the house, jumped the foot depth from the level of the terrace on to hard rough ground, with both feet together, crossed this to where a rock towered from the end of it and, stepping on to a slab, pointed to a thin stream of clear water pouring out of a crevice in the rock just by her head, then to where the water fell to the side of the slab and disappeared down another crevice between two small boulders.

'It's easy, see, isn't it?' she said. 'You put your pail there and it's full in a jiffy. It's the same water that we get lower down, but it's the devil of a job to get at ours. Dad's promised to pipe it, but Vin's going to see to it himself this year when he's got time.'

'Could . . . could we see the house, do you think, I mean, inside?'

Moira looked up at Constance. 'Surely,' she said solemnly, and without more ado she led the way back to the terrace, stepped over the edge of the plastic tablecloth, turned her back to the oak door, bent well forward, then, bumping the door with her small buttocks, said, 'There! It's a knack. It's never locked; it's just on the sneck.'

Constance wanted to laugh. It was a long time since she had really wanted to laugh. Then she forgot the child for a moment, for she was standing in the middle of the room between the open door and the staircase. It had looked an interesting room from outside, but from this angle it was fascinating. She was looking towards the window to the left of the door, from where there was a shallow raised dais standing out about eight feet.

'Look at the fireplace, Mother.'

She turned and walked slowly to where Peter was standing looking down at a great iron basket, the bars rusted and worn thin at the bottom through years of service.

'Through here is the eating-room.'

They now followed Moira through a doorway and entered a room as long as the first, although not quite as wide. This,

37

as Harry and Millie had described it, was the huge kitchen, with the open range and the hook hanging from the chimney, together with a rusty oven to one side and a pot boiler to the other. There was one article of furniture in this room, and that was a long table. It was definitely hand-made and, like the grate, had seen much service.

'Come away upstairs; you get a grand view from the windows up there.'

Upstairs, they walked through the three rooms which ran one into the other. They were on one side of a narrow landing situated above the kitchen. At the front of the house there were two bedrooms and, as Moira had said, they had a spectacular view. The view from downstairs had been wonderful enough, but from these windows you had the impression you were afloat in the great expanse of sky.

She turned from the window and looked at Peter. His eyes seemed to be waiting for hers and he said quietly, 'If it was only for week-ends it would be wonderful. It's . . . it's so peaceful, isn't it?'

After a moment, while she continued to stare at him silently, she made a small motion with her head. Then going past him and the child, she walked slowly down the stairs; and in the long room she stood gazing at the fireplace before moving on to the terrace. And there she turned to Moira and said, 'Would . . . would you take me to your father?' As she spoke she visualised the big fellow Harry had described.

''Course. Tell me' – Moira cocked her head on one side – 'you taken with it?'

'Yes, very much.'

'Truly?'

'Yes.'

'Aw, Hannah said she felt it in her bones that somethin' good would happen the day. She feels lots of things in her bones . . . Hannah. Me mother sometimes says they're wrong 'cos she gets mixed up with the weather . . . Hannah.'

They were now climbing the hill from which the spring

flowed, when quite suddenly they came on to a pathway that emerged from woodland to go downhill towards what looked like a huddle of houses inside a stone walled compound.

'There's a quicker way down,' said Moira, pointing to a steep zig-zag trail to the left, 'but I'm not allowed to take it. The boys use it mostly, and it wears the seats of their pants out. It's made their backsides as tough as the soles of their feet. It's no use latherin' Joe and Davie, Dad says; they feel his belt no more than a duck's feather.'

Constance turned a quick warning look on Peter as a suppressed giggle came from him, yet she had to suppress a laugh herself. Perhaps the child wouldn't mind being laughed at, but you never knew.

As they descended the hill the situation of the houses behind the stone wall became clearer. There appeared to be four cottages in a row, with two others and a huddle of buildings opposite, and the nearer they came to the enclosure the more her amazement grew. The whole setting resembled a medieval hamlet, an isolated hamlet walled and protected against intruders.

Having reached the bottom of the hill they crossed a piece of rough ground and passed through a gap in the stone wall that had once held a gate of sorts. The grunt of pigs came to them, and chickens strutted lazily about the yard. A dog with a shaggy coat came towards them but didn't bark, and Moira put her hand on its head and said casually, 'This is Rip.' Then in a voice that seemed much too big for her body she yelled, 'Dad! Dad! I've brought some folks.'

'What's that you say?' A woman put her head out from one of the outhouses to the right of the yard. She was evidently washing clothes, for her great thick arms were covered with soapsuds. 'Oh, what's this now?' She was wiping her arms on her apron as she crossed the yard towards them, a woman, Constance guessed, of around fifty, and unmistakably Irish.

'The folks were looking at the house, Hannah. They might take it. Where's me Dad?'

39

'In the kitchen, the last I saw of him. Your mother was seeing to his foot.'

'Come away. Come away in.' Moira smiled broadly at Constance, and Hannah, nodding to Peter, said, 'It's interested in the house, you are? Well, that's good to know. Sean!' She was shouting now as she led the way through a low door and into a small room that was stacked with boots, shoes, wellingtons, and odd-sized coats. Then through yet another small room; obviously a storeroom, for it was full of sacks of potatoes, above which were racks holding vegetables. Finally they entered what was evidently the living-room, and for the first time Constance saw Sean and Florence O'Connor, and Sean was certainly not the big fellow of Harry's description. The man was of medium height, thin, and with a head of thick grey hair, making it appear large. His wife, who had been attending to a cut on his foot, was also thin. But she was tall, even stately, and whereas Sean O'Connor's voice and attitude stamped him immediately as Irish, his wife was unmistakably English, Northumbrian English, and of some breeding.

'This lady's after the house, Sean,' explained Hannah.

'Good afternoon,' began Constance; then added, 'I . . . I hope we're not intruding.'

'Not at all; be seated.' Florence O'Connor pointed to a wooden chair to the side of a large table, its top bare and white; then she stooped and picked up a tin dish from the floor, and as she stood straight again she inclined her head down towards the man who was hastily pulling a sock on to his foot, and said, 'This is my husband.'

'How do you do?' Constance too inclined her head.

'He's for it. He's taken with it, Dad.'

All eyes were now turned on Moira, and her mother's voice came at her sternly, saying, 'Moira!'

'Sorry. Sorry, Mother.' The round face drooped for a moment, only to come up again, a smile splitting it, as she said quickly, 'Well, *he* likes it.' She jerked her head towards Peter. 'They both like it fine. . . Don't you?'

Before Constance could reply Sean O'Connor put his head back and let out a deep laugh. 'That's me girl! The only one in the family with a business head on her shoulders . . . Sit down, sit down.' He was pointing towards Peter now, then added, 'You're the son, I suppose?' and without waiting for confirmation he turned to his wife and said, 'Put the kettle on, Florence.'

'I was about to.' Florence O'Connor moved towards the open range and placed the kettle in the heart of the red glowing fire that gave the room, on this hot day, the atmosphere of a bread oven.

'Now, are you really interested in the house?' Sean O'Connor stood up and made a painful grimace as he began to pull his boot on. 'You're not just passin' by?'

'Yes, I'm really interested.'

'You know . . . of course you do, for Moira there is sure to have told you, the water's outside, but like wine it is. I'm tellin' you that, and it's worth the short distance you've got to go for it. You'll find nothin' like our water in a tap. An' you also know that sanitation is nil? as also is the lightin'? You know that?'

'Yes; it was obvious, all of it.' Constance smiled as she spoke.

'Ah well, now we know where we stand. Put those three unimportant things to one side and you've got the finest house in the county, even though I'm sayin' it meself. A house of character. My wife was born there, weren't you, Florence?'

'Yes.' Florence O'Connor came to the other side of the table and looked at Constance. Her face held a composure, although there was a shadow of sadness behind it. Constance thought she was a woman who wouldn't waste words, and she found it difficult, at this stage, to associate her with this rough-spoken, merry-eyed, congenial Irishman. She could quite imagine her saying, That is all, O'Connor, and the man touching his forehead and leaving the room. Florence O'Connor's voice, like her face, had a controlled quality. She

41

was saying, 'And my mother was born in the house; and her mother, and grandmother. It was built in 1822, because this place —' she spread her palm upwards — 'became too small for the family.'

'Oh, aye,' Sean put in now. 'The Wheatleys reared grand families; eighteen, one of them ran to; and, you know, this very place and the wall around it was built in the seventeenth century. Would you believe that now? And ten families were housed inside it at that time, and all Wheatleys . . . Aye, they were a fine family, and they built well. This place will be standing when the buildings being thrown up everywhere today are rotting again. But now, to get back to The Hall—'

'You call it The Hall?' Peter's voice held a note of surprise and Sean O'Connor turned towards him and said airily, 'Shekinah Hall, to be exact.' He pronounced it She-ki-nah.

'What a quaint name,' said Constance. 'What does it mean?'

'Oh, its meaning is simple; it means to dwell . . . A dwelling place, you know.'

'We call it Snow Hall,' put in Moira on a laugh, 'because once you get in there in the winter an' it snows hard you can't get out again . . .' The words trailed away under the eyes of her mother, and Sean cried, 'There! they would hang you, wouldn't they? children . . . they would hang you. If I didn't love you I would murder you at this minute.' He was leaning towards his daughter, and although she looked concerned because of the look her mother had cast on her, she laughed into her father's face and asked, 'Shall I go and get Vin?'

'Yes, away you go, you little witch, and fetch him. We can do nothing without Vin.'

'I'll be getting back to me wash,' said Hannah now.

Constance had forgotten about the woman who had ushered them in, but now she turned to see her still standing at the side of the door, the position she had taken up when they had entered the room, and she saw Florence O'Connor turn her head towards her quickly and say, 'No, Hannah; you must be here. And anyway I'm going to mash some tea.'

'Aw, that's different. Who could walk away with a brew in the offing?' Hannah now walked across the room to the window and sat down in a high-backed wooden chair, rolling down the sleeves of her blouse and buttoning her cuffs. She could not place her in the scheme of this household. She must be a servant of sorts, not a relative. No, she didn't think she was a relative. Aiming to find out in what relation the Irish woman was to the Irish man and his English wife, she said to Florence, 'Have you a large family?'

Florence O'Connor was at the fire now, pouring water from the big black iron kettle into a large earthenware teapot, and her voice came low and muffled as she said, 'We've had ten children.'

'Ten! That *is* a large family.' Constance smiled and nodded at Sean O'Connor and he nodded back at her, saying, 'It's an even number, anyway. And we like children; we both like children very much.' The smile had gone from his face and his voice held a serious note now, and it seemed to alter the man completely; his manner no longer placed him in the role of farmhand but as the master of the house.

There came the sound of Moira's laughing voice from the other room together with a heavy tread, and Constance looked towards the door and saw, standing behind the child, the man Harry had described.

He had to bend his head to enter the room. He was wearing corduroy trousers and a checked open-neck shirt, and he looked first at Peter, who was sitting directly opposite the door, then down the room towards Constance.

As Harry had said, he had a granite-like face, all protruding bones. His mouth was large, the lips full and, in comparison with the rest of the features, soft. From this distance his eyes looked colourless, but they were directed hard on her and she felt her own waver under his gaze. She could understand Millie getting a fright at the sight of him. He was so big, hard-looking, and remote. That was the word that described him, remote.

43

His father was saying, 'This lady here, Mrs . . . ?' But he paused on the name and Constance prompted, 'Stapleton.'

'Oh aye, Mrs Stapleton. She's interested in the Hall, Vin.'

'Oh yes?' The tall figure moved a step forward. 'You've been over it?'

'Yes.'

'And you like it?'

She looked upwards at him now. 'I like it very much. I . . . I don't know whether I could live in it permanently, but . . . but we could use it for week-ends to start with, that is if . . . if I can meet your price.'

'Well; well now.' It was Sean speaking again. Moving up to his son's side, he said, quickly, 'It's cheap as houses go. Fifteen hundred, we want for it.'

Constance's attention was drawn back to the big man's face. He was now staring at his father, his mouth slightly open as if he were about to say something abruptly; then he brought his eyes to her again and waited.

A house such as the one they were discussing would have fetched around six thousand if it had been situated near a town and had the essentials of water, light and sanitation. As it was placed, it was just a well-built structure set in a very inaccessible spot in Northumberland. They were asking enough. A thousand, she had thought. Very likely it had been more than fifteen hundred for, from the son's expression, his father's statement had come as a surprise to him.

'And that's for a quick sale, mind. It's worth two thousand of anybody's money.' Sean O'Connor was now walking towards the fireplace, and Constance noticed the expression on his wife's face. He did not meet her eyes, but went on, 'We're hard-pushed, else we wouldn't be parting with it. No, not for a minute. But needs must when the devil drives.'

'Have this cup of tea.' Florence O'Connor was handing Constance a blue-rimmed china cup and saucer. Constance and Peter had just emptied a flask a short while ago, but with her usual courtesy she took the cup, saying, 'Thank you very much.' She watched Peter doing the same. She was glad he hadn't refused, although he didn't care much for tea.

She raised the cup to her lips and was about to sip at it when she became aware that Vincent O'Connor was still staring at her, so she stared back at him, and it was to him she spoke and not to his father when she said, 'Would you give me a little time to consider it? I'll . . . I'll write you this evening, whichever way I decide.'

He stared at her a moment longer, then said, 'Very well,' and on this he turned about and walked abruptly from the room, dipping his head quickly as he went through the doorway.

The next minute her attention was brought to the large woman sitting by the window. She was now unloosening the buttons of her cuffs and quickly rolling her sleeves up again as she pulled her heavy body out of the chair, and she spoke apparently to no one in particular as she said, 'He's vexed; you shouldn't have done it. Your legs are not long enough to straddle mountains; you should have left the going to him.'

'Hannah!' Florence O'Connor spoke the name as she had done that of her daughter earlier. It was a censure and no more words were necessary to voice her disapproval.

Hannah paused in the doorway, her face lost in the shadow from the next room, and her voice was a mumble as, still speaking in metaphor, she said, 'When you gollop your food the belly sends it all up again; then what've you got?'

Sean O'Connor, his face red, was looking at his wife now, and she was looking at Constance, and she said, 'I'm sorry, I haven't offered you anything to eat. A little currant cake? it was freshly made this morning.'

'No, thank you; we . . . we just had lunch on the terrace.' Constance made a motion upwards with her hand to indicate the house.

As Florence turned again towards the fire, where her husband now stood with his hand on the mantelpiece, Constance made a silent signal to Peter, and together they rose to their feet.

As they did so there was the sound of young voices shouting across the yard, and presently from the outer rooms came racing two boys. One was the image of Sean O'Connor, small, thin, brown hair; the other, taller, black-haired and dark-eyed. They were closely followed by a girl in her teens, black-haired like her brother, with brown eyes and thick cream coloured skin. She came in running, her head back, her mouth open, crying, 'They pinched my—' Her voice trailed away and she looked at the two strangers standing in the kitchen, just as the two boys were looking at them; and Florence, moving towards them, said, 'Davie, just look at the sight of you. Where've you been?' Then turning to Constance but stretching her hand back towards the girl, she said, 'This is my daughter Kathy. This is Mrs Stapleton, Kathy. She has come with a view to buying the Hall.'

'Oh!' The girl nodded at Constance, then said, 'How do you do?'

'How do you do?' replied Constance. 'This is my son Peter.'

The girl looked at Peter and said, 'Hello,' and likewise he answered, 'Hello.'

'My . . . my daughter is training to be a nurse.' It was with evident pride that Florence was speaking now. 'She's doing children's nursing for a year until she can get into the General Hospital. She's not yet eighteen. This is her day off.'

'Oh yes.' Constance nodded at the girl, who looked somewhat embarrassed, and she asked her, 'Where are you studying?'

'Newcastle.'

'Oh, we live there.'

'You do?' The girl was smiling at her now. Then she turned and smiled at Peter, and he said, 'It's a small world after all.' And it was as if his words held a depth of wisdom, the weight of which was silencing them all, because no one spoke for a moment, until Constance said, 'Well, we must be going. I have enjoyed meeting you very much, Mrs O'Connor.' She held out her hand, and Florence O'Connor took it and they smiled at each other. Then she was shaking hands with Sean

46

O'Connor, who was now strangely quiet. His verbosity seemed to have deserted him even to the point of saying farewell, for he mumbled only a word, then turned away and stood looking down at the fire.

Florence O'Connor escorted them through the two small rooms and into the yard, where she checked Moira from accompanying them. And so they passed out of the gateless gap in the wall and walked across the field and up the hill. They didn't speak until they were quite sure they wouldn't be overheard, when Peter said, 'That's a bit steep, I think. And apparently they wanted more. They all seemed surprised when he stated the price.'

'Yes, I noticed that.' Constance nodded. 'But of course, as he said, if it were near a town it would bring a good deal more.'

'But it's not near a town . . . Still, the point is, do you like it?'

'Yes, I like it. But I've got to think about it. It has to be furnished and . . . and we couldn't live here in the winter. We'd have to have some place in town and that would mean keeping two places going. In the long run it would be as expensive as our present flat.'

'Yes; yes, I suppose so.' He put out a hand and helped her up and over a rise; then he stopped and, looking at her, asked, 'What do you think of them?'

She smiled at him, then turned and looked down on to the walled compound. 'It's difficult to say, having met them for only a few minutes. They're . . . they're quaint.' She shook her head. 'That isn't the word, but I've never met anyone like them; I mean, a family like them.'

'Nor I. But they seemed happy. Look how that girl came running into the room chasing the boys . . . Odd.' His face became straight. 'You don't know these kind of people exist,' and he swept his arm in a wide circle as he enlarged on this: 'They could be in another country, sort of uncivilised . . . Oh no –' he jerked his chin to the side – 'I don't mean that, and not backward either. Oh, I don't—'

'I know what you mean. I'm as puzzled as you are. Come on, we'd better be getting back; it's a long walk to the car.'

She was panting slightly when they rounded the side of the house and stepped up on to the terrace, and they both stopped again, for there, standing by the doorway, apparently waiting for them, was Vincent O'Connor. He walked slowly towards them and without any preamble he said, 'My father made a mistake about the price.'

'Oh!'

'You won't take it at fifteen hundred, will you?'

'Well. Well, as I said, I would like time to consider.'

'That's what most folk say when they want to get out of an embarrassing situation. If you need time to consider you'll consider against it . . . Is it only the price?'

She turned and looked over the wide, wild landscape before saying, 'No; not, not . . . entirely.'

'I need the money, so you can have it for a thousand clear. Whatever expenses are involved in the transaction you would have to cover them; I want a thousand. The thing is, I want it now.'

She was looking up into his face. His eyes were grey with brown flecks in them. They seemed to her to be the wrong eyes for the face, as was his mouth. The bony structure of his face should have been the setting for two black eyes, or cold steely blue ones, and his lips should have been thin and straight. The whole face was a contradiction, a strong contradiction. She had the idea at this moment that he was willing her, a stranger, to provide him with a thousand pounds.

'It's a deal.'

His two front teeth nipped quickly at his lower lip.

The face did not move into a smile, nor did he thank her. All he said was, 'You won't be the loser. You can't go wrong at that price.'

'No. No, I suppose not.' She turned and looked at Peter and put the question in two words. 'All right?'

'Fine.' He was smiling widely at her. 'For me, I can't wait to

48

get settled in. I wish I wasn't going . . .' He paused before adding, 'But I can come up every week-end.'

'How soon can I have the money?'

She turned quickly from Peter and looked at the man again. 'Oh, well . . . well, I haven't got my chequebook with me. I can't leave a deposit but I can let you have it tomorrow. Can you come into Newcastle? I'd have to see my solicitor, of course. It should be done through him.'

'What time?'

She was wavering in her mind, for he was going ahead like a racing car. 'Whatever time you like,' she said. 'What would suit you? You'd have to get in to town.'

'I can be there at ten.'

She wanted to smile. He wasn't going to waste a minute. Nor was he going to give her time to change her mind, apparently. She said now, 'Well, you see, I'll have to make an appointment; I don't know whether my solicitor will be free at that time.'

She saw the dark shadow dropping like a blind from his eyes over his entire face, and in an effort to lift it she said quickly, and as if explaining to someone who knew nothing about solicitors and their ways, 'Well, you see, it isn't always convenient. He may be able to see us or again he might make a later appointment, but . . . but if you'll call at our flat – I'll give you the address – I'll be able to tell you what has been arranged. In any case, I could give you a deposit to show that I am in good faith.' After a pause she added, 'You have your own solicitor, I assume?'

His lids were lowered now. He was staring at the rough flagstones of the terrace and she could not see what impression her words were having on him, but he said quietly, 'No, I haven't. It could all be done through your man. I'll be there at ten.'

As she handed him a card from her bag she said, 'Your . . . your father; he'll be with you, I mean, to make the necessary arrangements for the transaction? That is if we can see the solicitor tomorrow.'

'No, it'll be my mother. It's her house.'

'Very well.'

It was his mother's house but he had said that he wanted the money. She was slightly puzzled.

'I've left the door open.' He nodded back towards the house. 'You might want to look around again.'

'Thank you.'

He inclined his head by way of farewell, then walked abruptly along the terrace. But at the end he stopped and, turning, asked, 'Which way did you come?'

'We . . . we left the car near Woodpark.' She pushed her arm backwards.

'Woodpark!' His thick eyebrows moved upwards. 'That's all of two miles away. There's a nearer road, two in fact, one just below our place –' he jerked his head – 'and the other behind the house here. You can bring the car to within a few minutes' walk of the back.'

'Oh.' She smiled at him over the distance. 'That's good to know. I was just beginning to wonder how we would get the things here. Furniture, you know.'

'That won't be too difficult.' He turned abruptly and disappeared round the side of the house, and the next moment Constance found herself being whirled round the terrace in Peter's arms, and she laughed while protesting, then put her hand over her mouth. When she managed to pull him to a stop she looked along the terrace in the direction Vincent O'Connor had taken and she said, 'You shouldn't; he might . . . he might think we were laughing at him.'

'Why should he?' He was off again, running now, jumping over the remains of the lunch and right into the house. She followed him, her face bright, and looked at him standing at the bottom of the stairs, his arms outstretched, his hands gripping the knobs of the two balustrade posts. She waited to see what he would do next; would he bound up the stairs or continue his hilarious gallop down the length of the long room? But he did neither. His arms dropping to his sides, his body turned slowly and when he confronted her there was no

50

longer laughter on his face as he said, 'It won't be the same if *he* comes.'

'Peter!'

'It won't, I tell you, it won't.' He closed his eyes as he shook his head from side to side in wide sweeps. 'He'll change it; he'll put his stamp on it. Can't you . . . can't you give him the flat and leave him and come here?'

'Peter. I couldn't live here alone; at least, I don't think so. I'd . . . I'd have to see. I've never been alone. You see—' She moved towards him and haltingly, as she tried to explain, she said, 'You see, I need people . . . someone. You don't understand.'

'I understand.' He moved away from her and walked towards the raised dais footing the window. He sat on the edge of it and placed his elbows on his knees and dropped his hands between his legs as he said, 'You're alone all the time; you couldn't be worse off. I should have thought it would be worth giving him the flat to get rid of him.'

She walked up to him and stood over him. 'I hate to hear you talk like that. After all, he *is* your father.'

He looked up at her and his expression and words were not those of a boy as he said, 'I wonder how that came about.'

'Peter!'

'Oh, don't sound so shocked. But I'm telling you, leave him before it's too late or you'll be sorry.'

4

'You know what you are? You're a bloody vindictive bitch; a
quiet, refined, vindictive bitch.' Jim Stapleton was sitting at the
desk in his study, his forearms, tightly crossed, lying over some
scattered sheets of manuscript and his Adam's apple moving
swiftly up and down his short thick neck. 'You're trying to
break me, aren't you, trying to make me do something I'll be
sorry for, or, more to your point, I'll have to suffer for. You'd
like me to beat you up, or him, something that would put me
. . . put me along the line, say.'

'You wouldn't necessarily have to do that to be put along
the line.'

The retort had been dragged from her and she was sorry as
she heard herself saying it. She watched him lean back in his
chair. She saw the quivering of his hands, the tightening of his
face muscles, and she knew that his whole body was suffused
with rage, and as she looked at him she knew that what he had
said was right. She knew she wished, and had wished for a
long, long time, that he would do something that would act as
a cleaver between them. It was illogical, this way of thinking,
because she already had the cleaver in her own hands; she had
a weapon which, were she to use it against him, would
certainly put him along the line. Then why hadn't she used it?
Because exposure would reflect on her own inadequacy?
Partly. But the main reason was Peter and the shame he would

take on to himself; the shame of having a father who was not like other fathers. And yet, Peter alone wasn't the main reason; he was only part of it. There were so many other reasons why she stayed with this man, why she had borne with him over the years. Part of the answer lay in what she had said yesterday morning in the long empty room of the house: 'I don't think I could live by myself.' She had never, as yet, learned to live with herself, and so she feared having to live by herself. This feeling of being alone, she knew, stemmed from the day she learned that her mother wasn't coming back from her long holiday but was getting a thing called a divorce. The result of this was that she became a boarder in the convent instead of a day pupil.

It was in the convent that her need for people had gone underground. On the day the Mother Superior, looking at her across the large black desk, had said firmly, but kindly, 'You are a big girl now, Constance, and you mustn't follow Sister Mary Agnes about. When you try to get all her attention you are depriving others of it. You understand this, Constance?'

'Yes, Reverend Mother.'

'One of our greatest assets in life, Constance, is to be able to control our feelings.'

'Yes, Reverend Mother.'

'You are not a Catholic, child, so I cannot say to you, go and pray to the Holy Family and there you will find comfort, but I can say to you that you should pray, pray to be given calmness of mind and decorum of manner.'

Decorum of manner? She had achieved decorum of manner, so much so that it could drive Jim mad, but calmness of mind . . . ?

She did not realise that she was standing with her head drooped, her chin on her chest and her eyes closed. She had not heard him get up from the desk. It was the awareness of him standing close to her that brought her to herself again. She opened her eyes but kept her head lowered as he talked. Because of her barbed thrust, she had expected his wrath to pour over her, but he was ignoring it, acting as if she had never said it; instead, he was telling her he was sorry for his outburst. Somewhere in the back of her mind she recognised the strategy of his attitude.

'You make me say these things, Connie. I . . . I don't mean them, you know I don't, but I ask you, was it fair to do this off your own bat, buy that place and never let me know, and then expect me to go and live there? You know yourself, I can't stand the country.'

As she swerved slightly his hand came on to her elbow. The whiteness of her face worried him for a moment. 'Sit down,' he said. 'Look, sit down. I'll get you something.'

She sat quiet until he returned with some brandy in a glass and after she had sipped it he said, 'Feel better?'

She inclined her head.

He now drew up a chair and sat opposite her and after a moment he asked, 'What's it like?'

She looked down into the glass and swirled the brandy round it before saying, 'It's very well built.' Her voice was shaking and she swallowed before she went on, 'But isolated. It has beautiful views. It's . . . it would just do for summer living.'

'But you said we'd have to get rid of this?'

'Yes, yes, because I must get the capital up again. I thought . . . I thought if we got eight thousand seven hundred and fifty for it, and we should with all the fittings and carpets, we could get a bungalow, a small one around three thousand, and the remainder would bring in another two hundred a year or so. Then if we sold one of the cars, that would be at least another hundred, and in the new place the living . . . well, it would be reduced to a minimum, just food and transport into the town; the rates are negligible, no phone, or electric bills.'

He rose to his feet and paced the room before he said, 'I like this flat; I've done better here than I've done for years . . . Oh, I know.' He shook his head as if he were aiming to throw it off his shoulders. 'I know I haven't hit it again, but that isn't to say I haven't done good work.' He punched at a large parcel on the desk which had just come by post. It was the sight of the parcel itself that had waxed his anger into white heat, and on the matter of the house that she had bought, he had vented upon her his disappointment of yet another returned manuscript. His fingers tugging at the sticky tape, he now uncovered five hundred quarto sheets which represented to him a year's labour. Clipped on to the title page was a letter. He picked it up slowly and read it, but before he had finished the first paragraph his whole manner underwent a change. His face alight, he was bending down to her, his mouth opening and shutting before he brought out, 'They've taken it! He's taken it. He just wants one or two alterations. He's been abroad, that's why I haven't heard. Three hundred advance, he's given me.' He straightened up and looked at the letter again, saying before he resumed reading it, 'He's not breaking his neck, but nevertheless he's taken it and it'll sell; I know it'll sell,'

When he had finished reading he shook the letter. 'I've done it, Connie. I'm back.' His face was only inches from hers and slowly he bent forward and kissed her.

As his lips touched hers she did not shrink. Anyway, there was hardly time, because the kiss had been quick and light, a mere brush of the lips. And now he was sitting back smiling at her. In this moment he appeared a different being, and although she could no longer forget his real character she was grateful for his lapse into happiness. And when he said, 'I'm glad of one thing, anyway. It's proved to you that I've really been working this past year, that I haven't just been sitting in here on my backside twiddling my thumbs,' she replied, 'I never thought you were.'

'Oh.' He smiled wryly as he wagged his finger at her. 'Anyway, it doesn't matter; I'm in again. Look, will you read it and let me know what you think?'

'Yes, yes, of course.' It was almost six years since he had asked her to read any of his work and it might be six years again before she had another opportunity, unless she could say that she liked what he had written. Anyway, it must be an improvement on his last three books or they wouldn't have taken it. 'Is it set in the north?'

'No. No.' The tone was defensive once more. 'I told you years ago I'd finished with that. Look, Connie.' He was bending towards her. 'I've said this before and I'll say it again. I'm not going to be dubbed a regional writer, even if I never make a go of it. But I have. I have.' He flung out his arm in the direction of the desk. 'I knew I would . . . Regional writers!' He was pacing up and down again. 'Ten a penny. That's what they are . . . And mind' – he turned and pointed his finger at her – 'Our Harry can talk until he's blind about the virtues of Hardy and Bennett and the rest of the old brigade, and the new brigade an' all, Fillman, Cooksy, and that lot. That kind of writing is dead. Oh, they make me sick, as sick as our Harry makes me when he goes on, glorifying the back streets and the blowsy women –'earts of gold. Real Geordie characters; taking a pride in using a dialect that nobody else on God's earth, only their own kind, can understand. You should hear what they say about them down south. They get the same kind of treatment as a secondary modern school kid would get from an Etonian, polite condescension. The term "worthy" is even tagged on to them. I tell you I know what I'm talking about. I had some of it with my first . . . You should know, anyhow . . .'

He was away, well away again on his protest against his early environment. She could have said, as Harry had often said to him. The only decent thing you have ever written was in that first book, and that was full of northerners, north-eastern northerners, not those of the Yorkshire Dales or Cumberland, but the conglomeration of northerners who filled the towns that hemmed in both sides of the river. But what was the use; there was no point in aggravating his bitterness, the bitterness of being ignored. He had come back to his birthplace, where he imagined he should have been fêted . . . even if only as 'local boy makes good', but after one brief mention in *The Journal* he had been filed for further reference, if and when he made the grade again.

He stopped suddenly in both his walk and his talking and stood gazing down at the manuscript; then looking at her, he said, 'I want our Harry to know. Do you feel up to going round there tonight?'

'Yes. Yes, of course.'

'And we'll take Peter. Where is he, by the way?'

'Oh, he just went for a run out, but he'll be back. And he'll come; he likes going to Harry's.'

'Yes. Yes, he likes going to Harry's.' His voice held a bitter note again.

As she rose to her feet she knew she had said the wrong thing. It was seldom they could talk for more than a few minutes without her saying the wrong thing.

He let her go without further comment and she went into her room and lay down on the bed and, her thoughts again reverting to yesterday, she remembered Peter's words: 'It won't be the same if he comes.' And she knew it wouldn't, and she wondered if, up there in that house, she could learn to live with herself, and by herself.

5

Four rooms on the ground floor of a two-storey building, one of eighty such dwellings that formed Bickley Street. Like everybody else in the street, Harry described his home as a house, not a flat. The sitting-room was like ten thousand others in the town; the furniture could be seen in any shop window that boldly advertised deferred payments. It was the antithesis of Constance's lounge, yet she always felt at home here, perhaps because Millie and Harry made you so welcome; and tonight more than usual.

Harry had been genuinely pleased to hear his brother's good news, although Constance knew that, later Jim would say that Harry had put on a good face and that underneath it he was seething.

During tea, Harry had laughed and joked about what Jim would do when this one hit the paperbacks, and then became a film . . . The first one had, and this was a comeback after years in the wilderness. Jim, Constance knew, hadn't appreciated his brother's simile, but he had made himself smile.

Suddenly, the outer door burst open; then the room door was flung open and Ada banged into the room. Her handbag was flung on to the sideboard, and she pulled off her coat and head scarf and in a high-pitched giggling voice greeted everyone with: 'Well! The gathering of the clans. Hello, Uncle. Hello, Aunt Connie. Oh! Hello there, big boy.' She saluted Peter with

58

an old soldier's hand to her brow, then rumpling her father's hair as she passed him to follow her mother to the scullery, she said, 'Hello, love-of-my-life.'

'I'll love-of-your-life you in a minute.' But there was pride in Harry's voice, and even in the assumed sternness of his expression as his eyes flicked from one to the other the while he said, 'She's a girl, isn't she?'

'What's to eat?' Her voice came from the scullery, and Harry said with a sigh, 'Oh, to be young again and with the chances they have today.'

'Where's she working now?' Jim asked; but before Harry could answer, Ada's head came round the door and she cried, 'At Woollards, Uncle. But not for long, I'm tellin' you.'

As her father and Jim laughed the head disappeared, but the next minute she came back into the kitchen carrying a tray. Banging it down on the table, she seated herself and pushed a piece of ham into her mouth, saying, 'All women over thirty should be shot. What do you say, Uncle?'

There was a moment's hesitation before Jim said, 'I agree with you,' after which he glanced in Constance's direction and gave her a wry, shamefaced sort of smile that was meant to be reassuring.

'Honestly?' Ada chewed vigorously on a mouthful of food, swallowed it, then went on, 'She's so damned refeened is Miss Nesbit, the head of the department, you know. She talks like this—' and, pursing her mouth, she mimicked, 'Miss Stapleton, are you aware that you are on duty and a customer is waiting? Get along. Get along . . . Coo! she's an old twit. She makes me want to spew—'

'Ada! We'll have none of that talk.'

'Aw, Mam, what's in that? it's nothing. Anyway she does . . . she does, Uncle.' She was bending forward and grinning, addressing herself solely to Jim. Then pulling herself upright again she looked from Jim to Constance, and then to Peter, and asked, 'Any special reason for your visit? Not that I'm inhospitable; I'm just askin'.'

'Well, there're two reasons.' Her father was nodding at her. 'Your uncle's got another book on the go. I mean, it's coming out.'

'Oh! Good for you, Uncle.' Ada jumped up from the table and, throwing herself on to Jim's knee, put her arms around his neck and kissed him. It could have been a childish action, but Ada was eighteen and none of her actions was childish.

Constance's expression did not change as she watched her husband's arms encircle his niece and return her kiss.

When Peter spoke, it was as if he were trying to drive a wedge between his father and his cousin. His voice high, he gave the second reason for their visit: 'That's not all. Mother's bought the house out in the wilds, the one Aunt Millie and Uncle saw last week-end.'

Ada was standing on the hearth rug now looking at him. 'No kiddin'!' she said. 'For a week-end cottage?' This last remark was addressed to Constance and Constance replied, 'Well, not exactly; we might live there for most of the year.'

'But I thought it was at the back of beyond.'

'Yes, it is rather.'

Ada looked at Constance in silence for a moment. Then shrugging her shoulders, she returned to the table and continued her meal. Her silence on the subject seemed to condemn the whole idea of the house as a permanent habitation. As a week-end cottage she could see it as bearable, but to her, anyone preferring to live outside the town was barmy.

The conversation now became stiltedly general. Ada went on eating, and it wasn't until she had finished and pushed the plate away from her that she turned to Peter and said, 'I hear you've got a car.'

'Yes; that's right.'

'I haven't seen any invitations flying around.'

As her mocking gaze stayed on him he swallowed and said, 'I've hardly driven it myself yet.'

Ada now rose from the table and dusted some crumbs from

60

the sharp rise of her breasts, the while saying, 'I've got some new records; want to hear them?'

Peter did not answer; Ada kept her record player in her room and he certainly did not want to be in there alone with her. Once before he had gone in to hear her records, only to come out flushed to the ears. But his Uncle Harry was now saying, 'Go on, man, and do a bit of twisting; it'll do you good. You never go to dances, do you?'

'No, Uncle.'

'Well, it's about time you started. Go on with you.' And he jerked his head towards the door and his daughter, and there was nothing Peter could do but to follow Ada. As he passed his mother he did not look at her; he knew that she wasn't looking at him but that his father was.

In the room Ada said, 'Shut the door, or you'll have me mam yellin' along the passage. She can't stand the groups; they drive her barmy. Coo! What it is to be old.'

After she had put on a record she turned and straightaway walked towards Peter, who was standing by the window, and leaning close towards him, she thrust her face upwards until her nose was touching his chin, and above the din of the music she cried, 'What's the matter with you? Sit down. I won't seduce you.'

He closed his eyes as he said to himself, Oh God! She's off again. Although she was only a few months older than he she seemed, and always had seemed, like someone of another generation. He had no way of combating her, or her quick-fire talk.

After he had seated himself she sat on the bed and faced him. Supporting an elbow in one hand, she grasped her chin with the other and, moving the skin back and forth, she said, 'You know what's the matter with you, don't you?'

He made his expression superior and his voice careless sounding as he replied, 'I know there's lots of things wrong with me but time, I am sure, will erase them.'

'Not if you don't get out of your nappies an' grow up.'

61

He could do nothing to stop the flush covering his face, and it brought from her a high laugh. 'You know—' she placed her fist into her small waist now and, her expression changing to a sneer, she said, 'you know you're just like me Aunt Connie; all bottled up inside, frightened to let herself go. She'll snap one of these days. I'm tellin' you, she will.'

'Don't talk rot.'

'I'm not talkin' rot. I've been around; I know, I've seen people. An' if you keep the kind of stuff bottled up in you that she keeps bottled up, the cork pops. It's bound to some time or other.' She dug her thumb into her black lacquered hair. 'She'll go barmy.'

He now pointed his finger to the record player and said in a sarcastic, superior tone that only youth can use to youth, 'Perhaps you haven't noticed, but that record is running itself almost off the player, Miss Socrates.'

'Miss who?'

'Socrates. I thought you might be related to him. He, too, used to pretend to be ignorant, then come out with something devastatingly wise.'

'Come off it.' She flicked her hand at his face. 'Just because you're goin' to college, don't come that high stuff with me. An' let me tell you something else: just 'cos I don't know what you're talkin' about, doesn't make me feel awful; I'm not like me dad. If he doesn't know something he gets a guilty feeling about it and has to dash to the library to find out all the whys and wherefores . . . But not me. That kind of clut doesn't affect me. Me, I'm goin' to live. Do you know what livin' is, Peter boy?'

When her face was thrust at him again he said, with studied calmness, 'I thought I was going to hear some records, but if you would rather we discuss philosophy, it's okay with me.'

'Aw, chitterlings!' she said as she pushed her hand flat against his face. Then she went to the little table and switched off the record player, indicating her irritation with him. She now changed the record, saying over her shoulder, 'This is an old one of the Stones, but it's me favourite.'

As the raucous noise filled the room she turned about swiftly and, facing Peter, her body all movement now, she said, 'Come on, let yourself go.'

Peter shook his head. 'I can't do that.'

She waggled herself up to him. 'Anybody can do it, even a baby in a nappy can do it.'

He glared at her. At this moment, above all else, he wanted to slap her across the face; not to utter a word but just slap her across the face. But when he felt her hands on his, pulling him up, he knew he would have to go along with her, because were he to walk out and back into the living-room she would follow him and show him up in front of them all. He bent his arms at the elbows and slowly he moved his body.

'Oh, shades of the Charleston!' She covered her eyes for a moment. 'Let yourself go, man . . . bend your knees!' Her hand shot out and grabbed his tie and he was jerked towards her. His body touched hers and bounced off it again before he wrenched himself from her grasp, saying, 'Don't be a damn fool! You're mad.'

As he straightened his tie her cavorting increased, and she shouted above a sudden loud blare of the music, 'Bet you ten to one I could have that off you in ten seconds.'

'What! What did you say?'

'Your tie.' She pointed: 'I could have it off you in ten seconds.'

He was standing still now looking at her, and he said scathingly, 'It's you who wants to grow up. You're like a dippy thirteen-year-old; you're still wolf howling after the groups . . . Grow up! Huh!'

'Dance!' She waggled her small stomach in front of him. 'Let your belly loose.' Once again her hands flashed out and grabbed at his tie; but this time he resisted her, and strongly, and now in the struggle, managed to grip her hands, and the next minute they were sprawled across the bed, she underneath

63

him with her body shaking convulsively as he struggled to free himself.

He had one hand behind his head tearing at her hands, while with the other he was prising himself up from her chest when the door opened and a voice cried sternly, 'Aye! Aye! What's this? Come on now, enough of that! Come on.'

When her hold slackened, he pulled himself up from the bed, then ran one hand through his hair, at the same time trying to straighten his jacket with the other. He could not look at his Uncle Harry. His whole body was glowing with a painful heat, and he kept his head down as Ada pulled herself up, saying, 'It's all right, Dad, man; we were going round and we fell, that's all.'

'They're going.' Harry's voice had a flat sound. He motioned his nephew towards the door, and Peter went past him . . . still with his head lowered.

Harry now looked at his daughter and he closed the door quickly before he asked her softly and urgently, 'What happened? Was he up to any tricks?'

'Oh, Dad!' She put her hand across her mouth. Then going to him and looking up into his face with wide-eyed innocence, she whispered, 'It was as I said; we were dancin' around, an old-fashioned one, you know; they're doin' it now like you used to do, and we slipped on the mat there—' she pointed backwards.

'You're sure?'

'Of course I'm sure. Anyway, can you imagine Peter attempting anything naughty?' She took her fist and punched it gently against her father's jaw.

He seemed to ignore the fact that her words and the act that accompanied them were in any way insinuating. To him, everything she did had a touch of naive innocence about it. If he had come into the room and found her stark naked he would have believed her if she had said that the situation had been forced on her. He said now, quietly, 'You be careful. Still waters run deep, you know. Even if your Uncle Jim *is* my brother, I know he's a rake at heart, and Peter's his son. So I'm warning you. Don't tease him or give him an inch. Now mind what I say.'

'All right, Dad.' Her face was serious and when he turned and left her, pulling the door behind him, she stood with her shoulders pressed against it, her belly thrust out, and after a moment her mouth slowly dropped into a wide gape and she became convulsed in a spasm of soundless laughter. God! Men were barmy, all of them.

After her mouth had closed her expression altered. The laughter left her face and she looked down at her belly. Then, her mouth opening wide again, she murmured, Why not? God! Why not? Her dad coming in like that. Why, yes. What more evidence did she need?

She went and stood near the bed and looked down at the rumpled coverlet, and her lips made a spitting movement, and on it she brought out two words laden with derision: 'Cousin Peter!' she said.

6

On Wednesday of the second week in August Constance moved into the house. Legally she should not have taken possession until all the paperwork had been completed, but it was Sean O'Connor who said, 'Get your bits and pieces in any time you like, otherwise you'll miss the fine weather.'

Florence O'Connor had endorsed this; and Hannah had said, 'I'll scrub down for you, and I'll put the gang in with a wire brush or two over the stones of the fireplace, for they're smoked black in parts.'

Yesterday she had driven out and told them that the furniture would be arriving today. She had come to Wheatley's Wall, as the O'Connors' home was called, by the lower road, and in the kitchen she had found Sean O'Connor and Florence. Sean was sitting reading, because, he explained, his toe was giving him gyp. Florence O'Connor had been baking and she pressed Constance into taking tea with new bread, and explained that the children and Hannah were all up at the Hall getting it tidy, as they had promised.

Over the past four weeks Constance had been the recipient of kindness such as she had never before experienced. All the O'Connors seemed pleased that she had taken the house; all, that is, except for the big fellow. Vincent O'Connor had spoken to her only twice since he had made the deal with her on the terrace. First, when he and his mother had called at the flat; the second time when Jim had come to see the house and she had taken him down to the farm, as she had come to think of the huddle of cottages inside the stone wall. She had occasionally caught sight of him at a distance, but he hadn't gone out of his way to acknowledge her or to give her the time of day. But against the combined warmth of the rest of the family she could ignore his churlishness.

And now here they were, but again with the exception of Vincent, all helping to carry the seemingly thousand and one articles up to the house. Sean helped the three removal men with the heavy pieces of furniture, while Hannah, at one end of drawers full of linen and bedding with Michael and Davie at the other, went crabwise up the grassy hillside, yelling at each other as if poles apart.

As Biddy, the fifteen-year-old daughter, twin to Michael, dashed past Constance down the hill, followed by the youngest boy, Barney, their faces broad with laughter, their voices high, their legs leaping from one mound to another, she thought, with not a little amusement, that they were all enjoying the arrival of the van as if it were a fair rather than a pantechnicon full of second-hand furniture.

She had spent the last month exploring antique and second-hand shops, because she knew that Shekinah would reject anything new within its walls; the furniture that was to go into it must be weathered and mellow, or it would not fit.

Barney ran past her now carrying a frying-pan in one hand and a steamer in the other, the shaggy-haired dog bounding by his side. It would have been easier, she felt, for the men to have shouldered the tea-chests full of kitchen utensils, but the children had taken it upon themselves to empty them on the rough road below and she hadn't the heart to stop them. For this seemed indeed a fête day for them . . .

It was two hours later when one of the men said, with a grin, 'Well, that's the lot. You're all set now, ma'am; and do I understand we've been invited down below for a cuppa?'

'Yes; Mrs O'Connor has been kind enough to make you some tea.'

'Well, it'll be very acceptable; so we'll be away then.'

'I'll see you before you go.'

'Sure. Sure,' said the man and, followed by the other members of his gang, which now included Barney, Joseph, Davie and Michael O'Connor, they went out of the house, leaving behind only Moira and Biddy. The two girls suddenly became quiet and a little shy; at least, Biddy did. Moira's silence, Constance assumed, was merely respectful awe of the furniture, for she was walking from one piece to another, fingering it in an appreciative loving way, as if she liked furniture. She turned from the tall black-oak dresser standing against the wall to the right of the fireplace and said, 'What did you call this again, Mrs Stapleton?'

'A Welsh dresser.'

'It's nice. It'll look lovely when you get your plates on. It's a bit like our dresser, but nicer.'

'Mother will be expecting you down there,' said Biddy suddenly.

'Oh yes . . . Yes, of course. But I'm an awful sight, and so dirty.' Constance flicked at the specks on her plain blue print dress, then clapped her hands against each other, and as she did so Moira walked slowly towards her, saying casually, 'Oh, you're all right; it doesn't matter what you look like up here. That's the beauty of it. That's what Hannah says. Hannah says you could look as dirty as a fiddler's pack and nobody would notice, but you look all right.' She smiled disarmingly at Constance, then added, 'Dad always says you can't mistake gentry; they can go about in sackcloth, but it doesn't cover them up.'

It was a covert compliment, an Irish compliment. They had likely been talking about her . . . Gentry indeed. It was nice to be taken for gentry. Or was it? She guessed that Sean O'Connor's idea of gentry wouldn't be the same as his wife's;

he would stick the label on anyone with money, and she knew that he was under the impression that she herself was well endowed with the latter.

Going down the hill, Biddy remarked, 'Your husband will find it all done when he comes back,' and Constance replied, 'Yes; yes, he will.'

'Hannah always says that the best way to get rid of a man is to show him some work; they're all a lot of lazy—'

'Our Moira!' Biddy's voice came as a high reprimand, and Moira answered quickly, 'Oh, don't sweat yourself, I wasn't goin' to say anything I shouldn't. I was just going to say lazy beggars.' She now glanced sideways up at Constance, and Constance was forced to smile down at her.

'Is your son still in Switzerland, Mrs Stapleton?'

Biddy had put the question tentatively, and Constance answered her without smiling, saying, 'No, Biddy; he . . . he should be in Germany now. I should imagine they'll be walking in the Black Forest this week.'

The fifteen-year-old Biddy had shown a marked liking for Peter during his visits to the house, and now she wouldn't see him again before she left for Hexham, where she was to stay with a distant cousin of her mother's and start work in a local draper's shop. She was suffering the pangs of first love and Constance didn't laugh at her, even inwardly.

As they passed through the gap in the wall, it was to see Hannah waddling across the yard carrying a tray, on which was a small teapot and a cup and saucer. She was on her way to Vin's workshop.

Constance was curious about the workshop; she didn't know what Vincent O'Connor did there, and as yet she had not asked. This was another facet of decorum; the withholding of curiosity.

Hannah called to her: 'You must be dead on your feet. Away in with you; I'll be with you directly.'

The greeting did not require an answer but Constance smiled and nodded at the woman. She liked Hannah; you couldn't help liking her. That was another thing. She didn't know as yet what position Hannah held in the O'Connors' household, or who she was. There was only one thing evident; she seemed to be needed by them all, because someone was always calling, 'Hannah! Hannah!'

The kitchen was crowded. The men sat at one end of the table, Sean with them; the children were sitting on the fender, and on the clippie mat before it; and Florence O'Connor stood at a side table with large shives of buttered currant bread, and as Constance entered she turned to her and said, 'Well! It's done?' and Constance answered, 'Yes, and I'm not sorry.'

'It's all grand furniture she's got, Mother,' put in Davie above the babble. Although he was thirteen, and there were two boys younger than himself, he was the smallest of all the O'Connors. As Moira had stated with her disarming frankness, their Davie was undersized, but he was bright for all that.

As his mother said sternly, 'Mrs Stapleton, Davie,' he slanted his round black eyes towards Constance and replied on a hick of a laugh, 'Aw, she doesn't mind: Mrs Stapleton is such a mouthful; we should find a name for her.' Again his glance slid up to Constance, and as they all laughed she laughed with them. Everything and everyone was so free and easy here: it was like being dropped on to another world, and finding yourself surrounded by a different species.

She was gratefully drinking a cup of tea when Hannah entered the kitchen and, seeing the children all sprawled around the fire, she cried at them, 'Away up out of that! the lot of you, sittin' clucking there in the middle of the day like fleas in fleece. Come on! Come on! Up with you.' And she hauled Joseph up by the collar and slapped at Michael's head, and, in their various ways, they groaned, saying, 'Aw! Hannah man, give over; leave be;' but they obeyed her.

'I want wood in' – she was digging her finger into Michael's chest – 'and don't forget it's bath night. And you, Davie, and you, Joseph, get those pails in your hands an' start luggin' that water up here.'

70

Protesting but laughing, they were bundled from the room; even Biddy and Moira; and as Moira went out of the door, with a backward glance towards her, Constance wondered yet again at the situation where this untidy woman could order the children about, and which elicited not one word of censure from their mother. On this occasion, at least, she would have expected Florence O'Connor to say, 'Oh, let the girls stay; they have been working hard,' but no; Hannah shooed them out, and Florence made no protest.

The men, too, rose and followed the children; and Constance went with them; and when they reached the house again and she had tipped them substantially they showered her with good wishes. Then, for the last time, they made their way down the hill to the van, and she was alone in Shekinah.

Standing in the middle of the long room, she looked about her. Tonight she would have to sleep here by herself; not that she hadn't slept by herself for years, but there had always been someone in the house. Two days ago Jim had gone to see his publisher and he wasn't due to return until tomorrow; and even then he might not come out to the house. What would happen if he refused to stay here for even a short time? She knew the atmosphere would be lighter without him, but with Peter soon to be away at university, except at week-ends, would she be able to bear living on her own all the time?

Of a sudden she felt very tired. She couldn't remember working so hard as she had done this past week or so, and, as Jim hadn't been slow to point out, she wouldn't have a Mrs Thorpe doing for her out here. He had given her a month, at the outset, to cope with a Calor gas oven, supplemented by a kitchen range that she must feed with wood and coke if she wanted hot water; and he had laughed at the idea of her being able to light a Calor gas lamp in safety, let alone deal with the intricacies of a Tilley lamp. He had pointed out, with heavy sarcasm, the discomfort of getting out of a warm bed and walking at least twenty yards to the lavatory, such as it was.

With a feeling of tiredness, all the drawbacks attached to the

71

place ranged themselves before her like an array of obstacles she knew she'd never be able to surmount. Slowly, she lowered herself into a large, old-fashioned, upholstered chair, and, lying back, she closed her eyes and placed her hand across them and told herself not to be afraid; this feeling was just a reaction. But her thoughts began to race. She wished Peter were here. He hadn't wanted to go on the walking tour, but he had made the arrangements with two other students weeks previously, and she had insisted that he keep to them. If Jim did not come out tomorrow night – if, in fact, he did come out at all – would she be able to stay until Peter returned? She answered this question by telling herself that she could, if necessary, go back to the flat each night to sleep.

A movement in the doorway made her sit bolt upright. Florence O'Connor was standing looking at her.

'I'm sorry. I didn't mean to startle you.'

'Oh. Oh, you didn't. I . . . I was just feeling a little tired.'

'Naturally. May I come in?'

'But of course, of course.' Constance held out her hand in a wide sweeping movement to the older woman, then said, 'You know, somehow I'll always think that this is really your house.'

'That's very nice of you, Mrs Stapleton.' They were standing looking at each other now. Then Florence O'Connor moved her gaze round the room, and after a while she said, 'Davie was right.' She smiled her hesitant smile. 'You seem to know what the house needs; I somehow thought you would.'

'Thank you. I'm . . . I'm glad you like the things, but they aren't properly set yet. I need more rugs, too, and tomorrow I'll hang the curtains. Would you like to see upstairs?'

'No, no; I won't trouble you now. I just thought I would come up and say you are very welcome, if . . . if you understand.'

Again they were looking at each other, and Constance said softly, 'Yes. Yes, Mrs O'Connor. I understand, and I thank you.'

Florence O'Connor turned away from her as she said, 'I never thought I'd be able to tolerate anyone taking the Hall; it holds so many memories for me; but . . . but it's all right.' She turned again towards Constance and the smile on her face was a little more relaxed. 'Would you mind if I look in the kitchen just to see what you need in the way of wood and oil? You see this will be an entirely different way of life from what you've been used to. There are things you will find that are as necessary as air, such as dry wood, water, and oil. You always want to keep a good supply of water in. The children will get it for you, and the wood, too, on their way to school, but I don't want them to become a nuisance to you. I have warned them they must not come over unless they are invited.'

'Oh, no. Oh, please don't stop them coming, not any of them. They'll be company for me, especially Moira.'

'Oh, Moira. Moira talks too much.' Florence again smiled. 'But I think I should warn them, because if you give them the slightest encouragement you'll never have a moment's peace. You see, they don't meet many people this far out, except for the occasional hiker.'

'But they must be used to coming up to the house?' said Constance as they entered the kitchen.

'Oh, yes. The boys camp out up here in the summer, and Vincent lived here for a whole year on his own.' Her voice stopped abruptly, and she changed the conversation, saying, 'Your gas cylinder isn't connected up.'

'Oh, no.' Constance clicked her tongue. 'I meant to ask the men to do it. Oh, dear.'

'Don't worry, that's easily seen to. My husband or Vincent will fix it in a few minutes.' Florence now pointed to the side of the fireplace, saying, 'They've got you some wood in, but that won't last long on that fire. If you intend to stay any length of time I'll see they get a stock in for you.'

'Thank you. I'd be grateful if they would. We may be coming and going until the late autumn. I'm . . . I'm not sure yet.'

73

'Your husband isn't taken with the venture, then.' It was a plain statement.

Again they were looking at each other. Then Constance, her eyes lowered, said, 'Not very. But, of course, he hasn't tried living in the country.'

Florence O'Connor nodded, then turned and entered the long room again and straight out and on to the terrace, and there she stood in silence gazing over the hills, until she remarked quietly, 'It's the most beautiful view in the world.'

'I've come to think so too.'

Again there was silence between them. Then Florence O'Connor, once more facing Constance, said softly, 'Don't be lonely. Come down whenever you feel you want company. It isn't good to be too much alone. And if you want anything, or help, you just have to ask; we're all there,' and before Constance could thank her yet again she had turned and, her grey head held very erect above her thin straight back, was walking across the terrace.

It was some minutes before Constance went back into the house and to the big chair once more, where she again covered her eyes with her hand, but this time for a different reason. She could almost say she felt happy, with a sort of happiness she had never experienced before . . .

Half-an-hour later she was upstairs making her bed when she heard the voice from down below saying, 'Hello, there.' From the top of the stairs she saw Vincent O'Connor. He was dressed, as she had seen him once before, in a dark grey suit, with a blue shirt and matching tie and black shoes. Without the heavy boots and rough cord trousers and coat he didn't look quite so huge, nor did his face look so big; perhaps it was because his hair had been brushed into some semblance of flatness. As she neared the foot of the stairs he said, 'I've fixed it.'

'You mean the gas cylinder?'

'Yes.'

She hadn't heard him coming into the house and he ex-

74

plained his presence by saying, 'I knocked on the back door but you weren't about.'

'Oh, that's all right.' She had been quick to reassure him: if he had been so used to walking in and out of this house it would be difficult for him to get out of the habit.

'See that the gas is turned off at the cylinder every time you've finished with the oven or the grill plate.'

'Yes; yes, I will.'

'Have you used Calor gas before?'

'No.'

'Then be extra careful.'

Again she said, 'Yes; yes, I will.'

He turned his back on her and walked to the door, where he paused, saying, 'You'll be on your own tonight?'

'Yes; my husband's in London, and my son, as you know, is on holiday.'

'You won't feel easy. I've told the boys to bring Rip up, and his box. Nothing, or no one, will get past him. But –' he glanced at her across his shoulder – 'I can assure you no-one will try up here; nevertheless you've got to get used to that fact.' He turned fully round now and his face seemed to soften, as did his voice, as he said, 'I hope you'll be happy here; I've never known anyone who has lived in this house who wasn't . . . I mean, permanently in it.'

'Thank you; I'm sure I shall.'

'The children will bring you milk in the morning when they come to fetch Rip. As my mother has already told you, you only have to ask for anything you want, and if we've got it, it's yours.'

She smiled at him and drew in a long breath before she said, 'I can't tell you how grateful I am to . . . to all of you.'

He stared at her in silence for a few seconds, then said, 'I won't be back until the week-end. Goodbye.'

'Goodbye.'

As she had watched his mother, so she now watched him stride along the terrace. But he seemed to cover the distance in half a dozen steps. She moved her head slowly. Were there ever people so kind? Even he, in his grumpy, hard-faced way, was kind. Where was he going for the next two days? It didn't seem right somehow that he was dressed up for town. He looked very presentable; yes, indeed, different altogether from when he was in his working clothes. She wondered why he had wanted the thousand pounds so badly. Perhaps he wanted to get married and it was for a house . . . But in that case he could have had this house. Not necessarily so, he might want to be nearer his work . . . But didn't he work on the farm, in the outbuilding? What did he do in the outbuilding? She had never asked, and as yet no-one had vouchsafed the information.

The following morning she was awakened, in a strange bed, to the sound of muffled voices rising from the terrace. With sleep still on her, she stretched her limbs and thrust her hands high above her head. She had slept soundly all night. Amazing. She hadn't done that for years . . . And by herself, too.

The voices swept the remaining sleep from her and she sat up and, leaning from the bed to the window-sill just a foot away, she stretched her neck and put her head out of the open window and looked down on to the children below; at Joseph who had a milk can in his hand, and at Davie who was saying, 'Don't leave it there, man, leave it round the back; she'll find it as she goes to the lav; she's bound to go there first.'

'Shut up! both of you,' Moira said in a loud whisper. 'She must still be dead asleep . . . Mind what mother said, and Hannah. Come on, leave it there. You take Rip.'

'It hasn't got a lid on,' said Davie. 'The tits'll be at it.'

'Then you should have thought about a lid,' whispered Moira. 'Come on with you now; we don't want to upset her by pokin' our noses in on the first day or else we're finished.'

'Look who's talkin' about pokin' noses in!'

On Davie's 'Huh!' Constance called, 'Good morning,' which caused three bright faces to upturn to her, and they all said, 'Aw! good mornin'.'

76

'Did you sleep all right?' asked Davie.

'Yes; better than I've slept for years. The air's wonderful.'

'I could make you a cup of tea,' said Moira, a suggestion which brought a none too gentle push from Davie, which could be taken as, Who's pushing noses in now!

'You didn't feel frightened with Rip being here, did you?' Joseph asked.

'No; not at all. And he never barked once.'

'It was Vin's idea.' Joseph nodded up at her. 'He's gone to Manchester.'

'Oh, has he?' said Constance politely.

'For the machinery,' Moira put in.

'The machinery?' said Constance.

'Yes. You know, for the workshop. And you know what? He might bring back electric light.'

'Don't talk dippy.' Again Moira was pushed by Davie. 'Bring back electric light!' He brought his disdainful glance from his sister and, looking up at Constance, explained, 'He's after a second-hand generator. He doesn't know if he'll get it, not with the money he wants to pay, 'cos he's after a second-hand Land-Rover an' all, 'cos ours has had it. But if he does, he'll be set.'

'Yes, yes, of course,' said Constance, nodding as if she understood the whole situation.

'An' you know, if he got it an' we got electric light he could run it here for you. What do you think of that?'

'That would be wonderful, Davie.'

There was a mumble from Joseph now. Constance could only see the crown of his head. Then she was looking down on Davie's crown and his words were mumbled too, but from them she made out that he was denying anything and, from Joseph's mumblings, that they had been told to keep their mouths shut.

'Would you like me to make you a cup of tea, Mrs Stapleton?'

Constance smiled down at Moira. 'It's kind of you, but I'd like to lie in a little longer.'

77

'Oh, you'd have no need to come down and let me in; I could push the front door open as I showed you.'

'Sticking nebs in.' Davie's voice was high and Moira turned on him, crying, 'Aw! you, our Davie.'

'Come on!' said Davie, dragging his sister by the shoulder. Then lifting his gaze, he said off-handedly, 'Your milk's there. I'd get it afore the birds spot the can.'

'Thank you, Davie; I will.'

When she lay back on her pillows her face was alive with laughter. What more entertainment did one need than to get two or three of the O'Connor family together, the natural, uncomplicated O'Connor family?

And that was how she thought about them until early evening, when Jim arrived. He came in and caught her unawares in the arduous task of rubbing wax into the dry floorboards of the long room. He stood staring at her down the length of it; then walking slowly towards her, he said, 'Well, now I've seen everything. You scrubbing a floor!'

She got to her feet and, putting the lid on the polish tin, said stiffly, 'I'm not scrubbing a floor, I'm rubbing polish into it.'

'Takes the same effort.' He smiled at her now. 'Well!' He looked around the room; then walked to the dresser in the far corner, and from there to the side of the fireplace, where he ran his hand over a Victoria inlaid work table. And now, thumping the well upholstered back of the couch that was set opposite the fireplace, he said, 'Put this on the outskirts of Newcastle and I'd say you'd done a fine job.'

She made no comment on his remarks but asked, 'Have you had any tea?'

'No; but it doesn't matter. I stopped for a drink on the way up.'

She sat down in the big armchair and pulled off her rubber gloves and dropped them on to the floor. Then looking at him, she said, 'Well, how did you get on?'

'Oh!' He unloosened the lower button of his coat, then flapped his hands under the sides of it as a man wearing tails

78

might do. 'Not too badly at all. They were very civil. I saw Conway himself. He was extra civil. He smells another *From The Seed All Sorrow* in this one . . . and making a tidy pile for himself . . . Aye.' He rubbed his hand over his chin and dropped into the chair opposite her, adding, 'When I think what they must have made out of that first book it makes me see red.'

She had the answer to this but, as usual, she kept it to herself, for whatever they had made, it would have gone to defray what they had lost on his second, third, fourth and fifth efforts.

'If this one is filmed they'll likely want to read it on the radio, like the last.'

'Did he say the film people were interested in it?'

'No; but you never know. It's as good as my first, and if it's filmed I'm going to make a stand all round. By Jove! I am this time. What? Twenty-five per cent to them and ten per cent to the agent? Not likely!'

Before she could check herself the words were out, setting a spark to his highly inflammable temper. 'Well, you should understand that if they didn't publish a book first it would never reach a film company.'

'Hah! Hah! There speaks the publisher's daughter. You were well trained; I'll say that much for your father.'

She knew she had said the wrong thing. She rarely discussed his work with him, but when she did it nearly always ended up in a row. Yet she couldn't sit silently always and listen to his bigoted, one-sided approach to everything that didn't please him.

She rose, saying, 'I'll make some tea.'

He followed her towards the kitchen, asking, 'Is there a bed ready, or do you want me to go back to the flat?'

'There's a room all ready for you if you want to stay.'

'God! You make me sound like a guest, and not a very welcome one at that.'

'I'm sorry.' As she turned to him, both her voice and her manner told him she was sorry, and he said in a mollified tone, 'Well, do you want me to stay or not?'

79

She did not say, It's up to you, but, 'Of course I would like you to stay.' As she made the tea she also endeavoured to make conversation. 'What time did you get back?'

'Oh.' He was walking round the refectory table and examining the set of four hide-seated, high-backed dining chairs, and he said hesitantly, 'Well . . . this morning.'

'You travelled overnight?'

'Yes; you know I always prefer a sleeper.'

'You've been at the flat all day?'

'Yes, yes' – it sounded as if his attention wasn't on her or on what she was saying – 'except for a stroll I took this afternoon.'

'Have you started on anything fresh?'

'No, not really. I've been revising one of the old ones, but now I am wondering if I should do a sequel to *The Temper of The Steel*. That's what I'm calling the new one . . . Talking of stories, real and imagined, do you know anything about that lot down there?'

He came and stood at the other side of the cooker, and she raised her eyes to his as she asked, 'You mean the O'Connors?'

'Yes. Who else?'

'Only that they're most kind, all of them.'

'There's something fishy about them.'

'Oh, really!'

He answered her remark with, 'Now look, don't get on your high horse; I'm just putting two and two together.'

'What do you mean, putting two and two together? And fishy? What are you talking about?'

'As I said, there's something fishy going on down there.'

'What makes you think that?'

'Well, I stopped for a drink just outside Gunnerton. There were three or four fellows in the bar and there was talk about some youngster who had broken both his legs and almost his neck too after falling down one of the crags. They said he went climbing in ordinary boots, which is asking for trouble. But that's by the way. I got talking to one old boy, one of the locals, apparently, and I happened to say I'd bought—' He stopped and, screwing up his eyes, bounced his head at her, saying thickly, 'All right. We, or let's go further and say, you . . . Will that suit you?' He had opened his eyes and was looking at her again, and she answered quietly, 'I never said anything.'

'No! No! You didn't have to, but you should have seen your face. Lightning couldn't have been quicker than the change in your expression . . . Well, to continue. That's if you want to hear.' He turned from her and went back to the table and, sitting down, he said, 'When I mentioned this house, the old boy pricked up his ears and said, "Oh, Shekinah. So you've taken The Hall. Well, well now. There's a story if you want to write it."'

She had her back to him so that he could not now see her expression, but knowing he had given himself away, he paused. He was never long in any strange company before letting it slip that he was a writer. It was a harmless weakness, this, but it had always made her squirm. His voice took on a harsh note as he went on, "I'd be careful of that big fellow if I were you. I never liked him from the minute I saw him. Don't give him any rope."'

'Rope?' Her voice was indignant and she turned her head quickly over her shoulder to look at him.

'Oh, you know what I mean . . . keep him in his place. After all, what are they? Apart from the mother they look like a lot of Irish gypsies, and she couldn't have thought much of herself to marry a fellow like O'Connor. You've only to listen to him for five minutes to know that he's the type of Irishman that will neither work nor want.'

'Don't talk like that about them!' She was facing him across the table now, her voice unusually brisk. 'I've told you, they've been more than kind to us.'

'Keep *us* out of it.'

'All right then. They've been more than kind to *me*.'

'They've only been kind because they've made money out of you.'

'They didn't make money out of me. All things taken into consideration, I got this place very cheaply.'

He closed his eyes again, saying patiently, 'All right, all right; we won't go into it. But I'm telling you. This old fellow down there suggested things weren't all they should be.'

'What did he say?'

'He wouldn't say anything clearly, but he asked if I'd seen Big Vin, and I said, if he was the eldest son, yes. The old fellow put his head back and laughed. Then he asked about the fat one, Hannah, and his enigmatic remark just before he left was very telling. "It couldn't happen in a town, mister," he said; "it could never happen in a town; they wouldn't let it live." So what do you make of that?'

She turned back to the stove, a feeling of disquiet in her now, in spite of herself. She didn't know what to make of it, but this she did know: she liked the O'Connors, yes, even the oldest one . . .

It was at around half-past seven when Moira and Biddy came up with another can of milk and a pat of home-made butter. After they had put them on the sideboard they stood looking somewhat shyly at Mrs Stapleton's husband. They were seeing him, not only through their father's eyes, but judging him on Hannah's comments; they hadn't heard their mother or Vin say anything about Mr Stapleton. But tonight he looked different, not so stiff; he looked jolly, and he came and stood between them and put his arm around their shoulders and asked them their names, asked how old they were, and told Biddy that she was too beautiful to be lost in the country. And Biddy hung her head and blushed. Then Mrs Stapleton handed them the can, unwashed, and she told them to thank their mother for the butter, and to tell her that she would be down tomorrow.

They had expected to stay awhile. They had intimated as much to their mother, and she had said, 'Well, only half an hour, mind. And don't make a nuisance of yourselves.' But now they were almost being shooed out of the door, like

82

Hannah did the hon.., and, going down the hill, Moira said to Biddy, her head well up now, that she thought she knew why Mrs Stapleton was cross. She didn't know much about life, except that it began with birth and ended with death, but she did know that women didn't like to hear other women being called beautiful by their husbands. They could be jealous. She had learned that much already.

7

For her first two weeks in the house Constance lived at peace with herself. She pushed out of her mind the fact that there could be anything wrong with the O'Connor family. She also thrust to the back of her mind the scene in the kitchen after she had hustled the children through the doorway, and the fact that because of it Jim had flown into an incoherent rage and returned to the flat.

The following day she had gone down the hill to the O'Connors' and invited Biddy and Moira up to tea with her in the afternoon, and as far as she could determine all was as it had been with the family.

Two evenings later she saw Vincent O'Connor returning home. At least, she saw the old Land-Rover threading its way, like a small black beetle, on the curving road, far away over the fells, that led to the farm.

That day the children had informed her that their father was going to meet Vin at the station. They had been in a state of high excitement waiting to know if their brother had got the 'lectricity, for it would be wonderful to have 'lectricity, they agreed, the boys because it would give them light, and the girls because it would give them hot water and, as Hannah had said, they might even wash the clothes with it.

On the Saturday morning Biddy and Michael, Davie, Joseph and Moira had stormed up the hill and she had gauged from their tangled, excited conversation that Vin had done a splendid deal; he had got not only a generator but also a lathe, and a saw that would go by 'lectricity, and a polisher . . . and oh, many more things. And what, Constance had enquired, did he need all these things for?

They had gaped at her. Didn't she know? Vin made animals, lovely animals. He cut them all out of wood, by hand, and sent them away to a firm, which firm put the finishing touches to them, polished them and painted some of them. But they were daylight robbers, the firm, as their father and Hannah were always telling him, as if he didn't know himself. And then there came that stroke of luck a few weeks back when their mother's cousin from Manchester was passing through and he stopped to look them up, and he saw what Vin needed. Tools and 'lectricity to drive them, and he knew where Vin could get these tools second-hand for a quarter of what they would cost new, and then he could have a real business on his own and nobody could cheat him. And that's why they had sold the house to her, and now didn't she understand?

She understood . . . What could be wrong with such a family? Nothing. Nothing. They were as open as the wide sky that covered them.

A week later Sean took her to see Vincent O'Connor's workshop. The shop was but two little cottage rooms made into one. Along two sides of it, from floor to ceiling, were shelves and on them were carved animals of every shape and size. She had gazed at them in silence for a long while before saying, 'And he has carved all these by hand?'

'Every leg, feather and rump, all himself. He's an artist, is Vin. If he was up there in London he could make his fortune, but London's not for him, so he chips away for pennies. But not for much longer, not for much longer. When the machinery comes he'll be set; we'll all be set.'

'How long would it take him to carve that?' She pointed to a lion standing about four inches high, with its mane looking so real you could expect it to stir in the wind.

'Oh, a thing like that, a full day. Yes, a full day. He often sits at it for hours at a stretch; he gets lost in it. I tell you he's a fine artist, is our Vin.'

The sound of the door being thrust open turned them both towards it, and Vincent O'Connor stood there with his hand on the latch staring at them, and his father said to him, 'Aw, there you are, boy. I was just showin' Mrs Stapleton some of your handiwork; I thought you were away over the hills for a stride.' He moved slowly towards the door and Constance imagined that he sidled past his son. 'I'll away now; I've got those pigs to see to. There's always somethin', always somethin'.'

Vincent O'Connor, now standing by the corner of the table, looked at Constance and said brusquely, 'I don't allow visitors in here as a rule.'

A slight flush tinted her face. 'Oh, I'm sorry. I had no intention—'

'Oh, I know you had no intention of intruding; it was my father; he should have more sense.'

'You don't like anyone to see your work?' It was a tentative question.

'Not . . . not this kind.'

She blinked at him, then turned to the shelves and on a surprised note, said, 'Not this kind? But these are beautiful; only a sculptor could carve like this.'

'I'm no sculptor.'

'Well, what would you call this work?'

He turned his huge head, and his eyes ranged along the shelves as if he had never before seen what they held, and then he said stiffly, 'These are the work of a whittler.'

'You're too modest.'

'I'm not modest, either.' There was a raw, hard quality to his voice now, making it match the expression on his face, but she told herself not to be deterred by his manner and so she asked lightly, 'Well, would you call yourself a whittler?'

'No; I would call myself a wood carver.'

He was a difficult man to be nice to, she decided.

She walked towards a shelf that held nothing but horses, the tallest about twelve inches high, the smallest no taller than half an inch. There must have been at least fifty animals on the shelf and her eyes ranged along them, then lifted to a high corner bracket where, standing alone, was a carving almost concealed in the dim light of the workshop. When she finally focused on the piece she felt a sense of shock. She was gazing at a lamb being born, carved in wood. So real, so elemental was the carving that the strain of the animal evicting its young almost became an embarrassment; the birth pangs were in the sheep's drawn features. The knife had even indicated the slime on the struggling body of the lamb.

'Well?' His voice coming from just behind her made her start. 'Do you like it?'

She had to wet her lips before she replied, 'It's a very fine carving.'

'But it shocks you?'

'No, no, of course not. Why should it?' She turned towards him just as he reached up to the shelf and brought the carving down and held it at face level, saying again, but quietly now, 'It shocks you.'

'It doesn't shock me. I have a son, so why should the birth of a lamb shock me?' To her annoyance her voice had a prim sound, and it rose as she added, 'Does it give you any satisfaction to produce work that shocks people?'

When he did not answer but continued to stare at her she said, 'I think it would have been better if you had let the lamb be born.'

'Ah! There we have it. There we have it.' He was wagging his head at her. 'Better let the lamb be born. Aye, that's been said before. Get it over, get all pain out of the way. Why didn't you let the lamb be born?' He was mimicking her refined tone now. Then his voice harshened: 'Because this is how things are; this is the way we came out, you and I, slime-covered and

87

strugglin', giving pain. We're born in pain and we retaliate by givin' it back. All our lives we give pain to somebody.' He stopped for a moment and stared into her straight face, white now, only her wide-stretched eyes showing colour. He nodded to her. 'But on the whole women have it easier than men because they can give the blasted thing birth. They get rid of a lot of pain by giving birth. They call it part of the joy of motherhood. But there's no such compensation for the man. He just goes on hurtin' and inflictin' pain to justify his existence. And don't tell me –' his voice was very soft now but he was wagging his finger almost in her face – 'don't tell me that a man is compensated by his children, by his son, say . . . Is your husband compensated by his son Peter? No; not on your life.' He was staring down into her eyes, and when she made no answer he said, 'Do you know something? Your husband's afraid of his son, and your son despises his father.'

Her face whitened even further under his gaze: she was filled with indignation and anger. Jim could be right about him. She was searching for words with which to cut him, put him in his place when he said, 'I . . . I've gone too far?'

Now she could say, 'I think you have, much too far, Mr O'Connor. Besides, you don't know what you're talking about.'

'No; no, I don't.' His head drooped. 'I'm sorry. You see I . . . I so rarely talk to anybody, and . . . and never in this place –' his eyes looked upwards under his lids and swept the room – 'this place is too full of my thinking. It's . . . it's about the only place I can be meself. You . . . you shouldn't have come in here. But it wasn't your fault; as usual, it was my father's.'

She turned from him and walked stiffly towards the door; but before she could open it his hand went across her shoulder and kept it closed, and he said with a note of pleading in his voice, 'Don't . . . don't let this make any difference across the road, will you?' He nodded in the direction of the house. 'My mother lays great stock on you being up in the Hall. She's never had company, I . . . I mean her own kind to talk to, for years.

Please. It . . . it won't make any difference?' His head came down and he was looking into her face, and she answered stiffly, 'No, no, of course not.'

He straightened up and opened the door, and she walked past him and into the yard. There was no-one about and she didn't knock on the house door but went swiftly through the gap in the wall and up the hill.

After entering the house she stood at the foot of the stairs, her hand pressed tightly against her cheek. Her whole body was shaking. He was a strange man: intense, full of bitterness, too. He had been hurt in some way and the hurt had apparently seared his mind, because bitterness had dripped from his every word. But to say that about Peter and Jim . . . Her hand slowly dropped from her face and she turned about and walked to the big chair and sat down. But he was right; every word he said was true. Still, that didn't give him the licence to say it, and him only a stranger. It was odd, odd how he had talked. The feeling of disquiet returned to her. It would indeed seem that there was something just not right down there.

Later, as she sat on the terrace in the dusk wishing that tomorrow was here, when Peter would be home, even wishing that Jim might put in an appearance, as he had done twice during the past week, Vincent O'Connor came round the corner of the house and towards her. He was carrying in his hand a brown-paper parcel, and on his approach a nervous tremor filled her. She made herself sit quietly, and when he stood before her he handed her the parcel, saying, 'I'd like you to take this as a peace offering.' He was smiling. It was the first time she had seen him smile and it transformed his face. His voice, too, had a gentle quality. This wasn't the man who had confronted her in the workshop.

She took the parcel from his hand. She knew what it contained before she opened it; but she undid the string and looked again at the straining sheep; and now she thought it looked beautiful, and good, and very, very human. She said quietly, 'It's . . . it's very, very kind of you, but I can't take it.

Not because—' She, too, was smiling now. 'I'm not annoyed any longer, but it's too fine a piece for you to give me. If it had been one of your little horses or lions I would have accepted it gladly.'

'They're trash, commercial stuff. I wouldn't offer you any one of them. If you're no longer annoyed you'll take it; but if you're still mad then you'll hand it back.'

'Put like that, what can I do?'

She went to rise from the low deck chair but had difficulty in pulling herself up because she was holding the wood carving. His hand came down towards her elbow, but he didn't touch it; instead he took the carving from her, and, with both hands now on the chair, she pulled herself up, and when silently he handed her back the carving she took it, saying, 'I'm . . . I'm very grateful to you. It'll sit on the mantelpiece beautifully.'

She passed him and was walking into the house when she realised he wasn't following her, so she turned and said, 'Won't you come in for a moment?'

He crossed the threshold and stood just within the doorway and watched her walk down the room, then place the carving on the mantelpiece; and when, standing back, she surveyed it and said, 'It seems to have been made especially for there,' he answered quietly, 'It was, many years ago.'

'Really!' She turned towards him.

'Yes' – his chin was jerking – 'it's funny how things work out, but that piece was made for that very mantelpiece.'

She watched him now walking towards her. He wasn't looking at her, but went past her and stood in front of the carving and gazed at it, and she didn't ask why he hadn't placed it there before. But once again there came back to her a feeling of disquiet.

'I'm about to make some coffee; would you like a cup?' It was what she would have said to a visitor to the flat, and it seemed quite as natural to say it to a guest in this new house, but from the surprised look he turned on her she might,

90

she thought, have been making an indecent suggestion to him. 'No. No, thank you,' he said quickly.

As he walked back towards her, he asked, 'When will your son be back?'

'Tomorrow; and I'll be glad, because I miss him very much.'

He went past her now and towards the door, saying, 'You shouldn't stay here alone. Not that anyone would interfere with you, nothing like that, but it's not good for you to be on your own; it's . . . it's not good for anyone to be on their own.'

'Well –' she forced herself to smile and speak lightly – 'after tomorrow I won't be,' and she made a further effort to say, 'My husband would have been here but he's working on a new book, and it's strange –' she gave a little laugh – 'but he can't write in the country; he's got to be in the middle of town. You'd think writers would need the quiet of the countryside, wouldn't you?'

He was staring at her from the doorway and he nodded, but didn't give her an answer.

She followed him slowly on to the terrace, but stood apart from him as she followed his gaze across the hills that were purple in the fast-fading twilight.

'If you can't find peace here, you'll find it nowhere.'

'What?'

He turned his head slightly and repeated, 'I said, if you can't find peace here, you'll find it nowhere.'

Why must he stab at her with such truisms? He talked as if he knew all about her life, her inner life. He made her uncomfortable, and that was putting it mildly.

'Good-night.' He was walking away, and she answered to his back, 'Good-night;' then returned immediately into the house and locked the doors and went to bed.

Her displaying of the carving on the mantelpiece had repercussions. They began when Davie and Joseph brought the first batch of wood to the back door and stacked it under the lean-to. They would be starting school on Monday, they informed her, and their mother said they must bring a supply up because the nights would soon become chilly. It was when Davie carried some wood into the house to fill the big rope basket that rested at the side of the fireplace that he saw the sheep with its lamb. His arms still piled with the wood, he stood staring up at it; then turning to where Constance was entering the kitchen, he shouted at her, 'Where did you get that?'

By the time she reached the fireplace he had dropped the wood into the basket and was again staring up at the mantelpiece.

'Vincent gave it to me.'

'Our Vin!?'

'Yes.'

'He gave you that?'

She nodded now.

'But he wouldn't.'

She looked down into the round black eyes, so like his father's, and she said, 'Well, he did, Davie, I didn't steal it.'

'No. No. You wouldn't steal it,' he said; then he went out.

There was quite an interval before the boys came up the hill with the next pile of wood, and when she offered them hot chocolate, for which she discovered they had a particular liking, together with some biscuits, they drank and ate in comparative silence, saying only, 'Ta,' and 'No, no; I don't want any more. Thanks all the same.'

During the afternoon she went several times down the rough path to the end of the garden, round by the outhouses and the closet, which had defeated her in her endeavours to eliminate its particular odour, through the small patch of what had been a vegetable garden, and on to the hill that overlooked the rough road below to see if Peter was coming. He should have arrived in Newcastle by the early morning train and she had expected him to come straight out to the house.

It was mid-afternoon when, returning to the house once more, she found Florence O'Connor on the terrace. She was taking a stroll, she said, just to stretch her legs, and she had looked in to see if she needed anything. Mr O'Connor was going into town in the morning, so could he bring her any groceries? Had she enough oil?

It was very kind of her, Constance had replied, but she herself would be going into town tomorrow; she needed to go to the flat. She had laughingly added that at times she forgot she had to look after two homes now; the purchase of this house had brought on a particular kind of amnesia. Would Mrs O'Connor like a cup of tea?

Florence O'Connor had accepted and had sat in the long room drinking the tea and talking about her childhood spent in this very room. Only once had she glanced towards the mantelpiece, and that was when she first entered the room. Constance had seen her do this, and had expected her to make some comment, but she hadn't referred to the carving in any way, and so, remembering Davie's surprise at seeing it, she refrained now from alluding to it. The feeling of disquiet was back.

Then, at six o'clock, Hannah climbed the hill and came along the terrace. She was carrying a blackberry and apple pie;

she was sure the boy would be hungry after his long journey.

Constance told her that Peter had not yet arrived and that she was rather worried; if he didn't come shortly she would take the car down to the main road and phone the flat.

Without invitation Hannah walked from the terrace into the long room and exclaimed in a high voice, 'It's beautiful you've got it. Never have I seen it looking like this. Now, why didn't we ever think of hanging red curtains at the windows?' She fingered the material. 'It's fine velvet. I guess that cost a pretty penny. *That's* the reason we didn't hang such curtains at the windows.' She put her head back now and laughed, and her large breasts shook.

'Would you like a cup of tea, Hannah?'

'No, no; thank you all the same.' Hannah turned her beaming face towards Constance. 'You know, I never drink anybody else's tea but me own or Florence's, unless I'm parched, that is. You know, the English, no offence meant' – she brought her head forward – 'but the English can't make tea. Water bewitched and tea bedamned it is that most of them turn out.'

Constance was laughing heartily now. 'I'll let you brew your own, Hannah. It's all yours,' she said, holding out her hand towards the kitchen, and Hannah, laughing louder now, said, 'No, no. Honestly, I'm runnin' half the night out of me warm bed. Like a hare I go across the yard, the skitters it gives me.'

Oh! Oh! Like a hare I go, the skitters it gives me! Constance had never belly-laughed in her life, but she wanted to do so now. The very sight of Hannah filled her with mirth, and this was a feeling strange to her. She had the desire to link her arm and draw her to the couch and say, 'Talk, Hannah, just talk, because I want to laugh, really laugh.' But now Hannah had turned her head towards the mantelpiece and was staring at the carving, and again Constance waited for some comment about it. But as Florence O'Connor had reacted, so did Hannah; an ignoring of the fact that an apparently well-known piece of carving had found its way from Vincent's workshop

94

on to her mantelpiece. She should have said to both Florence and Hannah, as she had said to Davie, 'Vincent gave it to me,' but because she sensed there was something behind it, some significance, some embarrassing significance, she said nothing.

Her face still bright, Hannah turned to her now, saying, 'An' you're settled right in, then?'

'Yes, yes. Until the bad weather starts, Hannah.'

'Well, that could start from any time next month an' go on right up to the beginnin' of March . . . We'll miss you when you leave.'

'Yes, and I'll miss you, all of you. And this house, and meeting the family.' She hadn't known whether to say 'your family' or not. 'It has been a wonderful experience, and . . . and you've all been so kind.'

'Aw.' Hannah flicked Constance's arm with her fingertips. 'It's easy to be kind to some folks, very easy,' and she finished the compliment with a bob of her head, then sauntered towards the door. But it was on the terrace that she said, 'Well now, I'll be goin'. If I don't get down there soon that lot'll be in bed with their boots on. It's school for them on Monday, thanks be to God.' And then, the smile slipping from her face, she gazed at Constance and said, 'I shouldn't say that, it's a lie. I'm never happy unless they're around me feet kickin' up a shindy. Truth to tell, I dread the day the last one leaves home, because then they'll all be grown up.'

Constance dared to probe now, asking, 'You've been here a long time, Hannah?' And Hannah stared back at her, and it was a moment or so before she replied, 'A long time, Mrs Stapleton, a long time. Good-night to you.'

'Good-night, Hannah.'

She was as wise as ever. A long time . . .

It had turned seven when she stood on the hill and at last saw the red open car bumping along the road, and she went hastily down to meet it.

'Hello, darling.' After holding Peter in her arms she kissed him and he kissed her back. 'Where've you been? What time did you get in? I've been expecting you since lunchtime.'

He walked by her side up the hill, saying, 'I got in this morning but I was so tired I went to bed.'

'You've been in bed all day?'

'No, no.'

She looked at him closely as they walked in silence for a time; then she said, 'Is anything wrong, Peter?'

'Wrong? No, no. What could be wrong?' He was smiling fully into her face.

'Have you had a good time?'

'Oh.' He pressed his lips together and jerked his head. 'Great! Absolutely great! We've decided to go again next year, only for twice as long. I'll tell you all about it later.'

As they entered the house through the kitchen door she said, 'You saw your father?'

He threw his bag on to the table and there was a definite pause before he answered, 'Yes.'

Swiftly she pulled him round to face her. 'What's wrong, Peter? There's something wrong.'

'There's nothing wrong.'

'You've had words with him? A row?'

'No.'

She swallowed; then moistened her lips. 'Is he in the house?'

'He was when I left.'

'Was he there this morning when you arrived?'

'Yes, yes. I got him out of bed.'

'And . . . and you've had no words?'

'No, no; I've told you. We were very polite to each other.'

She sighed, then asked, 'Are you hungry?'

'Yes.' He turned now and looked round the kitchen, saying, 'Oh, you've got it fixed. Oh, I like this. I say!' He went towards the open grate in which a wood fire was burning. 'Does this work?'

'Yes. It cooks beautifully too, and heats the water in the side boiler, with the help of some coke. Go and have a look at the other room while I make the tea. Or would you prefer coffee?'

'Coffee, please.'

When he left her she stood for a moment gazing after him. There was something troubling him and it concerned his father. She was sure of that. They must have had words, although he'd said they hadn't.

A few minutes later he returned to the kitchen and his enthusiasm had lifted the blank look from his face. 'It's splendid! Really splendid. I knew you'd make it comfortable, but not like this. The orange rugs and those red curtains; you'd imagine they'd clash, but instead they look wonderful. The whole place looks warm. It'll be marvellous in there in the winter.'

'But we won't be here in the winter.'

'Oh, no. Have you found a place yet?'

'No, but then I haven't looked. I must, though, and very soon. I don't suppose I can stay here later than October.'

'Do you think you'll have sold the flat by then?'

'I don't know. In any case we'll have to have some place in town to go into first; you couldn't possibly come out here in the winter even . . . even if I decided to stay on.'

'Look.' That strange expression was on his face again, and his voice was urgent now. 'I've told you, you're not to take me into account. In any case I'll be living in. Don't you worry about me in any way; do what is going to suit you, and just you.'

She saw his jawbones tighten on the last two words and she said again, 'Peter, tell me, please, what's wrong? And it's no use saying nothing's happened between you and your father, because I don't believe you.'

He turned from her, but swinging quickly round again he said, 'I'm going to say this once more. You should divorce him, for he's no use to you.'

'Peter! Don't talk like that. I hate to hear you talk like that.'

'Well, you're going to hear quite a lot more of it in the future. I don't know how you stand it for you're neither married nor single.'

She stared at him. He had only been gone from her for three

97

weeks but he seemed to have developed into a fully grown man in that short time. Perhaps his education had been widened when he was abroad. She rejected the thought. No, whatever had happened she was sure Jim had had a part in it.

After he'd eaten his meal she reopened the matter of finding a place in the town and said, 'I think I'll go in tomorrow. We could go round looking at places. What about it?'

'I'll go in with you but I'll be busy in the afternoon.' He kept his eyes on his plate. 'I've got an appointment. It's about some work I've got to do before I go up.'

'So late? You didn't say.' She was staring at his bent head.

'Well, I didn't know until this morning; there was a letter awaiting me at the flat.'

She knew he was lying.

'I've got to see this fellow at the Hancock Museum.'

'Will it be open?'

'Oh yes, yes.' He glanced up at her and smiled. 'You don't stop studying because you're on holiday, you know.'

'No.'

'Oh, I forgot to tell you. I saw Kathy O'Connor, the one that's nursing, you know.'

'Really!'

'Yes; I stood her a coffee.'

'You didn't! That was very, very generous of you.'

They were both laughing now.

'Well, you know what I mean.'

'How did you meet her?'

'I was stopped at the traffic lights and there was a bus stop further on and I saw her waiting. We spotted each other at the same time and we waved, and so I asked her if I could drop her anywhere. She was going back to the nursery. She was having her two hours off or something.' He wagged his head, drained his coffee cup, then ended, 'After spending a couple of bob I dropped her at her quarters, and that was that.'

'You mustn't throw your money about.'

He wafted his hand at her; then after a moment said, 'She's rather nice.'

'Yes, I should imagine so. And she's very pretty.'

'Well.' He lay back in the chair, stretched out his legs and again he said, 'Well,' and his hairless chin flattened itself as he paused to consider this statement. Then he gave his verdict. 'I suppose she is, in a way. And you know something?' He was looking up at her as she poured out more coffee. 'She's good company. We laughed all the time we were together. The O'Connors are all like that, aren't they? You always find yourself laughing. How are they, by the way?'

'Oh, they're all very well; just the same as when you left them.'

As she sat down again he looked about the room and said, 'You know, I can't get over what you've done to this place.' Then getting up and strolling to the mantelpiece he asked, 'Where did you pick this up?' He was looking at the carving and she rose and came to his side and she, too, looked at it before she said, 'I didn't pick it up anywhere. Mr . . . Vincent O'Connor gave it to me.' She kept her eyes on the group as he turned his face towards her and asked, 'Why did he do that?'

'Oh, I don't know; just to set the mantelpiece off, I think.'

'Did he buy it for you?'

'No, no.' She turned and was now looking at him. 'He carved it. He's got a workshop full of these things. That's his job.'

'No kidding!' He picked up the carving and, after turning it about one way and another, he said, 'I don't know much about the ins and outs of this kind of stuff but I should say it's a fine piece of work. He's caught the whole feeling of the thing.'

She stared at him; unlike herself he hadn't been shocked by the elemental starkness of the group.

She asked softly, 'Have you ever seen a lamb born?'

He glanced at her. 'No, not until now. You know –' he was

99

drawing his finger over the back of the straining sheep – 'I bet you this would cost something if you went to buy it. It's a beautiful piece of work. The fellow's clever.'

'Yes, I think he is.'

'You would never guess it to look at him, although I got the impression that he ran the place down there, and not his father.'

'I think you're right there too' – she nodded – 'I think he makes the decisions.'

He put the carving back on the mantelpiece, saying, 'I've got an idea that work and the old boy don't agree.'

'I've had something of the same idea myself.' They smiled at each other; and presently he asked, 'What about sleeping here, how do you find it?'

'Wonderful,' she said. 'Not a sound.'

'You weren't afraid to be on your own?'

'Not after the first night; and on that night the O'Connors brought the dog up with his box and left him outside.'

'That was thoughtful of them.'

'Yes; they're all very thoughtful.'

'I think you should give a special vote of thanks to Aunt Millie and Uncle Harry for finding this place for you, and the O'Connors.'

'Yes, I must. And I'll remember to do just that when they come out on Sunday.'

He got up abruptly, then went to the window and looked out into the deepening twilight, and without turning he asked, 'Will they be bringing Ada with them?'

'I shouldn't think so. Why?'

'Oh, nothing. Only you know I can't stand her . . . I think I'll go down and show myself to the O'Connors.' He glanced back over his shoulder.

'Yes, I would do that; they'd like to see you, I'm sure.'

'You coming?'

'Not tonight. I'd better stay put in case your father comes.'

The blank look took over from the smile on his face and without further comment he turned from her and left the house.

Constance arrived at the flat the following morning about eleven o'clock and found Jim just finishing his breakfast. He greeted her quite affably and, asking her if she would like a cup of coffee, then enquired where Peter was. 'Oh, he's gone to buy some books,' she said, then paused before asking, 'Did anything happen here yesterday?'

'Happen?' He screwed up his face at her. 'What do you mean, happen?'

'Well, did you have a row or anything?'

'Me have a row with him? No; why should I? I saw him for only a short time. He came in early, had something to eat, talked a little about his trip, after' – he stressed the word – '*some* persuasion, as always. Then he went to bed. I didn't see him at all after that. Why do you ask?'

'Oh, nothing.'

'Don't be stupid; it can't be nothing, woman, there's a reason why you asked. Has he said we had a row?'

'No; he said you didn't.'

'Well, then, that endorses what I've just said, so why should you think we had?'

'He . . . he seemed upset about something, that's all.'

'For God's sake stop babying him . . . Upset!' He shrugged his shoulders, then said, 'Oh, by the way, Millie phoned this morning; she wanted to know if you were likely to be in town. I told her I didn't know your movements, or words to that effect.' He bowed his head gravely towards her, then added, 'But I told her that if you did come in I'd tell you and perhaps you'd go round.'

'Yes, all right. Have you seen anything of them lately?'

'Not since the night we were at their place.'

'They're coming out on Sunday. Will you be there?'

101

'I don't see why not. Why miss a happy family party?'

She gave him no answer to this but asked, 'How's the work going?'

'Pretty well.'

She allowed another pause before she said, 'I've come in to look round for a flat, or a bungalow.'

He stared at her blankly. 'I'll never forgive you, Connie, if you sell this over my head.' His voice was quiet.

She rose to her feet and turned her back towards him, saying in a hopeless tone, 'How many times do I have to tell you before you believe me that the money is running out and fast. You've got to come to terms with it; it has to go.'

'You can cut down. Look, do away with Mrs Thorpe; I can do what cleaning there is to be done. You know I can look after myself. That's one thing you must give me credit for; if I've got to I can. You must admit, I'm having plenty of practice lately . . . Look, Connie' – his voice took on a pleading tone – 'I'll sell the car.'

She turned and stared at him, and with pity in her gaze now. She wished, oh, she wished she could do what he asked, if only to keep the peace, but she knew it wasn't possible. In two or three years' time, if he added nothing to the exchequer, they would really be in trouble. 'It's no good,' she said flatly. 'It's the overall cost, and I've told you I must build up the capital.'

'But I'm in again.' He spread his hands wide. 'Another year and I'll have money coming in. I can get the three hundred advance tomorrow if I ask for it.'

'Three hundred advance, and a year before the book comes out. We're living at the rate of three thousand a year . . . !'

As she turned from him his bark almost brought her from the ground. 'Blast you and your money!' The words seemed to bounce off the back of her head, and when she reached her room his voice was still coming at her. She stood, her eyes flicking nervously from one object to another. The whole block would hear him; the Thompsons below would be able to pick up every word.

Her hands clasped tightly together, she found herself longing to be back . . . up there. Life was different up there. In that house she could cope; here, with his voice still upbraiding her, she felt she would go to pieces at any moment and scream.

A few minutes later she was driving along the main road towards Millie's . . .

When Millie opened the door to her she stared at her blankly, then said, 'Why lass, you look as white as a sheet,' but allowed Constance to pass before asking, 'What's the matter?'

'Oh, the usual, Millie, money. He must think the bank manufactures it for us alone.'

In the living-room Millie said, 'Sit down; I'll make a drink. I . . . I didn't expect you so soon after Jim told me you weren't at home.' She went into the scullery and Constance called to her softly, 'Is there anything wrong, Millie?' But it was some seconds before Millie answered.

'Yes, Connie,' she said. 'Yes, indeed, there *is* something wrong.'

'She's pregnant then?'

'Aye, she is.'

'You're sure?'

'Yes. And that's not all. There was hell to pay here last night. And it went on until the early hours.'

'You mean with Harry . . . he knows?'

'Yes. And he'll never be the same again. But she didn't say who it was until . . . until this morning, just afore he left for school.'

'Is . . . is it anybody you know . . . local?'

As Millie stared at Constance there was no movement in her, neither in her hands, nor in her head, and her stillness brought a wave of sickness into Constance's body; it was so strong that she almost retched with it, and she heard a faint voice whimpering inside her, saying, No, no! not that. Oh my God! Not that. She could see Ada throwing herself on to Jim's knee the last time they were in this room.

Both their faces were the colour of lint now. Then Millie

whispered, 'I'm afraid, Connie; I'm afraid he'll want to kill him.'

The whimpering voice inside Constance said, Oh God, how I wish he would. Then Millie's next words brought her to the edge of the chair, her mouth agape, her face strained with astonishment at what she was hearing. 'That night you were here, Harry went into the bedroom. You remember? when she was playing her records. And he found them on the bed together. He told me after . . . I'm sorry lass, I'm sorry. I'd rather it not be him for the world . . . I don't blame him, I don't, believe me.'

'You mean . . . you mean Peter?' Constance's voice was actually on the edge of a scream. 'Peter and Ada! No! No! Millie, no! Never.'

She was experiencing feelings of relief and shock at the same time. But she could tackle the shock. Peter couldn't stand Ada. She stood up, crying at Millie, 'I won't believe it, Millie! not for one moment. Do you hear me? It was never Peter.'

'I think it was, Connie.' Millie's voice was quiet. 'I'm sorry, lass, but I think it was. You see, Ada has always been sweet on him. He doesn't know that, but she has, and . . . and up to lately he's never given her any encouragement. But you never know with youngsters. I told you, Harry said he found them on the bed together, and they hadn't been in the room a few minutes.'

'I won't believe it. Do you hear me, Millie? I won't believe it. I'll see Peter now . . . now! I'll bring him round . . .'

Her hands shaking, Millie straightened her apron and said, 'I think it would be wiser to keep him at home, Connie, until Harry turns up, as he will after school. He'd have been round at dinnertime only he's on dinner duty. And another thing; I told him I didn't think Peter was back from his holiday yet. But he was going round anyway.'

As Constance walked stiffly towards the door, she said, 'Did she actually say it was him?'

'Yes, Connie. I'm sorry. Oh, I'm heart sorry, lass. I would

rather she had named anybody in the world but Peter. He's such a good lad. I don't blame him, I don't; I know what she is: she would take a clothes prop down if it had trousers on. She's me own, and I say it, but she's no good. You can't get him to see it though. He's besotted with her: she can twist him round her finger like she can almost any man. As you know, Connie, I've had this since she was thirteen and I've never known a day's peace, and I've had to put a face on things because of him. He's always laid so much stock on her; if there had been another one it might have been different. But you know all this. You know all this.'

'I still don't believe it, Millie.' Constance's voice was quiet now, but there was less conviction in it, for she was remembering Peter's manner when he arrived at Shekinah yesterday and which had made her think he'd had a row with Jim. And she was also remembering the night of his birthday, when she found him with the nude pictures on his bed.

At the door she said from between tight lips, 'Do you think Harry'll come straight round from school?'

'Yes; yes, I do, Connie.'

'Then will you come round to the flat with him, Millie, for I . . . I might have to say things that he won't believe unless you are there to confirm them.'

Again they were staring hard at each other, and after a moment Millie said sadly, 'I understand; and I don't blame you.'

'What! What did you say?' Peter was yelling as he pushed his hands through his thick hair. 'You must be joking!'

'Peter, I'm . . . I'm not joking and . . . and you know I'm not. You were upset yesterday. I knew there was something . . .'

'Now look here!' It was he who was screaming now. 'That had nothing to do with it, nothing whatever. Good God! Talk about circumstantial evidence. I could tell you what was wrong with me yesterday, but . . . but I won't. I won't!'

'Tell me.'

'No. Anyway, that's beside the point. You mean to stand there and say openly that you believe that I . . . with her! Ada! I wouldn't touch her with a boat hook! You know I can't stand her. You know I can't . . .'

'Listen. Listen, Peter.'

He had backed from her and she held out her hand to him and implored, 'Listen to me, please.'

'I won't! I won't! You believe it! You really believe it!'

'I don't, Peter. But . . . but you've got to explain about the night in the bedroom.'

'The night in where?'

'When you went along to her room to hear the records and your Uncle Harry went in and . . .'

'Oh, Mam! You mean to say . . . you mean to say that he's accusing me because of that?'

'Not . . . not that alone. Ada says—'

'Ada's a liar!' He was screaming again. 'That night in the room she pulled my tie off and threw herself on me and whirled me round and we fell on the bed. That was it; that was all. We hadn't been in the room five minutes, so how could—?'

'He's going on the theory that if you were . . . carrying on . . .' She shook her head and screwed up her face against his expression. 'I'm only repeating what your Aunt Millie thinks. She says that if . . . if you were carrying on like that then . . . well, there must have been other occasions—'

'They're liars. I've not been alone with her for almost a year, and she was so forward then I swore it would never happen again. And . . . and that night . . . well you know yourself I was pushed into going along to her room . . . Look' – he stretched his neck out of his collar – 'I'm going along there this minute and I'll throttle the truth out of her.'

'It's no use; you won't find her there. Your Aunt Millie and Uncle Harry will be here any minute now. I've . . . I've been waiting for you to come in all afternoon to . . . to prepare you. Where've you been?'

106

He looked at her grimly for a moment. 'I told you last night. I . . . I had to see a fellow.'

Then, as now, she didn't believe him.

He stood leaning over the back of the couch as if he were easing a pain in his stomach, and from that position he asked, 'Does *he* know about this?'

'No.'

At this moment the key turned in the front door and the sound brought Peter's body stiffly upwards, and, going round the couch and sitting down, still with his back to her, he said, 'Go and tell him.'

When she didn't move he turned his bleached face to her and he repeated in a harsh whisper, 'Go on. Go on. Tell him.'

She went into the hall and there saw Jim taking off his coat. She waited for him to hang it in the wardrobe, before she said, 'May . . . may I have a word with you in the study?'

He turned towards her, his face no longer filled with anger as she had last seen it. 'What is it? What's the matter?'

She walked from him and up the four steps into his room, and he followed, and when he had closed the door he said again, 'What is it?' And Constance, hardly able to control her voice, told him.

At one period in the telling she saw a flicker of amusement cross his countenance, but in the main he took the matter seriously. 'She's an artful little bitch, that,' he said. 'And a tart, if ever I saw one.'

Her answer to this could have been, You should know, but then it really wouldn't have been applicable, for her husband didn't go in for tarts. She had often wished he had; it would have simplified matters. He said to her now, 'Has he denied it?'

'Absolutely. And I believe him.'

'Oh, you would. That's understandable.' Then softening a little, he added, 'But in this particular case I am inclined to agree with you. He wouldn't have the guts to go for her, not Ada. She could, though, have seduced him. She can rape you with her eyes, that one.'

Bitch; tart; seduced; rape; the words were all distasteful to her. She hated the people and the things they represented, and he seemed to sense this and said, 'Well, this should bring you down to earth, if anything could. These things happen.'

'I . . . I don't need anything like this to bring me down to earth, as you put it. And forget about me for the moment and think of what you're going to say to Harry.'

'What I'm going to say to Harry!' His voice rose. 'I've got nothing to say to Harry. If I know Harry it'll be he who'll do the saying. What I might say to him, though, is, he's asked for everything his daughter's got, because he's made a fool of her since she was born.'

'That won't help now.'

'Where is he . . . Peter?'

'In the lounge. He's . . . he's terribly angry.'

'Well, that's no proof of his innocence.' As he opened the door he paused and asked, 'What do you think she's after, money? Because she's a mercenary little bitch.'

'I think it's him she wants. Millie . . . Millie says she's always had her eye on him.'

'You don't say! Well' – his mouth fell open – 'well, I'll be damned. And this is one way of getting him. It's been done before, this trick, you know; it's as old as the hills. But if he's been with her he hasn't a leg to stand on.'

'He hasn't!' She snapped the retort and he said, 'All right. All right. Have it your way. You know. Oh, you know.'

Before they reached the foot of the study staircase the bell rang and they looked at each other. Then Jim, squaring his shoulders and buttoning up his jacket, marched to the door, and once again he opened it to his brother and sister-in-law . . . and Ada.

Jim Stapleton had always been secretly afraid of his brother. Harry knew too much about him; he knew all his weaknesses. He had probed the intellectual façade right from the beginning, and for that alone he could never forgive him. And then there was his other weakness, and Harry certainly knew about that.

108

But now Harry was no longer on top. Although he was looking the part of the enraged father, he was a man in a state of shock. Jim's victory took a form of superiority. He forgot for a moment it was his son who was concerned, but even if he had remembered, it wouldn't have altered his manner, for deep down he was gloating. His son was a prig, and this kind of situation was a great leveller of prigs. If he had to marry Ada, all to the good. It would get him out of the house and away from his mother. He had always felt that without his son forever in the background he could have managed his wife better.

'Well!' Harry growled the word out as he looked from his brother to Constance. His chin moved in little twitches; the action was almost like one that preceded tears. 'Where is he?'

'Harry. Will you come into the study for a moment and let us talk this matter over qui—'

'Now look, Connie' – Harry's voice had come like a blow – 'I'm talking to one person, that's all; one person I'm talking to about this matter. One person. Where is he?'

'He's in the lounge.'

Harry now stalked past Constance and his brother and pushed open the lounge door. Constance looked quickly from Millie's pathetic face to Ada, and as Ada stared back at her defiantly, she had the urge to take her by the shoulders and knock her head against the wall, to knock the lies out of her. Yet within the last few minutes she had recalled Peter's attitude when she told him that Harry and Millie were coming up on Sunday. He had asked if Ada was coming with them and she had remembered the look on his face when she said no.

A bellow from the lounge brought her springing towards the door to see Harry standing close to Peter as he shouted into his face, 'You're an underhand, dirty . . . !'

Peter checked his uncle's words with a thrust of his hand that nearly knocked him on his back, and also surprised him into silence.

'Don't call me a dirty . . . whatever it is you were going to say. Keep that word for your daughter.' He glared across the

109

room to where Ada was standing to the side of Millie and he used the phraseology that fitted the situation: 'You won't pin this on me, you loose slut, you.'

As Harry sprang forward, Jim grabbed at his shoulder and said heavily, 'Enough of that. Enough of that. Sit down. Sit down and calm yourself. This looks like being a long job.'

'It'll be no long job.' They were all looking at Peter. 'She's lying. She's a stinking, dirty little liar.'

'Mind, I warn you!'

Again Jim was holding Harry's shoulder, and now he bawled at Peter, 'Sit down! you. Sit down!'

But Peter did not sit down; he stood at the head of the couch, his fingers clawing into the upholstery, and he glared at his father. And Jim, glaring back at him, said, 'Did you hear what I said?'

'I heard all right.' The answer and the tone of it made Jim's teeth clamp together, but as he did not want any side issues he turned to Constance and Millie and called loudly, 'Sit down, sit down.' Then turning to Ada, who was standing with one arm across her breasts, her hand tucked tightly under her oxter, his voice dropping, he said, 'Sit down, Ada, sit down.' And he sat down. They all sat down, with the exception of Peter, and his father made no more comment on that but, taking charge of the situation, he said, 'Now then, what's this all about?'

'Look.' Harry screwed himself round in the chair and glared at him. 'This doesn't need any lead-up; she's pregnant.' He slanted his eyes towards his daughter: yet they did not rest on her face, but his fingers stabbed in her direction. 'She's pregnant and she says it's him.'

'She's a liar,' said Peter.

'Be quiet!' said Jim.

'I'll not be quiet, I'll say it till I drop. She's a liar. She's a liar.'

Jim's jaw worked stiffly as he glared back at his son, but then his attention was drawn to his brother again as Harry, forcing himself to look at Ada, said, 'Who's the father?'

110

They all watched Ada turn her head towards Peter, stare at him for a moment, then drop her gaze, and Peter's voice filled the room as he cried, 'God! I could strangle you.'

'And I you!' The words were deep and slow, coming from the depth of Harry's being, and after holding Peter's eyes for a moment he went on, still slowly, 'I mightn't have believed it either but for what I saw myself that particular night.'

'What you saw was what she manoeuvred. She pulled me round and on to the bed. She manoeuvred it. Anyway, is it likely that if I wanted to do anything I would do it there, within an arm's length of your living-room and any of you likely to come in . . . as indeed you did?' He bounced his head at his uncle.

'Some folks will do it in the street.' Harry's retort seemed to bleach Peter's face still further, but his answer came quietly and seemed to surprise them as he said, 'Yes, yes, I know that.' Then Harry's next remark brought him yelling again, for Harry said, 'You'll marry her, as young as you are. There's going to be no illegitimate bairns in my family, for there's enough filling the town as it is, but by God! I'm going to see—'

'Marry her? I'd jump off the high level first. Do you hear me? All of you!' Like a trapped animal Peter paced the back of the couch, still shouting. 'You can't *make* me marry her. Her! If I had to choose, do you know what I'd do? I'd rather marry a tart; any one of them in the town, save her. But there's no choice to make, because I'm not marrying her.' He now glared at Ada, and Ada glared back at him, and her small face was tight with suppressed passion. Had she given way to it, they would have needed no further evidence of Peter's innocence.

It was as Harry drew himself slowly and menacingly to his feet, thrusting off Jim's outstretched hand, that Constance spoke. Her voice trembling, she said, 'What about the other two, Harry? Why should Peter be forced to marry her for this one? There was no question of forcing the others.'

111

Harry turned slowly and looked down at Constance. 'What! What are you talking about?'

'I'm talking about the other times she's been pregnant.'

Harry stared at Constance, and as he did so his upper lip moved slowly back from his teeth, and the movement pushed his nose upwards, swelling the nostrils. Then his eyes crinkled at the corners and as he bent his head forward his throat swelled as if with words bunched there, but he said nothing for a moment. He turned his gaze from Constance to Millie; but Millie had her head bowed. And then he looked at his daughter; and Ada was glaring at Constance. When he again looked down on Constance he asked, 'Why do you say such a thing?'

'Because it's true.' She turned her head and said, 'It's true, isn't it, Millie?'

When Millie's head remained bowed, Constance looked at Harry again. She wouldn't have hurt Harry for the world. She had always liked Harry; she had wished at times that Harry had been the first man who had kissed her, and not Jim. She also knew, in a secret place in her heart, that Harry held a feeling for her that was nothing to do with the affection of a brother-in-law. Now she was going to cut him to shreds.

'Take your mind back, Harry,' her trembling voice went on. 'You remember when she came away for a holiday with me to Devon three years ago? She was fifteen then. Well, we didn't go to Devon, Harry, we went to London. And she had a baby taken away. It cost me nearly two hundred pounds, Harry. Then, when she had just turned sixteen, she fortunately had a miscarriage. I wasn't here, but Millie told me about it. She also told me that Ada tried to get rid of this one on another holiday, Harry. But it didn't work this time; she had to think of a way out. And so she . . . she picks on Peter, because . . .' Now Constance looked down, first to the right, and then to the left before adding, 'because she thinks that with Peter there'll be money. Also, by naming Peter, she could hurt me. She's never forgiven me because I . . . I did what had to be done for her for Millie's sake, not hers, and she was aware of this.'

When she lifted her head she saw that Harry was standing quite still. He looked pathetic, so pathetic that she could not bear to look at him any more, and again she lowered her head. She was aware of Millie getting up and coming to his side, and then she heard him ask quietly, 'Is this true, Millie?'

And Millie answered, 'Yes. Yes, it's true.'

She saw Millie's feet turn in the direction of Ada and she heard her say, 'She's me own flesh and blood, but she's bad. I've . . . I've tried to warn you but you wouldn't listen. She's lied. She's lied all her life, but you . . . you believed her. One thing I do know. If she had a baby every time she's been with someone the street would be running with—'

'Don't! woman. Don't!' Harry's head was bowed deep, his hands covering his face, and when Millie put her arm around his shoulder he thrust her off.

It was some time before he straightened himself again. Then, turning, he looked towards his daughter and slowly he approached her, and they stared at each other for a moment, before he said, 'What've you got to say?'

'Huh! They haven't left me very much *to* say, have they?' Her voice had a slight tremble in it, but her manner, as usual, was bold, and she glanced over her shoulder towards Connie and, taking on her voice, she said, 'Don't worry, dear, no one will ever know. I swear to you no one will ever know. You can rest assured that whatever happens it will lie between your mother and you and me . . . Thanks, Aunt Connie. And how right you are. I've never been able to stand you: you're so bloody smug and you're a sodding hypocrite—'

'Stop that!' Harry roared at the top of his voice. There followed a short silence before, wetting his lips, he said grimly, 'One last thing I'm going to ask you, girl. Is Peter the father of this one?'

Turning now to Peter, whose face was still bloodless, Ada's mouth curled with scorn and she said, 'That drip! God, he's too soft to clag holes with. He wouldn't know how—'

The blow sent her reeling, and as Millie cried out and rushed in front of Harry before he could follow it up with another, Jim went and picked Ada up from where she had fallen, and Peter, pressing his hand tightly across his mouth, dropped on to the couch. Only Constance remained where she was.

Dizzy from the blow, Ada held her head for a moment; then pulling herself from Jim's hands, she walked unsteadily towards the door and there, supporting herself against the stanchion, she faced them all, and cried, 'You lot! What do you know about it? You're old; you're all dead from the knees up. And him!' – she pursed her lips and glanced towards Peter – 'he's still in nappies, as I've told him before. As for him fathering a bairn. God! He couldn't father a newt. One last thing I'm gonna tell you.' She was addressing herself solely to Millie now. 'I'm goin' to live; no matter how, I'm goin' to do it. But now I've got you off me neck it should be easy. To hell with you! All of you.'

As she turned quickly about and crossed the hall, Millie darted from the room after her, and she reached her as she went out of the door. 'Where're you going?' she demanded.

Pressing the button for the lift, Ada turned a cold glance at her mother. 'That's my business from now on, an' don't try any court orders or think you'll put me into care, 'cos you won't find me. Anyway' – her lip curled – 'you won't try much, will you, 'cos you can have Dad back now. That should make you happy; you'll have him all to yourself.'

'You're a wicked, wicked girl!' Millie's face was twitching as if with a tic.

'Yes, I know I am. And I should do, 'cos you've told me that since I was knee high. You made me want to know what wicked meant, and I found out, so your teaching's come true, hasn't it?'

The lift came to a purring stop; the doors opened, and just before they closed Ada, nodding viciously towards her mother, said, 'And that'll give you something to think about at nights,

114

won't it? It's you that made me what I am in more ways than one.'

When Constance came into the hallway Millie had her face against the wall. She led her back into the lounge and helped her into a chair, and she brought Harry out of his daze by touching him on the arm and pointing towards Millie's shaking body.

Harry, his eyes blinking rapidly, stood for a moment staring at his wife. Then going to her, he put his hand on her head and said dully, 'Come on home . . .'

Five minutes later Constance, Jim and Peter had the flat to themselves again. Jim walked about the room for a time in silence before he said, 'I think I need a drink; what about you?' He looked at Constance, and she said, 'Yes, please.' Then he turned to Peter and raised his thick eyebrows and sat nodding at him, then remarked caustically, 'You've been lucky.'

'I wasn't lucky,' Peter was barking again, his face once more showing rage.

'All right, all right. Mind your tone. Who do you think you're talking to?'

'I'm answering you. Don't say I was lucky; I had nothing to do with it, so getting out of it wasn't lucky, it was justice.'

'Well' – Jim took a deep breath and pushed out his chest – 'we're not all lucky enough to get justice.'

He was near the lounge door when Peter said grimly, 'No, you're right there, you're certainly right there.'

Jim paused in his stride but did not turn; then he continued out of the room, and Constance, going to Peter, put her arms about him and pressed him to her. And he allowed her to hold him until he heard the faint clink of glasses, when he drew away, and as he did so she said softly, 'Be . . . be civil, Peter. He tried to help.'

She watched him turn away, his lip curling. She couldn't really understand his present attitude towards his father, for he hadn't previously been so openly hostile to him.

She sat down again. She felt drained and her emotions were

115

utterly confused; she was relieved beyond measure, yet she was sad to the depth of her for Harry and Millie; but mostly for Harry, for Millie could stand this; she'd had to stand it for years. Harry, though, would never be the same again.

When Jim returned to the room they drank in silence, and when Peter, without excusing himself, left them and went to his own room, she thought Jim would make some reference to his attitude, but he didn't.

After a while he said, 'This is going to make it awkward, there'll be no more to-ing and fro-ing after this.'

She did not reply. She knew what he said was true and that in a way he was glad. But she would miss the to-ing and fro-ing for, after all, Millie and Harry were the only friends she really had outside her home; she had never looked upon her bridge acquaintances as friends.

'Do you think she'll go back home?' he asked now.

'I shouldn't think so, but wherever she goes she'll likely fall on her feet.'

He rose, his glass in his hand and, looking down on her, he said, 'You kept pretty tight over her other lapses.'

'I promised Ada.'

'Huh! So much for promises. She must have thought you would keep yours though, or she would never have taken this chance. She's stupid, is Ada, at bottom, like her father.' He threw off the remainder of his drink, then left the room.

She was sitting alone now and staring out of the window. Yes, so much for promises; but it had saved Peter. She was sure that, if she hadn't spoken, Millie never would; she wouldn't have risked breaking Harry.

She had a sudden overwhelming desire to get back to the long room, to the windswept house, away from this existence that held the Jims and Adas, and the smirky, dirty dregs of living. In one way and another she had been smothered by such dregs for years. She got hastily to her feet. She would see if Peter would come back with her now.

She tapped on his door but there was no response, so she

116

opened it and saw him lying on the bed. He had his back to her and didn't turn round. She said to him, 'I thought about going back tonight; would you like to come?' It was some seconds before he answered and his voice was thick. 'No, not tonight,' he said, and she knew he was crying.

She wanted to take him in her arms again and comfort him, but she said with forced lightness, 'All right; I just wondered. There's no hurry. We'll go back tomorrow.'

In her own room she looked in the mirror at her long white face. She looked lost. She too now had a longing to cry, but she knew she couldn't, for tears were for the young or the old. She was neither one nor the other.

9

Constance drew the car to a stop on the bottom lane and sat back and relaxed for a moment; then she turned and looked over her shoulder at the parcels and packages on the back seat, and considered that with what was in the boot she would have to make three journeys up to the house.

This morning, when she had packed up, she had taken it for granted that Peter would be coming out with her; she was keenly disappointed when he said he wouldn't be coming until the evening.

She had also asked Jim if he would be joining her, but his excuse had been that he was going to do some work. And this he had tried to prove by forgoing his constitutional walk after lunch.

Her arms laden, she now mounted the hill and made her way up the tangled path to the back door; but then considered it would be easier to go round to the terrace and open the front door in the Moira manner than to unload her packages and get the key from her bag.

When she reached the house she was surprised to find the slim, dark figure of Kathy O'Connor sitting on the edge of the terrace opposite the front door, her feet dangling to the grass below.

'Oh. Hello, Mrs Stapleton. I . . . I just came up to have a look.' She spread her arms out, indicating the valley. 'I knew you weren't back. I hope you don't mind?'

118

'Of course not.' Constance shook her head, then added, 'Isn't it close? I feel boiled.'

'Here! Let me help you.' Kathy took some of the packages from her arms. Then Constance, turning her back to the door, gave it a jab with her buttocks, laughing as she said, 'Moira showed me this trick.'

As she dropped the parcels on to the round rosewood table to the right of the stairs, she looked about her, saying, 'I feel I've been away for weeks; it's wonderful to be back.'

'Funny how it gets you.' Kathy nodded understandingly. 'When I'm down there in the nursery there are times I get an awful homesick feeling. You know, you'd think I was a thousand miles away. You either love this kind of life and scenery or you hate it.'

'Well, you all love it,' said Constance.

'Oh no. No. Kevin, he couldn't stand it; it nearly drove him mad.'

'Kevin?' Constance put her head on one side, and Kathy explained, 'He's the one next to Vin. He's married and has four children. They come up for holidays, but he's always glad to get back, is Kevin, into the town, I mean.'

'He's in Newcastle?'

'No, in Jarrow. A week of it would kill me, but he loves it. His wife is from there, so everybody's happy. Shall I put the kettle on and make you a cup of tea?'

'That would be lovely, but I've got more stuff to bring from the car.'

'Oh, I'll help you, then.'

And so the rest of the parcels were brought up. Afterwards, Kathy put the kettle on and laid out a tray with quiet ease as if she were used to doing it in this house every day, and when the tea was brewed and poured they sat in the long room and drank it; and after a while Constance said, 'Peter was telling me he ran into you the other day.'

'Yes; yes, we had a coffee together. He's good fun.'

It was on the tip of Constance's tongue to say, You think

119

so? Instead, she said, 'Yes; yes, he likes to laugh.' She had always considered her son a very serious-minded boy; it was strange to hear someone label him as good fun, but she was glad that someone had. 'Is it your day off?' she asked.

'Half-day,' said Kathy. 'And don't I need it.'

'You like looking after the children?'

'Oh yes, I love it. But I think I'll like it better when I can work in the General. I can't do that, though, until I'm eighteen.'

'When will that be?'

'Next month.'

'How do you get in and out; I mean, from the town to here?'

'Oh; coming, I get a bus to Wark-on-Tyne or Woodpark, whichever one comes, and then I shank it from there. It's only three miles, but Vin always takes me back.'

Constance said now, 'He already has his work cut out as a chauffeur taking the children to school and back.'

'Yes, he's got his work cut out all right. They could go part of the way in the school bus from Haltwhistle, but he prefers to take them straight to Hexham.' Kathy's face became thoughtful for a moment. Then looking directly at Constance she said, 'He's wonderful, our Vin; he's wonderful, Mrs Stapleton.'

After a moment, during which she felt slightly embarrassed, although she couldn't say why, Constance said, 'I'm sure he is. He seems to take care of everything.'

'Yes, he does that. I don't know where they'd all be without him.' Her head turned slowly and she now looked towards the mantelpiece, although Constance felt the girl had been aware of what sat there from the moment she first entered the room.

'That's a beautiful piece, isn't it?' Kathy moved her head slowly.

'Yes, it is.' Suddenly Constance made up her mind to say something and, bending forward, she said, 'Kathy, I . . . I didn't want to take the carving but Vi . . . your brother put it in such a way that it was impossible for me to refuse.'

Kathy's dark brown eyes surveyed her but she offered no comment, and Constance went on, 'Well, I . . . I mean they all

120

seemed rather surprised when they saw it there, and neither your mother nor Hannah made any reference to it, which puzzled me. I feel that in some way it's of value and . . . and I'd like to return it, but—'

'Oh, don't do that, Mrs Stapleton, if he's given it to you, and he did give it to you. Don't, please don't return it; he'd be so upset. When Vin does anything it's final. You know?'

Constance didn't know, but she said, 'Yes; yes, I understand.'

Kathy now smiled at her. Then getting to her feet, she said, 'I'll have to be moving; they'll wonder where I've got to, for, you know' – her smile widened – 'they expect me to talk and tell them tales about the children every minute I'm at home. You'd think I spent my time at the pictures, the tales I've got to tell them, true and imaginary' – she nodded – 'especially me dad. He'd sit and listen all day to tales. That's the Irish in him. And, of course, he can tell his share himself.'

'Yes, I can believe that.' Constance laughed with Kathy. Then, together, they walked out of the door and with a word of goodbye Kathy ran along the terrace in much the same way as Biddy or Moira would have done. She did not, however, go round the side of the house and take the pathway down the hill; instead, she scrambled over the edge of the crag that was a short cut to the farm, the short cut that always left its impression on the boys' hind quarters. At this thought, Constance smiled to herself.

Her lips were still apart when she again entered the long room, and sat in the armchair opposite the window, letting herself swim in the view from it.

The past twenty-four hours were receding fast; it was as if the events in them had happened a year ago; the house was spreading a blanket of time between her life in the flat and the life within these walls. But she wished, after what had happened yesterday, that she didn't have to thank Millie and Harry for finding the house . . . Oh that girl! She was vile. Vile.

Of a sudden, the sun was gone, and the biscuit-coloured,

sloping stretches of land and mauve-tinted hills had turned to a steely grey. It's going to rain, she thought . . . What would she do when it rained all day, day after day, as it might do in the winter? And when she was snowed up for weeks on end? As the children had said, she could even be cut off from the farm below. What would she do with herself then? She couldn't read all the time, and there wouldn't be enough work to occupy her. If Jim didn't come, and it wasn't likely that he would in the winter, when he'd hardly stay a night now, there wouldn't be much cooking to do, except at week-ends for Peter . . . Well, she'd have to take up a hobby; she'd take up painting again. She'd been quite good at it in the convent, and embroidery, too. She could do that. She could also practise at the piano. That's if she could get a piano up here . . . That was a thought; a piano. She'd look round for a second-hand one, a smallish one, something that the men could manoeuvre up the hill.

She got to her feet and walked to the open door, and as she looked on to the empty terrace and the greater emptiness of the land beyond that stretched away to meet the heavens, she became awed by the vastness and the silence, and she found herself wishing that she *could* persuade Jim to come and live here. It would solve everything. But attached to this wish was an unpleasant truth and she made herself face it. The only reason she wanted him to come and live in this house was so that *she* might live in it all the time. She desired his presence at any time only as a means to ward off the soul-stripping feeling of aloneness. She had put up with the unspeakable for years simply because she was afraid to be left entirely alone. Peter, she had recognised, was but a stopgap to her fear; he would leave her some day to marry. Then, if she didn't have Jim, what would she do?

She despised herself.

Just then, a thin veil of rain came over the hills, so she went in and closed the door on it, on everything.

10

It was the day Constance decided to go for a walk that she met the priest.

She had felt restless all day, and worried, too: Peter's manner was puzzling her more and more. He seemed disturbed about something: she was sure it had nothing to do with Ada's accusation; nor was he worried about starting his first term at university, for she had challenged him with this. The trouble lay, she was sure, with his father. From the beginning, there had never been any love between Jim and his son, and for this, at times, she felt she was to blame, because she had done nothing to make the boy even like his father. It had been impossible for her. That Peter had always been respectful towards Jim, she knew was because he was a little afraid of him. But over the past few days – in fact, since his return from his holiday – his manner towards Jim had undergone a change for the worse.

Last night he had been quite cheerful and they had gone down to the O'Connors and he had talked with Kathy again. He had even taken her back to the nursery. But today, the set look was on his face again. When he announced he was going into Newcastle before lunch, Constance thought that perhaps he had made an appointment to meet Kathy; but he hadn't said, and she hadn't asked.

As yet, Constance had not explored the countryside; the only distance she had been from the house on foot was to the wood. It had rained heavily in the night and for most of the morning, but now the sun was shining. It was even hot, and steam was rising from the ground. It was as if she were walking on the clouds themselves.

After she had walked for about two miles she crossed a fast flowing burn and gauged that she was on Allerybank Moor. To the right would be the village of Falstone. Some day, before the bad weather set in, she would walk to Falstone or Stannersburn. She had been to Falstone by car and found it delightful, but today she felt she had gone far enough, because she wasn't used to rough walking.

It was as she retraced her steps over the stones on a narrow part of the burn that she saw the priest pushing his bike up an incline. He was a dark-haired young man with a thin, ascetic-looking face. His Irish accent was prominent as he greeted her politely, saying, 'It's a beautiful day it's turned out.'

'Yes, it has, Father.' The spontaneous way she gave him his title caused him to look at her closely, and with a smile on his thin lips he said, 'You're a Catholic?'

'No, Father. No, I'm not a Catholic.'

'No? I could have sworn you were, though you're not from these parts. You're just on holiday, then?'

'No, I'm not on holiday, Father. From now on you could say I *am* from these parts. I live up in Shekinah Hall.'

'Oh, you do, you do?' His face brightened. 'You must be Mrs Stapleton? I'm Father Shelley.'

'Yes, I'm Mrs Stapleton, Father.'

'Ah! Ah! That's it, I knew there was something. I had a feeling I'd met you before; it was their good description of you. You know' – he leant his head towards her and his voice dropped to a whisper – 'when you ask some people if they're Catholics they take it as if you are accusing them of being a Communist or something.'

She laughed, and he said, 'I'm on my way to the O'Connors now; it's a long trek to the next downhill run. Good-day

124

to you. We'll doubtless be meeting up again.'

'Good-day, Father.'

As the black-clothed figure pushed the bike up the slope of the moor she sat down on the bank of the stream and gazed into the water, where it gurgled around a group of rocks.

More than once she had been tempted to enter a confessional box and unburden herself to a priest: not that she could receive absolution, but just so that she could speak about this dark thing that shadowed her life. But it would have meant asking, What should I do, Father? Should I leave my husband or should I stay with him? And when she was asked the reason could she have said, even through a dark grid, because he has a weakness for young girls? No, it would have been impossible to have betrayed him, even to a stranger.

She must have sat on the bank for nearly an hour before starting on the return journey, and she was feeling weary as she neared the end of it. But she knew she had only to round the foot of just one more hill and from there she would see the house.

It was at that point that she heard Hannah's unmistakable voice yelling, 'Well! you've found me. So what you goin' to do?'

'If your conscience wasn't troubling you, you wouldn't try to hide.' It was the priest who spat the words at Hannah, which caused her to bawl back, 'Who's hidin'? I was goin' for a walk!'

There followed a short silence, during which Constance remained still; there was something about the exchange that appeared utterly private, and she hesitated whether to show herself or retrace her steps and get to the house the back way. Then she heard Hannah say, 'All right, all right, there'll be no peace until you have your say, but don't forget, I've heard it all afore and you're wastin' your time. But if you intend to try again, I'd get off me legs if I were you, for it looks like being a long session.'

Constance moved slightly so that she could see the priest. He was looking down on Hannah as if he hated the very sight of

125

her, and no doubt this feeling was engendered by his inability to bring her to her knees, for she now laughed scornfully at him as she said, 'Well, I'm waitin'; you're wastin' precious time. Come on, Patrick, you might as well get it over with.'

'Don't you dare call me Patrick, woman.' The priest's jaws were clamped together now.

'And why not?' Hannah's head went back and she gave a loud, coarse laugh. 'You wouldn't like me to call you Mister, would you now? And you'll wait a hell of a time afore I call you Father . . . What did you say?' She brought her head towards him. 'Thank God for that? . . . Well, you said somethin' and it sounded pretty like it. An' I repeat, an' I've said it to your face afore, I'm not callin' you Father. Father Bateman, aye. Any day in the week I'll give him *his* title, because he's a priest of God, but not you.'

Father Shelley's face was livid and for the moment he could not speak. Instead, he had to listen to Hannah laughing up at him from the grass and saying, 'It's right what I'm tellin' you. Oh but, for God's sake, don't let the thought make you pass out. Come and sit yourself down; you'll be able to upbraid me easier that way.'

Father Shelley gulped in his throat before he said, 'I haven't sought you out to hold a conversation with you, but to tell you that you must get yourself to confession and the sacraments, as well as your Easter duties, long overdue, before it is too late. You're getting no younger, remember that—'

'Aw, you don't have to remind me. And it's a pity, I say, because it stops me showing the results of more sins.'

Father Shelley's voice was harsh as he said slowly, 'I'm a priest of God and as such should have forgiveness in me for you, but I haven't; nevertheless I must try, but at this moment I can only see you as a loose, brazen woman. You told me once that Father Bateman said that your kind were Christ's own chosen people; well, I don't see eye to eye with my superior on this matter, for to me, woman, you are a sink of iniquity.'

'Don't you call me woman, I'm warnin' you. Me name's Hannah Kerry.'

'Well, Miss Kerry' – the priest's words came weighed now as though prophesying – 'there're only two things sure in life: birth and death. You've achieved one and the other is fast approaching you. Remember that: the other is fast approaching you, and ask yourself if you're going over with your soul as black as the coals of hell. Ask yourself that in the quiet of the night.'

Constance was amazed at what she had heard, yet at the same time she didn't fully understand it. What had Hannah done? She knew that Catholic priests, especially Irish ones, could put emphasis on actions such as adultery, far away and above the censure entailed outside the church. She had no doubt in her mind that the priest was accusing Hannah of adultery. Yet Hannah was a middle-aged woman, a motherly person whose only apparent attraction was her sense of humour. Had Hannah in her early days had an affair with someone? And if so, would the priest be keeping on at her now about it? Everybody had their troubles, but somehow she wished the O'Connors had escaped them. It disturbed her to think there was disharmony in that household. She remembered yet again Jim saying, 'They're a queer lot down there.'

She stood for a moment uncertain what to do. She didn't hear either of them leave, but after a time she imagined the priest had made his departure following his last words, so with a deep breath she stepped quickly from around the butt, prepared to show surprise at Hannah sitting on the grass. But the hillside was unoccupied.

Some time before she reached the house she saw Hannah sitting on the corner of the terrace. She greeted Constance over the distance, calling, 'Aw, there you are. You've been for a walk. I came away up to see you.'

'Yes,' Constance managed to call back airily. 'I wanted to explore the countryside. I'm sorry I wasn't in. Have you been waiting long?'

127

As she approached her, Hannah said, 'No, not very long. To tell you the truth, I thought I'd catch you about to go into town, and I was after a lift.'

'Oh, you want to go into town? Well, I'll run you in.'

'Well, not into town exactly; I just wanted to go as far as Birtley.'

'Birtley!' Constance raised her brows. 'But that's miles away; on the way to Durham.'

'Aw.' Hannah threw her head back. 'Not that Birtley. Oh, not that Birtley; I mean the little village yon side of the river. It'll be no more than fifteen minutes in the car.'

'Oh, I'll be pleased to take you. Would . . . would you like to go now?' She hoped Hannah would tell her there was no rush, for she was dying for a cup of tea, but Hannah did say she would like to go now. 'If it wouldn't be puttin' you out too much,' she said.

Constance went into the house to pick up the car keys, and when they were both seated in the car Hannah, with disarming frankness, said, 'I never thought I would take a likin' to the body who would buy the Hall, but I've been proved wrong. An' I'm speakin' for all of us.'

'Oh, Hannah.' Constance backed the car down the lane and to a spot where it was wide enough for her to turn, and as she swung the wheel round briskly she did not say, That's very nice of you, but, 'You don't know how happy that makes me feel, Hannah. Happy and wanted.'

'I'm glad, I'm glad.' Hannah was nodding her head. 'Do you know that's the best thing in the world; to feel wanted, I mean. Nothing's any good to you unless you are wanted. I've always been wanted.'

'I'm sure you have, Hannah.'

'I was never anything to look at; I was always a fat hulk of a lass, and me clothes never fitted. Look at me coat here, for instance.' She pulled at the baggy grey coat she was wearing. 'And I never had much taste for clothes, even as a lass. Never much in me head, either. But what I lacked there I made up for

128

here.' She slapped her heavy breasts. Then the smile sliding from her face, she gazed through the windscreen as, in a deflated tone, she said, 'An' I've done no harm to anybody, not really, except meself an' one other.' She turned her head. 'If you go by your own conscience you can't go far wrong, can you?'

'No, indeed, Hannah, you can't.'

'Of course, we've all got different kinds of consciences, some more tender than others. Mine's tough.' Her head was back and she was laughing again.

She was still laughing when Constance dropped her off at the spot she indicated on the outskirts of the small village, and as she stood in the road Constance said, 'Shall I wait for you?'

'Oh, begod! You might have a long wait, at that. But it's kind of you.' She put her face down to the window. 'Aye, it is. But no, I'll get a bus back. Thanks all the same.'

'But you won't get one until after eight, Hannah, and then it will only take you as far as—'

'Don't you worry, Mrs Stapleton, don't you worry your bonny head. And it is a bonny head.' She put her hand through the side window and touched Constance's brown hair, and Constance, laughing but embarrassed, said, 'Oh, Hannah.' You could hardly answer anything else to this woman but, 'Oh, Hannah.'

Constance watched her walk along the road towards some cottages, then she turned the car about and went home, wondering not a little about who Hannah was going to see in Birtley, and wondering, too, if it was connected with what the priest had said to her, for despite her laughter, she seemed disturbed.

Her feet were aching when she got into the house; in fact, she felt sticky all over, and she decided that, after she had something to eat, she would attempt the Herculean task of filling the boiler to supply enough water for a bath.

It was just as she was making the fourth journey with the bucket that Vincent O'Connor made his appearance. Without

129

a preliminary greeting he asked, 'Have you seen Hannah?'

'Yes.' She looked up at him where he stood on the rise above the stream. 'I took her into Birtley about half an hour or so ago. Is . . . is anything wrong?'

He stared at her for a moment. Then stepping down from the bank, he took the bucket from her, saying, 'No, no,' and turned his back on her, moving swiftly up the slope to the back door. As swiftly she followed him, and as he put the bucket down she said, 'Thank you.' Then, 'I wondered how she would get back, but she said she would get a bus.'

'Yes, she'll get a bus.' He nodded at her. 'I'll get the boys to come up after school each night; they'll get the water in for you.'

'No, please don't. They have little enough time to themselves after school, and the nights are drawing in so quickly. Anyway, the more I do it the easier it becomes. I reckon three journeys will give me a shallow bath.'

'Yes.' He inclined his head to her in a form of farewell; and as he made to go she said, 'The children tell me the machinery's come. Have you got the lathe going yet?'

'No; it'll take time to set up.' His face creasing into a wry smile, he said, 'I'm having to see about electricity in the house first.' He jerked his head back. 'They're not so concerned about the generator running the machinery but what it'll do inside.'

'I can understand that. It'll be wonderful for them to have electric light.'

He pulled at his chin between his finger and thumb and, his expression serious now, he said, 'The young ones suggested that I might be able to bring the light up here. I'm sorry, but that's out of the question; the house is really too far away.'

She felt a twinge of disappointment, but she covered it by saying quickly, 'Oh, that's perfectly all right.'

'You could get your own generator going, though.' He looked down towards the sheds. 'One would go in there fine. You want to talk to your husband about it.' He was walking down the path as he spoke.

'Oh; I'm afraid he's not mechanically minded. But it's an idea; I must think about it.' She found she was having to shout to him and the realisation brought the colour to her face and her fingers to her lips.

As she waited for the water to heat she stood on the terrace and saw, far away down the valley, the black dot of the Land-Rover winding its way to the main road, and as she watched it she realised that Vincent wasn't going in the direction of Birtley but towards Haltwhistle. She began to wonder about Vincent O'Connor. He was an odd man altogether, his manner brusque and forbidding, although when he smiled, as a while ago, he showed an entirely different side of himself. Doubtless this was the side of him that captured his family's affection; 'He's wonderful, our Vin,' Kathy had said.

It was almost dark now and she had just lit the lamp when she had another visitor. She opened the door to see Sean O'Connor standing there. He had the usual smile on his face and his voice was high as he asked, 'I . . . I was just wondering, Mrs Stapleton, if Hannah had stepped in for a moment?'

'No, Mr O'Connor. Hasn't she returned yet?'

'No, no. But it's early yet. It's the buses, you know; we thought she might have missed the last one.'

If that was the case, Constance thought, why would they expect to find her here?

Then Sean said, 'There's a short cut across the hills and if she missed the bus she might wend her way in this direction; an' I was thinkin' that it would be a long walk and that she would be tired by the time she reached here and had stopped for a crack. Aw well, I'll be trippin' down again. Are you all right, Mrs Stapleton?'

'Oh, yes, Mr O'Connor, thank you.'

'Nothing you want?'

'No, not at present, thank you.'

'Did you know we'll soon have electricity to the house?'

'Yes. Vi . . . Vin was telling me.' She hesitated on the name, not having used it before.

131

'Oh, aye. He's doin' a grand job down there. It'll be the making of him; the making of us all. There's good times coming, good times, Mrs Stapleton. We're all set now.'

'Yes, yes, I'm sure you are.'

'How's your husband?'

'Oh, he's very well, thank you.'

'Has he been workin' hard on those books?'

'Yes; yes, he's writing another one now. It's taking up all his time.'

'And your boy? Now there's a grand lad for you. He's something to be proud of, that boy, with the air of a prince. That's what I said to young Michael yesterday. "There's somebody to copy," I said: "just look how that young man deports himself."'

'Oh, Mr O'Connor, I'm afraid you mustn't hold Peter up as an example to anyone. He's like any other boy, very ordinary.'

'Aw, it's well you look at it like that. It isn't all those that see their sons as ordinary. Now I must be off. But one more thing' – he lifted his hand and shook it as he talked – 'if Hannah should happen to drop in, would . . . would you let us know?'

The request seemed strange, to say the least, but she said, 'Yes. Yes, of course, Mr O'Connor.'

A few minutes later, as she was about to scoop the water from the boiler into a pail, before carrying it to the newly acquired hip bath, she thought, I'd better wait a little while in case she does come. There was something odd about the whole business.

Another hour passed and she still hadn't taken her bath. When the clock struck nine she thought, Well, I've waited so long, I may as well wait now until Peter arrives.

It was half an hour later still when Peter announced his arrival in a most odd way, a way that startled her, for she heard his voice calling from a distance, 'Mother! Mother! Are you there, Mother?'

She rushed to the back door and stared out into the

darkness. And then she heard his voice again. 'Mother! Are you there, Mother?'

She went flying down the path, and groped her way round by the lavatory, crying, 'Where are you?' and Peter's voice came from close by, saying, 'Here! Here!'

When she reached him she gasped out, 'What is it? Are you hurt? You've had an accident?'

'No! No!' He was gasping too. 'Look, it's Hannah. Help me with her.'

As her hands groped over the inert body half lying on the ground, she muttered, 'What's . . . what's the matter? What's wrong with her?'

'Lord, need you ask? She's as drunk as a noodle. I nearly ran her down about two miles along the road. She came staggering across. God, she did give me a fright. I tell you I nearly ran her down. And . . . and this is the first time she's stopped talking.'

'Come on! Come on! Hannah; you're nearly there.' And he hauled at her again.

'Nearly there,' muttered Hannah. 'Nearly there. Home . . . comes . . . the . . . pigeon.'

When they reached the lavatory they propped her up against it to get their breath, and Hannah began to laugh. She laughed until every part of her body shook like a jelly. And they shook with her as they half-carried her up to the house and through the kitchen, finally laying her on the couch in the long room. There Hannah lay gazing up at them, her body still shaking; but then the expression on her face changed and the tears burst from her eyes and her mouth opened in a wide gape as she lifted her wavering hand towards Constance and began to gabble: 'It was him. Confess, he said, confess. 'Tis . . . n't wrong, 'tisn't wrong to bear children, is it, now? Fair question. Is it, now?'

'No, Hannah. No, of course not.' Constance turned to Peter, who was still trying to regain his breath, and pulling him aside she whispered, 'Go down and let them know; they've been looking for her.'

'She's been on about the children all the time,' he whispered back at her. 'Do you know what she's talking about? She says they're all hers.'

'What do you mean?'

'All the O'Connors. That she's their mother.'

'Don't be silly.'

'I'm telling you. I couldn't get her up and off the road and into the car because she wanted to explain everything to me.'

Constance glanced quickly towards the couch and to Hannah's hand that was waving in the air, and again she said, 'Go on down and tell them. Quickly now.'

'Where's the torch?' said Peter; 'I've forgotten mine, and nearly broke my neck trying to get her up that hill.'

'In the kitchen drawer.'

Constance returned to the couch where Hannah was still muttering and crying. Her tears were making rivulets through the dust on her face, and her hands were covered in mud, as was her grey coat, and from the looks of her shoes and stockings she must have stepped into a quagmire. Her voice broken by her sobs, she appealed to Constance: 'No sin . . . no sin, was it, to have children? Arranged . . . arranged it was. Florence, she got the name. Florence got the name; Mother, they call her. But they're mine. Every blasted one of them is mine, from here . . .' She thumped her stomach. Then taking her hand and covering her eyes, she moaned, 'Oh God! Sin, he called it; sin. But it brought me solace . . . it brought them all solace. It did. It did, because they're all happy. Let him say what he likes, my sin has brought them solace.'

'It's all right, Hannah. Don't distress yourself.' Constance took hold of the waving hand and gazed down at the fat, drunken, unsightly looking woman. Hannah had evidently got drunk to blot out the priest's tirade against her, that of being the mother of all the O'Connors. It seemed an utter impossibility. Florence and Sean appeared to be a devoted couple. Although she was of a class far above him, it was evident to anyone with eyes that she was more than fond of him, and he of her. But then there was Hannah's attitude towards the

134

children: she had an authority over them. But yes, she had brought them all happiness through her sin. Solace, she called it.

At this point she heard footsteps on the terrace, and Peter appeared, followed by Vincent O'Connor.

When Hannah stopped her gabbling and crying long enough to realise that the big figure bending over her was Vincent, she flung up her arms and clutched him, blubbering, 'Aw! me lad, me lad. I waited for you on . . . on the moor. Vin will fetch me home, I said. Vin will fetch me home.'

'Come on, get up!' Vin put his arms under her shoulder blades and hoisted her to her feet, and there she hung on him, babbling again, this time about the priest. 'He's the one that'll end up in hell . . . No rest. Never lets me rest. No peace from him.'

'It's all right. It's all right.' Vincent's voice was low and soothing as if he were talking to a frightened child.

'I'll not fear him; I'll not fear him, Vin.'

'No, you've got no need to fear him; the day of the priest is over. Come on, now, don't worry.'

'He said the church would—.'

'Don't worry about what he says. I've told you afore the church is the refuge of weak men like him who enjoy frightening women.'

As he led her stumbling down the room, Hannah swung her body round towards Constance, crying now, 'He's me son! Me eldest. I don't care who knows it. Do you hear? Do you hear?'

'Quiet! Quiet now!' Vincent's voice thundered and it brought Hannah whimpering again, saying, 'All right, all right. Home! we go. They'll be waitin' for me, waitin' for Hannah, for their mother. I'm their mother, Vin . . . Aren't I their mother, Vin?'

Vincent avoided Constance's eye as she stood by the open door. He was almost carrying Hannah now, and she did not follow them on to the terrace or render any assistance and with a small movement of her head she checked Peter too from offering further help. But not until Hannah's voice had almost faded away did she close the door; and then she looked at Peter, where he was standing at the foot of the stairs. As she went towards him on the way to the kitchen he said, 'It's true, then.' His voice was low and awe-filled, and she passed him, saying, 'Possibly. But it's no business of ours.'

He followed her into the kitchen, whispering, as if he might be overheard, 'But who would have thought it? And, and how could he . . . I mean, Mr O'Connor?'

'I don't know, Peter.' She turned and looked at her son, her face blank. 'And we mustn't probe; it's their business.'

He watched her as she stooped to fill the kettle from the watering-can, and he continued to watch her as she filled a pan with some milk, then lit the gas. She was upset about it. But why should she be? As she had said, it was none of their business. Actually, at this moment, he thought it was rather funny, but when he would come to think about it later he knew he would likely see another side to it, because it meant that the whole lot of them down there were illegitimate, and that included Kathy . . . Well, what about it? It didn't matter to him if she was illegitimate twenty times over; he wasn't going to get himself involved with girls of any kind; that business with Ada had put paid to attachments, light or serious, for many a year to come. He was still shivering inwardly from the impact of the accusation. He was also shivering inwardly from another feeling, anger against his father. He gazed at Constance as if he had never seen his mother before. Why . . . why had she stuck him all these years? She had so much class. It showed in her figure, her face, in all of her. Besides which she was nice. My God, if she found out about this last business, she would go mad. But wouldn't it be better for her to know? Then she might do something definite before she was too old. And she *was* getting old; she was thirty-seven . . . But she had found out before and she had done nothing. It seemed as if she was afraid to let him go. Yet what life had she with him? He couldn't understand it. It was beyond him.

136

'Are you going to have a wash?' she said, looking over her shoulder. 'There's some hot water in the boiler.'

'I could do with a bath. Look at me; I'm muddy right up to the eyes.'

'Go and get your things off and I'll fill the hip bath for you.'

'Thanks,' he said. 'That'd be marvellous.'

'Will you have your coffee now or wait until later?'

'I'll wait until I've had a wash.'

She pulled the milk off the stove; then ladled the hot water out of the boiler into the buckets and with it she half-filled the bath.

As Peter came into the kitchen in his dressing-gown there was a knock on the front door and he said softly, 'Shall I see who it is? It's likely . . . one of them.'

'No; you get your wash, I'll see to it.'

When she opened the door, there stood Vincent O'Connor, and after only a slight hesitation she said, 'Won't you come in?'

He walked past her and into the room and straight down to the couch, and from there he looked round at her and said, 'She's messed up all your covers.'

'Oh, that's all right; they'll wash.'

'I'm sorry about all this.' They were standing behind the couch looking at each other, and she did not take her eyes from him as she said, 'It's perfectly all right; it's . . . it's none of our business.'

'You're very polite.' His mouth twisted just the slightest. 'But it doesn't cover the fact that you are shocked again.'

'Shocked again?' Her eyes widened. 'Why should I be?'

'For the simple reason that to all intents and purposes my father has two wives.'

She blinked. And now she did take her gaze from his, and, walking to a chair, she sat down, saying, 'Won't you take a seat?'

He turned from the couch and sat on a straight-backed wooden chair that was set against the wall near the window. He looked like someone sitting in a waiting-room and she was

137

forced to say, 'Oh, please, not there. Make yourself comfortable.' She pointed to the chintz-covered chair to the side of the fireplace, but he said, 'This'll do me.'

Then he asked abruptly, 'Do you want to hear about it?'

'Oh!' She was blinking again. 'It's as I said, it's—'

'I know, I know.' He nodded his head sharply at her. 'It's none of your business. But I want to put things straight, put them right in your mind, because they concern my mother.' He now put his hand up and ran his fingers through his hair; then said, 'This is where the explaining starts . . . Hannah, as you have already guessed, is my mother, but she's not my father's wife. And we've always called his wife Mother, even . . . even when we knew she wasn't, because that's the way they wanted it, the three of them. It was rather . . .' He now rubbed first one side of his chin and then the other with the palm of his hand, and he looked towards the stone fireplace before he went on, 'It was this way. My mother was a Wheatley. The Wheatleys were of good standing in these parts. The place below didn't always look as dilapidated as it does now. There was a good farm attached at one time, and they had enough money to build this house and set up their large families in good careers. They all had big families, all the Wheatleys. Right up to my grandfather and grandmother; they only had one, and she was Florence . . . It's funny but I always think of them as my forebears, yet I haven't a drop of their blood in me. But so that it won't be more confusing still, I'll refer to them as if they were my kin. When Florence was young the Wheatleys weren't as prosperous as they had been, but they sent her away to school to be educated. She was sixteen when her mother died and she came home to look after her father. And she was only eighteen when he went, and there she was alone, but for the farmhand, Sean O'Connor.' He wetted his lips and stared at her for a moment in silence before going on: 'Sean was only two years older than Florence; he was a good-looking man in those days, I'm told, and amusing, as he still is; and what was more, he was a great reader. If he had been as good at his work as he

138

was at his reading, the place would have been paying today. But there' – he moved his head slowly – 'if that had been the case she'd likely never have taken a fancy to him. Anyway, he was someone to look after in the short winter days, and someone to talk to during the long winter evenings, and she fell in love with him and he with her, and they were married. And you could say that they almost lived happy ever after. Yes, in spite of everything . . .' His voice trailed off but his eyes still held hers; his face had that granite look about it again.

She said softly, 'You . . . you needn't explain any further; it's perfectly all right, Mr . . . Mr O'Connor.'

He stared into her eyes until she became embarrassed; then quite abruptly he said, 'I haven't explained anything yet; I haven't come to Hannah. She, Florence, lost her first child. She had to have it taken away, and after that she knew she would never bear another. She was very ill at this time. It was then that my father sent over to Ireland for a distant relative of his, Hannah Kerry. Florence and she got on very well, but the need for children was with Florence . . . and my father, and whether they planned it or not I don't know, but he became close to Hannah and' – he looked sideways for a moment – 'I was conceived.'

He now dropped his hands between his knees. 'When I was born, Florence stipulated one thing: I must be given their name and I must look upon her as my mother . . . Then Kevin came and . . . and I think Florence rebelled, because Hannah went back to Ireland and didn't return for ten years. Then it started all over again. I . . . I think by this time Florence had become a very wise woman; that's all the explanation I can give for her acceptance of the situation. You know the rest . . .' He waved his hand back towards the window. 'The results are running wild; and strangely enough they're all happy. I don't think you'd find a happier family if you searched the countryside.' He paused and moved his head slightly, then said, 'You don't believe me?'

'Oh, yes, yes. That . . . that is what struck me when I first met you; I mean, the family; you all seemed very happy; well, certainly free.'

'They're free, all right.'

'Do the children know?'

'Yes; they were told at an early age and they have accepted it. And the strange thing about them is they all still look on Florence as their mother. It was different with Kevin and me, for we were brought up by Florence alone. But we, too, accepted the situation, for we loved Hannah. We all love Hannah, and she knows it . . . But at times it's not enough for her, like today, and it just needs someone like Father Shelley to lift the lid. It must be two years ago since he cornered her, and the same thing happened. She hasn't been a practising Catholic for years; nor has my father, nor I. Kevin kept it up, and the children go to a Catholic school. I've little time for priestly patter and less when I see what effect it can have on Hannah, although she professes not to care for God or man. But her conscience starts working overtime when they get at her. Not that Father Bateman – he's the one that usually visits – not that he ever speaks to her unkindly; but this one, instead of being in today's priesthood, he should have been in the Inquisition.'

When he stopped speaking she found she had nothing to say, and there was silence between them; and she was relieved when she heard Peter call from the kitchen, 'Shall I make the coffee, Mother?'

She called back, 'Yes; yes, do, Peter. And bring an extra one for Mr O'Connor.'

'You . . . you won't let it make any difference in your attitude?' Vincent's hand was pointing towards the window.

'Of course not.' Her face was straight.

'If you're here long enough, you'll hear things from time to time.'

She smiled slightly now. 'I doubt it, not right up here.'

'You'd be surprised. There's a bush telegraph that operates in this land; its wires run through every pub in every village;

but it doesn't always get the messages clear.'

He rose to his feet abruptly now and walked to the mantelpiece. Resting his elbow on it and one foot on the raised hearth, an attitude that was so natural he must have done it thousands of times, he stood staring at his carving. He appeared to be so at home standing there that it was almost embarrassing. Constance was turning towards the kitchen door and hoping that Peter would soon bring in the coffee when, with his eyes still on the carving, Vincent said, 'There's something else you should know; one more thing. If . . . if I don't tell you, you'll hear it through some other channel. It could be the bush telegraph or the grocery cart, or on market day, or even from a hiker on the fells. They might say to you, "Where does that big fellow live, the stone-faced fellow, who killed that bloke, you know?"'

As her mouth fell open and her eyes stretched, her heart seemed to jump against her ribs with the impact of his words. He was still standing in the same nonchalant position, but his head was turned towards her now and he was saying softly, 'They could easily ask that of you; it has been asked before. Time seems to make no difference . . . You see' – he brought his arm down to his side and his foot on to the rug and, turning and facing her, he said, 'I once did time for killing a man.'

As her fingers slowly grasped at her dress where it made a hollow in her lap, Peter came in from the kitchen carrying a tray on which stood three cups of coffee. He was wearing his dressing-gown; his hair was wet and his face looked bright and very young. He said, 'Oh! that was lovely . . . Oh, I've forgotten the sugar.' He put the tray down on the table at the head of the couch and went back into the kitchen, and as he did so Vincent O'Connor took a step from the fireplace and, leaning his body towards her, said under his breath, 'For God's sake don't be afraid of me, there's nothing to be afraid of. I . . . I just thought I'd better tell you. I'll explain . . . I'll explain some other time.'

'There you are.' Peter had the sugar basin in his hand. 'Do you take sugar, Mr O'Connor?'

'No; no, thank you.'

'You're like Mother; she doesn't, either. It's poison to me without sugar.' He handed the cup to his mother and for the first time during the last few minutes he looked at her face; then, as he handed the cup to Vincent, he looked at him, and as he said to him, 'I hope it's not too strong for you,' he thought, Now what? They both look strained.

'Thank you. I like it strong.'

The coffee was almost scalding hot, but Vincent drank his almost immediately, standing while he did so. Then putting the cup and saucer back on the tray, he said, 'I'll be getting back, if you don't mind.'

Constance rose to her feet but did not speak, and Vincent, looking at Peter, said, 'Thank you for being such a help tonight. I don't know what would have happened if you hadn't found her; she doesn't usually come by that road.'

Peter jerked his head, indicating it was a mere nothing.

'Good-night.' He was looking at Constance, and she, looking back at him, answered, 'Good-night.' And when he had gone, closing the door quietly after him, she went and sat down on the couch and said, 'Get me a drop of brandy, Peter, will you?'

'Brandy? Are you feeling faint?'

'Yes; yes, a little.'

When he returned with the brandy, he dropped on to his knees beside the couch and, holding the glass to her lips, said, 'You look like death. What is it? Something he told you about Hannah?'

'No, no . . . Oh, I suppose so. It . . . it was rather a shock.'

'Oh Lord! Mother, don't be so stuffy. Look, you won't let it make any difference to . . . to your going down there?' He seemed anxious that it shouldn't.

'Oh no.' She shook her head.

'You know.' He looked away from her. 'You know, it's

142

funny, but it doesn't matter a damn to me, not in the least, I mean, Sean O'Connor having, as it were, two wives.'

And that, when she had time to consider it, she knew would appear odd, for did he not hate his father practising the same game? Yet there was a difference; Mr O'Connor's weakness lay with a woman, not immature girls.

'What did you say?'

'Nothing, nothing; I . . . I was only thinking.'

She pulled herself up on the couch and drained the last of the brandy from the glass. She knew she had muttered Vincent O'Connor's words aloud, but Peter hadn't caught them. She turned her head and looked towards the mantelpiece and the carving, and all of a sudden she felt sick, and afraid; very afraid, with a new kind of fear. And it wasn't because Vincent O'Connor had admitted to killing a man.

PART TWO

1

It was a week later when the O'Connors celebrated the installation of electricity in the house. As yet, it consisted of a solitary bulb hanging from a cable attached to a bracket inside the kitchen door, but to all of them it was as exciting as if they had struck oil right in the middle of the yard.

Vincent came out of the shed where the generator was installed; he was wiping his hands on an old rag and he looked across the yard to where his father was leading The Duchess into the byre for her afternoon milking. The boys were scattered about the yard doing their chores: Joseph at the chickens, Davie humping wood, and Michael taking swill to the pigs. Kathy and Moira were inside helping with the tea, a grand meal that was not only meant to celebrate the electricity but to show the folks up above what a real Northumberland spread was like.

Vincent went into his workshop and, throwing the piece of rag on to the bench, sat down on a wooden stool and, out of habit, took up a knife and began whittling at a piece of wood. After a moment his hands became still and he looked down on them. He should get changed, he supposed; his mother would expect it. But what would . . . she up there expect? Nothing. Nothing. It wouldn't matter to her how he was dressed. Why had he told her? They were getting on all right; soon they would have been able to talk, at least he to her. She, it would seem, found no difficulty in talking to anybody, but from now on she would find great difficulty in talking to him. Why hadn't he gone up and explained? He could have done so any day during the past week. Why in the name of God had he told her in the first place? On top of the other, it was too much for anyone to stomach. Aw, what did it matter, what did it matter, anyway? He pushed savagely at the half-chipped piece of wood on the bench and it slithered along the surface to come to rest against the edge of the polisher. It was the best thing after all; it had killed the seed before it had had time to fertilise. He was mad; he had been mad for the last month. He wished to God she had never seen the house. But now she mightn't like the flavour of her neighbours and it was more than likely she'd disappear back into town for the winter. Then, come the spring, he wouldn't be surprised if she sold the place. Well, perhaps that would be the best thing.

He looked about the workshop, admiring the newly acquired machinery. Once upon a time he could, if he had wished, have broken away, but it was too late now. In selling the house he had forged one more chain around himself, for now he would be expected not only to support them but to make them rich. He sighed and the tension in him seeped away . . . Rich. If he managed to clear fifteen pounds a week they would consider themselves rich. It didn't take much to satisfy them, and up to a few weeks ago that's all he had wanted to do But now . . . He rose abruptly.

As he went through the storerooms he heard Florence saying, 'That's about the last, I think;' and when he walked into the kitchen she turned to him and said, 'Oh, there you are; I was just going to send for you. You'd better get changed.'

Kathy, standing at the sink, asked, 'Are you wearing your dinner suit or just going lounge?'

He thrust his fist out and tapped her gently on the chin; then after sluicing his face he turned to her and said thoughtfully, 'There's Great-Grandad's kilt still in its box; I was wondering if the occasion warranted it.'

148

Kathy's laugh filled the room and she thrust her face up to him. 'I bet you wouldn't dare!'

'Well' – he scrubbed at his neck with the towel – 'it all depends on the size of the bet.' She laughed again; then said, 'Do you think they'll come?'

'Why not?'

'Oh' – she smoothed back her hair – 'after what I heard about the other night.'

'That won't make any difference to them.' It was Florence speaking.

'Well, I don't know.' Kathy walked to the fireplace, and Florence said, 'Why should it? Anyway, she's accepted.'

'She's a bit starchy.'

'Starchy? I wouldn't say she's starchy.'

Both Florence and Kathy turned towards Vincent. He was hanging the towel on a hook to the side of the sink and with his back to them he said, 'Him now, the husband. Well, I can imagine him getting high-handed and picking his company, but not her, or the boy. At least, I don't think he would.'

'Oh, you've no need to wonder about . . . the boy; he'll be here.' Kathy had her head on one side, and Florence, looking at her, said, 'You've seen him again?' For answer Kathy just nodded, but did not speak.

'Well, well.' Vincent was smiling as he walked down the room between the long, laden table and the fireplace, and again he put out his fist and gently punched Kathy, then asked, 'Is it his car, or him?'

'Oh!' She tossed her head and said candidly, 'At the present moment the car's got it; it's a great saving in bus fares. And he always stands me a coffee. That's another saving. And on Wednesday it was a fair sized tea, brown bread and white.' She nodded solemnly, and on this they all laughed.

After Vincent had left the room, Kathy walked to the table and, running her finger round the edge of a plate, said, 'He's funny, you know, Mother. He's so proper that you could laugh. But . . . but I don't.' And she glanced at Florence, who,

149

standing stiff and still now, said, 'And I hope you don't, Kathy!'

'Well, I said I didn't.' Kathy shook her head. 'But he's always bobbing up and down if anybody comes up and speaks, and pulling doors open for you. Not that I don't like it, but . . . but it sort of stands out, especially in a coffee bar where they all know you.'

'I can only think that's all to the good. With the majority of them looking a cross between ancient Britons and Druids with their long hair and Adam's apples, I should think he would stand out.'

Kathy's laugh again filled the kitchen, and Hannah, coming down the narrow stairs which led directly into the room at the far end, shouted, 'What's this I'm missin'?'

'Oh' – Kathy turned towards her – 'Mother's just said that the boys today look like a cross between ancient Britons and Druids.'

'And begod! she's not far wrong. The last time I was in Hexham there was one who stepped off into the road and nearly under a car, an' I said, "Be careful there, lass," and he turned an' looked at me, an' begod! I was so flabbergasted I couldn't even laugh.'

'And neither did he, I bet,' said Kathy.

'No, no, of course he didn't. If you're not sure of your sex, it reacts like a restrainin' factor on you. Stands to reason.'

Smiling quietly, Florence said, 'Go and get them all in, Kathy, and see they're cleaned up. And tell your father to come along.'

Kathy went to do Florence's bidding, the while Hannah, as Vincent had done, walked down the side of the table, saying, 'Aye, it looks grand, Florence, grand. And that smell; was there ever such a smell in the world as roastin' suckling pig? I bet they've tasted nothing like it. Nor your ham.' She continued her walk, round the end of the table and up the other side. 'Everything looks lovely; it's going to be a grand night. There's nobody can set out a spread like you, Florence.'

Florence turned slowly from the stove and went and stood

by Hannah; and she looked down at the table as she said quietly, 'It's all right, Hannah, it's all right. I keep telling you it's all right.'

There was a short pause before Hannah, her lips working one over the other, muttered, 'I'll never forgive meself, and them so nice. If they don't come I'll die.'

'If they don't come, they don't. We lived before we had their company up there and we'll live again.'

'But . . . but you like them up there. She's a change, an' your kind. I've shamed you, but more so I've shamed meself. I tell you I'd rather have cut me tongue out than . . .'

Florence's narrow hands fell on to Hannah's shoulders and she pulled her round to face her, and they looked at each other. Then Florence said softly, 'You know, Hannah, we never speak of this, but for your peace of mind I'll tell you something . . . You've brought me much happiness, Hannah, happiness that I'd never otherwise have known.'

The round eyes, lying deep in the sockets of the fat face, became misty, and Hannah said brokenly, 'And much heart scald.'

'We all have heart scald, and I have been amply repaid for any you gave me. Now' – her voice took on a brisk note, and her fingers tightened on Hannah's shoulders, and bending towards her she said, 'No more of this now; we haven't time to rest on tears, talk and emotion. We know where we stand, we two, don't we? We're a family.'

'Aye, we're a family.' Hannah's voice was trembling. 'An' you have a fine family, Florence; everyone of them's a credit to you.'

There was a tightness in Florence's throat as she turned about and began bustling at the stove again. Only someone with Ireland deep in their bones and heart could have done that, passing the flesh of their flesh on to another in an effort to bring them comfort. To an outsider the gesture might have seemed naive in the extreme, but to Florence it was, and always had been, an act of heroism on Hannah's part. Let those

151

outside the house, in the hamlets, on the farms deep in the valley, in the villages and market towns the length and breadth of the county, let them have their say about the set-up at the O'Connors' farm. Let them pity her – as they did – as much as they liked, but no one of them would dare say a word against Hannah Kerry in her presence. Hannah had made life full and satisfying for her in a way that she would never have experienced had her marriage taken its natural course, for Sean's love would, she felt sure, have gone the way of all men's love; it would have cooled.

> Love, it is teasing, Love, it is pleasing,
> Love is a pleasure when it is new.
> But as it grows older and days grow colder,
> it fades away like the morning dew,

ran the old ballad, and there were never words so true. At this stage of their lives there would have been only forbearance between them, whereas now he gave her a love tinged with adoration. No one knew Sean O'Connor as she did, not even Hannah. No, not even Hannah. She knew he had no love for Hannah; he had used her to give him sons and daughters. He was kind to her; he would stand no-one saying a wrong word to her; but for love, he had none to give her. Yet Hannah loved him. That was the pull that had brought her back across the sea again, not only to see her children, but to see their father. One would have thought that these two from the same country, the same county, should have come together, for they were of like temperament: they never did today what could be put off till tomorrow; they had no money sense; they liked to sit and talk and laugh. Their wants were few, their pleasures simple, the height of them being an occasion such as tonight. But only the one had been attracted to the other, and that was Hannah's cross. And when chided, as she sometimes was by the priest, as had happened the other day, she retaliated by going on a drinking bout, because only when in drink had she

152

the courage to claim her family, because in doing so she inflicted pain.

'Do you hear that lot?' Hannah was pointing towards the room off the kitchen. 'The Durham Light Infantry isn't in it.'

'Send them along to the other end to get cleaned up,' said Florence hastily, 'in case they should come upon them.'

'Come on, away with you!' Hannah stood at the connecting door. 'Do you hear me! the lot of you, along the bottom end and wash yourselves, before I flivver you. An' I want your faces shinin' like spit on a barn door.'

'Right down there?' protested Barney.

'Aye, right down there,' said Hannah, grabbing him by the ear and pushing him towards the far door that led into the next cottage. 'And you two,' she yelled at Davie and Michael, 'stop your carry on this minute. If you want to brain each other do it outside.'

'I'm not playin' second fiddle to him' – Michael was pushing at Davie – 'I'm older than him.'

'Second fiddle!' Davie was choking with laughter. 'You're bloody lucky to be in the band at all, never mind second fiddle . . .'

'What's that?' The voice behind them brought their sparring to a halt, and when the question was repeated, Davie looked up at Vincent and said under his breath, 'It slipped out. But it was him; he's always punchin' . . .'

'I'm not, our Davie; it's you. 'Cos you think you've got brains I've always got to play second . . .'

'Both of you! You heard Hannah, didn't you?'

They went past him now, with Joseph coming up in the rear, and they all grinned as they looked up at him, and Davie of the ready tongue said, 'That's your best suit, our Vin. Are we to have a ceilidh after, or . . . ?'

Vincent reached out and grabbed his young brother by the ear and pulled him forward, and lowering his face to the boy's eye-level he said, 'No, we're not havin' a ceilidh after, but I'll

153

tell you what we might have: we might have a session in the byre where I'd take somebody's pants down and lather his backside for giving me his old lip. How about it?'

Davie's face stretched into a wide grin. 'Aw, give over, our Vin. Look, leave go of me; in a minute the water'll be so mucky I'll have to start carryin' again.'

'Listen to me,' said Vincent, quietly now. 'You behave yourself at the table, mind; no fun and games with company here. You understand me?'

'Aye, Vin.'

Vincent pushed him away and Davie dashed after his brothers, and he, aware that both Florence and Hannah were staring at him, left the room without further words.

At the outside door his father passed him, saying, 'Three gallons she's given us the day. We can't grumble at that now, can we?'

'No,' said Vincent. He stood on the step and looked around the yard. It was filled with sounds; the sound of the generator behind the closed doors of the shed; the muffled grunts of the pigs; the quarrelling and clucking of the hens; the conversation of pigeons on the roof; the lowing from the cow byre. The combined sounds used to be as sweet to his ear as the sound of a symphony to a music lover.

He watched Kathy enter the yard through the gap in the wall, and when she reached him he said, 'Any sign of them?' and she shook her head. He looked at his watch. 'It's early yet. Six, just turned.'

'Did she say they would come?'

He looked puzzled for a moment. 'Mother sent Moira up yesterday and she came back with the message that they would be pleased to come.'

'Hasn't she been down since . . . since that night?'

For a moment he didn't answer, but then said, 'She went back to their flat the day after and she . . . she didn't return until the day afore yesterday.'

'But Mother says she usually comes down every day for

154

something or other. It's funny she's never shown her face since that night.' Kathy jerked her chin upwards now. 'Well, if that's put her off she must have a weak stomach. That's all I can say.'

'That didn't put her off.'

Kathy turned and looked up at Vincent. He had his hands thrust deep in his pockets and was staring straight ahead, and she said, 'You . . . you didn't tell her about it?'

'Yes; if I hadn't, somebody else would've.'

'Oh, Vin, you're mad.'

'Aye, perhaps.'

'How did she take it?'

'I don't know. I had just finished telling her the bare facts when the boy came on the scene an' I couldn't go on.'

'You just said . . . ?'

'I just said that . . . that I'd killed a fellow.' He sighed. 'And there was no time for further explanation.'

'Well!' Kathy's face stretched and she shook her head slowly. 'Candidly, Vin, I'm surprised she said she'd come at all. Oh, our Vin. You are a fool. Nobody as much as remembers the affair; it's over and done with.'

He looked down on her and his voice was quiet as he said, 'Except Mr and Mrs Ridley.'

After staring up at him she moved to his side and leant her head against his arm, saying, 'Oh, Vin, Vin, don't torture yourself any more. He asked for it. Everybody said so at the time.'

'Aye, at the time; but people have a habit of changing their minds and opinions.'

'Look' – she turned her face up to him – 'as soon as you get the opportunity tell them up there about it, the whole thing.'

'Perhaps.'

'No perhaps, Vin.' She tugged at his arm. 'You make yourself right with him. Have a chat with him.'

'Him? No!' He shook his head slowly, a look of surprise on his face. 'You couldn't talk to him, explain anything. Her, yes, but not him.'

'You don't like him?'

155

'No. No, I don't like him. I didn't from the first minute I saw him. He's a big head, a nowt, really.'

'That's funny. Mother sees him in the same way, and so does Hannah; but Dad thinks he's a nice chap.'

'Yes, yes, I know; but then he thinks most people are nice.' As they smiled at each other, he lifted his hand and said, 'Ssh! there's somebody coming.' There was a faint sound of voices from beyond the wall and through the opening appeared the guests. Vincent moved back into the sorting-room and Kathy walked slowly through the dusk to meet them.

They were all seated at the table: Florence at one end, Sean at the other; Constance sat on Sean's right, and facing her sat Vin; next to Vin was Moira, and next to her Michael; then came Kathy and Jim Stapleton; on Florence's left sat Hannah, and next to her and opposite Kathy was Peter; Davie and Joseph filled in the space between him and Constance.

They could scarcely see one another because only the firelight illuminated the room, but everybody seemed to be talking at once. Then Sean's voice, rising above the din, called, 'Now have you all got something in your glasses?'

To this there came a chorus of, 'Aye. Yes, yes.' Then Sean's voice again. 'Well, Vin, we're ready.'

Vin rose from the table, took an electric bulb from a shelf on the dresser. Then, reaching up, he fitted it into a socket protruding from the wall.

And then there was light.

'Hu-rray! Hu-rray!' The boys were bouncing up and down in their seats.

Sean had his glass held high. 'Drink! Drink! all of you,' he cried, 'to a miracle, Vin's miracle.'

Edison himself scarcely received such acclaim as did the solitary electric bulb and the man who had run the wire into the house.

'A miracle indeed!' Vin's reply was scornful, but he smiled as he raised his glass with the rest, and Constance, looking him

156

straight in the face for the first time since his words had awakened her into a new awareness, answered the smile, if tentatively.

'I think I'd rather have the lamp,' said a voice.

The babble of voices faded away to hear Sean demand, 'What's that you say, Moira?'

Moira, her eyes screwed up, was staring over her shoulder at the bulb and she looked towards her father now, saying, 'I would rather have the lamp, Dad.'

'I thought that's what you said. There's gratitude for you.'

'Well, it's softer, sort of.'

'Of all the ungrateful . . . !'

'She's right.' Vincent was nodding down the table at his father. 'She's absolutely right; give me the lamp any day in the week.'

'It only wants a shade.'

They all looked at Constance, and she smiled as she said, 'That big carboy in the storeroom would make a lovely lamp with a nice shade on.'

'The big wicker bottle, you mean?' Hannah was bending forward over the table looking towards Constance.

'Yes, Hannah; the wicker-covered bottle.'

'You don't say.'

'Yes; they make lovely lamps.'

'Well, now; well, now, that's an idea. Isn't that an idea?' Hannah looked across at Jim, and he, finding an opening at last, took hold of the conversation.

'For myself' – he inclined his head towards her – 'I don't think it would be suitable for this kind of house. I would . . . well' – he now put his head to one side – 'I think two wrought-iron standard lamps, one at each side of your big fireplace there' – he nodded towards the open grate – 'would be more in keeping. You want to keep things in character.' He now gave Kathy the benefit of his smile. 'Lamps or 'lectricity, for you?' He stressed the 'lect' and she laughed back at him and said, 'Lect-tricity for me every time, mister.'

157

Jim received this rejoinder as if it were pure wit, and as he laughed outright Peter stared at him from across the table, until Hannah, nudging him with her elbow, asked, 'Have you ever had suckling pig?'

'Suckling pig? No, no; I never have.'

'Aw well, you're in for a treat.' Hannah was now on her feet standing behind his chair, and the next minute she made him jump by letting out a bellow, crying, 'Which of you want your Yorkshire with gravy, and which with milk?'

There was a confused babble from the children and she counted heads as to their taste, stopping at Joseph and pointing to him, saying, 'You want it with gravy! But you always have it with milk. You're the bloke that never changes.'

'Well, you asked me, didn't you?' He cocked his face up at her.

'Yes, I know, but what's made you change, the night?'

'Just 'cos you asked me.'

'I'll ask you all right. Begod! I will.'

The whole family of O'Connors were laughing at some particular joke not understood by the guests. Even so, Constance joined in, as did Peter, but Jim's face remained straight.

'You're sure, now?' questioned Hannah further. 'Don't let me put it on, then you go and say—'

'Just give it to him, Hannah,' said Florence; 'you know he's having you on.'

'Havin' me on, is he? I'll swipe the hunger off him if he's havin' me on.' She flapped her hand at him.

Florence now turned to Jim and said politely, 'Excuse me,' then rose from the table and went to the oven, from which she brought out a huge dish on which lay a complete suckling pig, surrounded by roast potatoes, braised carrots, onions, and parsnips, and as she laid it before her husband she turned to Hannah, who was standing by Constance's side, and said in a whisper, 'Perhaps Mrs Stapleton doesn't care for Yorkshire either way, Hannah.'

Constance had never had a meal preceded by Yorkshire pudding, with or without gravy, or milk, but if it were only to please Hannah she said, 'Yes; yes, I would like some, Hannah. What do you recommend? Gravy?'

'Aye, it's best with gravy. The young 'uns like it with milk, some of them . . .' She cast a glance up the table, which caused more laughter.

'Then I'll have it with gravy. Thank you, Hannah.'

'And you, Mr Peter' – Hannah was bending over Peter – 'gravy or milk?'

'With gravy, Hannah, please.'

'And Mr Stapleton?'

'Not for me, thank you, not for me; I'm . . . I'm looking forward to that' – he nodded to the dish in front of Sean – 'I don't want to spoil it.'

'Aw, Florence's Yorkshire won't spoil a meal.' But she did not press him, as she had done Constance, and soon they were all supplied with a plate on which reposed a large portion of Yorkshire pudding floating in either milk or gravy.

To her end of the table Florence now carried a ham that resembled a porcupine, for skewered all over it were chunks of roast pineapple resting on orange rings; and this dish did bring an exclamation of admiration from Jim. The air of condescension that was underlying his thin air of cheerfulness vanished for a moment and he said, 'That looks marvellous! I've never seen one done like that before.'

'Wait until you taste it,' cried Hannah. 'Nobody can do a fruit ham like Florence.'

'Be quiet, Hannah, and get the vegetables.'

As Florence and Sean carved, Vincent went round the table filling the glasses from an unlabelled bottle. When he came to Constance he said, 'It's peach; my mother makes it.'

She tasted it, then said, 'It's lovely; and very potent.'

'Aye, it is that,' put in Sean, now handing a plate down the table and calling as he did so, 'Do you like stuffing, Peter?'

'Yes,' Peter called back; and Sean, bending his head towards

159

Constance, said, 'The tree they come from must be all of fifty years old. And that's another miracle; it growing here. But it's sheltered in the corner of two walls and it gets good feeding, and what sun there is falls on it full. Oh aye, them peaches are another miracle. An' there's nothing like their brew for relaxing the nerves and warming the heart.'

Constance was endorsing in her mind all that Sean was saying because, of a sudden, she was feeling relaxed. She could look at Vincent without that queer tightening of her stomach muscles; she could even look down the table and see Jim entertaining his end of it, making them laugh, and not think, as she had done when she heard him discoursing on wrought-iron standard lamps, of what they would have said if they had heard his opinion of them, spoken in no small voice, a few minutes before they left the house up above: Why the hell did they have to go down to that series of shacks with that lot of gypsies? That was his opinion of the O'Connors, and without his having the knowledge either of Hannah's place in the household or of Vin's confession. What his reactions would be when he found out, she didn't dare to think. Well, he wouldn't find out from her, or from Peter, the part he knew.

The main course was followed by an apple pudding with mouth-melting crust and dollops of fresh cream.

Afterwards, Florence, rising from the table with the graciousness of a town hostess, said, 'Would you care to come into the parlour for coffee?'

Her voice was almost cut off with Hannah bellowing, 'Not you, not you lot! You sit where you are and you'll help with the washing up, every blasted man-Jack of you.'

There were groans and chit-chat from the boys as the elders left the table and followed Florence into 'the parlour'. They entered the room by one of the two doors leading off from under the staircase. It extended over the ground floor of one cottage, and it presented to Constance a fascinating picture of a Victorian sitting-room or, as Florence called it correctly, a parlour. There was an inlaid wooden-framed couch in faded

fawn tapestry with two matching chairs; there was a blanket
box couch with a single head and drop foot covered in tapestry
that had once been red; there was a circular table with four
claw feet in the middle of the room; across one corner stood
an upright piano in a fretwork frame; in the opposite, also
standing crosswise against the walls, was a cabinet filled to
capacity with what Constance instantly recognised as Coalport
china. A heavy ornate sideboard stood to the side of the
window, and on each end of this stood a crystal ornament, the
shimmering light on the glass reflecting a thousandfold in the
ray of the lamp that was set between them. Another lamp with
a pink oil bowl resting on top of a slender stem was placed at
the centre of the circular table. The floor was entirely covered
with the remains of a good Wilton carpet. The fireplace was of
rough stone, similar to the one up at the house, and in front of
it was a filigree brass fender with a black iron bottom. To
complete the picture, standing opposite the couch on a sofa
table was a tray of delicate cups and saucers, more Coalport.

When, with the exception of Hannah and Kathy, who were
still in the other room, they were all seated there fell on them
that awkward silence that often descends on a company, until
Jim bridged it by heaving a big sigh and saying, 'All I want to
do now is to lie back and smoke; which, in my own way, means
I've thoroughly enjoyed a fine meal.'

He inclined his head towards Florence, and she smiled back
at him; and now Sean said, 'Finest cook in the county bar none,
that's my wife.' And he jerked his head towards her.

'Do you keep many pigs, Mr O'Connor?' asked Peter.

Sean screwed round in his chair to look at him. 'As many as
ten sows will give me in a year, boy.'

'We passed a great flock of sheep when we came up
yesterday. They were over by Allerybank Moor,' said
Constance. 'They had clean faces and legs. I haven't seen any
like them before.'

'No; no. They're the Scotch half-breeds; as you say, a clean
face and legs. They'd be Tennent's. No, I keep the black-faced.

161

You can't better them; they'll stand hail, snow and flood water, and come through. And that's the opinion of many around here. They've taken the prize again and again at the Royal Highland Show, you know . . . Have you ever been to the Royal Highland Show, Mrs Stapleton?'

'No; I'm afraid I haven't.' Constance smiled at Sean and he, putting his head back, said, 'And why for would you now, unless you were interested in livestock? Up to these last few weeks I'd like to bet you could hardly tell the difference between a goat and a sheep, and that you thought a Galloway was a pit pony.'

'Well, isn't it?'

'There, what did I tell you?' He laughed loudly. 'No, no; it's a breed of cattle they rear in these parts.' Sean, giving the impression of being a knowledgeable farmer, was enjoying himself.

At this moment Kathy entered the room carrying a tray on which stood a heavily ornamented silver coffee pot and matching jug. She set them down on the table to her mother's hand and Florence, looking up at her, said quietly, 'Fetch Hannah in. Tell her to leave things . . . fetch her in.'

A few minutes later Hannah followed Kathy into the room, saying, 'I'm not goin' to sit on me backside all night with that lot to face out there, so don't try an' persuade me otherwise.' She was wagging her finger towards Florence, and Florence, smiling gently at her, said, 'Well, sit yourself down for a minute and drink a cup of coffee.'

Whilst pouring the coffee, Florence enquired of her guests whether they required black or white; then, the cups filled, she handed them to Vincent, who in turn handed them first to the guests, then one to Hannah, another to Kathy, and last, he served his father. With a cup in his own hand he now stood at the end of the couch. There was room on the couch, but he did not seat himself until Hannah, who was seated the other side of Constance, looked up at him and said, 'Take the weight off your legs, boy, and sit yourself down.' And after a

162

moment's hesitation he took his seat at Constance's side.

To the right of them, seated in an armchair, was Jim Stapleton; and on a hassock to the side of him sat Kathy; and opposite, but some distance from her, was Peter, with Sean seated to the right of him.

The conversation divided itself: Sean began to ask Peter questions about the work ahead of him at university, and Peter answered, but every now and again he would turn his attention to his father, who was making Kathy laugh; Florence, from her chair by the end of the couch, talked intermittently with Hannah, and Hannah, seated next to Constance, brought her into the conversation; but no words passed between Constance and Vincent O'Connor.

The general conversation was flagging again, apart from that between Jim and Kathy, when the door opened and the three youngest boys and Moira pushed each other into the room. Rushing towards their mother, they chorused, 'We're off to bed, Mother,' and one after the other they kissed her on the cheek. Then, still pushing and giggling, they gave the same salutation to Hannah.

'Quiet now!' admonished Florence sternly. 'Say good-night to Mr and Mrs Stapleton.'

'Good-night, Mrs Stapleton. Good-night, Mr Stapleton. Good-night, Mr—' They looked enquiringly at Peter; then Joseph and Davie pushed at each other again and drooped their heads, and Peter, smiling, said, 'Peter'll do.' Again they all laughed, and then they went scampering out of the room.

At this point Kathy looked across at Vincent and said, 'It's nearly time, isn't it?' And he, looking at his watch, answered, 'Yes, I suppose so.'

'You're going back to Newcastle tonight?' Jim was bending over the side of the chair gazing down into Kathy's upturned face, and she nodded brightly at him, saying, 'Yes, we must be in by ten-thirty.'

'Oh, then I'll drop you there.'

Before Kathy could make any response Peter, his voice high

163

and seeming to thrust him up out of his chair, cried, 'No! No, you won't. I'll take her back.'

There followed a moment of dead silence in which Peter stared at his father, before he drooped his head.

Kathy rose from her low seat and, looking first at Peter, and then towards Jim said, 'Thanks . . . Thank you both, but Vin always takes me in.' She walked across the room and as she passed Vincent, she said, 'I won't be a minute,' and he, rising to his feet, nodded at her, then followed her out.

Jim Stapleton's face was a dull red; his mouth was set in a grim line and he sat staring fixedly at his son, while Hannah gabbled to Constance about the strictness of those places that treated the staff like bairns; in on the dot or else you were for it, up on the carpet in the morning. And the work the poor lasses had to do! Not satisfied with making them care for dozens of bairns, they gave them books to fill. And what did they expect them to put in the books? It was the case of trying to fill a full pail all over again, for what they had to write was practically a description of what they had been doing all day. Did you ever now, did you ever?

A few minutes later when Kathy came back into the room to say goodbye, the Stapletons were on their feet ready to go, and she stood in front of Constance and said quietly, 'Goodbye, Mrs Stapleton.'

'Goodbye, Kathy.'

Then she turned to Jim and said in the same tone, 'Goodbye, Mr Stapleton.'

'Goodbye.' He did not say her name and there was no smile on his face now.

Kathy turned to Peter and she looked at him hard for a moment before she said, 'Goodbye, Peter. Be seeing you.' And he answered, 'Goodbye, Kathy. Yes, be seeing you.'

Kathy now took leave of her mother and Hannah, kissing them both warmly, and Florence said to her, 'Goodbye, dear, and mind how you go,' while Hannah said, 'Slap all their backsides for me, do you hear? good and hard.'

Kathy laughed and touched Hannah's fat cheek gently with her fingers. Then she turned to where Sean was waiting for her, and he put his arm round her shoulder, laughing as he said, 'Come on; I'll see you off the premises.'

Saying, 'I've had the most lovely evening: I don't know when I enjoyed a meal more,' Constance held out her hand to Florence, who took the praise as her due, answering quietly, 'Thank you, Mrs Stapleton. I . . . we've all enjoyed your coming down.' She inclined her head towards Peter; and then to Jim; and Peter, offering his hand, said, 'That goes for me, too. I've enjoyed every minute of it.' His expression did not entirely bear out his words.

Then it was Jim's turn. 'Goodbye, Mrs O'Connor' – there was a smile on his face – 'I can only repeat what I've already said; you put on a great spread.' There was a slight note of condescension in his manner now and Florence inclined her head but said nothing. And now Hannah was shaking Constance's hand and laughing as she did so. 'Shaking hands as if one of us was off across the water, when the morrow, so to speak, we'll be chit-chatting over the wall.' She moved to Jim now but did not extend her hand as she said, 'But you, sir, you'll likely be off the morrow; you're not so inclined towards desolation. That's how you see it, isn't it?'

'Well, well, not exactly.' His voice was stiff. 'But to be quite truthful, I prefer the town.'

'Yes, I thought so, I thought so.'

They were now all moving towards the door when Hannah, walking by Peter's side, halted him by a light touch on the arm, and when the others had passed beyond hearing she said to him under her breath, 'I've never thanked you for the ride the other night.'

There was slight confusion in Peter's face and he began to say, 'Oh, that's all right,' when she slanted her twinkle-deep eyes at him and flapped her hand in front of his face, and followed this with a deep chuckle. 'Aw, it's a wicked woman I am. Do you know that, a wicked woman.'

'I would like to believe you,' said Peter gallantly, 'but I'm sorry, I can't.'

Hannah stood gazing at him. 'It's like your mother you are, just like her; you take after her in every way.'

'I'm glad you think so, Hannah.'

'I do. I do. Come on. Come on, away with you.' She pushed him as if he were one of her youngsters.

When they were in the yard Florence asked, 'Have you a light, or would you like the Tilley?'

'It's all right,' said Constance; 'we have two torches. You have one, Peter, haven't you?'

'Yes, Mother.' He flashed on the torch and saw his father already walking across the yard. There were more goodbyes, then they followed him.

A few minutes later, Sean, coming into the kitchen, said, 'What do you think of that now? I just came round the end of the wall and there's him going on ahead as if the devil was after him, and her and the lad coming up slowly behind. They haven't had time to have words, now have they?'

'They've had them already,' said Florence.

'What do you mean?'

'The boy, and him, when he jumped in and offered to take Kathy home.' Florence now turned and looked at Hannah where she was standing with her back to the fire, her skirt pulled up exposing the back of her knees to the flame. 'Didn't you notice it?'

'I did that, and it reminded me of what our Vin said the other night: that there was no love lost between that father and son. There's somethin' fishy there. The more I see of him, the less I like him. I've got a feeling he's no better than meself, for all he writes books. But her now. I've taken to her, if you know what I mean?'

'Yes, I know what you mean, Hannah.'

'Do you know somethin'? I wouldn't be in her shoes for all the tea in China.' They were talking to each other as if Sean weren't there, and he suddenly made his presence felt by

166

saying, 'Aw now, don't take things too far, both of you; the man's merely a town type and, as such, not understandable to the likes of us. But still' – he rubbed his chin – 'it was odd like, that bit of exchange atween them, as you say. Do you think' – he looked at Florence. 'Do you think he's gone on our Kathy? The boy, I mean. Oh my God! the boy I mean.' He was laughing loudly now, and Florence answered, 'Oh no, not at all; he hasn't had time.'

'Oh, talk sense, woman, talk sense.' Sean had accompanied his words with a smile, and taking a pouch from the mantelpiece, he sat down and put his feet up on a cracket to the side of the hearth. 'Anyway' – he looked at Florence – 'you let them see how things should be done and they were impressed. Oh aye, they were impressed. And who wouldn't be? That was indeed a meal, a grand meal.' He patted his stomach; and Florence, taking from the dresser a candlestick that held a half-burned wax candle in its holder, said, 'Well, I must away to bed, I'm very tired. Good-night, Hannah.'

'Good-night, Florence.'

'Good-night, dear.'

Florence O'Connor made her way to her room and left the other woman with her husband for a few minutes, which she usually did at times at the end of the day such as this. After all it was Hannah's due; and it was all she got at this time of her life.

2

Vincent stepped down from the Land-Rover and walked slowly towards the workshop, and as he was about to enter the doorway Hannah called loudly across the yard, 'I've just made a brew up,' and he nodded to her, saying, 'I'll be over in a minute.'

From the cow byre his father also called to him: 'The Duchess is niggly this morning; only just over a gallon.'

'Oh yes?' Vin nodded back at him absent-mindedly, then entered the workshop, leaving the door open, knowing his father would follow.

When Sean entered the shop he said immediately, 'Do you think you'll be able to do this, Vin? I mean all on your own? Even with me helpin' with the packing and such it's going to be some job, and it's gettin' the crates to the railroad.'

'I have my eye on a second-hand truck.'

'Oh, begod! Now you're talkin'.'

'And you know, Dad' – Vincent took off his jacket, then set a lathe in motion, before he added, 'we went into all this. You're going to pull your weight?'

'Now who said I wasn't? Aw, be fair, boy; I'll pull me weight, every ounce of it. But what I was just thinkin' is, if the concern grows . . . ?'

'It isn't off the ground yet. We'll talk about it growing when it starts to pay its way.'

'Yes, yes, boy, you're right, you're right. And here's me standing jabberin' instead of gettin' down to it. But . . . but I heard Hannah back there sayin' she had brewed up. Come over and let's have a cup or so afore we start, eh?'

'You go on; I'll be over in a minute.'

'Right you are.'

Left alone, Vincent switched off the machine and stood staring at it: there was something he had to do and he wouldn't rest until it was done. Kathy was right. Why blacken himself further than was necessary? He'd go up and explain. It couldn't alter what he had done, but it would show her why he had done it . . . But what if he was still there? He remembered hearing him say something about going off first thing in the morning. Or was it the boy who had said that? Well, he could dander up with the milk and if he was there he could say he had come up to see how they were all faring, to make sure they weren't suffering from the after-effects of the rich pork . . .

A few minutes later, Sean, entering the yard to give Vincent a shout, saw his son going out through the gap in the wall with a milk can in his hand, and he walked slowly after him and watched him mount the hill to the house. When he returned to the kitchen he looked at Florence, and then at Hannah, then back to Florence before he said, 'He's gone up above.'

Florence made no response; she just stared at her husband while Hannah put her fingers across her mouth and muttered, 'Oh, Holy Mary. If anybody in this world asks to be crucified, it's him.'

Vincent, his step slow, was approaching the side of the house when the sound of raised voices came to him. Only once before had he heard her voice rise above a level tone; that day in the workshop when she was angry. But now she was shouting; yet what she was saying was incomprehensible to him. He halted at the corner where the terrace began and he looked towards the stone wall which was muting the voices. After a moment of staring he was about to retrace his steps when a voice, no longer muted, came from the terrace, crying, 'Well, I've warned you! You keep him out of my hair; I've enough to put up with from you and your nagging. And another thing. You carry out your threat about the flat and you'll see what'll happen. Mind, I'm warning you!' As the footsteps pounded swiftly away towards the other end of the terrace, Vincent leant against the wall and pulled his lower lip tightly in between his teeth.

It was a good five minutes later when at a brisk pace he marched along the terrace and knocked on the door. When Constance opened it, he stared at her for a moment without speaking: she hadn't, as he had imagined, been crying. Her eyes were not red, but they seemed to have grown to twice their normal size, their brown hue appearing almost black against the whiteness of her face.

'Hello,' he said.

'Hello,' she answered, and hesitated. 'Won't . . . won't you come in?'

He passed her and stood in the middle of the room, saying, 'I just called in to see if you had all survived last night.'

'Oh, yes, yes.' Her face moved into a semblance of a smile; then she added, 'We . . . we had a lovely evening. We all agreed on that; we enjoyed it thoroughly. My son went into town early this morning and . . . and my husband has just gone. You've just missed him.' Her voice was low and her words rushed and when she had finished speaking she blinked several times, then looked over her shoulder towards the window. 'It's a beautiful morning. There was a mist first thing. I suppose it's telling us we're nearing autumn.'

'Yes, it won't be long. To my mind it's the best time up here; even better than spring.' He turned and walked to within a few steps of her and looked out of the window. His back was towards her now, and he said, 'Once you've looked upon those hills in the autumn they've got you for ever.' His head moved slowly round and his eyes slanted towards her, and there was a slight smile around his lips as he added, 'So you'd better look out.'

170

She turned from his gaze and walked towards the fireplace, saying, 'I'll likely be going down into town in a week or so; I'm . . . I'm looking for a flat.'

'You are changing flats?'

'Yes. The one we have is much too large.'

Walking towards her, in his abrupt way he asked, 'Are you afraid of staying here by yourself?'

She was looking him full in the face, and she did not answer for a moment, for she didn't really know whether or not she would be afraid to stay here alone in the winter. But before she could say anything to this effect he was saying, 'Is it because of what I told you the other day?'

'Oh no! No!' Her reply had come quickly.

'But it shook you?'

She turned her eyes from him and after a pause said, 'Yes. Yes, it did at the time.'

'That's . . . that's what I really came up about. It was no social call; I wanted to explain.'

'There's no—'

He lifted his hand quickly: 'Don't say there's no need,' he said; 'you can't just say you've killed a man and leave it at that; I must give you my reasons. By the way, did you tell your husband?'

'Oh no.' She shook her head firmly.

'Nothing?'

'No. Nothing.'

'Not about the situation with Hannah?'

'Of course not.'

'But your . . . Peter knows. Didn't he say anything?'

'No, no. Peter wouldn't say anything.'

His eyebrows rose. Then he said, still abruptly, 'Can we sit down for a moment?'

'Of course. But believe me, you've no need to explain anything. If it's painful—'

'It'll be more painful if I don't tell you the ins and outs.'

'Very well.' She sat down stiffly at one end of the couch, and

171

he sat down in the chair opposite, to the side of the empty fireplace. And he looked at the fireplace for some time in silence before he said, 'This room's nice any time of the year, but when there's a fire in that grate it's wonderful.' Turning to her and noting the expression on her face, he said, 'I'm not sidetracking anything, I'm going back to the beginning. You see, it really all started with me imagining what it would be like sitting in this room on a winter's night with my wife by my side.'

There was another pause, during which he kept his eyes on her face; then he began again: 'I'm a conservative sort of fellow, I imagine, and although both my parents are Irish I think my early environment among these hills and fells set my character. Like the people round about I didn't make friends lightly, and when I loved, the pattern was more set still.' He now joined his hands together and, putting his elbows on his knees, brought his big chin to rest on his broad knuckles. 'I'd known a particular girl from when I went to school, and it was understood that one day we'd marry. I knew there was nobody else for me, and I thought there was nobody else for her, but one thing I've learned, you never know what's in another person's mind, no matter how close you are to them. Anyway, at twenty-five it looked as if we'd still have a long time to wait. I was working as a carpenter over in Hexham, and at the same time trying to get a farm of sorts together down below. My father, as you may or may not have gathered, is a good-natured but feckless man. Well, with all this, there wasn't much leisure time, you understand. But the more important thing to me during that period was the lack of money. You see, they sort of relied on me down there, and there was no chance to save until a way presented itself to make quick money. I'd heard that the crews of the oil tankers were coining money, and the trips were short. I reckoned I could earn as much in three months as I could in a year at my own job. Two trips, no more; six months and I'd have enough on which to get married and pass on a little down below.' He moved his head slowly now on his fists and said

172

under his breath, 'That's as far as I looked ahead, just getting married. I . . . I knew that I could scrape a living of sorts around here, and not for a moment did I imagine myself staying at sea longer than six months. Anyway, to cut a long story short, I signed on, and I had my first taste of the ocean. I'd never been partial to the sea. As a distant setting to scenery, yes, but not otherwise . . . Have you ever been on board ship for weeks on end?' He looked at her, and she nodded and said, 'Once, for five weeks.'

'And it didn't want to make you go berserk?'

'No; I rather liked it.'

'I thought I'd go mad every day. There was no place you could stride to. Oh, you could walk round the deck but I always had the desire to walk off the end of the boat when I came to it. Anyway, I should have been back from the first trip in under three months but there was an explosion on board when we were in port and one of the crew was killed. Incidentally, it was a fellow I'd become pally with, the only one I really liked. It . . . the way he died shook me and I knew, money or no money, that once I was back home there would be no more sea-going voyages for me. We were held up in that place for nearly three weeks because we had to send over here for one of the company to come and estimate the damage, and just as the repairs got underway the fellows went on strike. Anyway, by the time we docked in the Tyne, I'd been away nearly five months.'

He sat back in the chair now and again he turned his eyes towards the window and looked across the fells before saying, 'You know what I did when I got off the bus at Wark?' He waited a moment, and when she didn't reply in any way, but just continued to stare at him, he said, 'I flung myself down on the hillside . . .' There was another pause before, from deep down in his throat, he muttered, 'Can you imagine loving earth so much that you rub your face in it?' Again he waited; and when again she remained silent he went on, 'Although I was bursting to see them all . . . and her, I walked the long way

173

round, and when I saw the waters tumbling over the shale and glimpsed the red deer and saw the kingfisher once more my cup was full . . . or almost.'

He coughed; then, his tone changing, he said, 'I walked in on them just as if I'd walked out half an hour gone, and at first I thought their behaviour was because I'd given them all a gliff. It wasn't until I mentioned Mary that I guessed something was amiss; but I didn't put any questions until I was changed and ready to go down to Harbottle to see her. It was then that my mother suggested I'd better wait for her to come up . . . Ah, well!' Again he coughed. 'Anyway, I couldn't get any real sense out of them until I cornered Dad outside the house. And then he asked me' – his eyes flicked sideways now, then he gazed at the floor as he said, 'had I got Mary with child?'

He was nodding towards the floor now. 'My answer to that was to stalk over the hills to find her. But she wasn't in the house, and her father told me to let things go the road they had taken; I'd kept her waiting too long, anyway. I didn't see her for three days although I went over every day and hung about on the outskirts of the village. And then I saw her . . . and him too. It was when I was meandering home in the dusk. I was on a rise just below Falstone and there in the distance I saw them together. They were a good way off and it could have been any couple, but no, she had red hair and it stood out like another setting sun in the twilight.'

Now he took a handkerchief from his pocket and wiped his face; after which he returned the handkerchief to his pocket and looked at her for a moment before saying, 'I didn't ask any questions, I just hit him; and he came back and he hit me. He only hit me once. The next minute I had lifted him from the ground and thrown him down again. We were on the edge of a scree cliff, and he rolled and went over. I don't know whether he was dead before he rolled over or not, but he was dead enough when they found him.'

He stood up now and walked to the fireplace and, lifting his hand, he traced the back of the sheep and the lamb gently with

174

his finger. 'They were kind to me at the trial. They brought it in as manslaughter, unpremeditated, that was the extenuating factor. But you know' – he turned towards her – 'if I hadn't finished him off then, I would have at another attempt.'

She shivered inwardly as she rose to her feet but she did not take her eyes from him as she said, 'I don't think you would; it was in the heat of the moment. And . . . and I can understand how you felt. And I'm sure they would too. That's why they found you not guilty.'

'. . . Not guilty?' he repeated. 'No, not guilty of murder, but guilty of manslaughter, for which they sentenced me to seven years in prison.'

He straightened up from the mantelpiece and stared at her, as she stood with her fingers pressed tightly across her lips, her head moving slowly from side to side, and he said, 'Oh, don't be concerned like that; it's all over. I did a little over five years.' The corner of his mouth twisted upwards as he added, 'It's a good job after all I'd had that apprenticeship of living in close quarters on an oil tanker. But' – he again looked away from her – 'when I came out I knew I would never grow a day older inside until I died. How old do you think I am?' His face was turned towards his shoulder and she looked at it, from one big feature to another, at the prominent cheekbones over which the skin looked stretched, at the wide grey eyes with the lines running deep from the corners, at the long thin nose. She did not look at his mouth, because that did not indicate his age, being the softest part of his face, and she said, hesitantly, 'Well, about . . . about thirty-five.' He gave a wry smile and said, 'You're quite close. Even though I look older, I'm thirty-four.

'Any road, what does it matter?' he went on and thrust out his arm towards the window. 'That's all that matters to me, just to be able to look at that, and to walk out there until the day I actually die. And then' – he turned round to her, his face smiling gently now – 'I've no doubt I'll haunt it.'

He watched her expression change. There came a trembling smile to her face and her lashes began to blink rapidly – they often did, he had noticed, when she was disturbed – and now her voice held a cracked note of laughter as she said, 'It's very early in the morning for a drink and I've only sherry and brandy, but would you like one?'

The corners of his mouth spread as he nodded slowly at her. 'Yes, thanks, I could do with a drink; brandy, if you please.'

He watched her walking down the room towards the kitchen, her step quicker than usual. Then looking at the carving on the mantelpiece, he walked slowly to it and again fingered it gently.

But he was standing gazing out of the window when she entered the room carrying a tray on which stood two glasses of brandy. After handing one to him she raised the other, saying quietly, 'To happier days.' And he repeated her toast, 'To happier days.' And when his glass touched hers the whiteness left her face and she flushed deeply.

They had almost finished the drink when, rolling the stem of the glass backwards and forwards between her fingers and thumb, she looked at it as she said, 'May I ask about . . . about what happened to the girl?'

'Oh! She married the fellow's cousin. They live on the South Tyne somewhere, Hebburn or Pelaw, round about there.'

'How long ago was all this?'

'Nearly ten years gone. I've been free now for just over four years.'

She looked through the window, out into the wide expanse of sky. 'When you come to an isolated spot like this you don't imagine that anything has touched the people for . . . well, for generations.'

'People lived here before they lived in towns; and things happened; things have always happened . . .'

'Vin! Vin! Our Vin!'

Joseph was pelting along the terrace, and Vincent as quickly moved to the door where the boy threw himself on him, gasping, 'It's me dad; he's nearly taken his finger off with the scythe. Me . . . me mother says to come, to come now.'

176

Vincent seemed not to be very perturbed at this news; in fact he smiled as he said to the boy, 'All right, go on back; I'll be down directly.' Then turning to Constance, the smile still on his face, he said, 'What did I tell you? Things are always happening. My father is what you would call accident prone. There's another name for it, in fact two; an Irishman would say, "Aw, it's because he's Irish;" but the English would have their own definition. I'll leave you to guess what that is.' He nodded. 'Whenever Father gets tired something happens to one of his extremities.'

When she laughed aloud he laughed with her. It was a deep, rounded sound.

'Goodbye.' He nodded at her. 'And thanks for the drink.' He paused as he was turning away, and, his voice low, he said, 'You'll not be frightened of me any more, will you?'

The laughter left her face and she looked straight into his eyes and said quietly, 'I was never afraid of you . . . Vin.'

For one moment longer he looked at her; then he left, closing the door behind him. She walked slowly to the mantelpiece; and she, too, fingered the carving.

3

Even though it was the end of October, Constance was still at the house. The days were much shorter and the nights long, but so far the time had not hung heavily upon her and she had had no opportunity to be lonely.

The part of the day she enjoyed most was early evening when, the lamps lit and the fire blazing, she would sit on the couch and have tea, after which she would read. This would be on week-days. From Friday evening until Sunday evening she had the company of Peter.

Rarely a day passed but that one or other of the O'Connors didn't come up the hill, even if she had been down earlier, perhaps to ask if they wanted anything bringing back from Newcastle or, on the other hand, to enquire if Vin would bring her something. If Vincent ever did an errand for her he always brought it up the hill himself. Twice he had come to the door when Jim was in the house. On these occasions his visits had been brief. But when she was alone he would stay for ten minutes or so; although he never stayed long enough for anyone to come and fetch him.

This particular evening she was sitting with her feet upon the couch and a book in her hands, although she wasn't reading, but was thinking about Jim. It was five days since she had seen him, and then they had spent the time rowing. The agent had written to say that her husband had been rude to

178

some prospective buyers when he took them to see over the flat: and would it be possible for her to be there the next time he made an appointment to view? So she arranged to be there. And it was after the people had left, having promised to buy, that Jim had let his rage run loose again.

At times lately, she had felt a little guilty at staying so long at the house and letting him fend for himself, but following the latest scene she told herself she would feel guilty no longer: there was a room waiting for him at Shekinah; in fact, three rooms that ran into one another. They made an ideal suite; if he wouldn't take advantage of them, that was up to him.

In Felling, she had seen a new bungalow she liked and she had asked him to go with her to look over it, but he had refused. Well, soon he'd have to make his choice, and she hoped, deep in her heart she hoped, that he would prefer the bungalow.

It was a quiet night but she had been so lost in her own thoughts that she hadn't heard anyone approaching along the terrace. So, when the door opened abruptly, she turned her head, startled to see Peter entering the room.

Swinging her legs from the couch, she hurried towards him, saying, 'What's the matter? I wasn't expecting you, it being Thursday,' then stopped when she saw his tightly drawn face. Jim again. He'd had another row with his father, one that had been brewing for weeks past. She sighed and said, 'Have you had any tea?'

'No; and I don't want any; not yet, anyway.'

'Here, give me your coat, and go to the fire.'

When he was seated on the couch she sat beside him and, touching his hand, said, 'Come on, tell me.'

He slumped against the back of the couch and, biting on his lip, turned his face from her.

'What is it? Tell me what's happened.'

'Ada.'

'Ada?'

'Yes. I'll kill her. I'll . . . I'll—'

179

'What has she done now?'

'Told Kathy.'

'Told Kathy what?'

'Oh, for God's sake! Mother. Don't be so dim. What would she tell her that could upset me?'

'You mean? . . . She couldn't!'

'She could, and she did.'

'Where? When?'

'Today, in a coffee bar.' He pulled his hand down over his face and held his chin tightly for a moment. 'I've been seeing Kathy pretty often recently. We've . . . we've been to the pictures, and around.' This was the first she had heard of their meetings. 'It was during the lunch hour. It's her half-day. She was intending to come out here and return early and we were to go to the theatre. Well, we were sitting there, and she says, "There's a girl over by the counter who keeps staring at you. Do you know her?" And when I looked, I saw it was Ada. Well, you know how I . . . how my face goes red. Well, I felt myself turning a beetroot colour, and the next moment Ada comes up to the table and says' – he sucked his lips in tightly – 'she says, "Hello, cousin. Long time no see." And when I didn't answer her she bends down to Kathy. "You want to be careful of him," she whispered. "Fast as they make them. He'll burn your cylinders out. I should know; I"' – he found difficulty in going on – '"I've got a bellyful of him," and she patted her stomach.'

Constance stared at him. His face was drained of all colour and for a moment she thought he was about to cry. She moved her head slowly. 'What did Kathy say?'

'Nothing.'

'What did you do?'

'Nothing.' He sounded ashamed. 'I wanted to scream at her, choke her, but I knew that's what she wanted so that the whole place would be in an uproar. She just stood there waiting, so' – he lowered his head – 'I . . . I scuttled out like a frightened rabbit.'

180

'And Kathy?'

'She came out a minute or so after. I asked her to get into the car, but she wouldn't.'

'What did she say?'

'She asked me' – his voice cracked and he coughed – 'if I was the father of the baby, and I said, "No! No!" but she didn't believe me. I told her I loathed Ada and always had. She still didn't believe me.'

'Did she say so?'

'No, she didn't need to . . . Oh God!' He dropped his head into his hands. 'I feel sick, sick to the bottom of my stomach.'

She, too, felt sick to the bottom of her stomach. That girl! And he was helpless against her. She could do this any time they met; unless she herself put the matter into the hands of her solicitor. But then that would upset Harry. And in any case, she would have to be found first. She said soothingly, 'Kathy will understand. Give her time. When she has time to think, she'll know you could never have been with a girl like Ada . . . or any girl.'

'How? How will she know?' He was on his feet, bending towards her. 'It doesn't leave a mark on you, you know. If you've been once, twice, or forty times with girls, it doesn't tattoo you.'

'Peter!'

'Well, you sound like something left over from the Stone Age. The fellows in my form last year, Pete – you remember Pete and Mickey. Well, Pete started when he was thirteen, and he's had twenty-seven different girls since then. As for Mickey, he's stopped counting. So how can you tell! And remember you liked them both; you said they were . . . nice boys.'

Peter straightened up and they stared at each other. Yes, she had liked them both. Nice boys. Nice boys. She was old; yes, she was old, indeed something left over from the Stone Age.

'I'm sorry,' he said.

'It's all right, I understand.'

And she did understand. In spite of his big talk he had never

181

as yet been with a girl. 'It doesn't leave a mark,' he had said, but in fact there *was* a mark on him, the mark of virginity. And it was there through the fear that once he started, he'd acquire tastes similar to those of his father.

'Are you going down to the O'Connors?' she said.

'No, of course I'm not. Do you think I am a fool? She'd spit in my eye. She wouldn't get into the car, remember.'

'She's . . . she's had time to think it over. Did you go to meet her later?'

'No. Do you think for a moment she'd have been there? Oh Mother!'

She was silent, until he suddenly said, 'I'll be getting back.'

'What! But you've just come. And all that way! You must have something to eat.'

'I don't want anything . . . Oh, I'm sorry.' He put out his hand and touched her shoulder. 'I'm all het up. I tell you I could throttle that cheap, dirty little pro. That's all she is, a —'

'Don't . . . don't upset yourself. It'll all come right.'

'. . . In the end? Yes, I know.' He moved his head slowly. 'About as right as your life has . . . Oh, I'd better go else I'll just go on saying I'm sorry.'

He picked up his coat and hat and made for the door. She put her hand out towards him, only to allow it to fall again. He wanted action; that was the way the young tackled their problems, with movement. It scattered them to a certain extent. She had sat still under hers, like a hen on eggs; and doing that she had hatched fresh nerves, to be strung tight and played on.

She kissed him and let him go.

'Mrs Stapleton's been down. She was askin' if you'd pop up and see her. Didn't she, Florence?' Hannah looked from Kathy to Florence, and Florence said, 'Yes. She's seemed rather troubled lately. By the way, how's Peter?'

'Oh, he's all right,' replied Kathy.

'Where's he taken you this week? To the pictures?' asked Hannah.

'No, no; he's been busy working.'

Hannah looked at Florence; then seeing Vincent standing near the door, she caught the signal from his eyes and changed the subject.

'Are you goin' to miss the bairns a lot?' she said.

'Yes, I suppose so.'

'Aw, but then you'll be so taken up with being in a real hospital you won't have much time to think about anything. Oh now, won't it be grand to see you all decked up in uniform . . . you must get your photo taken right away.'

And so they talked hospital until it was dark, and then Vincent came into the kitchen, and looking at Kathy, said, 'Hadn't you better go up there? The time flies; you'll soon have to be thinking of getting back.'

She returned his look, then said, 'All right' . . .

It was five o'clock when Kathy went up to the house, and at six, when she hadn't come down, Vincent walked slowly up the hill and stood by the spring and waited. He waited nearly another twenty minutes before he heard the murmur of voices and Kathy's quick tripping step clapping the stones. When she came off the terrace he swung his torch in a double circle to let her know he was there, and she called, 'Vin?'

'Yes.'

'I'm sorry I've been so long.'

'That's all right.' His voice was light.

'It spoils your evening, having to take me right in.'

'What evening have I to spoil?'

He took hold of her hand and led her across the top of the hill, and as they were about to descend he said, 'Well?' and she stopped and said hesitantly, 'It was just about Peter.'

'I gathered that much. But what about him? You've had a row?'

183

'No, not really.'

'Then what?'

'Oh, I can't explain, Vin.'

'Why?' She had never before said that, and he felt there should be nothing she couldn't explain to him; he had practically brought her up. They were very close, perhaps because he had walked the floor with her for the first three months of her life. She had cried from the moment of her birth, and each night he took over from Florence and Hannah and allowed them to rest in turns.

Kathy had been the second girl born to Hannah after her ten years' absence. The other had died within a month of birth. All Hannah's girls had cried during their first three months of life, yet the boys were born placid and happy. Even Vincent had been born so. He said again, 'Why can't you?'

'Because' – she peered up at him through the dark – 'it would . . . well, it might upset you.'

There was a pause before he said, 'Has he . . . ? Did he . . . ?'

'No, no!'

'Well then, what?' His voice was harsh now. 'It must be something unusual for her to want to see you about it. What has he done?'

'He's done nothing. Well, at least . . . Oh, he's done nothing, nothing, I tell you.'

'Out with it.'

'Well, you're not going to like it, our Vin, so I'm telling you.'

'Well, I'll be the judge of that. Go on.'

So she told him; and when she had finished he said, 'What did she have to say?'

'She said he loathes Ada, always has, but that she's always had her eye on him. She's had two babies before this one. Constance says she's bad. I . . . I said that people weren't naturally bad because they had babies; I said Hannah had ten.'

'That's different.'

'That's what she said. But how?'

184

'Hannah wouldn't go into a café and do what you say that one did. She sounds vicious.'

'Well, yes, she was . . . horrible, dirty. Not dirty-looking, but just when she spoke.'

'Yet you believed he'd been with her?'

'Yes. No. Well, he ran out of the place. He . . . he looked scared.'

'He had reason to be, I think. Anyway, so you've dropped him?'

'No; he's dropped me. I turned up that night and he wasn't there, and I haven't seen him since.'

'You like him?'

'Yes. Yes, I suppose I do.'

'Would you mind if it were true?'

'No, not really, after I've thought about it. Men look upon this thing differently from us. Look at Dad. He's been an education in different kinds of love. He doesn't love Hannah, yet we're all hers. It doesn't follow, does it?'

'No, it doesn't follow.'

After a few moments of silence they began to walk down the hill again, and he said, 'What kept you so long?'

'Oh, we got talking. You know I really like her. I used to think she was starchy, but it's not so. She's very unhappy, though.'

'Did she say so?'

'No, of course not. But then, she doesn't have to; it's in her eyes. They're very alike, Peter and her . . . all keyed up. He's always talking about her; at least, he was at first. I used to get a bit fed up listening to him. But he never mentioned his father. I've got an idea he can't stand him.'

'What does she want you to do?'

'She didn't say. She only wanted me to know the truth.'

'And now you know it?'

'Well, it's up to him. I'm not going to go running, Vin.'

When he didn't respond, she said, 'Well, you wouldn't want me to, would you now?' and he answered, 'All I want for you

185

is to be happy, whether you run to it or walk. But don't let it slip past you; don't wait too long; don't wait for money, or anything else, marry young. It might not work out, but in the long run it's the lesser of two evils.'

'Oh, Vin.' She laid her head against his arm, and again she said, 'Oh Vin.'

4

'I'm sure it'll snow before mornin',' said Hannah, rubbing vigorously at the dry blacklead on the stove.

'No, it isn't cold enough,' said Florence. She was stirring warm sugar and yeast in a basin prior to pouring it into the well of flour in the big earthenware dish.

'It's over three weeks since we had the last fall,' said Hannah, 'an' the roads have been as clear as a new pin for a fortnight now. You would have thought she would have come up, now wouldn't you?'

'Perhaps she's been busy with their new bungalow.'

'Aw, she's had that long enough to have everything ship-shape twice over, and she said she'd be up for Christmas. Then her not sending even a line; just that ordinary card. And there's the bairns with all their bits of presents for her.'

'There's likely a reason,' said Florence, her hands deep in the flour now.

'Aye, and I bet it's him. If only our Kathy had still been friendly with Peter we'd have known all about everything, but not a word do you get out of her these days. She's like a blank page; no excitement, no tales, and her in a big hospital. But you remember how Moira said the Stapleton man went on when he saw missy coming over the fell with Vin. It was the day Vin went out after the sheep, you mind, when Sean thought they had foot-rot, and it was just that one of them had gone lame.'

'Yes; yes, I mind.' Florence's voice had an impatient ring to it.

'Well, now, it was just a chance meetin', wasn't it now? It couldn't have been anything more.'

'Of course, Hannah, of course; it was just a chance meeting. And we've been over this before.'

'Yes, I know. But I keep wondering why he went on the way he did – the Stapleton man, I mean – just because he had been waiting half an hour.'

'Mind you,' said Hannah, changing the subject, 'even when I'm worried at the back of me mind, there's a sort of excitement at the front, if you follow me, something that gives me the urge to pull up me skirts and do a bit of a jig.'

Now Florence stopped kneading the dough and, resting on her doubled-up fists, she leant over the dish and her body began to shake with silent laughter, and Hannah, her head drooping to one side, also started to laugh; then Florence gasped, 'Oh, Hannah, you're incorrigible.'

'And what's that?' said Hannah, wiping her mouth with the back of her smeared black hand.

'Oh, it just means you're a case.'

'Oh, is that it? But you know, Florence' – Hannah now went to the sink and began to wash her hands and her voice took on a serious note – 'I'm right concerned at the back of me mind most the time because Vin's actin' like a cat on hot bricks, an' that's not him.'

'It'll pass, it'll pass. It's got to pass.'

'Well, I hope to God you're right.' Hannah rubbed a lump of soap up and down her plump arms. 'But what if it doesn't?'

'It's just got to,' said Florence firmly. 'There's no hope at all for him up there, in no possible way. You can see it for yourself, can't you? Chalk and cheese.'

Florence had turned her head to speak directly to Hannah, who was now standing with her back to the sink, drying her arms on a coarse towel, and Hannah said, 'And he's the cheese; which, unlike the chalk, is palatable, but of no great value, only to us. But why, I ask the God above, should he be so unlucky? What's he done to deserve it? He's done nothing all his life but see to others, other people. Now hasn't he, Florence?'

'Yes, yes, Hannah, he has.' Florence was looking down at the dough again.

'There's no justice,' said Hannah, flinging the towel from her. 'Or' – she stopped as she neared the table and, her head to one side, she enquired of Florence, 'or is he bein' dealt the justice that should have come to me; the sins of the fathers?'

'Now, none of that, Hannah, none of that. That's silly talk and you know it.'

'Aw, Florence.' Hannah took in a deep breath. 'I'm not so sure. An' you know what? I would die this minute, yes, I would lay me life down if I could see him gettin' a bit of happiness, just for a little while, just a little while, whether it was right or wrong.'

'Mother! Hannah! Mother!' Moira's voice, accompanied by Barney's, came from the yard, and then both children came pelting into the kitchen and pulled themselves up at the corner of the table and pointed their hands upwards before they had breath to say, 'There's a light on. There's a light on up there.'

Florence and Hannah looked quickly at each other, and Hannah said, 'Well, now. Well now, they're back.' And Florence, turning to Moira, asked, 'Where's Vin? Is he still in the workshop?'

'Aye,' Barney put in quickly; 'and Davie's gone to tell him. We were all up on the crag and we saw the light from there.'

'Will we go up, Mother?' Moira asked, and Florence said, 'Yes. Yes, go and see if they've got plenty of wood.'

'Oh, they have, they have,' said Barney; 'our Vin made us cart up loads.'

'Yes, yes, of course,' said Florence. 'Well, take them up some milk. Ask your father to give you a canful.' She did not add,

And see who's up there; they would give her this information when they returned . . .

Across the yard Vincent, too, waited for the news as to . . . who was up there.

It was almost half an hour later when the children returned and Davie came dashing into the workshop, crying, 'Oh, Vin! You should see what she's brought us. Every one of us has got something. And Mother and Hannah's got table lamps. They're lovely.'

'Good.' Vincent straightened his back from the bench and asked quietly, 'Have they all come?'

'Mister isn't there, just missis and Peter. And Peter says, will you go up and help him with the table lamps 'cos he's frightened we'll break them. Oh, they've got heaps of things.' About to rush out of the door again, Davie paused; then as if Vincent were at the other end of the yard, he shouted, 'She's been ill in bed!' Then he was gone.

Ill in bed. That was it. He had never thought about her being ill; everything else, but not that. The air he drew into his lungs brought a lightness in him and quickly he switched off the machinery, rolled down his shirt-sleeves, dusted the wood shavings from his trousers and, after taking his jacket from the back of the door, put it on. Finally, before he left the workshop, he ran a comb through his hair. He had no mirror; anyway, he very rarely looked in a mirror because he didn't like what he saw there.

As he was crossing the yard his father called from the byre, 'They're back, then?' and he nodded. That was all.

When he rounded the corner of the house and stepped on to the terrace, the wind meeting him in full force, he thought, Why didn't I light the fire today? Every day except today.

He tapped on the oak door and waited for his knock to be answered. It was Peter who opened the door to him. His face looked bright, as was his greeting: 'Hello, Vin,' he said. 'We've just arrived.'

'Yes, yes, I see that. And most of our family has too, by the

190

look of it.' He nodded to where Moira, Barney and Joseph were gathered around the couch. Then he turned to Constance, who was sitting there. She had her head turned towards him; then she rose to her feet. 'Hello,' she said.

'Hello,' he answered.

'It's . . . it's a bit late to wish you a Happy Christmas' – she waved her hand towards the round table which was covered with packages – 'but . . . but I'm in time for the New Year.'

'You haven't been well, I hear?'

'No, I had 'flu. I thought the last time I had it was bad enough, but it was nothing like this. One often calls a cold 'flu, but this was the real thing.'

He stared hard at her. Her face was thin and wan, the brown eyes seeming to encompass it. 'Do you think it wise to come out yet?' he asked.

'The doctor said she should stay indoors for another two or three days.' Peter turned from where he was kneeling and pointing out the merits of the engine in Barney's train set.

Vincent looked back at Constance and she smiled faintly and said, 'I just had to get out; the bungalow seemed so small and cramped after the flat and . . . and I was longing to be up here again.' She moved her head slowly and looked about the room.

'I can understand that. And it would be all right if the room was warm, but that fire' – he nodded towards the grate – 'it won't give out real heat for hours yet. I . . . if I'd known you were coming I would have lit it this morning; it's been on most days.'

'Oh, thank you.'

'Your best plan is to come below straight away and stay there until we get that fire roaring. Come on! you lot.' He turned abruptly to the boys and Moira. 'Take whatever you've got to take and get going . . . Now, what's to go down?' He was addressing Peter, and Peter said, 'It's these cartons.' He pointed to the two-foot-high cardboard boxes.

'Well, leave those to me; you see to your mother. The wind's come up and it'll lift you off your feet. Wrap up well.' He nodded towards Constance; then stooping and picking up a carton in each arm, he went towards the door, and the children, their arms laden, followed him.

'Shall I leave the lamp on?' Peter called to Vincent; and he called back, 'Yes; it'll be all right. We'll be up again shortly.'

Turning to Constance now, Peter said, 'Shall I bring your coat and things downstairs?' He sounded excited, and she said, 'No; I want to go up. Light me a candle.'

In her room she slowly took her fur coat from the wardrobe and just as slowly put it on. Then she wound a scarf round her head. She had to stoop to see her reflection in the dressing-table mirror. Framed in the dark fur collar and the deep blue scarf her face looked like that of a ghost, and she said, 'I'm home; and here I'm going to stay.'

5

'It's the finest New Year's Eve I've ever known,' said Hannah. 'Just look at that table. Has this kitchen ever seen anything like it?' She pointed to where the long, wooden kitchen table was covered with a snowy white cloth and where at each end, standing between plates of food, was a table lamp of like pattern, their cream bowls holding pink satin shades. And even though the flexes were attached to the low ceiling, along which they ran to a socket on the wall, this did not detract from their appearance. 'And to think,' said Hannah, 'that with a mere turn of the switch you can light up the bowl as well. I've never seen anything like them in me life. They're too good for a bedroom. Don't you think so, Vin?'

Vin, coming in from the storeroom on his way to the parlour, his arms full of bottles, said, 'What's that you say?' and Hannah repeated her words.

'Well, you wouldn't be using them on that table every day of the year, would you?'

'No, of course not; but I can see them adornin' the parlour.'

'You were given them for your bedroom, so use them there.'

'You're right, Vin, you're right. But I'll never go to sleep for lookin' at them . . . Listen to them in there!' she said to Florence.

'They're gettin' going already. By, that's a fine radio of Peter's; no hum on that one. Aw, did you ever see a lad as happy? And our Kathy; I'll never forget her face as it lit up when she came in that door and saw him standin' there right by the table. And to think of our Vin bringin' her all that way and never letting on one word to her that he was here an' waiting. It was the gliff she got; she'd no time to show him a different face. He seems older. Don't you think so, Florence?'

'All of two months,' said Florence.

'Aw, you know what I mean. And he's a good boy, looking after his mother since he finished term. And fancy him tryin' to tap Michael as to whether Kathy had talked of seeing a lad lately – Lord God, he didn't know what he was doing, for Michael was the very boy to spin him the yarn she'd seen twenty. It's as well that Moira was within earshot or that one enquiry would have been his last . . . How long have we got to go now, Florence?'

'Oh, another twenty minutes I should say. The clock in the parlour was set right at dinner-time.'

'But you know that one gallops,' said Hannah.

'Well, even if it does,' said Florence, 'we'll hear the bells.'

'Aye, we might; and we might not, with the wind and the snow fallin' as it is. I told you we would get it. Now didn't I?' Hannah walked to where Florence was piling sandwiches high on a plate, and she asked quietly, 'Are you happy this night, Florence?'

It was a moment before Florence said, 'Yes, Hannah; very happy.'

'We've seen some New Years in together, we two, haven't we?'

'Yes, we have, Hannah.'

'I've got a feeling about the coming one, Florence.'

Florence made room for the plate on the table, then returned to the long bench and began to fill another plate. Presently she stopped what she was doing and looked at Hannah. 'Your feeling, Hannah . . . I hope it's good,' she said.

'I don't know, Florence.' Hannah shook her head. 'I don't know. It's a funny feeling, not sad like, and not happy. I just don't know; I never had a feeling like this afore on me on New Year's Eve. And yet . . . yet I want to dance. You know? Perhaps it stems from the worry that's on us both.'

'Yes, Hannah, yes; it could be that.'

'Ah well, the old one's near out, so let's forget it tonight, eh? . . . He's happy, Florence . . .'

'I pray it may last,' said Florence, going to the table once more. 'But I can't see how it can.'

'Me neither, Florence. Me neither. But I join me prayers to yours, nevertheless . . . Listen! there. That's Kathy laughin'. Isn't it grand that she's got tomorrow off, an' at this time an' all? We've got them all here except Kevin, Florence, and it's natural that he should want to bring it in in his own house, isn't it now?'

'Yes, of course,' said Florence: 'quite natural.'

'By the way, did you see our Biddy cockin' her cap at Peter? Quite brass-faced she was. If it wasn't that the boy can't see anybody in his eye but Kathy, I'd have skelped her into the middle of next week. An' listen to her now; that's her singing that song again. That's what comes of them living in the town and seeing that television.'

Biddy's high young voice penetrated through the kitchen now, singing, 'I say, No! no! no! It ain't me, babe, it ain't me you're looking for.'

Florence did not stop to listen to Biddy's voice, but, taking off the apron that covered her one and only best dress, she said, 'Do you think she's really enjoying it?'

Hannah did not ask whom she meant, but answered immediately, 'I'd swear on it. Why, there's even some colour in her face the night; and when Kathy and her dad did the jig she clapped and laughed with the rest of them. Oh, she's enjoyin' it fine, Florence.'

'I shouldn't think it's her kind of entertainment. But there, she seemed pleased to come down. Well now' – she looked around her briskly – 'have you got the piece of coal ready for him?'

195

'Yes, Florence; it's here.' Hannah pointed to the side hob, where a lump of coal lay on a newspaper.

'And there's the new loaf,' said Florence, pointing to the bench. 'He'll get the bottle himself. Well, now, I think we'd better go in.'

When they opened the parlour door the noise struck them like a wave. Seated in various positions on the mat around the big fire were Barney, Joseph, Davie, Moira, Michael and Biddy. On the couch sat Kathy, Sean O'Connor, and Constance, while Vincent sat in one leather chair and Peter in the other.

'Quiet! Quiet a minute!' Florence tried to silence the children; then turning towards Vincent, she said, 'There're only a few minutes to go.'

Vincent got to his feet and reached over Peter towards the sideboard, and, picking up one of the bottles he had brought in, said, 'Well, I'd better get stacked up.'

The boys pushed at each other and began scrambling up, and Michael cried to Davie, 'I'll be a first-footer next year. Vin said I can be when I'm sixteen.'

'Oh aye!' cried Davie back at him as they rushed towards the door. 'But it'll be lemonade you'll have in your bottle, or milk. Oh aye, milk,' he ended scornfully.

'Whist!' cried Sean. 'Stop makin' such a racket or none of us will hear it come in at all.' He turned to glance at the clock. 'It says three minutes to. Do you confirm that, Mrs Stapleton?' Constance looked at her watch and said, 'Mine says four; but it could be wrong.'

'Aw well, three or four, what does it matter, it'll be in a minute. Come on, all of you, into the kitchen!' Sean now turned and held his hand out towards Constance to help her up from the couch, saying, 'We should use the house door' – he pointed to the door at the far end of the room – 'but it's the devil of a job to get open and, more than that, to get closed again. It's swollen with age and years, like most of us,' and he brought her hand to his chest in a natural gesture – 'so we first-foot through the door we use every day of the year.'

As Constance entered the kitchen she saw Florence placing a white loaf in the crook of Vincent's arm and then handing him a piece of coal partly wrapped in paper. She watched him put the bottle of whisky under his other arm before taking the coal; then he was pushing through them all towards the store-room, and they all cried different things at him: 'Bring in a good one, Vin.'

'Make it a rich one, Vin.'

'I want to pass my exams, Vin.' This was from Kathy.

'Me, too, Vin.' This from a transformed Peter.

'See I win the pools, Vin,' from Biddy.

'A motor-cycle, Vin,' from Michael. On and on, what they wanted him to bring in the New Year.

'Good luck to us all, Vin,' was his father's wish; and Hannah's was, 'Peace on the house, Vin.' Only Florence and Constance made no request of him, and as he opened the door the snow swirled in. Sean forced it shut, stood with his back to it and faced his family, all illuminated, not by an electric bulb, but by the Tilley lamp that was hanging from the ceiling. And he became quiet, as they all did, while they waited for Vin to bring in the New Year.

When one of the boys coughed, Sean admonished him, 'Quiet now! Hold it, otherwise, with this wind blowin', we won't hear a sound of them.'

The minutes passed, and still no sound of bells permeated the thick stone walls; and the next sound that came to them was a fist being hammered on the door and Vin's voice crying, 'Open up there! Open up!'

Sean pulled the door open, shouting, 'We never heard them,' and Vin cried, 'I just caught a tinkle. A Happy New Year! A Happy New Year!'

For the next few moments there was pandemonium, as they all retreated with him back to the kitchen, and there, laying down the coal and bread but still holding the bottle of whisky in his hand, he greeted them one after the other. 'Happy New

Year. Happy New Year, Mother.' Then Hannah, her arms up round his neck and answering his greeting with, 'An' many of them, lad. Many of them.' She did not, even on this occasion, call him 'son', for so far she'd had only a small amount to drink. Then Kathy and Moira were clinging to him, followed by the boys. No kissing here, just a gentle punch to the side of the head and their answering punch to his stomach: 'Many of them, Vin. Many of them.'

'May all your wishes come true, Michael.'

'Thanks, Vin. And yours, and many of them. Many of them.'

Then Peter. A handshake here: 'Happy New Year, Peter.'

'And to you, Vin. Happy New Year.'

Now he was facing Constance, and after a moment's hesitation he held out his hand and said quietly, 'A Happy New Year to you.'

'And to you, Vin, a Happy New Year.'

When he let go of her hand the pressure and the warmth from it remained on her fingers.

A few minutes later they were all in the parlour again and Sean was crying, 'Now, does everyone have a full glass, Florence?'

'Yes, yes,' she called back excitedly. Then, forming a ring, they all held their glasses up towards the middle. The children's glasses held home-made wine; the adults', among whom Florence had included Kathy and Peter, held Scotch whisky.

Now all eyes were turned on Sean as head of the house, and he, with a great flourish, lifted his glass high, crying, 'Here's to all of us!' And they answered, 'Here's to all of us!' Then they drank.

'Come on, come on. Let's eat!' shouted Sean now. And eat they did . . .

At half-past one there was nothing left of the spread in the kitchen; in fact, the whole room was transformed. The long table was standing upended in the corner near the sink, the chairs had been pushed back round the wall, the rugs rolled up and the stone floor was given over to dancing.

With his hands cupping the side of his mouth-organ, Vincent played jig after jig, and reel after reel, which Sean usually led, and into one he had coaxed Florence. There was no need to coax Hannah or the children, nor yet Kathy and Peter.

Constance, seated now to the side of the fireplace, her knees against the warm oven, laughed and clapped and gave no thought to the morrow. She kept telling herself that she had never been so happy in her life.

Kathy came across to her looking flushed and happy. Putting her hands on her knees, she said, 'If we put the gramophone on, will you waltz? Peter says you're a cracking dancer. By the way' – her eyes twinkled – 'he doesn't take after you in that way; he has size fifteen feet. Did you know that?' She pushed at Constance's shoulder as she laughed, and the action was very much like one of Hannah's.

'Oh, I couldn't dance, Kathy,' said Constance. 'Don't worry about me. I'm happy just watching you.'

'Nevertheless, we'll have a waltz,' cried Kathy. 'They're all old-fashioned records, but what does it matter?' She dashed to the bench where a box gramophone had been placed and, putting on a record, shouted above the din, 'We're going to have a waltz.

'Come on,' she called across to Constance. Then grabbing Peter's hand, she swung him over the rough floor, and to the strains of *Over the Waves* she counted, One, two, three; one, two, three' to him while the others watched and laughed.

Vincent tapped the mouth-organ on the palm of his hand and put it in his pocket. Then, rubbing his hands with his handkerchief, he approached Constance, and looking down into her upraised face he said, 'Shall we try this one?'

Constance seemed to be rooted to her seat; she also found that she couldn't answer him; but he held his hand out and she placed hers in it. Then, with his arm around her waist and she with her hand on his shoulder, her step fell into his and she found herself almost sailing over the uneven floor. She wondered where he had learned to dance. Then Sean gave her the answer. His voice came to her above the chant of the children singing.

Neither of them spoke as they danced; nor did they laugh. After the record had droned to an end and they had danced on for two steps more, Constance, her face now pink-hued, gave an embarrassed laugh as she glanced to where Florence and Hannah were sitting side by side, and she called to them, 'I thought I'd forgotten; it's years since I waltzed.' She now almost overbalanced, and Vincent's hand came on to her arm. As he led her to her seat by the oven, she, still looking towards Florence, said, 'That proves I'm out of practice.'

'No, no,' said Florence kindly, nodding at her. 'A good dancer is never out of practice; once the music begins you always remember what you learned. That 'flu still has a hold on you.'

There followed a moment's quiet in the kitchen, which was broken by Kathy crying, 'Come on! Hannah; it's time for a song.'

'Oh no! not now, child; I'm not in form. Me chest's wheezin' like a rusty barn door.'

'Now was there ever a New Year's mornin' when you didn't sing?' said Sean. 'Up! with you now and get crackin'.'

So Hannah stood up, amid warnings of, 'Ssh! now ssh! Quiet!' and in a voice that was deep and rounded and heart-tugging, she began:

'Love me a little, I'll make it last;
Love me a little, I'll draw on the past.
Don't go away and leave me alone,
Life is death when on my own.

'Once we sat quiet, no need for words;
We walked the streets and saw gold everywhere;
Now the silence is but a sword
And the gold is worry and work and care.

'Once we were young and life was right,
But the years came, and years are stark.
Your love has gone in the long, long night,
And mine, I hug to me in case of flight.

'Love me a little, I'll make it last;
Love me a little, I'll draw on the past.
Don't go away and leave me alone,
Life is death when on my own.'

The song was from her heart; it was her life. It was beautiful and moving and oh, so true; but it wasn't a wise choice for the occasion. Something in it touched the life of each of the five adults in the room and brought a stillness to them, and as Hannah, resuming her seat amid the applause, said, 'Now, why did I have to go and sing a sad one like that?' there was an exchange of glances between Vincent and Kathy that brought Kathy to her feet, crying, 'Can you play a samba, our Vin?'

'How does it go?'

Kathy now la-lahed the tune to him while performing the accompanying steps. 'It's great fun. We did it the other night at the dance.' She turned to Peter. 'Come on. Anybody can do it.'

Peter now placed his hands on her hips and joined his steps to hers, which brought howls of laughter from the children, and Biddy cried, 'Show me!' And she put her hands on Peter's hips; then, her head on one side, she shouted to Kathy, 'There's a barn-dance at the Blacks' next week.'

'Which night?' cried Kathy between singing the tune to help Vincent.

'It's on Thursday.'

'Oh good-oh!' cried Kathy. 'I think that's my night off.' Then turning to Peter, she laughed up at him. 'If it is, I'll take you. I bet you've never been to a barn-dance?'

'No, never.' He was laughing widely back at her, looking deep into her eyes and lost to all but her.

201

'Oh, it's great, a barn-dance.' Then she turned to Vin. 'That's it, that's it. You've got it. Come on, all of you; get behind. Look; you just do this.' She took two steps to the side, kicked and thrust out her hip; then two steps to the other side with an accompanying thrust of a hip. 'That's all it is. Come on, now. Come on, Hannah. You, too, Mother. Come on, Mrs Stapleton. Dad, you follow on at the tail end. Aren't you coming, Mrs Stapleton?'

She looked towards Constance again, and Constance, shaking her head and laughing, replied, 'I've done all I can tonight, Kathy. Go on, I'll clap.'

And so she clapped and Vincent played the mouth organ, and when Kathy went to lead them all out of the kitchen, Vincent jumped up ahead of the crocodile and led the way round the furniture in the parlour, along the passage into the next cottage, through the children's quarters, and into the cottage beyond that, which was known to the family as 'Mother's place', right to Hannah's room at the far end of the buildings, and back again. Meanwhile, Constance sat alone in the kitchen, and as she cast her eyes around the shambles, she wondered at the pulsing, vibrant life that inhabited this house and the O'Connors. They were all alive. They had comparatively nothing, yet they were living, every one of them; even Vin, after all he had gone through. Oh yes, Vin was alive; underneath his granite exterior he was very much alive. She had felt the strong life in him as his hand had held hers; and, remembering it, she shivered and thought, I've been dead for years.

It was half-past three when Peter, Kathy and she went up the hill. The snow had stopped and the wind had died. A moon showed fitful gleams behind scudding clouds. Peter and Kathy, overflowing with home-made wine and the joy of meeting up again, were running ahead, pelting each other with snowballs.

Vincent, once they had all left the level ground and had begun to climb the hill, put his hand under Constance's elbow, and it remained there until they rounded the bushes near the rock from where the water sprang. And it was as she said, 'It's been a wonderful, wonderful night; I'll never forget it for as long as I live,' that he pulled her to a halt, and in the thin moonlight he gazed into her eyes. His hands holding both her elbows now, and his voice deep and soft, he murmured, 'A Happy New Year, Constance.'

It was the first time he had used her first name and he waited, perhaps for a rebuff, for her to withdraw from his touch. But when, looking back into his eyes, she said, 'And to you, Vin,' he knew that he hadn't been wrong. The next moment he was holding her close, pressing her thin body fiercely to him. When his lips, moving over her face, found her mouth, her whole body stiffened for a moment. Then, with a depth of feeling that surprised and even shook her, she was returning his kisses, returning the pressure of his body, holding him to her tightly, tightly. The weakness left by the influenza was as if it had never been; she was filled with a strength that was frightening. But, as quickly as had been its coming, it left her. Now she found herself struggling within his grasp, pushing her hands against his chest. Then she was standing with her shoulders and head drooping forward, and he was holding her clenched hands, saying over and over, 'Constance. Oh, Constance.' When her head drooped lower, he whispered, 'It wasn't your fault. Don't take the blame; it wasn't your fault.'

After a short silence, during which Kathy's high-pitched squeal came to them, he said, 'I knew this would happen from the first moment I saw you. But don't worry; I don't expect anything in return. It's hopeless, I know, for as Hannah says, there's all the difference between us of chalk and cheese. But I . . . I knew I'd have to tell you sometime. I just wanted you to know.'

She turned blindly from him, and as she stumbled in the snow his hand again cupped her elbow; but now he was holding it close to his side.

As he helped her up on to the terrace Kathy was crying from the far end, 'Cinch! Cinch! I give in.'

At the door Vincent called quietly, 'Come on, Kathy; it's time we were going down.'

'Right, Vin.' Then she was shouting back at Peter, who was poised with a snowball in his hand, 'Look; I've got my fingers crossed. Cinch!'

'Cinch? What's cinch? That's a new one to me.'

Peter now came to the door, where Constance was standing within the shadow, and his face stretched with pleasure as he said, 'Isn't it a marvellous night? It's been a marvellous night altogether. I can't remember ever having such a good time. I want to go . . . whoopee!' He let out a yell and jumped into the air, and Kathy gave out her high, gay laugh.

From out of the shadow Constance said softly, 'Yes, yes; it's been a wonderful night. We'll see you later, Kathy.'

'Yes, Mrs Stapleton. We're going sledging on the hill . . . Nine o'clock sharp, mind.' She flapped her hand towards Peter.

'Nine o'clock it is,' he replied. 'And if you're not up I'll come and pelt your window.'

'You'd have a job to find it among our lot. Coo! wouldn't he, Vin? Goodnight, Mrs Stapleton.'

'Good-night, Peter,' said Vincent; then after a pause, he spoke to the shadows and said, 'Good-night,' and Constance replied, 'Good-night.'

When they were inside and the door closed, Constance said, 'Don't turn up the light, Peter; put it out. I'm going straight up; I'm very tired.'

'Are you all right, Mother?' He came to her side, his face still alight, and she said, 'Yes, I'm fine.'

'It's been a wonderful night, hasn't it? They're all wonderful, aren't they?'

'Yes, they're all wonderful,' she said.

'I was a fool not to see Kathy sooner. You said I was and

you were right. You're always right. I love you.' He had his arms about her and kissed her, and she said with a break in her voice, 'You're drunk, Peter.'

'Am I?' He laughed aloud. 'I think I am just a little, but . . . but isn't it nice? Look; swear to me that life's going on like this for ever and ever. Swear.'

He was swinging her round, and she said on a broken laugh, 'I swear.'

He stopped suddenly and, taking her by the arm, he guided her up the stairs, then groped his way in the darkness of the landing to her door. 'Good-night, darling,' he said. 'And a Happy New Year . . . And I do love you, I do.'

'And I you.' She pushed him gently and laughed, adding, 'Don't forget to put the lamp out.' Then she was in her room, where she could see reasonably well, for the moon had escaped the scudding clouds. Going to the window, she stood looking out over the cold snow-covered land; but she felt warm, really warm.

Within the past few minutes she had been told twice that she was loved, once without words. She put her hands up to her face and held it tightly. What had she done? And what was she to do now . . . ? Go to sleep. Go to sleep, came the answer. Don't spoil it with worrying. There'll be plenty of time for that later when the head is clear of wine. Chalk and cheese. Chalk and cheese, he had said. She went to sleep repeating it: Chalk and cheese. Chalk and cheese.

6

The atmosphere inside the house had been gay, but it changed completely towards two o'clock on the afternoon of New Year's Day when, quite unexpectedly, Jim made an appearance. Evidently he, too, had had a good New Year's Eve, for he was suffering a hangover which, from the slight glaze in his eyes, he had been treating with the hair of the dog. His mood was mixed: he was inclined to be jolly, yet his conversation was threaded with recrimination. 'New Year's Eve and left on my own,' he grumbled.

'I asked you to come up with us.'

'And chance being snow-bound?'

Her raised eyebrows brought from him sharply, 'Yes, yes; I know I've made it today, but it isn't a big fall as yet, and I thought I'd better tell you that I'm off to London by sleeper tonight. I received a letter yesterday from Conway. He's shown my book to the film bods and there's a very good chance of them taking it. They'll be having a preliminary pow-wow tomorrow, so I'm off tonight.' He rose from the chair and strutted down the room, and as he reached the far window he stepped up on to the platform and, raising his hands high above his head, cried, 'God! it's good to feel in the swing of things again . . . Perhaps' – he looked towards her – 'perhaps, if this comes off I'll be able to buy myself a decent flat.'

'I should do that,' she said calmly.

He walked back to her now, saying, 'Have you any idea what it's like working in that matchbox?'

'I've been in bed in that matchbox for over two weeks.'

'Yes, yes, I know all about that; but when you feel inclined you can get out of it and come up here' – he turned his head in a wide circle – 'and soar.'

'You're at liberty to do the same.'

'Oh, what's the good! You wouldn't understand if I were to batter it into you with a hammer. You've never understood anything about me, have you? Only what *he* needs . . . By the way, where is he?'

'He's down at the O'Connors'.'

'Oh. The O'Connors'. I've got some news for you about the O'Connors.' He now sat down opposite her and as he leant forward his face took on a jovial expression. 'I knew there was something fishy about that lot. You remember me telling you some time ago about a fellow hinting at something? Well, I got the whole story, just like that.' He snapped his fingers. '"Where are you off to?" asked one of the locals. Half-canned he was. "Up to a cottage of mine."' As he had done once before, he stopped and, closing his eyes and shaking his head, growled. 'All right, all right. What am I going to call it, my wife's week-end retreat?' He lay back and looked away from her for a moment. Then, unable to withhold the information, he said, 'Did you know that O'Connor keeps a woman down there? And I'll give you two guesses who she is.'

'Yes, I know.'

He straightened up and pushed his shoulders back. 'You do? You know that all the kids are hers?'

'Yes.'

'How long have you known it?' His voice was threatening.

'Oh, for quite some time.'

'And you never let on? You are a close bitch, Constance.' He shook his head slowly. Then, wetting his lips, he said, 'Well, you know that much; but I don't suppose you know that the big fellow's done time. He killed a bloke . . . And that isn't hard to imagine, is it? He killed a fellow and did time, and he's only been out a few years. Well, you didn't know that, did you?'

She was looking past him down towards the fire, but in the corner of her eye she could see the carving in the centre of the mantelpiece and she said slowly, 'Yes, yes, I know about that, too.'

She remained still during the silence that followed her remark.

'You mean to say you knew that and yet you never let on?'

'It was none of our business.'

'God Almighty! None of our business. Who told you, anyway?'

'. . . The mother.' The lie was smooth.

'Oh, the mother. Well, she would soften it, wouldn't she? But anyway, why the hell didn't you tell me?'

'Are you ever long enough in my company for me to tell you anything? Do you ever want to listen to anything I have to say?'

'Don't twist things, Constance; this is different.'

'It's gossip.'

'Oh! Oh! It's gossip, and you're far above gossip. You would be. Does he come up here?'

'Very rarely.'

'What do you mean, very rarely? Does he come up here?'

She rose to her feet as she said, 'No.'

'Well, see that he doesn't. And steer clear of him when outside too. No more strolling on the fells. Give him a clear berth, or you might be sorry.'

As she looked at him she wondered yet again at his egotism, at the trait in his character that not only allowed him to ignore his weakness, the weakness that had ruined their marriage almost before it had begun, but helped him to act as if the weakness didn't exist: he could sound morally right as he censured other men's actions. This wasn't the first time he had warned her against the attentions of other men. If the whole thing wasn't so tragic it would be laughable; laughable as one laughs at something unbelievable.

208

Before he could make any comment on the expression on her face, there came concerted yells from outside and the sound of the children running along the terrace.

The wind had blown the snow from the flagstones but was now forming drifts on the level ground below and on the fells, leaving dark humps here and there and showing black twisted lines where the burns still ran.

Constance turned to the window and watched Kathy, Biddy, and Moira taking their stand against the boys, and Joseph, Davie, Barney, Michael and Peter pelting them with snowballs from strategic positions, all the time uttering blood-curdling yells.

She wasn't aware that Jim had moved until she heard the door open; then from the window she watched him go to the edge of the terrace and shout, 'That isn't fair; it's two to one!'

They all stopped for a moment. Then they were shouting up at him; all, that is, except Peter. He stood silent, rolling a snowball between his palms.

As Biddy O'Connor looked up towards Mr Stapleton, she caught sight of his wife at the window, and she remembered the night Mrs Stapleton had pushed her and Moira out of the kitchen because Mr Stapleton had put his arms around her. So, adolescent sex being a cruel, groping thing, she ran towards the man on the terrace and threw a snowball into his face.

'You little devil!' Jim, showing the agility of a man half his age, jumped from the terrace, grabbed up some snow and pelted it back at Biddy. In response, Biddy threw another one almost from arm's length. Then Jim had hold of her. His arm about her shoulders, he picked up a handful of snow and scrubbed her face with it and when she turned and buried her head against his waist, he continued to scrub her until a snowball hit him with unplayful force on the side of the head, stinging him, and causing him to let go of Biddy.

One of the boys had thrown the snowball. He didn't know which one it was, but when he saw his son bending for more snow, he wondered; then he took his stand alongside the girls.

Grabbing up a handful of snow, he pelted it back at the boys. And this went on until Biddy again pushed some snow into his face. This time he did not grab at her, but just threw a soft snowball at her in return. After a moment, stooping once again, he scooped up more snow and flicked it to the other side of him, and as it splashed into Kathy's face she laughed and spluttered. Then she was throwing snow back at him. When he grabbed her and his arm went tightly about her waist, holding her pressed to his stomach, her laughter died and she began to struggle fiercely. But he, his mouth wide, his eyes dark, continued to rub her face with snow; that is until the fist came on to his cheekbone and brought the water spurting to his eyes, while his son's voice yelled crazily at him, 'Let go of her! Let go of her! Don't you dare touch her! Take your dirty hands off her! Do you hear? Let go of her!'

He was standing now with his arms hanging down by his sides staring into his son's enraged face, staring at the spluttering mouth that was still yelling, 'You! You! Don't you dare touch her!'

Without moving, his eyes he took in the children's faces. Now they were all standing in a broken circle about him, staring at him. Only the fact that they all, as if on a signal, began to run down the hill, as if to warn someone of the fracas, stopped him from thrusting out his hands and gripping Peter's thin throat. He pulled his coat into shape on his shoulders; then with his teeth clenched and his lips squared from them, he marched over the flat ground, mounted the terrace, and burst open the door with his whole body.

Constance was waiting for him. She had her hands joined tightly at her waist and when he came and stood before her, the spittle jumped from his lips as he gritted out, 'This is the finish! That . . . that young swine—' But whatever he was going to say about the 'young swine' was checked by Peter himself bursting into the room. His face was as white as the snow he had been playing with, and his body seemed to have grown inches. After pausing for a second he advanced slowly towards his father, and when he was an arm's length from him he stopped and, staring into his face, he said, 'If I see you lay a hand on her again I'll . . . I'll—'

'You!' Jim's Adam's apple worked violently; there was froth at the corner of his mouth. 'You . . . you bloody little whipper-snapper, you! Who the hell do you think you are? What do you think you're up to, eh? Eh?'

'I tell you' – Peter's voice was shaking, as were his face and hands – 'I tell you, before God, if you lay a hand on her again, as much as a finger, I'll kill you. I will.'

'For two pins I'd go out there and roll her, and she'd have her knickers off for me in less time—'

As Peter's fist thrust out, his father's hand caught him a blow that knocked him backwards against the table, and sprawling over it to save himself from falling, his hand came in contact with a fruit knife that was lying on a low wooden platter beside some apples. Peter grabbed at it, and kept it in his fist, and still leaning backwards against the table he spluttered, 'You're rotten; filthy, stinking. You always have been. Why she's stayed with you all these years, I'll never know; but she won't any longer because I'm going to tell her about the house in Quilter Street . . . number eighteen, and the walks you take every afternoon for the good of your health . . . for the good of your health' – he was straining forward now – 'with a girl young enough to be your *granddaughter*, you dirty—!'

As his father dived at him, Peter's hand came up and the point of the short knife just missed the thick neck, although the blade ripped through the shoulder of Jim's coat.

Constance was screaming as she gripped Peter's arm in an effort to stop him repeating the action. Then her voice trailed away as she saw Jim stagger back, his face lint-white, and grasping his shoulder. She watched him pull off his coat, then the long-sleeved cardigan he was wearing underneath, to reveal a patch of blood on his shirt. He stared at it, then slowly he pulled off his shirt.

The point of the knife had merely slit the skin on the fleshy part of his upper arm, although if his coat had not been made of thick tweed and cushioned by the pullover the injury could have been much worse. But even if it had been, Constance would have found it impossible at the moment to have gone to his aid. She stood there, still holding on to Peter, who was shaking now from head to foot, yet just as aggressive as before.

When Jim dropped into a chair and, glaring at Constance, yelled, 'Well, come and do something, can't you?' Peter grabbed at her, but slowly she disengaged herself from him, and went to her husband's side. Taking a handkerchief from her pocket, she dabbed at the cut; then pressed it on to the wound and forced herself to speak to him: 'Hold it there,' she said in a voice that was scarcely audible.

She now went into the kitchen and returned with a strip of elastoplast which she placed across the wound; then, again with a great effort, she said, 'It . . . it might need a stitch.'

'Huh!' He gave a cracked laugh. 'It might need a stitch, she says. He stabs me, and that's what she says, quite calmly: it might need a stitch.' He got to his feet and pulled on his clothes, wincing each time he thrust his arm upwards. When he was again dressed, he picked his tie up from a chair, and thrust it into his pocket, then went to the cupboard under the stairs and took out his overcoat and hat. Having put them on, he looked towards her and repeated scathingly, 'It might need a stitch. You don't care a damn if I'm able to drive the car to get down there. Not a damn you care.' He brought his infuriated gaze from her to Peter, and he surveyed him for some seconds before saying, 'As for you, you lying, mischief-making young bugger, if you were to get what you deserve, I should go straight down to the police and inform them that my son had stabbed me, that he attempted to kill me.'

'But you won't, will you? For I would tell them the reason why, wouldn't I? As for me being a lying bugger—'

'Be quiet! Peter. Be quiet!'

But Peter now thrust away his mother's hand and repeated, 'Lying bugger, am I? Well, for your information I've been

212

trailing you for weeks . . . all during the summer holidays.'

'Peter! Peter!' She stood in front of him. Then turning to Jim, she cried bitterly, 'Go on, get out! Get out! will you?'

His face almost purple with rage, Jim sounded as though he was choking on his words before he finally said, 'God! It's come to something, hasn't it? New Year's Day, to be knifed, then told to get out.' He seemed to throw his body towards the door and as he went out, banging it after him, she wondered yet again at his capacity for shifting the onus.

Turning to Peter, she put her arms about him and led him to the couch; and when they were seated he bowed his head, bit on his lip, then slowly and painfully began to cry.

Holding him to her, she stroked his hair but said nothing; and when the spasm was over he pulled himself from her and wiped his face, first with his hands, then with a handkerchief, and after he had blown his nose he muttered, 'I . . . I couldn't help it. He took hold of her and she struggled.'

'It's all right, it's all right,' she said quietly; 'I saw what happened.'

His head was moving slowly now, and he said, 'I've been wanting to tell you about him for weeks and weeks, but I didn't want to upset you again and . . . and I didn't really know if you knew about it . . . Did you?'

'No.'

'I thought you couldn't know and keep going on, yet I—'

'How did you find out?' she interrupted in a flat voice, the while she looked down at the white knuckles of her joined hands.

He rose from the couch and leant his forearms on the mantelpiece. Drooping his head on to his hands, he mumbled, 'It was the day I came back from my holiday. He had gone out for a walk over the moor, as he was always supposed to do, and then I saw him, right down by the Armstrong Memorial. He was hurrying with what seemed to be purpose; then he jumped on a bus that was going the Leazes Park way. I don't know what made me follow it.' He stopped for a moment, then

213

said, 'Yes I do. I've always suspected him since the last business.' Again he paused, but she didn't ask, How did you know about that? for she had already realised little had escaped him over the years. 'He got off at the end of Queen Victoria Road, went round by the Infirmary, and I thought I'd lost him, until I saw him entering the park. I left the car there and followed him. When he came out he cut into Barrack Road; then made for Arthur's Hill way; in and out of streets he went. He walked for a good ten minutes before he went up the back lane of Quilter Street. I didn't know then which house he went to, because when I got there he had disappeared.'

He stopped now and was silent for some time before she said, 'Go on; I want to hear all of it.' He lifted his head but with his arm still on the mantelpiece he asked, 'Will you leave him?'

'Go on and tell me what you know.' She was still staring at her hands.

He took in a long breath before drooping his head again. 'I had to follow him four or five times before I saw which house he went into. There's a factory wall that runs along the end, and on the opposite side of the front street, on the corner near the main road, there's a little shop, so one day I went in. There were two women there. I had seen one of them before – she had come out of her house in Quilter Street as I was standing on the corner – and this day, after I'd asked for some cigarettes, I asked if they could tell me the name of the people who lived at number eighteen. Then they looked at me, the two of them, and the woman who lived opposite said to me, "You take my advice and keep clear of that one." She kept on and on; she ... they thought I was after her, the girl, and the woman behind the shop told me to be sensible because' – he swallowed again, then ended in a rush – 'they said that the girl did not only work day shift but the night shift as well. She had the system well arranged, they said, and she was spoofing the old bloke that kept her. Her name was Phyllis Vagus.'

There was a deep silence in the room now. The wood shifted

214

in the grate and sent up a shower of sparks. There was no sound from outside.

'I'm sorry,' he muttered. 'But . . . but it's better you should know. Anyway' – he turned from the mantelpiece and looked at her now – 'you'll leave him, won't you? This'll be the finish?'

As she stared blankly back at him the dark bulk of Vincent passed the window, and he opened the door without knocking.

Constance did not turn to look at him, for her gaze was directed towards the fire, but she knew that he was standing close behind her; and over her head he said to Peter, 'Are you all right?' and Peter, after nodding, answered, 'I'm all right.'

Vincent now looked about him. 'Your . . . your father. Where is he now?'

'He's gone.'

Constance rose slowly to her feet, and as she passed round the head of the couch Peter asked anxiously, 'Where're you going?' and she answered dully, 'To make some tea.'

When they were alone, Vincent's eyes moved to the table to where lay the fruit knife and the blood-stained handkerchief and, looking back at Peter, he said, 'Don't blame yourself; Kathy told me what happened. She's very upset. I'd go down and have a word with her if I were you.'

'I couldn't.' Peter closed his eyes. 'It was all so rotten, beastly, and I . . . I acted like somebody mad. And coming on top of the other business.' He glanced at Vincent. 'They think we quarrelled, parted over . . . did she tell you?'

'A little.'

'God! She must think we are a right lot.'

'She thinks none the worse of you. As for being a right lot, most families have skeletons. We've got more than our share. Go on down; she's leaving in an hour, as you know. I'll stay here until you come back, but I'll take her in today; you're in no shape to drive the car; and anyway your mother needs company. Go on, now.' His voice and his expression were soft.

Peter looked up into the large face, and after moving his

head from side to side he said quietly, 'There's a reason why I acted as I did . . . I can't—'

'I know there's a reason, and there's no need to say more. Go on, now.' He put his hand out, and touched Peter's shoulder. 'But don't be more than half-an-hour; I want to get her in and be back before it's dark. I think there's another fall of snow coming.'

Peter turned slowly away and picked up his long scarf, wound it about his neck, then pulled on his coat and left.

When Constance re-entered the room she stopped for a moment as she saw that Vincent stood alone in front of the fire. He said, 'He's gone down to say goodbye to Kathy; she's due to leave shortly. He won't be long.'

As she placed the tray on the table she was overcome by a fit of shivering. It started in her jaws, passed over her chest, down her arms and into her legs, and caused her to drop limply on to the couch.

Going to the tray, Vincent poured her a cup of tea, then silently handed it to her, and when she had drunk it and the shivering had subsided somewhat, she looked at the fire as she said, 'He . . . he could have killed him if the knife had been big enough.'

'Well, it wasn't, and he didn't; and he'll never attempt it again.' She raised her eyes to his, and he went on, 'He's still a boy; his action will wipe out all the bitterness that he feels towards him.'

When she still stared at him, he said, 'I know. I know. I told you before that if I hadn't done it the first time I would have tried it later; but this was different: Peter was fighting for his mother, I was fighting for a wife. There's all the difference in the world. There's something primitive rises in you when someone you imagine is going to share your life is taken from you, or . . . or marred in any way.'

Slowly he lowered himself on to the couch, although at a distance from her, and he leaned back and stared at the fire, and the silence that fell on them did not yell aloud in the room.

But she began to recall the events that had occurred in the early hours of this morning, and as she pictured yet again her clinging to him and returning his kisses with all the fervour of which she was capable, her body began to burn and she hoped that he wouldn't put his hand out and touch her, for she was afraid she would repulse him. The joy of New Year's morning was over. It might have continued throughout the day if Jim hadn't put in his appearance, but in one way she felt it was as well he had. At least it had put a stop to her madness, to the winter madness that seemed to fill and surround this house.

But she needn't have worried about Vincent making advances to her, for after lighting a pipe he sat puffing intermittently, his head forward on his chest. He could have been sitting in his own kitchen, so little notice did he take of her. The silence went on and on and she found she could not break it.

She felt a sense of relief when Peter returned. He was hardly in the door before Vincent got up and left, without saying either 'So long,' or 'Goodbye.' He did not even look at her, but just walked out. And Peter said, 'Is there anything wrong; I mean, with him?' and she replied, 'No. Nothing.'

7

On the Tuesday morning Constance said to Peter, 'If I'm not back tonight don't worry; I may not be able to get everything done today.'

'Are you going round there?'

'Yes.'

She had turned away as she spoke, and he said, 'You shouldn't go alone, I should be with you.'

'I don't want you with me. I'm calling on Aunt Millie; she'll come with me.'

He said nothing to this, then asked, 'What then?'

'I don't know yet.'

'You don't mean you would . . . ?'

'Peter.' She had her back to him and she bowed her head. 'Whatever happens, I'm staying here permanently.' As she pulled on her gloves she said, 'There's plenty to eat. I'll . . . I'll bring more supplies back with me.'

'You're not fit to drive,' he said; 'and the roads are like glass.'

'I'll be all right, don't you worry.' She turned and looked at him without smiling. 'Look after yourself. If I don't see you later today I'll see you tomorrow. Don't come out.'

'I'm coming down with you,' he said firmly as he dragged on his coat; 'at least as far as the car. And you may not be able to get it going.'

As it happened, Constance got the car going with little

trouble, and as she drew away she lifted her hand to him in farewell, driving cautiously down the ice-bound road.

Because of the road conditions it took her almost two hours to reach the bungalow on the outskirts of Low Fell. Before she got out of the car she sat for a moment gathering her forces, in case Jim should be still at home. But as soon as she entered the bungalow she knew he was gone; the whole place showed evidence of his anger. Dirty dishes were strewn over the kitchen table and sink, while in the dining-room, which she had turned into a bedroom-cum-study for him, the wardrobe doors were open, as were the doors of the dressing chest; and she noticed that his pigskin case had gone from the top of the wardrobe. She made no attempt to clear up, but instead made herself a cup of black coffee. Then she got into the car again and drove to Newcastle and Millie's.

When Millie opened the door she put her hand to her cheek and said, 'Why, Connie! This is a surprise. A Happy New Year, lass. Come in, come in. Oh, I am glad to see you. It . . . it seems years. Sit yourself down; you look frozen. What'll I get you? A cup of tea, or coffee?'

'No, thanks, Millie; I've just had a coffee.'

Millie now sat down on the edge of a chair and stared at Constance, and she said, 'You look thinner, if that's possible, and you're as white as a sheet.'

'I've had 'flu, or something . . . How are you, Millie? And . . . and Harry?'

'Oh.' Millie jerked her chin. 'What do you expect? It's no use trying to paint the lily, is it? For meself, I find the house quiet, more peaceful altogether, until he comes in at tea-time. And the sight of his face! Well, no matter how I tell meself I'm not going to worry any more, the look of him knocks all the gumption out of me, and I tell meself that if it would make him any better, I'd have Ada back. Yet, you know Connie, I doubt if he'd let her inside the door now.'

'Have you seen her since?'

'No, I've never clapped eyes on her, Connie, although she's

about the town. Susan's seen her. She went into Ben's shop one day, Susan says, and judging by the order she gave, money was scarce, and Ben made her up a parcel, and she didn't say no to it . . . I worry about that, an' all: if she's gettin' enough to eat; if she's got any money. Yet, remembering how hard-boiled she was, I can't see her going short, not really . . . But . . . but about yourself? You're in some trouble, Connie, aren't you?'

'I was wondering if you would come with me, Millie. I want to go to a house in Quilter Street.' She looked away towards the blazing fire, with the fancy glazed, cloaked horsemen propping up each side of the bars, and said, 'Peter found out that Jim's keeping someone in Quilter Street. He followed him a number of times. But if I just go on what Peter says and tackle him with it, he'll deny it. He went to London on New Year's Day. I . . . I don't think he can have done much about it since he left me. He had a dreadful scene with Peter up at the house; Peter used a knife on him.'

'Oh my God, lass!'

'I want to see for myself, Millie; then I'll know what I have to do.'

'Aw, lass.' Millie got to her feet and went to Constance's side and put her arm around her shoulder. 'I thought that was all over.'

'So did I. Yet I knew it would never be over with him. As long as he breathes it'll never be over . . . Will you come with me, Millie?'

'Yes, lass.'

'You . . . you weren't going to do anything? I mean, you're not busy or—?'

'Oh, busy? I have so much time on me hands that I want to scream. I said I like it quiet, but you can get too much of that, an' all. Of course, lass, I'll come with you. And I'm so pleased to see you; I've missed comin' along.' She smiled at Constance, and Constance replied, 'And I've missed you, Millie.'

'I'll get me hat and coat' . . .

* * *

220

It took Constance only fifteen minutes to find number eighteen Quilter Street. It was a short street and, as Peter had described, the last house was cut off by a factory wall. She drew the car up within a few yards of the wall; then, glancing at Millie, she got out, and when Millie came round to her side they walked two steps across the pavement. As Constance knocked on the brown-painted front door her heart pounded painfully against her ribs.

There came the sound of distant laughter; then footsteps coming towards the door.

'Yes? What d'you want?'

Constance was unable to speak as she stared down at the baby-faced girl, whose appearance suggested she might be about nineteen, but who was more likely seventeen. Her eyelids were painted almost as black as her eyelashes; on her pouting lips was a light brown lipstick, and her fair hair was built up high on the back of her head.

'I said, what do you want?'

'Is your name Miss Vagus?'

'Aye, yes. What about it?' The voice sounded as common as its owner looked.

'I would like to speak with you. May . . . may I come in for a moment?'

'I don't know about that. Who are you, anyway?' She looked from Constance to Millie and back again to Constance. 'If you're sellin' anythin' I'm full up; I've got so much in me kitchen that I can't get in meself. You're not the one that was here the other day, offering fancy foundation, or corsets, or what-have-you?' She now turned her head over her shoulder and called along the passage, 'Is this the one that called the other day about the corsets, Ada?'

When a figure appeared at the end of the passage Constance and Millie both groaned. Then Millie, pushing the girl aside, was along the passage and standing in the doorway staring at her daughter. She shook her head at her as she said slowly, 'Oh, you! Oh, you!'

'What d'you mean? Oh, you!' Ada's protruding belly was pulling up her woollen skirt to a point between her legs, and she hitched the waistband further around the mound of her flesh as she cried, 'And I say again, what d'you mean? Oh, you! What d'you want here, anyway?'

'Who is it? What's it all about?' The Vagus girl was standing close to Ada now. 'Who are they, anyway? It isn't the one about the corsets, is it?'

Ada, looking at the girl, jerked her head upwards; then with the same quick movement she directed her thumb towards Millie. 'It's me mother.'

'Aw. Aw, now I understand.' The girl giggled. 'Well, don't let's all stand here as if we was queuing for the lav. Get into the room.'

Millie followed Ada, and Constance followed Millie. She glanced around at the cheap trappings, thinking it was more than likely her money had bought them. 'We didn't come to see Ada,' she said icily; 'we didn't know she was here . . . I came to see you.'

'Me? What do you want with me? I—'

'Phil' – Ada was standing with one hand on the place where her waist should have been, and she dropped her head to the side as she stated flatly, 'She's me Aunt Connie . . . remember?'

The girl now turned her eyes slowly on Constance; then her face seemed to be pulled downwards as her mouth dropped into a large O. When she closed it, making a motion as if she were biting into an apple, she brought her head forward and screwed up her eyes, not with concern, or embarrassment, but with laughter. Then, putting her arm around her waist, she half turned her body away from the two elder women and leant against the cheap sideboard, on which stood a number of bottles and glasses. After a moment, during which Constance stared at her, trying yet again to understand the urge that drove him to pick such types, the girl slowly turned

222

about and, with a bubble of laughter on her puckered baby lips, she cried, 'Well, what do you expect me to do? If you're in a sweat about it you should do things to keep him at home, shouldn't you? Like being nice . . . an' obligin'.'

It was like a child talking; her voice had a petulant ring to it. Her body, too, was as yet a child's body, or at best, that of an unformed young girl, her breasts mere buds. This was a late developer.

Constance could find nothing to say; she could only stand and stare at this girl. But Millie's reaction was different. She took a step forward and said, 'For two pins I'd skelp the face off you. You should have your nose rubbed in the gutter, you loose little bitch, you! As for you!' She turned quickly on her daughter. 'You've got yourself nice company, haven't you? An' tell me, miss' – she put out her hand and grabbed the front of Ada's dress – 'what are you doing here, anyway? You know what will happen if your dad gets wind of it; he'll come along here and there'll be murder done. He'll kill him . . . your Uncle Jim. You know that, don't you?'

Ada tore herself away from her mother's grasp, smacking violently at her hands as she cried, 'Well, let him do murder, an' then let him find out he's done it for nothing. You . . . you two' – she glared from her mother to Constance – 'saintly, middle-aged bags! You make me spew. You've got nothin' to give anybody, either of you; you're as dried up as sawdust, and you wonder why your men leave you, or are bored stiff with you . . . You!' She nodded at her mother. 'Your body's never seen daylight in its life; dressin' and undressin' under your nightie. Aw, God, a convent behind every window.'

As Millie's hand went up, Constance grabbed it and said, 'Don't! Don't, Millie.' Then she was glaring at Ada, and Ada was shouting, 'I can understand why he went off the rails living with you. You're like your son: both neuters; terrified of it, aren't you?'

When Millie again made to go for her daughter Constance

held her and cried, 'No! No! Millie,' and after a moment Millie's body sagged and she stood with her head bowed deep on her chest.

Turning now to Ada, Constance addressed her in a voice that shook: 'Regarding my son,' she said, 'I'd better tell you that if you speak to him again in public, or molest him in any way, I shall inform the police. Now understand this: I don't have to consider your mother or father any longer. You approach Peter just once more and I'll have you in court. And don't think the police will be unable to find you. And when they do you'll be put under protection.'

Something in Constance's face stilled Ada's tongue for the moment, but she continued to glare at her viciously. Transferring her attention to the other girl, and her voice heavy with scorn, Constance went on, 'As for you; you can tell my husband I called.'

'An' you know what you can do, missis?' The fair head was bowed towards her, anger filling the baby face. 'You can go to bloody hell's flames, that's what you can do.'

Both Constance and Millie stood staring at the girl. Then Millie, looking at her daughter again, said slowly, 'Get your things on an' come home out of this.'

'Huh!' Ada tossed her head back, then clapped her two hands on the front of her stomach. 'Did you hear her? Come home, she said. You didn't care a damn when you threw me out; you were glad to see me go.'

'You weren't thrown out; you went of your own accord.'

'Well, you didn't do much searching for me, did you?'

'It wouldn't have been much use, would it?'

'How do you know? You never tried. And I'm goin' to tell you somethin'. And you too, dear . . . Aunt Connie. If it hadn't been for your bad, bad man, I would likely be spendin' me nights in the station waitin' room. Aye, you can look surprised, dear Mama. When you're carryin' cargo in your hold you haven't much chance of a job of any kind. Oh, I know I could have gone to the hostel for wicked, unmarried mothers but, you know, I didn't fancy it, somehow.' She wagged her head vigorously and her shoulders and her stomach followed suit. 'Anyway, it was Uncle Jim who, gettin' off the night train, saw me coming out of the waiting-room bleary-eyed, and he brought me here. The wicked, wicked man took compassion on me and gave me shelter and food.'

'He likely got his payment.'

'You'd like to think that, wouldn't you, Mam,' said Ada now, quietly. 'It would make you feel better. But he didn't want any payment off me; he's got Phil, an' she supplies all his needs. But let me tell you, if he had asked I would have given it him; and I might yet.' She turned to Constance and curled her lip. 'Do you hear that, Aunt Connie? I might yet, and damn you and your police.'

Constance felt as if, after entering this house, all the blood had been drained from her body.

Millie's voice sounded a little distant to her now as she said, 'What do you intend to do with the child when it's born?'

'What do I intend to do with it? Bugger all. I don't even want to see it. It'll go the same way as every other child of sin goes. That's what you call them, isn't it? It'll be adopted; and good luck to it.'

'Where are you having it?'

'What does that matter to you?'

'Where are you having it?' Millie's voice was a roar. 'You'll tell me or I'll have the authorities along here before you can wink. Under-age girls living in a bad house . . . Take your pick.'

Biting on her lip, Ada said, 'The Royal. But don't you come an' see me, 'cos if you do I'll spit in your eye.'

It was too much. Millie turned quickly away as the tears rained down her face and, groping blindly for the latch on the front door, she allowed Constance, putting her hand forward, to open it for her. And then they were in the street again; and in the car.

Constance's hands trembled on the wheel. She knew she was in no fit state to drive at this moment, but she carefully backed the car across the street and drove away slowly into the main road, across another street and towards the park. There she brought it to a halt, and putting her hands out she gripped Millie's, saying, 'I didn't know, Millie, I hadn't any idea. I wouldn't for all the world have asked you—'

'Oh . . . oh, I know that, Connie,' said Millie brokenly. Then blowing her nose violently, she added, 'I'll take it, the bairn. It's what he would want. But as for her, she'll end up on the streets . . . End up, I say; she's there already. She's bad, Connie, bad. And where does it come from? Not from me, I know that. And not from Harry.' She leant back now against the seat and looked pityingly at Constance. 'And you. I'm heart sorry for you, lass. What are you going to do?'

'Get a divorce, Millie.'

'Yes, you should have done it years ago. Our Harry said that's what you should have done years ago.'

'Harry? Harry didn't know about this . . . I mean about Jim and—?'

'Oh yes, he did. Harry knew about Jim's capers long afore you did, Connie. I can tell you now 'cos it won't hurt you any more. But just after Jim was twenty, Harry said he got belted by a man because he wouldn't leave his daughter alone, and she still at school. There was nearly a police case about it. But Harry thought that once he got married it would straighten him out. Apparently it didn't, did it? Yet' – she paused – 'he took Ada in and never let on, not even to you.'

'Well, he could hardly do that, could he, Millie?'

'No, no, of course not . . . Still . . .' Millie paused again, and then asked, 'About what you said: had Ada been taunting Peter?'

'Yes, she caused a scene in a coffee bar when he was with a girl. She . . . she told the girl he was the father.'

'Oh my God! Oh, I wish she was dead.'

They sat quiet for a time; then Millie asked, 'Will you come home with me and I'll make a bite to eat?'

'No, thanks, Millie; I've got a lot to do. And anyway, I

couldn't eat.' She touched Millie's hand. 'But thanks all the same.'

'Where you goin' now?'

'To my solicitors.'

Constance started the car and when, a short while later, she dropped Millie at her door, Millie, bending down, said, 'No matter what happens, Connie, I don't want to lose sight of you.'

'You won't, Millie. Come out any time; from now on I'll be living up there.'

'All the winter?'

'Yes, all the winter, Millie.'

'It'll be pretty tough, lass.'

'I'll get used to it. And the O'Connors are near.'

'How are you findin' them?'

'Marvellous, all of them.' She shook her head. 'I . . . I don't think I'd be able to stick it if they weren't near; it's very bleak in the winter, and lonely.'

Millie nodded. 'Aye, yes, it'll be that. But there's worse things than loneliness, lass. Well, as soon as the weather breaks we'll be up, and by that time, if I get my way, there'll be three of us again.'

'I hope it turns out as you want, Millie,' said Constance, and she knew that it would, for Millie would move heaven and earth, if that were necessary, to get the child; not so much for her own sake, but for Harry's. Love had many strange facets.

It was dark when Constance reached the bungalow. She felt tired and ill, and cold, cold to the heart of her. She had seen her solicitor and set the wheels of a divorce in motion. She had also been to the estate agent who had sold her the bungalow and told him to resell it as quickly as possible.

If Jim's business trip concerning the sale of the film rights of his book was successful, then he could buy himself a house; if not, then that was his problem in the future, not hers. On acceptance of the book, he had received half of the advanced royalties, which amounted to one hundred and fifty pounds; the rest he wouldn't get until the book was actually published, perhaps in a year's time. Well, if he couldn't earn a living by his writing he would have to do what many better writers than he had done before: take up work of another sort, for he would no longer be supported by her.

After she had rested and made herself a light meal she set about stripping the bungalow of china and anything that could be packed in the car.

When they had moved from the flat she had taken nothing back to the house with her. Sticking to her original idea that the 'Dwelling Place' would reject anything modern, she had sold more than half the furniture but had kept all her china and ornaments, mostly vases and figurines, which were either Dresden or Sèvres and which had originally belonged to her father. Now she spent the evening wrapping them in underwear, blouses and jumpers. She stripped the cupboards of the dinner and tea sets; she emptied the cabinet of cutlery, making it easier for her to handle the case; then, on the point of exhaustion, she went to bed, and after a long, long wakefulness, finally fell into a fitful sleep.

By nine o'clock the following morning the car was packed to its limit, with the boot so full that the lid would not close. The last object she brought out from the bungalow was a nest of inlaid tables and these she placed on the passenger seat. Returning to the house, she sat down and wrote a short letter.

This is to tell you that after visiting 18 Quilter Street, I have started divorce proceedings. I have put the bungalow in the estate agent's hands; the remaining furniture will be sent to the salerooms. I am not leaving you without habitation; you had a choice of three and you made it. I don't wish to see you again.

228

She did not sign the letter, but put it in an envelope and placed it on the bare mantelpiece; then she went to the car and drove away.

As she left, it began to snow again. The nearer she got to the fells the heavier it became, and she prayed it would fall and fall and cut her off from the outside world and all in it, for now at last she had done what Millie had suggested and Peter had long insisted she should have done.

It wasn't until she drew the car to a skidding stop in its usual place below the house and sensed its atmosphere, together with that of the other house down in the valley, that she asked herself boldly if she would have had the courage to make the break, and cut herself off into aloneness, if it hadn't been that in this wilderness there was one particular O'Connor waiting for her? And she found she could answer, Yes. Yes, she would have done it this time, for there was only so much one could stand.

The sight of that girl, that low, foul-mouthed creature, and the thought of his daily visits to her, the afternoon meetings and the fact that he thought so little of her own intelligence that he had practically carried on this latest affair under her very nose, must have been the deciding factor . . . Well, it was over.

As she went to get out of the car she saw Peter come running and sliding down the snow-covered slope towards her, followed by Davie and Michael.

'Oh, am I glad to see you!' he cried. 'There's a snow warning; we thought you would never get back home.' He took hold of her hand and helped her up.

Home, he had said. She was home.

8

It snowed all through Wednesday night, but it stopped during Thursday morning and the sun shone, only for the radio to warn that there was more snow to follow and that it would be heavy.

Vincent had collected Kathy from the high road, where a bus had managed to get through earlier in the day, and half an hour ago he had dropped her and Peter on the main road near Black's Farm for the barn-dance, with the warning that they were to stay there until he came to pick them up, whether or not the snow became heavier. Should this happen, he might get the car down to the main road, but not up again, and they would have to make the latter part of their journey on foot.

This prospect had not deterred Kathy, because she knew Vincent could make his way up the windswept slopes; as she assured Peter, their Vin had the feet of a mountain goat.

But even on this return journey Vincent found difficulty in getting the Land-Rover back to the house, and when he entered the kitchen he went swiftly towards the fire, rubbing his hands together, and saying, 'I won't get her back up again the night, that's a certainty.'

'They shouldn't have gone,' said Hannah from her seat to the side of the fireplace.

'Aw!' Sean said, the while leaning over towards the fire bars and knocking the doddle from his pipe, 'let them enjoy themselves while they're young. And what's a bit of snow? This is nothing. Not yet a foot on the level, it isn't, and the drifts are neither here nor there. It's the melting and then freezing again that you've got to worry about. Isn't it, Vin?'

'Yes,' said Vincent. 'But it's blanketing down pretty hard now.'

'Ah, don't worry about them; they'll be just one of many down there, and if they can't get back they'll dance the night through. It's been done before . . . Remember, Florence, that year at the Freemans' do?'

Florence, knitting vigorously at a sock, nodded her head but did not look up at her husband. She remembered that year at the Freemans' do: it was the first time she had appeared publicly with her farmhand husband and the tongues had nearly wagged themselves loose.

'Who's up there?'

Florence turned her head towards Vincent and said, 'Moira and Davie. They all wanted to go but I wouldn't have it. The others are along in the back room; they've got a fire on and they're setting up the train. I told Davie to stay put there until their dad went up for them.' Florence did not add, or you.

'She looks ill,' said Sean. 'I don't think she should be out of her bed; that 'flu took her down.'

'Aye. Besides which, she's got something on her mind,' said Hannah flatly as she reached over towards the table and took a piece of home-made toffee from a tin. 'The bairns say she's brought a pile of china and stuff back with her, all lovely bits. When the snow clears I'll take a dander up and have a look at them. Davie says they're beautiful, an' he's got an eye for such things, has Davie.'

And Hannah was right. Davie had an eye for china. He was standing at the Welsh dresser pointing to a shelf on which stood three figurines in Dresden, and he said, 'I like colours; colours like their clothes'. I say to our Vin, "Why don't you paint some of your things?" but he won't.'

From the couch, Constance looked at the back of Davie's

head as she said, 'It would be a shame to paint any of Vin's work. It's a different matter altogether, a different kind of art, Davie. If you like figures like that, then you should go in for pottery. Can you draw?'

Before he could answer, Moira, who was curled up on the couch by Constance's side, with a large encyclopaedia on her knee, said, 'Oh, he draws lovely, our Davie. Vin says he should go to an art school somewhere.'

'Where?' said Davie, still looking up at the china; 'they're all too far away. Anyway, I want to be a doctor.' He had turned towards the couch and Constance said in some surprise, 'A doctor? You want to be a doctor, Davie?'

'Yes.' He came and stood before her and looked into her face. He, the smallest of the O'Connors, was thin and, as Moira had once described him, undersized, but he was undoubtedly the smartest of them all where brains were concerned, and in an unchildlike tone, he said, 'I want to, and I'd like to, but I know I'll not be able to stay on at school; though me dad says if our Vin makes a go of it down there' – he jerked his head – 'I'll have a chance. But Vin doesn't say so.'

'And you can't believe it until Vin says so?' asked Constance quietly.

'Well no.' Davie shook his head and, looking down, examined his fingernails, which were far from clean. 'Our Vin always knows how the land lies; he never bunks you up unless he means to keep you there. Dad's different.' He smiled now. 'He keeps hopin'. Our Kathy calls him "Littlewood's bright light". Kathy does the pools. She says if she wins she's going to build us a mansion and a swimming pool.'

Constance didn't want to laugh, she didn't even want to smile, but you couldn't be with one of the O'Connors for long and not smile; that is, with the exception of Vin. She hadn't seen him since New Year's Day, when he had sat by her side on the couch here, silent and dour.

'If I won the pools I wouldn't build a mansion,' said Moira;

232

'I'd come up here and live with you, Mrs Stapleton.'

Constance put her hand out and Moira hugged it and laughed, and it was at that moment the door burst open. They thought it was the gale and they all sprang round, no fear on their faces, because the children didn't fear the elements, nor yet did Constance. Then, almost as one, their expressions changed, and Moira, looking at Mr Stapleton from where she was kneeling on the couch, slid backwards and stood near Davie. Mr Stapleton was covered with snow, but it wasn't that which frightened her, it was the look on his face. And then he was yelling at them, 'Get out! Get out!'

They both looked questioningly at Mrs Stapleton, but she was gaping at her husband, so they sidled around the head of the couch, keeping a good distance from the man. Then Mrs Stapleton spoke. She said, 'Go and get your coats;' and they came back and walked behind her and moved sideways towards the kitchen; then, grabbing up their coats and scarves, they put them on as they again hurried through the long room. The door was still open and the snow was piling up on the mat as they went out, and Davie had difficulty in closing the door after him. On the terrace, he groped at Moira and pulled her along by the wall, but after passing the window, he drew her to a halt and whispered in her ear, 'We'll wait here a minute and see what he does.'

What Jim Stapleton did was to walk slowly towards Constance and stare at her, and for the first time she felt a real fear of him. When angry or frustrated he bawled or shouted at her, but now he was silent, suffused with a white anger that had bleached his face almost to the colour of the snow lying on the broad brim of his tweed hat. When his hand shot out and grabbed at the neck of her dress she cried, 'No! No! Don't! Let go of me! Let go!'

As he held her his lips mouthed words without sound, and then slowly he ground out, 'I should throttle you, but you're not worth swinging for, you sneaking, bloody prig, you! Coming home off a journey to that, a notice in the window,

233

and the place stripped. God! You were lucky you weren't there, because I would have killed you on the spot. As it is, I'm going to give you something to remember me by.'

'Let go of me!' She tugged violently away from him, and the front of her dress ripped downwards, and as she staggered back she cried brokenly, 'I've got enough to remember you by: a small fortune gone, a wrecked life, your lies, and your deceit, the fear of a policeman coming to the door for you. I . . .' Her chin trembled. 'I've . . . I've plenty to remember you by. And the latest, your filthy little prostitute whom you've kept supplied with my money so that – in case you don't know it – she could carry on her business when you weren't there—'

The flat of his hand caught her full across the face and sent her staggering against the wall, and she fell down by the side of the wooden chair. When he came at her again, she turned her body across the seat and grasped the edge of it. Now she was screaming aloud as his fists pummelled her. Once having lifted his hand it seemed he couldn't stop and he rained blows on her; he even pulled her head backwards by the hair and punched at her face; then finally he raised his foot and kicked her shins. But the excruciating pain that this must have caused only brought a moan from her now. And after that she became quite quiet . . .

Davie jumped off the end of the terrace with the speed of a hare, and Moira, whom he was still holding by the hand, seemed to fly through the air after him. He did not follow the path they had cut out during the day which led down the hill but, sitting on the slide at the top of a steep incline, he let himself go, yelling, 'Come on! Come on!'

The snow permeated through Moira's long stockings and knickers and made her yell before she fell into the drift at the bottom of the hill, and she pulled herself out of it, gasping and shouting to Davie. But Davie was no longer there; he was racing across the yard, yelling, 'Dad! Dad! Vin! Vin!'

When he burst into the kitchen he was so breathless and his head was wagging so violently that he couldn't answer them

234

for a moment, and they all shouting at once, 'What is it? What is it?'

'He's . . . he's killin' her. P . . . punchin' her all over, kicking her. Sh . . . she's lying down by the wall.'

'Who? in the name of God!' shouted Hannah.

'Mr . . . Mr Stapleton. He came in all covered . . .'

The boy's voice was drowned by Florence crying, 'No! Vin. Let your father go.' Then Sean was shouting, 'Wait boy, wait! I'll see to this.' But Vincent was already through the storeroom, dragging a coat on as he went.

'Go after him, Sean. Go after him.' Hannah's voice was high and panic-filled, and Sean, bounding across the room in his stockinged feet, almost jumped into his wellingtons, and as he dragged on his coat, Florence thrust a torch in his hand, saying, 'Do something, anything, only don't let them meet up.'

Before he went out of the door Sean grabbed at a piece of wood Vincent had left there earlier to be chopped for kindling. It was of seasoned timber but had a flaw in it. It measured about two feet long and three inches square, and Sean tucked it under his arm as he lumbered and slithered out of the yard. When he flashed his torch in the direction of the hill he could see the dark shape of Vincent climbing the hill, but being impeded by the soles of a pair of ordinary shoes, and twice within a few minutes he lost his foothold and went on to his knees. Because of this, Sean, in his ridged-soled wellingtons, was able to gain on him, and when at last he reached the top of the hill, Vincent was only a few yards away and he called to him, 'Listen boy, listen. Hold your hand a minute. Do you hear me?'

When Sean passed the window Vincent was at the front door, and the next moment they were both in the room, immediately noticing the crumpled figure on the floor, then the man who with great sweeps of his arm was scattering the china ornaments, figures and plates from the dresser. So much noise was he making that he hadn't heard their arrival and it wasn't until he sprang towards the mantelpiece and, after knocking a

235

Chinese vase to the hearth, grabbed the carving of the sheep and its lamb, that the voice thundered at him, 'Leave that alone!'

Jim Stapleton swung round. His face, no longer white, was suffused with an emotion that had gone beyond anger into the realm of destructive hate. He was holding the carving above his head as he cried, 'What the hell do you want?'

Vincent didn't speak, but his body stretched and Sean cried, 'No! I tell you, no!'

Vincent seemed deaf to his father's voice. His eyes were now fixed on Jim Stapleton and it was as he moved towards him that Stapleton cried on a high note, 'Christ Almighty! A bloody murderer like you. My God! That's why she did it; she hadn't the guts before. But for you, you!'

What followed next surprised Jim Stapleton as much as it did Vincent, for Sean, gripping the piece of wood in both hands, brought it down with all the force of which he was capable on the back of his son's neck and shoulders. The act silenced Stapleton and it also brought a spate of apologetic words from Sean, but no sound at all from Vincent who, after staggering forward, his hands cupping his head, turned around, and through his dazed eyes looked at his father gabbling on, 'It's the only way, Vin, the only way.' The older man was almost crying as he watched his son stagger towards the table and hold on it for support. So, ignoring Stapleton, he went to Vin and implored him almost tearfully, 'Leave this to me. Trust me, boy. Leave it to me. Go on, go on down home.'

Vincent's reaction was to pull himself up straight and give a violent shake of his head; but he couldn't rid himself of the effects of the blow.

'Go on now, go on, boy.' Sean pulled his torch from his pocket and thrust it into Vincent's wavering hand. 'Go on, go on down and tell one of them to come up, either your mother or Hannah. Go on now, boy.' His tone was coaxing and pleading at the same time.

As Sean made to lead his son to the door, Vincent again

shook himself; but, still under the effects of the blow, he allowed himself to be led outside. There, Sean pushed him gently a few steps along the terrace. Then, in the light from the window, he watched him step off the end of the terrace and move away into the darkness.

Stapleton was still staring hard towards the door when Sean re-entered the room and straightway picked up the piece of wood from the floor and again held it in both hands, and he said, 'I'll give you exactly a minute to get goin'.'

'Who the hell do you think you're talking to?'

'You know who I'm talkin' to: a dirty, cowardly skunk of a man . . . I'm givin' you a chance to get out, because when he comes to himself, he'll do for you. And I'm goin' to tell you this: I wish I had the courage to do it meself. Another thing I'll say. If it was possible to get the polis up here I'd have them like a flash of lightnin'. Now get out, and go the road you came. You got here by car and pray to God that you'll be able to go back the same way because, I'm warnin' you, I don't hold much for your chances if you're about when he comes round.'

Sean's attention was drawn to Constance as she moaned and tried to raise herself from the floor, but he did not go to her. He looked again at Jim Stapleton, who was still holding the carving in his hand. Then with a violent gesture Stapleton turned and flung it into the heart of the fire and for a moment stared at it as the flames licked around it. Then, picking up his hat, which was still lying on the floor, spattered with pieces of broken china, he pulled it on to his head and, buttoning up his coat, he walked past Sean without taking his eyes off him. At the door he hesitated, as if the wind-driven snow deterred him, but then, lowering his head, he went out.

Constance again groaned and now made an effort to get to her feet, and Sean, quickly putting his arms about her, said, 'There now. There now. Come away. Come away,' and he led her to the couch and sat her down. Then pressing her back and lifting up her feet gently he spoke as if to a child, saying, 'Rest now. Rest now. They'll be up in a minute, the women.' Bending

237

over her, he stroked the hair back from her bruised forehead and darkening cheeks, the while muttering to himself, 'God save us! It'll be black and blue she'll be the morrow, and all over. That swine of a man! Mad he was, stark staring mad. And look at this place . . . What is it? What is it, my dear?' He cocked an ear to catch the words she was trying to frame with her swollen lips, and he questioned her, 'Stop what?' Then he screwed up his face before saying, 'Don't worry, my dear; it's all over.'

When again Constance muttered, 'Stop . . . stop,' he said, 'Yes, yes, I'll stop with you. Of course, I'll stop with you. We'll not leave you, none of us.' When she moved her head and tried to rise from the couch he realised that he had got her meaning wrong and, pressing her gently back, he said, 'Now, now; don't upset yourself;' then he looked towards the open door, through which snow was drifting into the room, and as if he had heard something, he went swiftly to it, put his head out and peered along the terrace. But there was no sign of anyone coming up from down below. What was keeping them? She needed a woman, someone to bathe that face and put her to bed. Suddenly he put his hand to his mouth. Had he hit Vin so hard that he had collapsed on the way down? The only thing for it was to run to the top of the hill and shout down to them; surely they'd be on the alert. He glanced back into the room before running along the terrace and over the ground to the top of the hill, and there, cupping his hands, he cried into the white night, 'Hello there! Hello there! Vin! Vin! Florence!'

A thin voice came back to him from quite near, calling, 'Dad! Dad!' And as Sean recognised the voice of his son, Michael, he shouted to him, 'Where's Vin? Is he down there?'

'No, Dad, he hasn't come back.'

'God in heaven!' Sean turned his head first one way then the other as if looking for support; then he shouted to Michael, 'Don't come any further. Go back and tell your mother and Hannah they're needed up here, an' quick.'

'Yes, Dad. Yes, Dad.'

238

As Sean turned back towards the house he thought, What's happened? God Almighty! What's happened to him? I shouldn't have hit him so hard . . . Come on. Come on, you women.

It was as he ran back towards the terrace that he heard the wailing and it speeded his legs along it to the door, and when he thrust it open his eyes looked on the strangest sight, for there was Vincent sitting on the couch, and in his arms, held like a child, was the woman he had left just a minute or so ago. And her crying was like a horde of banshees; for it was high and weird, and from the heart.

'There now. There now.' Vincent was soothing her as he himself had done. 'Don't cry. Don't cry like that. Quiet now. Quiet.'

But Constance could not quell her crying, for she was crying the tears that she had suppressed for years. She was crying as she had cried only once before, and the sound she was making seemed to be issuing from every pore in her body, for it deafened her own ears; moreover, it assaulted her sense of dignity as it ripped open her façade and tore away her control. It brought her mouth open wide and the saliva flowing from it; it racked all her bones and sent her arms flailing the air.

'Get my mother,' muttered Vincent thickly.

'They're comin'. They're comin',' said Sean.

'Don't. Don't.' Vincent now tried to smother her head against his shoulder, but she fought him, and went on fighting him, and Sean said, 'Put her down.'

'No; she'll do herself an injury.'

When Florence entered the room she immediately stopped and gazed at the shambles; then she looked at the man she thought of as her son nursing Mrs Stapleton, and she struggling to be free.

'Lay her on the couch, Vin,' she commanded.

Vincent looked at Florence for a moment; then went to do as she bade. But now Constance clung to him. Her hands

239

clawing at his neck, she held on to him fiercely as her wailing mounted.

'In the name of God! In the name of God!' It was Hannah. Stepping gingerly amid the broken china, she went to the couch and gazed at her son and the second woman he had set his heart on, and she said, 'Poor creature. It's as Davie said, he kicked her all over. God above! Look at her poor face . . . Can't you stop her wailing?'

'Tell me how,' said Vin, looking up at her.

'See if there're any spirits about,' said Sean, nodding towards Hannah, who answered, 'You'll never get them down her. It's a doctor you want, with a needle. She's in hysterics, and if it's allowed to go on anything could happen to her.'

'Get me some snow.'

'What!' Hannah looked down at Vincent; and so did Florence, and she questioned, 'Snow, Vin?'

'Aye . . . yes. Bring me a dish in. You get it, Dad.'

'Snow?' Sean was scurrying towards the door when he turned and cried, 'Where do I get a dish?'

'Where do you get a dish! Where d'you think? Out here. Out here.' Hannah ran into the kitchen and brought back a plastic bowl and, thrusting it into his hand, she said, 'Look slippy.'

It took Sean only seconds to scoop the bowl full of snow from around the step and then he was at Vincent's side. 'Hold it closer, in front here,' said Vincent. He now took one hand from around Constance's waist and pressed her shoulder back; then, pulling down the front of her torn dress, which a moment before he had put back into place, he scooped up a large handful of snow and slapped it on to her bare chest, and followed it with another. A third handful he levelled straight into her face. And now she was choking, spluttering, and gasping, but her wailing stopped.

As they all stood looking down at her heaving body, Florence said softly, 'Get me towels of some sort, Hannah; and see if there are any water bottles in the kitchen; she could catch her death.'

A few minutes later Constance, lying on the couch, a rug about her, looked as if she had died.

'We'd best get her to bed,' said Florence. 'Will you carry her up?' She glanced at Vincent, and he answered, 'It's too cold up there; she'd be better here. You could bring some blankets down, and get those bottles going quickly.' He glanced at Hannah, and she said, 'Aye. Aye,' and went hurrying into the kitchen again, while Florence rushed upstairs.

Standing in front of the couch, Vincent gazed down on Constance, then turned to see his father gathering up the broken china from the floor. Sean glanced sidewards up at him but did not speak and Vincent, turning now to look at the mantelpiece, and at the empty space in the middle, said over his shoulder, 'What happened to it?' And Sean mumbled quietly, 'He chucked it in the fire.'

Slowly, Vincent lowered his head. The sheep and lamb, besides being the best thing he had ever done, was a talisman to him. From the first it had represented one thing, a home. For weeks now he had seen it resting in the place for where he had originally cut it, and now it had gone up in flames. It's going meant the end of something; what, he wasn't sure.

9

Sometime in the early hours of the morning Constance awakened, after being administered a dose of chlorodyne. It was a medicine Florence used to soothe the children and to send them to sleep when they had colds, or toothache, and it had enabled Constance to sleep for over six hours. When she tried to raise her lids they seemed to have weights on them and when she came to run her tongue over her lips she experienced an excruciating pain. She tried to remember what had happened, but all she could hear in her mind was someone crying. It was a loud, bawling, raucous cry, and she wondered why she should be hearing it. Then, her lids lifting, her eyes were attracted by the flickering of the fire and to the humped figure sitting in a deep chair to the side of it. Why was Hannah here? Her eyes moved slowly to the other side of the fireplace to see Vincent sitting there, his head on his chest, and she knew she was dreaming. Then the volume of the crying mounted even higher in her head, and with a feeling of panic she realised she was listening to her own voice. It was like a dream within a dream, and suddenly it came to her why she had cried so much. It wasn't only because she had shed in one deluge all the pent-up tears of years, but also because of Vin, and she didn't need to ask herself why she had cried for Vin. The crying again filled her whole being. It was soundless now, but so great was the pain of it, even worse than the pain of the bruising on her

242

face and body, that it blotted out her hazy consciousness.

When she next came to, the room was full of white light that hurt her eyes. A dark shape clouded it for a moment, then Hannah's thick and comforting brogue said, 'There you are; you've had a nice sleep, me dear. Now what you want is a nice cup of tea, and it's all ready for you. How're you feelin'?'

When Hannah stroked back her hair Constance had the feeling that her scalp was bare and raw. As she tried to move she moaned, and Hannah said, 'There now, there now; don't distress yourself. I'll just raise your head gently and you'll have this cup of tea. An' then I'll wash you down with warm water; there's nothin' like warm water for soothin' you.'

'Ha . . . Ha . . . Hannah?'

'Yes, me dear.'

'Pe . . . Peter.'

'Never you fear about Peter; he's fast asleep. They didn't get back until nearly eight o'clock. Vin went and fetched them. He'd had to shank it; he couldn't get the car out of the yard. The snow's two feet if it's an inch this mornin', an' the drifts are head-high, and it's still comin' down. Aw, we're in for a right one this time. There now, there now; take another sip. That's it, that's it . . . Aw, that's good. You'll feel better after that.' She placed the empty cup on the mantelpiece; then tucking the blankets gently under Constance's chin, she said, 'Are you warm enough now?'

Constance made a movement with her head, then said haltingly, 'Could I have some aspirin, Hannah?'

'Surely, surely. Where do you keep them?'

'Kitchen . . . cabinet.'

As Hannah moved away Constance muttered, 'What . . . time is it?'

'Oh, around eleven o'clock; the day's young,' replied Hannah on her way to the kitchen, where to Moira, who was standing on a chair peering out through the top pane of glass, she said, 'Any sight of them?' And Moira whispered, 'No, Hannah. But I saw me dad go over the hill. At least, I think it

243

was me dad; I couldn't make him out rightly, although it had let up for a time.' She turned her face to the window again, then cried softly, 'Oh, I think this is him comin' now,' and Hannah, went to the back door and she opened it and waited for Sean; and when he stood kicking the caked snow from his boots, she asked, 'Any sign of him?' For answer he just shook his head.

'God in heaven! God in heaven!' Hannah gazed up at the snow-laden sky; then looking at Sean's bent head, she said, 'Where is he, Vin?'

'Out lookin' at yon side. He wouldn't go at first, although he's away now.' Sean raised his head and they stared at each other. Then Hannah put her head close to his and whispered, 'Have you tackled him yet?'

Sean turned away from her gaze as he replied, 'No, no. How could I? And anyway, if that so-and-so couldn't get his car started, he might have tried to walk.'

'If he ever got as far as his car,' said Hannah slowly.

'Don't say it, woman; don't even think it.'

'What in the name of God *can* we think?' she whispered. 'The car's there an' no sign of the man, and him being a townie he could never have made his way along that road at night like that. I couldn't have done it meself; I doubt if Vin could, not in the dark, anyway.'

'Well, if he's there we'll find him.'

'Oh, I'm not worried about you finding him, but how you'll find him.'

He turned from her and made to go down the path again, but paused and said, 'Is the boy still asleep?'

'Yes,' she answered.

'Well, he'd better be told as soon as he wakes. I would give him another hour, then get him up. I'll try once more down the hill towards the moor, then we'll have to report it.' He looked at her hard. 'You know that, don't you? We'll have to get word down to the Charltons, an' they'll get a party of searchers goin'.'

244

'God in heaven!' exclaimed Hannah again; then closed the door and, looking to where Moira was standing wide-eyed, she said, 'It's all right, child, it's all right. Everything's goin' to be all right. Keep pilin' wood on that fire, 'cos I want the water nice and hot to wash Mrs Stapleton down, that's a good girl. Oh, aspirin!' She suddenly remembered what she had come into the kitchen for and went to the cabinet, and after looking down the shelves she found a packet of Aspro and returned to the room . . .

The tablets, together with the hot, wet flannel under Hannah's kindly hands helped to soothe, if not to eliminate, the pain in Constance's side and face. The amount of bruising on her body brought murmurings from Hannah, and she was still murmuring as she went across the room with the bowl, when Peter came hurrying down the stairs, sleep still heavy in his eyes.

'You shouldn't have let me sleep. Just an hour, I said.' His voice was hoarse.

'Ssh! Now don't fret, she's all right. She's just had a cup of tea and a wash. She's all right.'

When Peter reached the couch he gripped his own jaw tightly with his hand and screwed up his eyes against the sight of Constance's face standing out in relief against the snow light. She had been asleep when he got back and her face had been half covered, and the others had said, 'Don't disturb her.' He dropped on to his knees beside the couch and words failed him; he could only bow his head and lay it gently against her shoulder. But when she lifted her hand and touched his hair, he muttered, 'Oh . . . oh, if only I hadn't gone out.'

'It . . . it had to come.'

'What?' He lifted his eyes to hers and she made a small movement with her hand as if waving explanations away.

She had always known that Jim wanted to strike her, but he also knew that, should he lift his hand to her, it would be the finish: he wasn't foolish enough to strike the hand that was keeping him and his little mistresses. But when he was faced

245

with the fact that she had finally made the break, he had determined that he was going to give her a taste of the outlet of which he had deprived himself for years. Well, he had done it. It was over. All finished.

The last two words brought back an uneasiness to her mind. She was remembering something. It was connected with the awful crying. She could see herself now crying, shouting, and moaning. What must they have thought of her, the O'Connors? And Vin? It was at the sight of him that she had first screamed. When he had come into the room and looked at her over the couch she had stared back at him, and as she did so she had remembered trying to stop his father from turning Jim out. There had been an idea in her mind connecting Vincent leaving the room and Mr O'Connor telling Jim to go. As she lay on the floor she had been only vaguely aware of what had been happening, except for the fact that Jim was going outside where Vin was; then, at the sight of Vin looking at her over the back of the couch, the idea had been clarified and it had burst something in her head and she had cried out. It was then that she knew she wasn't crying only because of the wasted years, of her lost youth, of the cravings of her body, but because of Vin's stupidity, of his misplaced loyalty.

Slowly she said, 'Peter!' and when he said, 'Yes, Mother?' she whispered, 'Go down and see if his car's still there.'

'What!' He raised his eyebrows.

'Please.'

'But . . . but he couldn't be.'

'Peter. Go . . . go and look.'

He got slowly to his feet; then stood staring down at her before going into the kitchen and taking a coat from the back of the door. Hannah was at the table stirring something in a bowl, and he went to her side and quietly, because Moira was sitting near the fire, said, 'Has . . . has anyone been down below? She . . . she's asked me to go and see if his car's there.'

Hannah's hands became still and she jerked her head towards him. 'She asked you that?'

246

'Yes.'

She puckered up her eyes and looked at him in a puzzled way as she said, 'Now why should she?'

When he made no answer she turned her attention to the bowl again, adding flatly, 'You can save yourself a trail; it's still there. The keys are where he left them. They've been out these hours searching for him.'

Peter cast a glance back at Moira, and Hannah said, 'Oh, don't trouble what she hears; she knows all about it. She saw it all last night. It'll be a lesson to her. She's learned that education and learnin' can't prevent a man from being a beast, nor the lack of it make a man into one.'

After a moment he asked, 'What'll I say to her?'

'Nothing yet. Go on down and see the car for yourself, then you can break it to her gently that they're lookin' for him.'

'He . . . could he have walked to the main road?'

'If he was Vin he could've, or Sean, or, at a stretch, even me.' She cast a quick glance at him, and for a second a glint of humour showed in her eyes. 'That's if it was in the daylight and I was meself.' Then she ended soberly, 'But in the dark and him not used to the land, an' not bein' able to tell the road from the fells, or where there is a gully, it would be a miracle if he ever reached the main road.'

As he opened the back door she said, 'If he's fallen into a drift they won't come across him until it thaws, unless the dogs should find him.'

'The dogs?' He turned to look at her.

'Aye. Charlton's, or Fenwick's, at yon side of the moor. They're good at that kind of thing. They've found folk alive after days, if they managed to make shelter.'

As he made his way slowly down towards the outhouses he thought, unemotionally, I hope they're not in too big a hurry getting the dogs out.

It was the following day towards noon when the police sergeant arrived at the house. Constance was still sitting on the couch, but dressed now. Her face displayed a distorted blue and yellow mask, out of which her eyes gazed at the policeman as he said, 'It's getting on for forty-eight hours now. We have combed the hills for a good distance around, farther than he could ever have travelled. There's little more we can do until the thaw sets in.'

He stared down at her. Her face, as it was now, gave him no indication of her looks; he could only see that she must be tallish and have a fine figure, if you liked the modern lines, and that her dress was smart and stylish. There was something wrong here and they likely wouldn't get to the bottom of it until they found the husband. He had certainly said his good-byes to her, if it was the husband who had done it. And who else, up here? Down in the village they said he was a bit of a lah-de-dah; nothing bashful about him, at least about his own accomplishments.

To some extent Constance knew the trend of the police-man's thoughts, and she clarified them by saying, 'My husband and I quarrelled. He . . . You see, he had returned from London and discovered that I had started divorce proceedings against him.'

'Oh! Oh! Well, madam, that's none of our business, you know; but I can say I'm sorry you've had to undergo such treat-ment. Well, now, we're taking the dogs around Allerybank Moor, though I can't see him ever getting across the burn; he could have followed it up, of course, until he came to the castle, but only if he was a hillman. Not being one, I doubt if that was possible; and, anyway, it's in the opposite direction from that which he should have taken. But as you know, ma'am, all roads lead in a circle in a snowstorm and it's surprising where people find themselves.'

Still looking at him, she said, 'How long do you think this'll last?'

'You mean the freeze? Well, they said on the radio it will be another couple of days, although you never know, we might

248

have another fall after that. Try, though, not to worry, ma'am; we're doing our very best.'

'Yes, yes; I'm sure you are. And thank you.'

After the sergeant had left Hannah came into the room and said, 'Will you be all right if I slip down below for a minute or so?'

'Oh, of course, Hannah. And . . . and I feel it's an imposition you staying up here, because Mrs O'Connor needs you.'

'Not a bit of it, not a bit of it. And you know, it's like a holiday. In other circumstances I would be enjoyin' it, and as it is, I'm likin' nothin' better at the moment, but I just want to have a word with Florence. Barney's in the kitchen tending to the fire; just give him a call if you want anything, he'll be listening. But I won't be gone more than fifteen minutes or so.'

'Oh, please, please, don't hurry yourself, Hannah; I'm quite all right now.'

'Quite all right, you say? If you were all right now you'd be a sight to see when you're not feelin' yourself. Well, I'm away then.'

In the kitchen, Hannah hastily dragged on her coat and, putting a woollen shawl over her head, she knotted it under her chin, saying quickly to Barney, 'Now keep that fire goin'; there's meat in the oven and it's got to be cooked.'

'Aye, Hannah, aye.'

She now pulled on a pair of wellingtons that disappeared up under her skirt; then scurrying cautiously, she made her way outside and along the path that the boys had scooped out from the snow, around the brow of the hill, and down the other side. She was still scurrying when she entered the door. Kicking off her wellingtons, she hurried through the outer rooms and into the kitchen in her stockinged feet.

Florence, in the act of placing mugs of cocoa before Sean and Vincent, turned, as they did, towards her, but it was Florence who asked, 'They've found him?'

'No. No.' She looked from Sean to Vincent, then back to

Florence. What she had to say had been for Florence's ears only, but now they were all waiting. They knew her too well to imagine she had come down here for a cup of cocoa, or made the journey because she was feeling homesick. She dusted the snow from the bottom of her coat, then went to the fire and held up one foot in front of the bars before she said, 'I've . . . I've just found out why he lathered her.' She looked over her shoulder at them and added, 'She's divorcin' him. Apparently, he didn't know until he came home from London and to the house in Low Fell, and he tore up here and into her.'

'Begod! you don't say,' said Sean.

'Aye, that's the rights of it.'

While Hannah warmed her other foot there was silence in the room. No one proffered the fact that there must be another woman, because that would have been tactless and they all knew it. And they knew something else, Hannah, Sean and Florence; they knew that the news must have come as a shock to their son, and it was as if the thought drew their eyes to him, for when he looked up from stirring his cocoa there they were all gazing at him. Slowly he lifted his eyes from one to the other, and his voice held an indescribable note of bitterness as he said, 'And he needn't have killed him after all.'

Sean was the first to speak. He jerked up his tousled head, rattled his spoon in the cocoa and cried loudly, too loudly, 'Aw man, what you gettin' at now?'

'You all know what I'm getting at.' With a suddenness that startled them, he rose to his feet and kicked the wooden stool, on which he had been sitting, backwards against the wall. 'It's been in your eyes, your actions, and your every word since Davie came yelling into this kitchen: I mustn't go there because I wasn't to be trusted; then to be whacked with a lump of wood that knocked the sense out of me.' His eyes rested on his father, and Sean spluttered, ''Twas the only way.'

'The only way for what? To kill me? If that blow had caught me on the side of the chin just a little further up my neck, say here' – he dug his thumb at his jaw line – 'it could have finished me. But that wouldn't have mattered – it would have been poetic justice. But you had prevented me from making the same mistake twice, that's it, isn't it? Now you're all sweating blood because you know you didn't prevent it, and you know that I waited outside and when he came out I got him. That's what you think, isn't it? Go on.' His voice rang through the kitchen. 'Have the courage of your convictions: I did it once, so I'll do it again.'

'Aw, no, Vin.' Hannah was shaking her head pityingly, and he mimicked her, saying, 'Aw, yes, Hannah. Aw, yes. And now you're thinking it's all so sad, because if she's getting rid of him in her own way the coast would have been clear for me . . . *if* I hadn't gone and done it again . . . A . . . aw!' He drew the word out. 'The last two days and the looks in your eyes, and wondering what's going to happen to you all when I'm gone this time, eh?' He looked at his father. 'At least you won't be short of firewood; the workshop's full of it. And you'll have one advantage, electricity, wonderful electricity. You won't be so badly off during this next spell . . . which could be for life.'

'That's unfair, lad, that's unfair.' Sean's head bowed.

'Is it? Look into your heart and you'll see.' He moved away from them, hunching up his shoulders. Then at the door leading into the storeroom he turned to them again, his voice low now. 'And if she was divorced a thousand times over, and I hadn't done him in, it would be all the same, because as you once remarked, Hannah, in the hearing of the lads who are apt to repeat things unwittingly, there's all the difference of chalk an' cheese between her and me. And there you're right, absolutely right.'

The silence he left was broken by Hannah suddenly crying, 'Aw, God in heaven! What's one to believe, anyway?' Then bursting into tears, she tore open her coat and lifted her apron up and buried her face in it.

Sean slowly stirred his cocoa again as he looked up at Florence, and she, unable to meet his gaze, bowed her head and closed her eyes and murmured to herself, 'If only she had never seen the place' . . .

Vincent's anger had cooled by the time he reached the top of the hill. Instead of entering the house by way of the terrace, he went in by way of the back door.

Barney turned from the fire, where he was pushing pieces of wood under the oven, and said brightly, 'Oh, hello, Vin.' Barney was the only one in the family who did not know that their Vin had killed a man. Michael and Davie had imparted the news to Joseph on his twelfth birthday and they would do the same to Barney when *he* was twelve. But as yet the big man was just their Vin; he wasn't someone to whisper about under the bedclothes and say, 'I bet he could kill anybody if he liked. He could even kill two at a time by knocking their heads together.'

'There's a leg of lamb in the oven,' said Barney, 'and Hannah's makin' Yorkshire pudding.' He nodded towards a basin on the table. 'I'm stayin' up so as to have some.' The boy looked puzzled when Vincent said to him, 'Stay where you are,' then went into the other room and closed the door. He looked at it blankly for a moment. Of course he was staying where he was; Hannah had told him to. He returned to his job of keeping an eye on the cooking meal, and told himself that there was something up with their Vin.

Constance could not recall having seen Vincent since he had held her in his arms to still her screaming, and now the sight of him brought her body trembling. He stood at the foot of the couch staring at her, and she tried to turn away from his gaze. When he came to her side and asked, 'How are you feeling?' she answered, 'Not very good.' To that he said, 'Don't worry about your face; it'll be all right . . . after a time.'

'I'm not worrying about my face.' She met his gaze now.

'But you're worrying?'

Her lashes flickered, and he said, 'Aren't you worrying?'

'Yes; yes, I'm worrying.'

'About when they find him?'

'You could say that.' She was now looking down at her hands.

'Because he might have been strangled or battered to death?'

Her neck jerked up so quickly that it caused a pain to shoot down her spine and she winced.

'You saw it all in your mind's eye that night, didn't you? It was on your face as though in large print. *You* were thinking then as *they're* thinking now' – he jerked his head backwards – 'that it was all for nothing, weren't you?'

'I . . . I cannot remember what I thought. I don't remember much about that night.'

'But you remember that, don't you?' His voice was soft yet insistent. 'Do you remember looking at me with your face full of fear?'

She looked up at him now and into his eyes. 'If . . . if there was fear in my face it was for you, not because of you.'

He did not speak for some moments, and then he said, still softly, 'Will you tell me something, truthfully?'

'If I can.'

There was another pause before he asked, 'Do you think *I've* killed him?'

She was too long in answering, and his voice cut across the words that were on her lips. 'All right, all right,' he said, 'don't strain yourself. But when they find him, I'll tell you something.' And with this he turned from her and walked away.

As he was leaving, at the back door he met Hannah coming in. She clutched at his arm and said, 'Aw, Vin. Vin;' but he pulled himself from her hold and went down the hill and into his workshop.

253

10

That Sunday a band of volunteers scoured the vicinity of the house. At intervals Constance saw them from the window, looking like flocks of sheep drifting across the snow. This was the third day of the search. Whatever had happened to Jim, he would surely be dead when they found him. She could feel no pity, no sorrow. She didn't think there would ever be any regret in her for the way of his going; the way of his last goodbye had wiped all pity and compassion from her.

The weather report now said that there was an early thaw coming. She wished it would come soon. Yet part of her was praying for the freeze to continue, because even after what Vincent had said there was still a doubt in her mind.

By late afternoon the moving dots had disappeared from the landscape, and Hannah, coming in from the kitchen carrying a large tray laden with tea things, said, 'This is what we're needing. I think there's nothin' so comforting on earth at any time of the day, or night, as a cup of tea, an' there's hardly an hour of the day but one of us somewhere needs comfort.'

She pulled a chair up to the table on which she had set the tray and began to pour out the tea, talking all the while to Constance, who was sitting on the couch. 'I suppose it's the Irish in me that lays a great stock on tea. Next to whisky it is with some, an' placed well afore it with others. I remember back home many years ago there was an old priest in our

254

village, and he said the next time I broke the fast on a Friday he'd give me the penance of a tealess week. God above! He was a terror. He made no difference between beef and pork. The pig, so to speak, was a great temptation to me on a Friday; the rest of the week we were hardly on noddin' acquaintance, for then, you know, I didn't care if I tasted bacon, ham, or cracklin', but on a Friday I seemed to crave it. It was the obstinacy in me. Aw' – she turned and laughed at Constance – 'the priests always had a hard job with me. I remember old Father Lafferty saying one day that all the children in the world had been born innocent, except for me. He was a boy, was Father Lafferty. And talkin' of innocence, did I ever tell you that neat little joke about the young Irish lass who told her mother she had a pain in her stomach, an' the mother said, "It's likely an ulster; go and see the doctor," and away she went and saw the doctor. "Me mother says I've got an ulster in me stomach, doctor," she said, and after the good man had examined her he said back to her, "Away you go home, Bridget, and tell your mother, begod! she was right, it's an Ulster volunteer you've got in your stomach, and within five months he'll be marching right out of it."' Hannah's head was back and her mouth wide with laughter. Then she turned to see what effect her joke had had on Constance. Constance's eyes were bright but her face, as yet, couldn't move into a smile.

'It's funny, don't you think?'

'Yes, Hannah, very funny.'

'Aw, here.' Hannah's face and voice were now sober. 'Have this cup of tea an' get that nice bread and butter down you; it'll do you more good than my blarney. I'm only aimin' to cheer you up but, begod! it's not very cheerful I'm feelin' meself.'

'You're more than kind, Hannah. I don't know what I would have done without you these past days.'

'God provides, lass; God provides. I may not go to me duties but I believe that he never deserts us; no matter how low we've sunk his spirit speaks to ours. Aw, there I go.' She shook her head as she seated herself down by the side of the couch with a cup and saucer in her hand. 'You know, me flesh wants to shake with laughter when I hear meself yapping on about me spirit. The likes of me shouldn't talk about such things; we should leave it to the learned, and the priests, but' – she moved her head slowly – 'but you know, Mrs Stapleton, underneath the coarse flesh that holds the manner of me class, I feel this thing, this sort of connection with whatever there is, call it spirit, or what you like. In here' – she dug her finger into her chest – 'it isn't beyond me ken and comprehension; it's only when I try to put it into words that I feel I can't understand it, you know?'

'Yes, Hannah, I know.'

'I understand lots of things I can't put into words. I have feelings about things. I had a feelin' on New Year's Eve; it was a strange feelin'. I didn't think much of it at the time, but now I know I should have because it was the signal for this, all that's happened, though God knows I couldn't have done anything to prevent it, now could I?'

'No, Hannah.'

Hannah now took a long drink from her cup, and as she replaced it on the saucer she said, 'I love Vin, Mrs Stapleton. I love him the best of the bunch; perhaps because he was my first, perhaps because he's got in him a depth not in the others, for he had to bear the brunt of the situation I created right from the beginning, and he did it manfully. He has never said a harsh word to me about it in his life.'

'I don't think anyone could be harsh with you, Hannah.'

'Aw, why not? Because' – Hannah wagged her finger towards Constance – 'I know meself. Oh, I know meself inside out. Look at me.' She spread her hand out. 'Like a bundle of duds; no matter how Florence cuts me frocks out they just look like sacks on me.' She smiled. 'You see, I'm easy goin' an' lazy by nature and if it wasn't for Florence keepin' me up to scratch, aw, I don't know but I'd sit on me backside all day and let hairs grow out of me ears.'

'Oh! Hannah. Hannah!'

If only she could laugh. But would she ever again laugh at the O'Connors? Far from making her laugh, Hannah's efforts made her want to cry, not as she cried the other night, but gently. She had thought last night that if she could just sit and cry gently, it might wash away the sadness that was banked within her.

There was a sound of footsteps coming from the kitchen and as Peter entered the room Hannah cried, 'You're just in time, boy. Are you frozen? You look it. Come away; come away and get yourself warm. There's a roaring fire an' a cup of tea. That's what you want, a cup of tea.'

Peter came to the fire and held out his hands before he said, 'Yes, I could do with one, Hannah.' He did not look at his mother until he was seated on the pouffe at the side of the fire, and then he merely glanced at her and away again as he said, 'It's thawing fast. If it keeps up they say the moors should be pretty clear by the morning.'

Long before it was light, Constance was standing at the window, and when the dawn came up it revealed great patches of black land studded by snow-capped mounds. The hills and mountains beyond were still white, but the flat surround in front of the terrace was one dark mass of water-logged turf, and as the light grew she strained her eyes to try to spot what might be a shape lying on it. Even when she told herself he wouldn't be there, she still peered towards the road at the back where she was sure they would find him: deep in a ditch, perhaps, or, if he had wandered on to the fells, at the bottom of a natural snow-filled ditch.

She shivered as she walked across the room and opened the door softly so as not to wake Peter, but when she reached the top of the stairs she could see the room below illuminated by the fire and she knew that he was already up.

He was sitting in the big chair to the side of the hearth, and, on seeing her, he rose to his feet.

'How long have you been up?'

'Oh, just an hour or so.'

She walked to the fire and held her hands down to the blaze, and he came and stood by her side. Putting his arm around her shoulders he pressed her gently to him, saying, 'It won't be long now and . . . and then you'll know, they'll all know.' She turned her eyes towards him, and they stared at each other in the flickering fire. 'I know all about it,' he said; 'and I know you all think Vin finished him off.'

'You knew about . . . ?'

'Yes, Kathy told me. And I hope for Vin's sake he didn't do anything that night, yet at the same time . . .' He looked away from her before he added, 'I'm wishing he did.'

'Don't, Peter, don't.'

'You like Vin?'

'Peter!' There was censure in her tone.

'Oh' – he shook his head impatiently – 'I'm not blind. You've always thought I was blind, blind to everything. Anyway, if I hadn't guessed something from your manner I certainly would from his. I like Vin, no matter what he's done. I'm . . . I'm not just saying that because of Kathy. Right from the beginning, I've thought it's a man like Vin you want, not a creature like—' His voice trailed off as she gently pulled herself from him, and he ended harshly, 'Don't treat me as if I'm still in short trousers, Mother.'

'Oh, Peter.' She turned wearily towards him. 'Don't you understand this is something I can't discuss?'

'Well, it's a pity you can't.' Both his manner and his voice were impatient. 'Things are better aired. What happened the other night' – he pointed his finger towards her face – 'was just the result of you keeping things to yourself – or trying to – putting a face on it . . . I didn't mean that as a pun, but it serves to show what I do mean.'

He walked away from her, saying tersely, 'I'm going out; I'll be back as soon as I can.' He did not add, as soon as they find him.

*   *   *

258

But the searchers didn't find the body of Jim Stapleton. It rained heavily all morning and as the day wore on the snow melted like butter near a fire. It was dusk when the police sergeant once more knocked on the door, and when Hannah opened it to him and invited him in, his eyes were drawn to Constance where she stood supporting herself against the edge of the table, and he shook his head before saying, 'There's no sign of your husband in the vicinity, Mrs Stapleton. We've searched within a mile radius of this house: a full circle we've been. He couldn't possibly have got any further, and as I say, he's nowhere to be found.'

Constance's relief was palpable, but then she was attacked by a new fear as the police inspector said, 'We were wondering if he might be in one of the outbuildings down at the farm.' He turned to Hannah. 'You have a lot of odd places down there; do you think it possible he could have crawled into—?'

'God above, no! What put that idea into your head?' Hannah's voice was high, her tone defensive. 'We use every outhouse every day: coals, wood, feed, hay, the cowshed, Vin's workshop an' the wood store next to it, where the seasoned timber is; we're in and out of every nook and cranny every minute. If he'd been there one of us would have seen him, surely to God.'

'Well' – the sergeant jerked his head to the side – 'in any case I think we'd better have a look round just to satisfy ourselves. We'll away down now. I'll call on my way back, Mrs Stapleton.'

Constance nodded to him and watched him go out and join the men on the terrace, and then she looked at Hannah, and Hannah, her voice even higher now, cried, 'God Almighty! Who do they think we are? I ask you. Wouldn't we know if he had crawled into any one of them? And would he go into a dark outhouse with the lights of the windows beckoning him on? Did you ever hear any such thing?' She looked at Constance for confirmation. Constance said nothing, but slowly made her way to the couch and sat down. Hannah sat

259

opposite and talked intermittently, still in that aggressive high-pitched voice. She talked until the sergeant again knocked on the door; then she jumped up and went to it and said immediately, 'Well! Well, now?'

He looked at her hard; then coming into the room he addressed Constance, who was again on her feet, 'There's no sign of him down there. I don't know what to say, Mrs Stapleton. Can you suggest anything?'

She shook her head. 'Only that he somehow found his way through.'

'It would have taken a desperate man to get along that road on that night; everyone is agreed on that, Mrs Stapleton.'

She wanted to say to him, But he *was* a desperate man, yet deep in her heart she felt that his desperation wouldn't have guided him to safety in that storm.

'Mr Charlton's men are going to do another scouring tomorrow. You never know, there might just be some nook or cranny that we've missed . . . Well, good-night, Mrs Stapleton. I'll look in again tomorrow if we have any news.'

'Good-night,' said Constance; 'and . . . and thank you.'

Within a minute or so of the sergeant's leaving the house Sean came in, and Peter with him.

'I don't know what to make of it,' said Sean, 'I just don't. It's a mystery to me. There's not an inch of the countryside surrounding the place that we haven't tramped over an' poked into. All I can think is that he got to the river and fell in and was carried down. But then he would have come up against the boulders dotted here and there.'

'They say there're deep crevices in the river bed in places,' put in Hannah quietly, and he nodded at her as he answered, 'Aye, I know. But that's a long shot, the river. He would never have reached the river in the first place. It's in the opposite direction, anyway, to what he would have taken when he left the car.' He now said wearily, 'I'll be gettin' down. Good-night to you, Mrs Stapleton.'

'Good-night, Mr O'Connor; and thank you for all you've done.'

''Tis nothin'; 'tis nothin'.' He smiled at her, then left, repeating the words to himself now. ''Tis nothin'; 'tis nothin'. And it would be nothin' if that devil were to be found whole and unmarked wherever he is lying.'

As he made his way across the yard Vincent emerged from the workshop doorway. It was as if he had been waiting for him, and he called in a loud voice, 'And they didn't find the body in the woodshed either.'

Sean stopped in his tracks, then slowly approached his son, saying, 'Vin. Vin, give over torturing yourself.'

'I've no need to do that; there are plenty only too ready and willing to do that for me.'

They stared at each other; then Vin said, 'Who sent them down here?'

'In the name of God! man, they're lookin' in every nook and cranny; it was likely just a thought of the sergeant's.'

'Just a thought? Do you forget that Dickenson was the man who came and collected me before? Do you forget that there's not a calf dropped, or a woman pregnant in this valley, but within hours it's been mulled over in every cottage and farmhouse? Tom Collins saw me walking with her one day across the hills: they knew that her husband's visits were few and far between; they don't need to be told how to put two and two together: "He did a fellow in for one woman" – I can hear them saying it now – '"so what's to stop him doing it again?"'

'Vin, look. Come here, boy.' Although only half his son's size, Sean grabbed his arm and led him back into the workshop and, closing the door, he leant against it and said, 'Tell me from your own lips, an' I'll believe every word you say. Exactly what did you do when I pushed you out of the door a few nights gone?'

Vincent's jaws worked, the bones showing beneath the stretched skin. He looked straight at his father, and remained silent a moment before he said stiltedly, 'I reached the end of the terrace. I was dazed. I stepped off it and made my way towards the hill. Then I asked myself what I was doing going down at your bidding, so I turned back. But I didn't go on to the terrace again in case I'd be seen, so I kept below the wall. The pain in my shoulder was giving me gyp and my head was beginning to swim again, so I sat down on a boulder and dropped my head on to my arms. Then I heard the door open and I saw him leaving. I wanted to go after him but I still felt swimmy, and I knew I was glad I was in that condition, for I kept saying to myself, Let him go. Let him go. Then I found myself on my feet and I was on the terrace again going in the direction he had gone, and when I rounded the house I saw him down below playing a torch. Then the car lights went on, and I knew that by the time I got down the hill he'd be gone. But I didn't want to go down, I didn't want to meet up with him. Then the lights disappeared and I thought he had backed round the bend, although I couldn't remember seeing the lights move. I was dazed. At one period I thought I heard you shouting, then I made my way back to the terrace and went into the room, and as soon as Constance saw me she started to cry . . . scream. That's all there is to it . . . And you don't believe a word of it?'

'Aye, I do. I do, Vin; it's only I'm thinkin', where in the name of God did he get to? He must have put the lights on, then off again when he couldn't get the car started. How long do you think the lights were on?'

'I've no idea; it's all vague.'

'Did you hear him trying to start up the engine?'

'I think I did, but I'm not sure. The wind was howling.'

'He could still have been sitting in the car, then when you came back to the house?'

'For all I know, yes.'

'Do you think he could have made it to the road?'

'It's a mile to the road; I can't see how he could have done it in that blizzard.'

'Then have you any ideas at all?'

262

'No more than you have.'

'God Almighty! It's a mystery, if ever there was one. You know, it's my opinion he's sunk into the snow somewhere, into a ditch of snow, not necessarily here. He likely started to shank it – a big-headed type like him would think nothin' was impossible – and, instead of keepin' to the road, he wandered off down the slopes towards Wark, or Simonburn, for that matter.' Then shaking his head slowly at his son, he said, 'I'm sorry, boy, I'm sorry. I take your word; afore God, I take your word.'

'No, you don't,' said Vincent heavily. 'You'd like to, but you can't. You'll not be convinced until he's found, and without a mark on him.'

'Aw, boy! Boy!' Sean turned and groped at the handle of the door and went out, and Vincent sat down slowly in front of his bench and put his head in his hands.

11

On the following Tuesday morning Sergeant Dickenson paid his third visit to the house and, coming straight to the point, he said, 'There's no sign of your husband at all, Mrs Stapleton. The men have been as far as the river, although it's agreed that under the circumstances it's unlikely he would ever get that far. Still, they went. Also police officers have been to your bungalow. From what they gather, your husband was last seen there late on Thursday afternoon. The next-door neighbour said he came in and went out almost immediately again, and she says there has been no one near the house since. You can't tell us anything that might help us further, can you, Mrs Stapleton?' He looked hard at her, and she looked back at him, saying, 'No. I'm sorry. If I could think of anything I would tell you. All I know I've already explained to you.'

'Oh, well. Good-day to you,' he said; 'and I'll be keeping in touch.' . . .

And he did keep in touch. He came back at half-past three that afternoon, accompanied by Sean. Before speaking to her he looked at her closely. 'We've found your husband, Mrs Stapleton,' he said.

Involuntarily her hand went up to her throat and she wetted her lips as she waited.

'The news that he was missing on the fells in the snowstorm appeared in the papers, and this morning we had a phone message from a man in Durham who had just seen a report of the affair. He told us that on the night in question, Thursday, the fifth, he gave a lift to a man on the road just below Woodpark. He was in a state of exhaustion and said he had been wandering about for over two hours. He said his name was Stapleton. The man, he said, asked him if he would take him to Quilter Street, and since he was on his way to Newcastle he said he would. He said Mr Stapleton knocked on the door of number eighteen and a young girl, whom he took to be the man's daughter, ushered him in.' Here the inspector paused before going on. 'Acting on this information, Mrs Stapleton, we went to the house and there we found your husband. He said he had been in bed for some days because he had caught a chill from exposure. He' – the sergeant moved his head, first one way and then the other – 'he said that he hadn't read the report of his being missing, nor had he heard it on the radio or television. He said he had felt too ill over the past few days to concern himself about anything.'

As Constance lowered herself slowly on to a chair near the table, Sean went to her and, putting his hand on her shoulder, said, 'Well, now! Well, now! Isn't that splendid news?' and Constance looked at him and made a small motion with her head. Then the sergeant was speaking again. His voice showing slight embarrassment, he said, 'That's . . . that's all we can do about the matter, Mrs Stapleton. As far as we're concerned it's . . . it's closed.'

'Thank you.'

'Goodbye.'

'Goodbye, sergeant. And thank you again for the trouble you've taken.'

The sergeant inclined his head, then left, followed by Sean who, from the door, said quickly to Constance, 'I'll be back in a jiffy.'

Neither man spoke until they reached the end of the terrace, and then Sean said, 'Good news indeed; at least, in one way I suppose it is.' He and the sergeant now exchanged understanding glances. Then, bowing his head, Sean said, 'He wouldn't have been the first man to have been hanged on suspicion, now would he, Bill?' and the sergeant answered, 'No, Sean, no. Indeed he wouldn't. I'm glad it's all cleared up. Can you believe me?'

'Yes; indeed I can, Bill. Indeed I can. But at the same time I don't think it's any good news that fellow's alive. He's a swine of the first water, if you ask me. You should have seen that room as I saw it, and her, after he had finished with her. If I'd been big enough and strong enough meself, God knows what I might have done, because the desire was there all right.'

'I can quite believe you, Sean, for from the little I saw of him I took him to be a nasty piece of work all round. The piece he's got there, which that man took to be his daughter, well! If ever I saw one, she's one, and a dirty-mouthed one at that. Do you know what she said to me as I left?'

'I could think of many things,' said Sean.

' "Is his missis sweating?" were her words. That's what she said. She's a dirty little bitch. But he deserves no better.' The sergeant didn't repeat the remainder of the sentence: 'Cos she thought her boy friend had put another notch in his gun. He had no desire to stir trouble up in the O'Connor household; they'd had their share.

'They tell me he's a writer,' said the sergeant.

'So I understand. He made a splash a few years ago, then sank to the bottom, as most of them do with heads the size of his.'

'Where's his son?' asked the sergeant now, and Sean said, 'He was still lookin', the last I saw of him. He's a nice boy, him. Takes after her.'

'That's something to be thankful for, anyway. Well, I'll be off.' After stepping down from the end of the terrace he paused; then looking back up at Sean, he said, 'It's many years since I was up this way, Sean, and I hope it's many years before you see me again. When I come, it usually means trouble, and I don't wish that on you.'

'Oh, don't you mind. Don't you mind,' said Sean in his warm embracing way. 'Break the spell by payin' us a visit one Sunday afternoon in the spring. I can promise you a good home-made tea, right down to the butter and, as you know, you'll not find better views in the world than from these hills.'

'I'll take you at your word, Sean. Goodbye.'

'Goodbye, Bill. And . . . and as you're passin' through the yard tell the women to put a move on an' get up here, either one of them. You'll do that?'

'Yes, Sean. Goodbye.'

When Sean re-entered the room, it was to see Constance sitting exactly as he had left her. Going to her, he said, 'Come on up to the fire; you're sitting so far away you'll freeze. One of them is comin' up and you'll have a cup of tea together and a nice natter an' you'll feel better. And the boy should be back any minute now. I'll go out and find him meself if he doesn't show up within the next half-hour. Now there's nothing in the world to worry about.'

He continued to jabber as, with his hand on her elbow, he helped her to her feet and led her to the couch; and when she sat down she looked at him and, the whole of her face trembling, she said, 'The cruelty of people. He stayed there knowing . . . knowing that people would be searching, frozen to . . . to the bone; wet and . . . and weary.' Her voice broke and the tears now welled slowly from her eyes.

'There now, there now. Don't start to cry again; you know you'll only make yourself ill.'

She shook her head. 'I'm . . . I'm all right. I won't cry like that again. But . . . but the cruelty of him. You know' – she put her hand out and gripped his – 'he . . . he had heard about Vin but not . . . not from me, down in one of the bars. He would know that I would think' – she bowed her head – 'that . . . that you all would think . . .'

'There now, there now. It's all over.'

'He did it purposely. The cruelty of it. He could have gone on . . . kept it up.'

'No, no, he couldn't; somebody was bound to have seen him.'

'You . . . you don't know him, Mr O'Connor. He once wrote a story not unlike what has recently happened.'

'There now, there now. Don't distress yourself any further. Anyway, his plot didn't work.'

'It did, it did.' She wiped the tears from her cheeks with her fingertips. 'It worked all right, because I really thought Vin had done something to him. Vin knows this and he'll never forget it.'

'Well, take comfort.' Sean's voice was very low now. 'You're not the only one who thought that; we all did. Vin doesn't love easily, and there's a deep possessive streak in his nature. It's a raw kind of streak that you sometimes find among the men reared in this valley. Yet, as you know, there isn't a drop of Northumbrian blood in him; Hannah's as pure Irish as meself. My family goes back to the day of dot, pure Irish every man Jack of them. But there's Vin. He looks neither like me nor Hannah, and his nature, if anything, follows that of Florence, but mainly he seems part of the very land he lives on, blunt, raw and compelling, yet as the seasons, beautiful in their turn, for there's a depth of kindness and compassion in him. How else would he have been the stay of us all down there? Because you know, Mrs Stapleton, I've never kept me family, I've only bred them. I'm a lazy, indolent creature, and capable of only two good things, love and loyalty; and then the loyalty, you might say could be questioned when you think what I've subjected Florence to. Yet I've been loyal to her in me way because she has what love there's in me. Aw' – he shook his head – 'why am I talkin' like this to you? Psst! Here's someone. Psst!' He lifted his chin. 'Somebody's comin'. Now dry your eyes. Come on, dry your eyes . . . Ah!' He turned from her. 'It's you, Florence. I'm just tellin' Mrs Stapleton it's a good cup of tea and a crack she needs.'

268

Florence took off her coat and put it over a chair, before walking towards the fire and looking down at Constance. But she did not say anything to her; instead she spoke to Sean. 'Michael said Peter was up by the burn. He's gone to fetch him. When you go down will you tell Hannah not to forget to take the dish out of the oven, or it'll be kizzened up to carbon.'

'I'll do that, I'll do that, Florence. Well, I'll be off. I'll be seeing you.' He bent down to Constance, and he smiled at her while patting her shoulder, and again he said, 'I'll be seein' you.'

'Yes, Sean.' . . .

When Sean reached his own yard he did not go immediately into the house to deliver Florence's message, but went across to the workshop, and as he pushed the door open he called, 'Are you there, Vin?'

Vincent was bending over the bench pressing the neck of a kangaroo against a buffer polisher, and his father said, 'Did you see Bill Dickenson?'

'Yes, I saw Bill Dickenson,' said Vincent.

'And he told you?'

'Yes, he told me,' said Vincent flatly.

'Dirty swine that, isn't he? I don't mean Bill.'

'No, I know who you mean.'

'She says he did it on purpose.'

Vincent turned slowly to look towards his father and he said flatly, 'Does she, now?'

'Oh, boy! Boy!' Sean tossed his head. 'Don't take that attitude.'

Vincent's voice seemed to bounce off the wooden beams of the workshop as he yelled, 'What in hell's flames attitude would you have me take? To sit down and smile at all of you in turn, and say, "Yes, human nature being what it is, I understand that you always suspected me of repeating meself . . ." God! There wasn't one of you, from Mother downwards. Except perhaps Barney – and he doesn't know yet, does he? The others haven't yet told him the news about his big

269

brother's past life. Not one of you but thought I had polished him off. And now, because you find him alive and laughing at his little joke, you expect me to act as if nothing had happened.'

'All right, all right,' Sean now shouted back. 'I can't answer for the others, whatever they thought in their hearts, but me, yes, I did think you'd done it. If you had seen yourself going towards him, seen how you looked—'

'No matter how I looked, I had no intention of killing him. Yes, perhaps if there would have been no consequence to it I may have, and that's speaking the truth, but I've suffered the consequences of one such act and I'm not such a damn fool, so stark staring mad, as to go through it again. I tell you, I had no intention of even laying a hand on him; I wouldn't have let myself, just in case. Like you, I would have seen he got out. All I wanted to do was to protect her . . . and to take the carving from him . . . whole.'

'Well, that being the case, boy, you could have fooled me,' said Sean grimly now.

'And apparently I did. But how do you know how I feel about ever hitting a man again? You've never been inside; you don't know what it's like. I took an oath to myself that I'd never lay a hand on anyone in my life again and I've kept it; even without your blow, I would have kept it.'

Sean sighed deeply and said, 'You think you would, lad. You think you would.'

'Oh, God Almighty!' Vincent beat his forehead with his clenched fist; then, gripping the edge of the bench with both hands, he leant his big body over the cluster of animals lying there and cried, 'How can you expect her or anybody else to believe in me when your own don't?'

'I'm sorry. I'm sorry,' said Sean. Then, turning towards the door, he said, 'She's in a bad way; she's as shocked about this as she was when she thought he was dead.' He opened the door and stood for a moment on the threshold before he asked quietly, 'Are you going up?'

270

Slowly Vincent turned from the table, and as slowly he said, 'No; I'm not going up.'

'Aw, you're nowt but a damn stubborn fool,' cried Sean, and on this he went out, slamming the door behind him.

Vincent sat down at the bench and pushed the animals aside, then leant his elbows on the cleared space and pressed his face into his hardened palms.

12

Towards the end of February, Constance knew she would have to get away; the loneliness was engulfing her. She hadn't felt it so much up to the middle of January, when Peter's term began at university. And anyway, during those days she had felt too physically ill to pay much attention to this other feeling, which the daily visits of the children, the popping in of Hannah, Florence and Sean did something to alleviate. Now, during the week, she was on her own most of the time. Peter came up on a Friday evening and stayed until Sunday evening; that's if the weather allowed. A fortnight ago, the road had been blocked again and the week-end had seemed longer than the week, in spite of the visits from the O'Connors.

There had been the unexpected mid-week visit from Harry and Millie that had taken her mind off herself for a while. They had come on an afternoon and had brought Ada's child with them. It was a fortnight old and already it had brought comfort to Harry. But at first neither he nor Millie spoke about the child, for they were aghast at the sight of Constance's face.

'Our Jim did that?' said Harry; and when Constance nodded, he said, 'Where is he?'

Millie and Constance both refrained from looking at each other, but Constance said, 'In London, I think;' and he replied, 'London? Well, it's a damn good job for him he is. The cowardly swine.'

But even following this they spoke little of the child; there was embarrassment about it on both sides. It wasn't until Millie, under the pretext of helping Constance to clear away the tea things, followed her into the kitchen that she said, 'Do you think he looks all right?'

'Harry?'

'Yes.'

'Yes, Millie; better than when I last saw him.'

'He's been through hell. He never speaks of Ada. When I brought the baby home he didn't even ask if she was dead or alive. I'm glad, in a way, it's a boy; he'll likely be more sensible with it.'

'She showed no signs of wanting it?'

'Not her! Like nails, she is . . . By the way, how did you know he'd gone to London?'

'I didn't. I just said that in case Harry had heard of where he was staying.'

'Well, it was a good guess, 'cos that's where he *has* gone. She told me when I saw her; and it was with spite she said it. She said her Uncle Jim was in the money again . . . It looks as if they're taking his book for a film, Connie. It's a damn shame that you'll not get a penny of it after all the money you've spent on him these last years.'

'Oh, that doesn't matter now, Millie. And in a way I'm glad; he'll have something to tide him over.'

'Tide him over!' said Millie scornfully. 'Small fortune he'll get for it, likely.'

Constance smiled wryly. That's what everyone had thought when he'd got his first book filmed; they made guesses at five to ten thousand pounds and he had not contradicted them. Later he'd told them he had received seven hundred and fifty pounds for the film rights. Of course, that was seventeen years ago, but even if they'd given him two thousand this time, it'd not last a year, not at the way he liked to spend.

Before they left, Harry said, 'Don't be lonely, Connie. If things get too much, come and stay with us for a while.'

273

She thanked him and said she would do that, knowing that she never would. Yet when they had gone she felt more alone than ever.

She hadn't seen even the back of Vincent in the distance all these weeks. She might have seen him had she walked down the hill, but she wouldn't do that; nor had the O'Connors, Florence, Hannah, or Sean, suggested that she should come down.

For years her pride had been rubbed in the dust through her husband's rejection of her. For a long time she had been unable to look upon his choice of younger women as a defect in his character; rather, she had seen it as a defect in her own. Her looks, or her figure, did little to help her morale. She wanted to love, and be loved, yet she knew the need in her to love was greater than that to be loved, but the damming up of this outlet over the years now made it impossible for her to move towards Vincent O'Connor. In any case, she was seeing the situation in another light: If he had wanted her he'd had plenty of time to show it. Reviewing the incident on New Year's morning, she saw it now as between a single man and a married woman. Then she had been safe, as it were; soon she'd no longer be married, but because of his past and the treachery in it, he wasn't going to become involved again. At first she had put his attitude down to his anger against her mistrust, but six weeks was a long time to sustain such a feeling, she considered, at least under the present circumstances.

So she sent for the travel brochures, and Michael and Moira took the news of her intentions down the hill. They stood in the kitchen and looked at Florence, Hannah and Sean, and Michael said, 'She's going to Spain.'

'She said that?' asked Sean.

'Yes. Didn't she, Moira? She showed us the place on the map.'

'When is she going?' asked Florence.

'I don't know. I only took the things up to her this morning. I met the postie on the brow and he asked me to take the letters along, and there was this big envelope with the folders in and there was a letter in it, and after she read it she pointed to the place where she was goin', didn't she, Moira?'

Moira said nothing, only nodded her head.

Sean thrust his fist into the palm of his hand, making a loud clapping noise. 'That'll be the finish; once she goes she'll never come back. She'll put it up for sale. Mark my words, she'll put it up for sale. And the way it is now it'll go like a hot cake. Once she steps down that hill, for Spain or any other place, that's the last we'll see of her, I'm tellin' you.'

'Why don't you go and tell him?' said Hannah. 'If you don't, I will. Tell him to stop actin' the bloody fool.'

'And what'll be the result?' asked Florence quietly. 'Except to drive him further into himself. He'll come round in his own time.'

'And it'll be too late,' said Sean.

Florence didn't answer her husband but gazed at Michael, then at Moira, and after a moment she said to them, 'Do you think that at dinner-time you could begin chatting between yourselves on the subject of Mrs Stapleton going for a holiday to Spain?'

Michael grinned up at her. 'You mean off-hand, like?'

'Just that,' said Florence; 'off-hand, like. And you, Moira, could you do the same, talk back to him as Michael has said, off-hand, like?'

Now Moira grinned up at her. ''Course,' she said. 'And I'll talk to our Davie about it. He always says he's goin' to travel, that's if he makes a lot of money as a doctor; that's if he ever gets to be a doctor, 'cos—'

'All right, all right.' Florence checked Moira's gabbling. 'Leave it at that... Now, don't start straightaway' – she looked from one to the other. 'When you're half through your dinners, you, Michael, make a remark about . . . about wishing you could go to Spain, or something like that, the weather you know, and it being warmer there.'

Michael nodded at her quickly, saying, 'Don't worry, I'll bring it up.'

'He'll twig it,' said Hannah; 'you can't hoodwink Vin.'

'He won't,' said Michael, on the defensive; 'not the way I'll put it, you'll see. An' we won't look at him while we're talkin'. Remember that, our Moira.' He pressed his thumb into her arm. 'Don't look at him; look at Barney, or Joseph, or me, or anybody, but don't look at him; that is, unless he asks you somethin'.'

'Aw, you needn't worry on that score,' said Sean; 'he's not likely to ask you anything. Dumb he's become, blind, deaf and dumb.'

In the middle of dinner Michael addressed a remark about Spain to his sister Moira, and Moira told Davie about the wonderful place Mrs Stapleton was going to, and Barney asked if Peter would still be coming up at the week-ends, and Michael said he didn't think so, 'cos what would be the use? And when Joseph asked if she'd still want the fire kept on to keep the place warm, Michael again said he didn't think so. 'Bang goes me half-crown a week,' said Joseph, and Moira pushed him as she chastised, 'Aw, our Joe, that's all you think about, your half-crown.' And Joseph replied, 'Well, you don't refuse it yourself, do you?' and she said, quite heatedly, 'Well, I don't just go up for that, I go 'cos I like goin' up.' Then looking at Michael, almost in triumph she spoke her best line, 'It won't be the same when she's gone,' she said.

If the family expected any quick reaction they were disappointed. Vincent returned to his workshop, where he worked all afternoon. He came in as usual shortly after five, washed himself at the sink, then had his tea. But now his pattern of behaviour, they noticed with interest, changed, for instead of settling down to do drawings of more animals, or sitting to the side of the fireplace with a book about wood-carving in his hand, he returned to the workshop, and the elders looked at one another.

It was Sean who said to Michael, 'Go and squint through

276

the window in the storeroom and see if you can make out what he's doing.'

A few minutes later Michael scurried back into the kitchen, saying, 'He's comin' over again.' Then he settled himself quickly at the table while the others, each assuming a nonchalant air, proceeded to carry on as usual: Florence clearing the table, Hannah washing up, Sean seating himself to the side of the hearth with his feet on the fender. And so they waited. After a few minutes had passed and there was no sound coming from the storeroom, they looked at Michael and he back at them, and he said quietly, 'Well, he was. He came out an' he was comin' over.'

'He must have gone back, then,' said Hannah.

Florence now put her face against one of the small panes in the window above the sink and she squinted across the yard towards the workshop, then said, 'There's no light on.'

'He was carrying something in his hand,' said Michael.

'Something in his hand?' said Sean. 'What was it?'

'I don't know; it was wrapped up.'

'Well, whatever it was,' said Hannah, her face bright, 'if he brought it from the workshop he'd not likely be takin' it to the cowshed, or the pig sties, nor yet the hen crees . . . Are you thinkin' what I'm thinkin'?' She was addressing Florence as she walked towards her at the window and Florence said, 'I could be.'

They now looked at Sean, and he grinned back at them, saying, 'Then we'll only have to content ourselves, won't we?' and turned to look at his son, jerking up his chin as he said, 'You're a clever lad, Michael, a clever lad.'

'I wonder how long he'll be?' said Michael.

'I wonder, too; I wonder, too, son. But the longer the better. In cases like this the longer the better, son.' He put out his fist and punched Michael's shoulder, and Michael punched him back and they both laughed . . .

To Vincent, it seemed like years since he had walked up the

hill, and when he reached the terrace he stopped. The light was streaming from the window, and he looked at it for quite some time before he passed it by and knocked on the front door.

He heard her coming from the direction of the kitchen – that door had always squeaked; it was hung by bolt and spike and no amount of oil would ease it because of the weight of the timbers.

When she opened the door she stared at him. Then, her head drooping forward just the slightest, she said, 'Come in.' When he entered the room he saw that the layout was somewhat changed. There were two carpets on the floor now, one at each end of the room, with a runner between them going from the door to the foot of the stairs. The runner was yellow, and he wiped his feet carefully on the doormat before stepping on to it. After closing the door she passed him and walked up the room towards the fireplace. He followed her, noting that the couch was no longer opposite the fireplace but set at right angles to it, making the room seem even longer. He also noted that some of the china ornaments were back on the dresser – she must have glued them together again – and the two figures were on the mantelpiece, one on each side. But there was nothing in the middle.

'Won't . . . won't you sit down?'

He sat down in a chair opposite the couch. The parcel was on his knees, his hands resting on top of it. And not until she had seated herself did he speak. 'How are you?' he asked.

'Oh, much better; in fact, I'm feeling quite well.'

He looked at her. Her face seemed thinner, if that was possible. There were hollows under the cheekbones and her eyes seemed more sunken in her head, but there was no sign of discoloration on her skin. 'I hear you're going on a holiday?' he said.

'Yes, I'm thinking of going to Spain.'

'For long?'

'Oh, it depends if I like it there. Two or three weeks, a month; it all depends.'

He broke the ensuing silence with the rustle of the brown paper as he moved the parcel around his knee; then looking down at it, he said, 'And you won't be coming back?' Without lifting his head he raised his eyes and she looked into them. 'I . . . I don't know,' she said.

'You know all right,' he said softly; 'once you go, you go for good. You'll sell up here.'

'Perhaps.'

He shrugged his shoulders. 'You'll have no worry about selling this now. Somebody will take it as a real week-end place.'

'Yes, yes; I thought that.'

There was another silence before she said, 'If Peter was here all the time it would be different, but . . . but, as things are, it's rather lonely.'

'You haven't given it much of a trial.'

'You don't think so?'

'No.' Again he moved the parcel around on his knee. 'What will you do after your divorce?'

She uncrossed her legs and, bending forward, she picked up the poker and straightened out a piece of burning wood.

'I don't know; I . . . I haven't thought that far ahead. Perhaps I'll get some place near Peter so that he can drop in.'

'Peter may get married. Have you thought of that?'

'Oh, yes, I've thought of that; but he's very young yet; only nineteen.'

'Some are fathers at that age these days.'

'Yes, yes, that's true.'

'He's very fond of our Kathy.'

'Yes, I know, and . . . and I'm glad; but they're both very young.'

'You wouldn't put a spoke in their wheel, would you?'

'Oh, no. No, not at all. What makes you ask such a question?'

'I was just wondering.'

'Why? Why should you wonder about such a thing? I want my son to be happy.' There was a terse note in her voice.

'But you're going to live near him so you can keep an eye on him.'

'I didn't mean that; it was only because—'

'Yes I know, I know; because you're lonely. You'd be far lonelier if you left here, Peter or no Peter. You know that, don't you?'

'No, no, I don't,' she said bitterly. 'I can't feel more alone than I have done these past few weeks.'

'I should have thought you'd be glad to have been on your own.'

'I'm not . . . I'm not.'

'You would rather still be tied to him?'

'Oh no. No!' She shook her head and moved her body on the couch. 'I wasn't meaning that at all.'

'Perhaps you'll feel different when the divorce is through.'

'Perhaps.'

He now leant against the back of the couch, pulling the parcel further up his thighs. 'I would never divorce a woman.'

She stared at him.

'No matter what she did, I would never divorce her. Once I married her, it would be for good.'

'Even . . . even if your life was hell?'

'If I'd married her in the first place, then without her my life would be a greater hell than anything it could be with her.'

'You're speaking personally; it isn't the answer for everybody.'

'No; no, it isn't. But if people took their time and learned about each other aforehand then they would know whether they wanted to tie up or not; and once done, I can't see they would find out much about each other then that would make them want to separate.'

'It's a simple logic you have,' she said, her voice still terse.

'It answers,' he replied.

'Again, only for certain people. You never know what people are really like until you live with them day in, day out; and then they can still surprise you.'

280

He stared at her until her gaze dropped away. 'Perhaps you're right.' His voice was low, his words hardly audible now. 'What do I really know about it? It's all supposition with me . . . I wouldn't do this, I wouldn't do that. Like many another man I don't know what I'd do until I was put to the test, and that's what you're trying to tell me, isn't it?'

She didn't answer him now, but looked towards the fire. Then he brought her eyes to him again by asking, 'Are you wondering what I've got in the parcel?' He tapped the brown paper.

'No, of course not.'

'No, of course not.' His voice, though soft, was mocking.

'Well . . . well, it's none of my—'

'For God's sake!' He threw his head to one side, his voice loud and angry now. 'Don't use that phrase, it's none of your business; it's . . . it's such a polite way of shutting yourself off from everything, and shutting out everybody.'

As she rose to her feet he also rose, and he said, contritely, 'I'm sorry, I'm sorry.'

'You . . . you talking of me shutting myself off . . .' Her lips were trembling slightly but she stared straight at him as she stated flatly, 'It's six weeks, almost, since I saw you.'

Slowly he turned from her and, laying the parcel down on the chair, he went to the mantelpiece and dropped into his old stance, foot on the raised hearth, elbow on the rough stone of the shelf, his head supported on his hand, and he said, 'I know, I know. I couldn't get myself up the hill; I was so bitter. Still am, for that matter. The others could have believed I'd done him in and I could have taken it, but not from you. You see, I'd explained things to you, talked to you as I'd never done to any one of them, not even Flo . . . my mother. All they knew of what happened, they heard at the trial. I couldn't talk about it to them, but I did to you, so it hit me harder when I saw your reaction, when I saw you were terrified of me.'

'I wasn't . . . I wasn't terrified of you.'

He turned his head slowly away from his hand but didn't

281

look at her when he said, 'You forget that I saw your face. You forget that you screamed blue murder.'

'That . . . that was partly the pent-up emotion of years of frustration. I . . . I always felt that one day he would strike me, and when he did, it broke loose something within me; but I was also crying because . . . yes, because I thought you had killed him and I saw your wasted life, and . . . and mine too.' Her voice sank on the last words, and now he turned towards her and one slow step brought him in front of her.

'And mine too,' he repeated softly. He put his hand out and gently raised her chin, and his grey eyes took on almost the colour of her own when he said, 'We're different, we two, poles apart in one way, yet clamped tight in another. I know this; I've always known it. Down there they look upon us as chalk and cheese, and in a way they're right, but this other thing between us, this could level out the chalk and cheese. I want you . . . you know that, but what I said a minute ago I meant. If you married me you'd do it with your eyes open, wide open, for I'd never give you a divorce. For my part, I can say I'd never give you the handle, and no matter what you did I wouldn't let you go free. I mean this. So . . . so you've got to be sure, and it'll take time. No jumping in then finding the waters starting to freeze, because once you're in, you're in for life, Constance.'

Her name sounded strange on his lips, thick and warm. Tears were tightening the muscles of her throat again. She told herself not to cry.

'You don't say anything,' he said. 'Do even my words frighten you?'

She closed her eyes and bit hard on her lip as he went on, 'Take your time, all the time you want; I'm used to waiting. Go away on your holiday, and then if you come back, that'll be my answer.'

'Vin!' The name toppled from her mouth and she put out her hands and clutched at his. 'I . . . I don't need to go away, I know the answer; I always have for . . . for as long as you have.'

He gathered her to him, pressing her close, holding her silently. He did not kiss her, but just held her trembling body close to his. Then, gently, he held her from him and they gazed at each other; Constance into the big bony face, now with an expression on it she had never seen before, for the granite look had gone, the gauntness had gone. He turned from her and, picking up the parcel from the chair, he placed it in her hands, saying, 'Open it.'

There, on the brown paper, lay the exact replica of the sheep and the lamb. 'Oh, Vin!' She stroked the animal from the top of its head to the struggling feet of its young. Then handing it back to him, she said, 'Place it where it belongs.'

And when he had set it on the mantelpiece he turned to her again. This time he kissed her, and she him, hard and hungry, the both of them. And when it was over he said, 'I need you as you need me; we badly need each other. I sensed your need even before I faced my own! Well, we'll need no more . . . Oh Constance. Constance.' Again they were holding fast.

Now they were gazing at each other and laughing a little, and on a laugh he said, 'Will you come down with me? They are all sitting there on pins and needles. They got the children to give me the news at dinner-time that you were going away. They're all upset; Florence because she likes you, for she sees in you someone of her own kind, and Hannah because she loves you. Yes, yes, she does.' He nodded his head at her. 'Yes, Hannah really loves you. And Dad. Oh Dad, for many many reasons, because he likes you a lot, because he thinks you'll be good for me, and not forgetting the business.' He rubbed his fist gently against her jaw and, his voice almost identical with his father's, he said, 'A woman like you is a great catch, a great asset to the family, a woman who can throw a thousand down, just like that, for a house. Oh, she's very, very rich. Yes, Dad likes you in lots of ways. But he's well-meaning, always remember that . . . And the children; they like you for yourself, Constance, as I do, me being one of them . . . I love you for yourself. I love you. I love you, Constance. Do you believe that?'

She nodded dumbly at him and when she touched his cheek-bone with her fingers, he pulled her to him again and held her tightly before saying softly, 'Come on down and hear me tell them just that . . . And what do you bet there won't be a ceilidh in the O'Connors' kitchen the night?'